The Adventures of Don Juan

ALSO BY RICHARD GARDNER

*Grito: Reies Tijerina and the
New Mexico Land Grant War of 1967*

Scandalous John

Don *JUAN LUCERO-MONTESA*
hijo, *Dn. Angel Lucero-Ruiz*
y *Dna. Isabel Montesa-Murillo*
"No por Virtud, por Maña."
Anno 1619

THE ADVENTURES
OF
DON JUAN

RICHARD GARDNER

A Richard Seaver Book

THE VIKING PRESS

New York

To my profesoras, A to Z

DON JUAN: What are your dishes?

GHOST: Scorpions and vipers. Such is our diet. Will you eat?

DON JUAN: I would eat if it were all the asps in hell.

El Burlador de Sevilla
Tirso de Molina, 1621

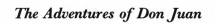

The Adventures of Don Juan

PROLOGUE

IT WAS inevitable that the king should hear of it, and soon he came from Madrid with his retinue and took the best balcony overlooking the stage of the Corral del Pollo Picando in Sevilla. It was Tirso de Molina's new play, *The Rake of Sevilla*, and in that summer of 1620, it was already a success with all sectors of society. Those who did not heartily praise it condemned it with equal enthusiasm. The men loved its hero for his unmitigated selfishness and rapacious charm, and the women found themselves attracted to the same qualities, but for their own reasons.

It was well known that the Third Philip had an uneven nature, and all eyes were upon the king as the performance progressed. But he appeared to have no single opinion. Now he rolled his eyes in surprise, now he clapped a hand to his codpiece and laughed, and now he looked judicious and fingered the Hapsburg chin.

On the boards below, the hero's lackey was protesting to his master: "Señor, you are the locust plague of women, and they ought to make the town crier proclaim your coming, thusly: 'All maidens, shun the man who outwits women and is the greatest girl guller in all of Spain!'"

To which the handsome actor who played the Rake replied, with a wink at the pit, "Begad! But you have given me a pretty name!"

While the alley was enjoying this, the king was gesturing for a nearby courtier to bend an ear. But because of their nodding plumes, there was no way to tell if His Majesty was laughing or frowning. However, this same courtier was soon to be seen making his way down from the royal balcony and past the stage, where the hero of the play was just performing a delicate rape upon a duchess, the which lady cried out, "Fire, O fire! I am burning!"

Finally the well-dressed hidalgo found his way backstage, where he spoke first to a thick-set personage who seemed to be an authority there, and was quite drunk.

"Ah, another fine gentleman come for a peek," said this individual, putting a finger upside his nose and rolling a yellow eye. "I suppose you want to meet an actress. But harken to the first commandment: Never mistake the play for the game, nor the hen basket for heaven."

"I am not here about ladies," said the courtier with a stern smile. "The king wants to meet the author of this play."

"The king!" The stout individual took up a flagon of his beverage and nervously drank. "No use to ask me, I am only an old runagate thespian. Better ask that one over there." He pointed to a figure in monkscloth lingering at the rear of the platform.

This monk was above the average height and oddly formed, with his bulk squeezed topside. As the courtier approached and offered a greeting, the monk turned, his face half hidden in the shadow of his heavy cowl, and what could be seen was not pretty, but neither was it dull. Fun and prayer in excess had left a striking battlefield. The nose was long, looked to have been stepped on, and drooped above a jutting chin. Very large and heavy-lidded eyes regarded the courtier with a kind of sprightly sorrow. "The author? I might be."

The courtier glanced about him at the small nun doing embroidery at a nearby table, and at the various actors pretending not to listen. "Then you are Windmill Nick? Your name is Tirso de Molina?"

"That is the name printed here," said the monk, plucking up a folio of the play and letting it fall open to the title page. "Who wants to know?"

"The king," said the courtier.

"Ah." The monk's face lost some color and he let go the folio and sat down on a stool.

"Now, now, there is not yet cause for alarm," said the courtier. "His Majesty only wants to know if you have used an actual person as model for this character in your play, this Don Juan . . . Tenorio. And, if such is the case, who and where that person might be." He bent a knee and

4

lowered his voice. "Whether or not he is alive, if you know what I mean."

The monk was silent a long moment, then turned up a narrowed eye. "I think you should tell me who you are."

"I am the Conde de Ortiz-Lucero," said the courtier. "Although you may not remember, we once met at a certain place of retreat outside Barcelona."

The monk's frown held a moment, then lifted. "The count, of course. I know the name, and I do have a dim recollection of meeting you. So you were a guest at my hostel, eh?" His eye gave a wild roll and he showed his teeth, but in an instant he was melancholy again and looked away. "But what if I have nothing to tell the king?"

"He will not believe you," the courtier replied. "He already has word that Tirso de Molina is only a nom de plume and not your baptismal name. Also, there is rumor that there is a diary, and he has sent me to see if it is so."

"And if I refuse?"

"Don't be foolish," said the other. "Refuse me, and he will only send another less likely to be sympathetic. You know his whims. Challenge him and he will go into a fit. Humor him, and he will soon forget. At least go through the motions. Give me something with which to satisfy his curiosity and soothe his suspicions."

Now he straightened up, a handsome man of indeterminate age, smiling and rattling his wig curls. "Besides, I am curious for personal reasons." He rested his hand on his sword. "You really have no choice, you know."

The boards bucked with the strutting of the actors out front, where the Rake was vigorously pressing yet another seduction. The monk looked toward the nun, and she considered the question in his glance. A wisp of close-cropped black hair escaped her headdress, and she pushed it back. Her starched blinders rustled softly as she gave a nod.

"Very well, there is something," the monk said at last, and got to his feet and led the way down a ladder to a box beneath the platform, from which he lifted out three battered books and gave them to the other.

The courtier laid the volumes out upon the boards. "And in here I will find the model for the consummate profligate, the merciless rake?"

A smile stirred the pouches of the monk's face. "There are various jackpuddings, coxcombs, and pornocrats. Even a certain renegade monk. Take your pick."

The courtier removed a glove. "Then, may I?"

"I cannot stop you." The monk sat on a bench. "Mind you, I do not claim to know who wrote this chronicle. But in a sense my play did spring from it. I will admit that much, but no more. Not that I believe it will satisfy His Majesty."

"We will take care of that when we come to it," said the courtier, wetting a thumb on a smile and opening the first book. And, while the monk waited and the play went on, he began eagerly to read.

DREAMS

1

Reports of the recent scandal at the Abbey of Our Lady of Infinite Sorrow at Valladolid prompt me to the reflection that only a Spaniard would cut off a nun's nose to spite his faith; and, indeed, that reflection, in the metaphorical sense, describes the central malady of my life and the cause of my greatest and final crime. Although I have been well known in my time as a profligate and fornicator, and as such you may know me now, I do not count venery as a crime, nor even rape, which is more often than not only social ineptitude resulting from an imperfect knowledge of women. I killed my sweetheart's father. It is for that crime that I have been tried by the secular authorities and condemned to hang at New Year.

However, before my final ejaculation, and since I have nothing else to do in this damned dungeon, I am taking the trouble to write down the story of my life. Not so that others might profit from my experiences, but because it was an exciting and entertaining journey, from a tight beginning to a fitting end.

Born I was, although I might as well have been shot from a cannon. I cannot be sure, of course, but an old bitterness persuades me that I did not take form in a womb awash with welcome, but instead grew to shape in cramped and inhospitable surroundings. Nor was I issued from a body quaking with creative abandon, nor merely dropped into this world with mechanical indifference, but was winced forth impatiently, with many a resentful scream and raging curse, like hard stool.

9

I seem to recall cataclysmic upheaval and desperate struggle reflected in an omnipotent eye, then sudden self-consciousness provoked by a sharp pain in the quick, as of mortal amputation, followed by a profound fear of a sound which it has taken me a lifetime to recognize as my own voice. And the light. I cannot forget the dazzling glow of that first promise, drawing me into life as the candle flame draws the moth.

I do not remember my father, but I have learned since that he was from a family of uncertain lineage and meager means, but through the help of a sympathetic priest he had studied to be an advocate and had been admitted to the provincial courts at the age of twenty-five, which was very young for such achievement. It was during a small banquet at the apartments of a magistrate of Sevilla that he consumed the several flagons of Rioja and two marinated lobsters which that same night caused his stomach to swell to uncomely proportions. A physician was called and, diagnosing the trouble as an inflammation of an appendage to the lower gut which he called Cleopatra's finger, he suggested opening the stomach and removing the troubled pouch with a razor. However, my father, being a self-trained barrister, engaged the bleeder in argument and by the Socratic method compelled him to acknowledge that the malady was equally susceptible to diagnosis as a temporary congregation of gases; and the doctor subsequently, and over my mother's uncertain objections, for she was scarcely eighteen, agreed to delay the operation for a day. Whereupon my father, being reassured of his persuasive powers, slipped into what appeared to be a deep sleep, and four hours later vomited and died.

I was an infant of six weeks at the time, and my mother's prompt response was to pass some of the wrench on to me. By sunset of that cruel day, her previously prodigal breasts had gone utterly dry. I was immediately seized by my first full-blown fit of furia. For five days I screamed and gnashed my gums and shook my small fists. I stopped only when I discovered my thumb, the which I immediately began to suck, a diversion to which I would cling well into young manhood. And to this day, and despite the fact that the compulsion has done much toward bringing me to the gallows, I cannot restrain myself when confronted by a well-formed breast and standing nipple, but must fall upon it hand and mouth, like a parched Moor upon an orange.

My mother was once very beautiful, there is no escaping that. My half brother has a miniature painted when she was seventeen, just before her marriage. Her hair is arranged in the fashion of the time, strongly influenced by the Genovese court, wherein a myriad of small curls cling closely to the skull, giving the impression that their wearer has just emerged from a bath of warm oil. Her eyes are large and dark and stare from the painting with virginal fixity. Although discreetly lightened by the painter, her complexion lacks fashion's chalky look, her lower lip is full and damp, and her rounded features hint at an incipient glandular looseness of the sort decried by propriety, but which I have always found to be quite moving. That is not to say there was ever the slightest suggestion of sensual inclination in her demeanor, only that signs of a certain inner ferment showed through the mask, like stains of volcanic potential on a granite hillside.

There is a dream which I had often as a child and still suffer on occasion, always after having dined on sea foods. I am in my bassinet and I am frightened, for she is there in the doorway of the nursery, dark of eye, dark of mouth, and chuckling. It is a beguiling laugh, roguish and coarse, low and savoring in her throat; and she glides toward me with unmistakable intent.

I have seen it since in the way she tickles the cat's belly: here pussums, here pussums, tenderly amused and gently patronizing, ready with a copper bell to tie to the tail. And poor old pussums comes purring to the mistress of his luxury, the wistful vengeance that pets. I start to tremble and my sheets are all of a sudden clammy on my shoulders. The sumptuous black shape of her looms over me, and I taste the nostalgic promise of wide welcome and warmth, yielding breast and bubbling milk, and I long to roll belly-up to the caressing claws and purr and bang my tail. But this is not the first time she has come like this, and I feel the delicate prick of sweet malevolence and suffer dim apprehensions of the bell, and I duck beneath the covers, longing to be pursued, terrified of betrayal. Her laughter spills wildly above me, and her fingers come dancing down the small cage of my ribs, searching out my belly and finding the button there.

11

I squirm, I squeal, but I cannot get away. I squeeze my eyes shut and clutch my little dingus as if to fix my body in place and steer my runaway mind. But my body will not stay still and my mind does not know what to do to end it. All it can tell me is that she does know, but will neither help me nor release me.

Dream In the end I surrender, giving myself up to the hysteria with a shriek of abandon, gasping, giggling, twisting my small prick until it burns, begging her to take her finger off my button. She does, and immediately I awaken in my bassinet in my dream in my bed wherever I am, to discover that my body is sheathed in sweat and that I am gripping my organ so tightly that all feeling has left it.

The silver had scarce been laid upon my father's eyes when there descended upon the melancholy scene the second woman in my life, my grandmama Celestina Trotaconventos des Puig-Tenorio, the famous lunatic. I can see her still, swooping through my childhood like that celestial pirate of those years, Saint Godfrey's comet. She wore an orange wig and painted her face, and from under the long black cape that was her nod to mourning, filaments of colored silk and taffeta streamed out behind like a flaming tail. Her nose was a powdered blade, her mouth a carmine daub, her eyes small and black, each with its fierce spark of unquenchable desire.

Flinging herself upon the corpse, she cried out that my mother had done wrong to allow my father to eat the lobster and was a murderess by neglect. Rushing to the bassinet, she snatched me up and tried to run away with me, charging that my mother was incompetent to raise me, by reason of immaturity and an empty head.

Did the compulsive chuckle bubble from my mother's lips? I know that she ran from the room, leaving the servants to remove the raging harpy. Following the funeral, she went into the country to recover herself, leaving me behind with my Aunt Carmen. But my grandmama was a wonder of passions and not easily foiled. No sooner was my mother out of the city than the old lady had my father's corpse stolen by grave-robbers, coated with beeswax, and otherwise preserved against the heat. And then she had me stolen away as well and took me to that painted caravan which she had got from the gypsies and kept near her villa on the banks of the Guadalquivir.

Although I was no larger than a suckling pig at the time, I could swear that I remember what followed. Certainly what has been told me since confirms the resultant feeling, that is of insufferable confusion and pain, not so much in my sockets as in my heart.

I was submitted to the attentions of a Mozarab wizard and gnostic who called himself Valentinus and was a specialist in matters of love. No doubt he wore the starry caftan and pointed hat of the professional cloudmonger and had a purple nose. Do I recall the pungent subfumigation of smoldering wormwort, the bubble and belch of the alembic, the tranced wheedling of the astrologaster as he bent to loosen my swaddling? I know that he read the wrinkles of my little dingle-dangle and otherwise practiced phallomancy upon me. He told my grandmama that I possessed four of the seven venal humours in excess and others in sufficiency, and that I would grow up to have a moderately large organ and a stormy love life. He said that I was a driven dream-child of Baphomet and was fated to love women more than most men do and any man should; and he was about to pre-scribe certain procedures and remedies by which I might avoid a bad end, when the door of the caravan burst open and my Aunt Carmen rushed in, accompanied by two armed aguaciles and a priest.

"Unmolest this infant's soul!" cried the priest, rushing forward to slap the wizard's hands away from my privy part and grasp me by my chubby arms.

Whereupon the wizard, in his desire to resist arrest, clutched me by the feet, and my grandmama cried, "He is mine!" and wrapped her arms about the waist of the wizard, while my aunt grasped the priest from behind, and the constables each took a side, and there ensued that awful tugging match which would come to typify my spiritual estate: the racking pain in my stretched soul, the bewildering ambivalence in my heart, the seesaw insistence of somebody else's contest, while my stiffening dingle waggles with each sway and lurch of jealous intention, and nearby, the mummy of my father lies under glass, a smile upon its waxen face.

To each man his rack, as they say in Al-Andalus, to each his dream of freedom. Is it any wonder that I came to look to my vital organ for surcease, since it seemed to be the only part of me that had a life of its own and was certainly the center and fulcrum of that deadly seesaw. For hadn't the wizard said as much, and hadn't the priest agreed?

Following the tug of war, *between women* the authorities persuaded my grandmama to restore me to my mother's arms and my father's bones to the ground. But that was not the end of it. Thenceforth she was likely to appear at our house on any day of the week, demanding that she be granted visitation rights and, in later years, that she be allowed to take me away for a day or more.

With what a contrary mingling of avarice and revulsion I came to view these visits. She always brought gifts: clay horses and tin rosaries, cakes and caramels, and once a fully articulated figure of the bull-baiter Pedrito. There was resentment and loathing in my mother's glance as the old lady plied me with plunder and flattery and prepared to lead me away. And yet my mother never once refused to let me go, and she never waved good-by, but always turned away as we were leaving, as if unwilling to acknowledge that she had allowed the abduction, yet equally unwilling to prevent it.

The old lady had commissioned, post mortem, a painting of my father, large and ingeniously made, with hollowed-out eyes that seemed to fix upon the viewer and follow him, should he retreat or advance, step to the right or the left. This icon she had fixed to the back wall of her caravan and flanked by votive tapers that swayed and sputtered with each lurch of the heavy chassis. After the toys and sweets, after the puppet show or the visit to the zoological gardens or to her marvelous friend the confectioner, there always came that moment when my grandmama pressed me into the shadows at the back of the caravan and began the distasteful ritual which was the price for all that had come before.

"Does Juanito know the pain that his poor grandmama has suffered in losing her only son?" she would begin, putting her powdered hand on mine. "Does Juanito know how precious he is to his grandmama, who has no one else left in the world but him?" she would ask, crushing me to her prodigious bosom. "Does Juanito know how very much his grandmama loves him, more than anyone else ever could, even more than his mama, who can always get a new husband, but poor grandmama can never get another son?"

Smothered in folds of flesh and taffeta, stifled by effluvia of incense and medicinal balsam, I would hastily nod my head and mutter some word of assent, for should I be tardy, her arms would tighten and her creamed lips increase their snail tracings upon my face.

"Give us a kiss, Yum Yum. Your grandmama is not too old for kissing and never will be. Feel that bosom, firm as any girl's, and each one a veritable milk factory when your father was on the tit. Do you know how much you look like him, in the chin and around the eyes, so round and rich and brown like the eyes of Our Señor in the chapel at Torrento de Lagrimas, where I nearly took my vows? Raise your chin and look at the picture and see how it watches you. Did I tell you that he came to me in the night again, that I saw him there in the bath water, smiling up from between my knees. Our dear, lost Angel, who died under such mysterious circumstances, who need not have died at all."

When I was four, my mother married again.

"Poor little orphaned Juanito," my grandmama wasted no time in telling me. "Now your mama has someone else, and couldn't possibly love you as much as your dear grandmama does."

The greatest joy of my infancy came on those occasions when my mother took me into the bath with her. In fact, the memory was long vital to my existence, like those recollections of an affluent former life which do so much to cheer up the poorer class of Buddhist.

I do not know how my mother came by her inclination to sanitary obsession. Bathing the body was no more approved of in Christian society in that day than in ours. But private exception was a habit with her, and somehow she had persuaded her new husband to install a Moorish pool and commode. There, she was another woman, as though only with her backbone cooked to compliant softness and the world and its memories obscured by drifting mists could she be free of the miasmic apprehensions which troubled her. What sweet rapture possessed me as she lifted me high and shook me, laughing at my bobbing dingus, then lowered me like a fat sausage into the steaming waters. No, there will never be a pleasure so pure and simple as to surpass it. She swings a leg over my head and lowers herself to the water gingerly, with engaging little oohs and ahs of protest. Her hips settle snugly behind me, and the

15

water rises above my navel. I pretend concern with my wooden boat, as her long soapy thighs rise shoulder-high to either side and her heavy breasts slip and slide upon my back, and she absently soaps and strokes, humming a scullery ditty.

> "Whistle while you scrub,
> Rub-a-dub-a-dub . . ."

O my God, how glorious to feel the slick and billowed friction of her, my little prick floating upward like an infant turnip, my bowels loose and ready in the warm water, and my heart so full of joy and gratitude that I long to cut loose then and there, to uncinch the noose of nurture and give birth, letting it nose out from between my legs like a baby muskrat and strain upward toward the light, pull free and come tumbling to the surface, Eureka! sluggishly bobbing and rolling in the suds, my very own offspring and unique personal creation; and when she has climbed from the tub and stands dripping above me, her long flank looming, the wet fruit of her breasts swinging as she bends to dry her feet, then to reach out and take it up, greasy and substantial in the hand, and squeeze it, warm and rich and rare, and hold it up to her, my votive offering and fundamental valentine, bulging out between my fingers: I love you, mama, and all I have to give, I give to you.

One afternoon not long after she had taken her new husband, I did it, abruptly terminating our last bath together, and, in truth, our last tender contact.

For the anus is the Devil's place, we are told, and the fundament the seat of death, and its fruit is the substantiation of evil and the stuff of the anti-Eucharist, to be taken by the damned at Black Mass and washed down with the Devil's own wine. The latter was called pee pee, the former was known as dirties.   *or dépent*

"Dirties!" she cried out in alarm, shrinking back from my offering. "Dirty, dirty, dirty!" she insisted, grasping me by the shoulders and pushing me at arm's length toward the marble slab at the back of the room. Here we were wont to seal our mortified bottoms to a snug, cold collar and expel evil from us with a righteous wince, turning quick to empty the water jar, then the last hasty glance and wistful farewell.

"Dirty, dirty, dirty!" she said hotly into my ear as we watched it plummet into oblivion. What had it done that it should be sent to Hell so soon after seeing the light? Why should this turd, my progeny, be cursed from birth to disintegrate in the running black bowels of the earth, claimed by the darkness and lost forever, forever to be forgotten?

Why, indeed, should any of us suffer such an ignominious and irreversible end?

"Dirty, dirty, dirty!" she supplied, her nipples cold and hard against my back.

It was at that same marble slab that my Aunt Carmen reports finding me kneeling alone one afternoon as if in prayer, and it is upon the basis of this and other occurrences that I gained an early reputation for having a deeply spiritual nature. The fact is that I was not praying at all; I had received a toy fishing pole on my saint's day and was trying to get my turd back.

It was, of course, too late, and I never tried again, for by the end of my fifth year I had begun to accept the assurances of my elders that what I sought was to be found in an equally unlikely direction, that is, straight up.

2

A DARK humour thickened the Montesa blood, and it must be from there that I got this inclination to melancholia, often followed by sudden elevation and a hilarious urge to commit indecencies. The same bent had certainly added many reckless knights, fanatical priests, and morbid widows to my mother's line, including her father, Don Salvador Ribera de Montesa, a Castellano, noted for his moods even amongst that brooding race.

Don Salvador had been the son of a successful Crusader and was himself a Knight of Santiago. But he had become disheartened by the neglect into which chivalry had fallen, which is to say, by the erosion of his personal fortune due to the failure of several expeditions which he had financed against the infidel Turk. There are indications that following his last journey he compromised his faith, becoming an Erasmian, perhaps even an iconoclast. Adan, the eldest of my uncles, proudly described how the old knight had expired of dropsy on the steps of the Burgos cathedral after refusing extreme unction, insisting that he had lost his way and was looking for a tavern to die in, and attempting at the last moment to skewer the sun with his sword.

In the later years of his life he was given to prolonged silences, which in bad weather might last two weeks, and I recall my mother telling of being taken as a little girl on long walks across the gray Castilian plain, with her father saying no word, only now and then lifting her up onto a wall and pointing out the black muscled shape of a fighting bull, which

18

father and daughter would then regard in silence, while the hot sun beat down on the backs of their necks.

"Once he had got my mother from the convent of Calatrava and put her in his house," she said, "your grandfather went immediately away to chase the Grail and other enticements. The longest he was home was two years, the shortest a month, seven times in all, and each time he got my mother with child. It is said that he kept another family in the Moroccos. My mother hated him, but I remember him as a tall, silent gentleman who held me firmly by the hand, the old devil."

And then, even as her eyes stared mournfully, the coarse, compulsive chuckle sounded, and she shook her head in mingled admiration and disgust.

It was from such moments that I early sensed that the love that women bear for men is often laced with loathing.

Whenever I became ill, whether it was with a light fever or the ten-day pox, my mother always included in my treatment that procedure known as putting the clyster, or irrigation. She submitted me to this Old Christian remedy whether the doctor had suggested it or not, and it wasn't until my mature years that I discovered that the treatment was properly prescribed only for a stopped-up bowel, and not for unrelated annoyances such as headache and pinch blister.

I can see her now, looming against the door of the bath in much the same way that she looms in the nightmare of the nursery, except that this time she is readying the trappings for a more elaborate ordeal: a leather bottle called the clyster bag, with an attached length of open gut ending in a horn nozzle called the clyster pipe.

The floor tiles are cold against my spine as I lie naked and waiting. She fills the bag with hot water from the kettle, greases the nozzle, then turns to look down on me, the tube kinked in one hand, the nozzle thrusting from the other. Her eyes are dark, denying access, and yet a small flame stirs in each, and I see it and sicken.

"Lift your legs." I lift them. "Higher." My pimpled knees touch my collarbone and I start to topple sideways and have to catch myself.

The first chortle bubbles from her lips and is quickly swallowed. "Here." She hands me the pipe.

19

When I was younger, she put it in, but now I put it in myself. The nozzle is cold and I complain querulously. She adds more grease, then hands it back. Still, it is not easy; I groan, straining, and again her laughter bubbles up and is suppressed.

"Push."

I push. Quick and cold, it slides in.

"Lie still." She reaches behind her to unkink the hose, and the first rush of water falls into me like fire down a well.

"Too hot!" I thrash, fluttering my hands.

Hilarity seizes her and again is suppressed. "You'll get used to it. Hold it now. Hold it just as long as you can."

I obey, filling slowly, eyes clenched shut, the edges of the tiles cutting into my buttocks. A spurt of turgid liquid squeezes out onto the tiles.

"Hold it!"

I hold it, through all the long ordeal of my childhood, expanding steadily like some overextended wineskin, moaning and groaning, filled to bursting, mutely waggling my hands and rolling my eyes, begging for release.

At the very last moment, just as I am about to explode, she nods her head. "Go."

Groping at my fundament, I jerk the nozzle out and scramble to my feet, reeling on the slippery tiles, finding the marble slab, slapping my buttocks down and letting go in one great murky deluge that burns from me like brimstone. And then I slump, gasping and quaking.

But it is not quite over. Again there is the sound of guttural laughter, and I look up to find her gazing mournfully at me, her hands at her sides, the clyster pipe thrusting from her skirts, bobbing sinuously as she struggles to choke back her hilarity, and dripping.

Yes, my mother was strange. No doubt she feared her own duende, and that is why there was no eccentric bent whatsoever in the character of the man whom she selected to relieve her widowhood: Don Diego Lucero, the famous carpet knight.

Poor Don Diego; he was a man of good breeding, high principles, and a short purse. Carved into the stone over his door was his family's escutcheon and the motto BY VIRTUE, NOT BY CLEVERNESS. Written in gold over our chapel in the cathedral were the words WORSHIP GOD AND SERVE THE KING.

From a family of noble blood but failed vigor and only moderate property, Don Diego sought to strike the powerful pose of his forebears while at the same time struggling to get the money with which to maintain that deception. Prevented by his reputation and the purity of his Old Christian blood from engaging in trade, he counted himself lucky to be royal agent at the Casa de Contracción, where his duties consisted of wheedling Philip's fifth from all silver that came from the Indies, while at the same time seeking not to turn the powerful merchants of the city against the Crown. Compelled to dance the various jigs of commerce without profit, he had at the same time to play the politician and curry favor, for he hoped someday to go to court. And yet he never stole and declined to backbite, and as a consequence was regarded with suspicion by most of the fallen nabobs and ambitious bumpkins who peopled the king's civil service.

To add to the irony, Don Diego was something of a dandy with his sharp black mustaches and slashed sleeves, and was never arrogant, but most often tolerant and cheerful. Yet if one looked closely, one might detect that chronic nervousness which plagued him, revealing perhaps the hidden fear that virtue might not be its own reward, that the king might be indifferent to his honesty, and God unaware of his love.

I could not hate him, but neither could I love him. And because I could not do the one, which I wanted to do, nor the other, which I felt I had ought to do, I did neither, but struggled instead to accept his pious beliefs and adhere to his adamant ethics. Which was not an easy task in light of my mother's opposite inclination.

My mother once confided to me with carelessly veiled pleasure that Don Diego had proposed marriage to her no less than thirty-seven times before she had accepted, and that even then she had dickered with him, insisting that her own property be kept in dower and exclusive to her, and exacting a promise that she would never be required to do any domestic drudgery beyond needlework and the supervision of meals.

She early developed a manner of disdaining his values even as she complied with his conjugal demands. At his insistence, she attended

Mass daily and confession once a week. We all went to Mass together two days of the week, and she would be the perfect picture of pious attendance, except that her eyes, in the shadow of her lace mantilla, stared in that fixed unfocus which indicated, not religious contemplation, but deliberate vacation of the moment. Priests acquainted with her through the confessional were wont to study her with veiled annoyance, and I have an imaginary picture of her seated in the confessional with that same vacant look in her eye, offering one or two random sins, then lapsing into absent silence, as though she had quite forgot why she was there.

For many years I pictured her as being essentially the same in bed with Don Diego. In anxious fancy, I saw her entering the bed as she entered the cathedral, like some perennial martyr. I saw her receiving the votive candles of his adoration with the eyes of a plaster saint, tears of glass on her cheeks. No doubt she complied with his requests, however eccentric, just as she gave all the outward signs of acceptance during that other communion, reciting all the proper responses, kneeling submissively, taking the Eucharist between her lips. And yet in either case she was not really there, I told myself; the spirit denied the body and stood elsewhere, looking away. I saw her face as he entered: the single wince, then bleak forbearance, her eyes staring past his shoulder as he began; the ritual droning on. I saw her offering a few random movements of the pelvis, as she might offer a paltry sin or two in the confessional, then lapsing into utter indifference, as though she had quite forgot why she was there.

In fact, I knew nothing about their bedlife and heard them at it only once. I was five years old at the time and had awakened in the middle of the night to find my cuckstool full. Stumbling out onto the balcony that ran the length of our sleeping quarters, I was about to water the stable straw below, when I detected unfamiliar sounds coming from behind their door. Pressing closer, I heard a duet of urgent grunts and sawing moans, the memory of which would stir me to a confusion of sickly rage for years to come.

Stumbling back to my room, I came upon my nurse, Ines, and my grandmama's groom, Catalinon, who was young enough then to hang about our servant girls in hopes the moon might be right. No doubt the two of them noted my wizened face and saucered eyes, for Catalinon asked me, "Why so pale, young master, have you had a bad dream?"

"Mama is not well," I told them fretfully. "I heard her just now from that man's room."

I saw their hands go to their mouths, but I only frowned the more at the bawdy twinkle in their eyes. "There there, never mind," said Ines. "Your mother and Don Diego are only having bedtime cocoa."

"But does it scald them?"

They doubled over, clutching at one another, but Catalinon managed to say, "Perhaps your mama has backache, and your new papa is exercising her spine."

"Rascal!" said Ines, giving him a push and a promising whinny.

But I knew better, and soon I was back in my bed, clenching the blanket in my fists and promising myself that when I grew up and was a man, it would be me and not Don Diego who gave my mother her enemas.

I was not wrong, however, in sensing my mother's indifference to theology and distaste for the disciplines of the Church. And yet, despite the skeptical inclination which her attitude encouraged in me, I was far from unsnared by religion's clever netting.

No doubt it was the colored cartoons which first excited my fancy. These little pictures were called *biblia pauperum* and came into my possession atop boxes of marzipan given me by my grandmama. Many were the hours that I pored over them, thrilling to the gaudy images and puzzling over their meaning.

One in particular I shall never forget: the Ladder of San Juan Climax. The ladder stretched from the lower right up across the picture and out at the upper left, each rung lettered in gold with the name of a virtue. Up this spindly and demanding path strode the saint, armed only with the benevolent end of a Crusader's broad sword, which is to say, a cross, but looking no less the proud and noble knight. Below, Satan's dragon belched fire, and scarlet sprites clutched at the saint's ankles, trying to pull him down with those other sinners who tripped and tumbled into the flaming abyss below. Above, a host of winged angels sang and prayed, urging him on. And on he went, mounting rung by rung, his blazing eye fixed upward toward the corner where the ladder exited into an enticing nimbus of that sort said to hover about the heads of saints and between the thighs of lady martyrs, and which had its center just outside the picture.

What was that mysterious hidden lambency? "Heavenly reward," Ines assured me. "See how it glows, Juanito. How much more beautiful, how much less dangerous than those cacodemons and their roasting coals below."

So deeply did this picture impress itself upon me that one morning, after having suffered the awful nightmare of the nursery and its chuckling nemesis, I tilted a chair against the wall and began to climb toward the blinding light of the window.

"Juanito, where are you going? Look at him, the child is an adventurer already. But you must come down now and drink your cocoa, for you are not old enough for climbing yet. First you must learn your prayers."

I got my formal religion from a succession of enthusiasts. There was always a priest about, of course. When I was six, the tutors began to come, and by my seventh birthday, I was going twice a week to the monks.

God, I learned, was the all-powerful Father, the first and last Judgment and Word, venting vengeful wrath upon those who defied Him, yet licensed beyond his own commandments, and an admitted lecher. "Woe unto the daughters of Zion that walk with stretched necks and wanton eyes; I shall smite with a scab the crown of the head of the daughters of Zion, and discover their secret parts."

In certain quarters it was claimed that He also was a God of forgiveness and love, but something informed me that anyone that powerful would not lack for respect and attention and would therefore have little need to love or forgive. I saw Him as the Absolute Father: He who gave me life but might withdraw it at any time, as He had taken it back from my father. He held me in His hand, and I must needs seek and earn his approval or die, not just once, but time after time in Purgatory. Later in my youth, as the idea of a God in human form became unacceptable to me, the Dominicans sought to guide me to a more rarefied appreciation of the Absolute, but I conjured instead my own secret image of Him as a great black rock the shape of a cow's heart and lying on its side, as large as a cathedral, smooth and faultless and something like the Wailing Wall of the Jews, but with accommodations on all sides.

A feeling of terrible loneliness and longing came over me at times, as when I awoke late from my afternoon siesta to find the sun gone and night too soon outside my window, and my good-night prayer yet to be whispered: "If I should die before I wake, I pray the Lord my soul to take." It was said that the one word, touch, song, secret that might quiet my dread lay in the dense center of the black rock of God.

But the stone was too clearly impenetrable, with no direct way to its heart. In fact, should I affront it or even get too close, it might roll its dark weight upon me and blot me out at once, rather than later. There was less direct access to the heart of the stone, they told me. I might earn God's acceptance and earn His approval by obeying the commandments of the Decalogue and emulating his stepson, Christ of the Cross, or at least one or another of the martyrs. I might, through a species of spiritual abnegation, receive dim benediction from within the stone. I need only disavow the Adam in me and resist the misguided invitations of Eve, deny the Devil and eschew his marvelous enchantments, decline to covet, hew to the truth, avoid adultery, and call God by his single name, striving always to speak well of Him. I might win the hereafter of peace that was surcease of dread and yearning, if I would learn to give more than I took, to crave the nails and invite the spear; in short, to drink my vinegar like a good little Jesus and call it blessed wine. The key to God's heart, it seemed to me when I was a child, was human sacrifice.

But I did not want to be a sacrifice. I did not want to leave our garden and die before I woke. Was there not some way that I might quiet this dread and still stay in the flesh, some solace to be found here on earth, some surcease to be discovered in the lambent fogs at the top of Climax's ladder?

"Someday you will meet the perfect girl and live happily ever after," Ines never tired of telling me. "Ah, love, it conquers all."

The other discipline in which I received formal instruction was, of course, the Code of Chivalry. Eventually I was taught such manly arts as tournament decorum, challenge forensics, dressage, and fencing. I also learned of the legendary exploits of such noble and fearless knights as Amadis of Gaul, Orlando Furioso, and the proud Cid, Rodrigo Díaz de Bivar.

Here again, as there had been one saint, so there was one knight who attracted me most, and he was Perceval del Santo Grial. For in his story there was a hint of something beyond the hot delights of battle and the satisfaction of plunder, and that was the Grail. Like the heavenly penumbra at the top of Climax's ladder, this Grail was a tantalizing mystery. Some said that it was the cruet in which Martha caught the Savior's blood, others that it was the inexhaustible dish whence came the food for the Final Supper.

But my book told me that a great king had been wounded and his land laid waste by famine, and so he had brought his priests and wizards together and they had set apart a stone chalice wherein there was blood, and a beautiful maiden to guard it and await the coming of the knight. And Perceval came with his lance and asked the right questions and received the answers to its meaning and use, and healed the king and returned abundance to the land. And when he rode away with his prize, the Grail was not gold or silver, nor any longer plain stone, but a sweet and warming glow in his loins and heart.

Chivalry did not come naturally to Don Diego, if indeed it does to anyone, but was an acquired taste, like flagellation or the wearing of corsets. He was attracted to it because it was the published code of those he thought to be his betters: namely, his forebears. Had not a Lucero been the first Visigothic knight to be eviscerated in the Holy Land during the Second Crusade? Had not the first Count Lucero received his title as a reward for leaving his head with al-Mansur at Zamora; and had not ten Luceros died in the subsequent struggle to evict the infidel from the peninsula? Had not succeeding generations of Luceros devoted themselves to the persecution of the remaining Moors, the entrenchment of the nobility and the Church, intermarriage and land neglect, and the proud and pious decline toward bankruptcy?

Was not he, Don Diego Lucero, except for his brother, the count, the last living repository of that fine tradition? And did he not find himself forever at fault in its eyes, since he could not help but be aware that the willingness to die in defense of privilege's high ideals involved the risk of never again enjoying its benefits?

Although he had not stepped a lance nor jousted since his youth, he attended all the tournaments, kept his sword well polished and sharp, and often marched with it as a quartermaster-captain of the Knights of Alcantara, Sevilla chapter.

I have vivid memories of him seated in the candlelight on the night before a parade, fondly rubbing his blade, while I looked on in envy and admiration. Before I had a sword of my own, he liked to remind me, I must learn the proper care and honorable employment of the weapon. I must learn to clean and wax the steel, never to use it for prizing open boxes or digging out calking tar, and always to hand it over hilt first.

A sword was to be put to its proper use only in defense of honor, he explained, whether that honor be represented by one's good name or religious beliefs or person or property, or the person, property, or good name of those women deserving of such defense, that is, those committed to chastity. When challenging a wrongdoer, I must always give him notice of my intention and the opportunity to offer apology, and if he was unarmed or I had other advantage, I must do my best to correct the imbalance by procuring a sword for him, fighting with one eye closed should he be one-eyed, and otherwise narrowing the odds so that I might better know that I was a gentleman and not a mere brawler.

I was eight when I first defended my honor. My mother had given birth to Don Diego's child a year previous, and little Paco was old enough to walk and talk and was very much the darling of the household, which may account for some of the wrath which I brought to the encounter.

My antagonist was the son of one of the more powerful brokers of the city. He was a large boy who appeared to be made of gobs of salt pork, always had snot under his fingernail, spoke clumsy Spanish, and hated slender, well-spoken boys with pruned fingernails like myself. "Maricón" is what he called me, jabbing his thick forefinger into my breastbone.

27

"Your father sells short and cheats widows," I told him, quoting Don Diego. Then I pushed his hand away and bent to retrieve my pen case.

"You don't even have a father!" he taunted, putting a boot to my bottom and shoving me into the sewage.

Getting to my feet, I declared as I had been taught, "I must warn you, sir, that I am demanding satisfaction. Prepare to defend yourself."

Whereupon he knocked me down again, this time with a kick to my middle, then trod on the center of my back, grunting obscene threats to my fundament. I tried to roll out from under him, but he weighed half again as much as I, and even as I managed to twist onto my back, he fell with his full weight upon me, his fat legs to either side of my head, his fetid breath upon my face. Did my demon take hold of me? I know that the furia blinded me and everything went red. "En garde!" I cried, and sank my teeth into him, grinding through the muslin to the gristle beneath.

He arose with an eerie grace, like a puppet on a wire, then went shrieking off down the cobbles, clutching his offended parts.

I picked up my pen case and went proudly home, yet something cautioned me not to mention the matter to anyone there. Within the hour, the broker appeared at our door, a servant carrying the moaning boy; and the enraged merchant denounced me to Don Diego, complaining that I had crushed his only son's huevos and terminated his family line. As it turned out, the boy did not lose his bollocks just then, but some years later to the public hangman as a result of having been apprehended in a graveyard while engaged in the constupration of a dead priest, although he afterward maintained that he had only been attempting to confess to the corpse.

My resistance to this monster's attentions filled Don Diego with nervous rage, an emotion he was in the habit of disguising as disappointment with my performance as a man. It seemed that I had affronted the high principles of chivalry by attacking my opponent in a most unorthodox and intimate manner. Applying oneself to another's parts, however crude the provocation, was not the act of a knight and gentleman.

But that was not all. I had long been enamored of the wooden mannequin my grandmama had given me: a representation of the bull-baiter Pedrito, noted for bending the tails of enraged bulls in such a way as to cause them to defecate in time to the roars of the crowd. More than two feet tall and dressed in the garish rags of the arena, this doll had become my imaginary soulmate, and I confided all my secrets to it, including certain barbaric impulses felt toward my half brother. Moreover, the mannequin was equipped with a hinged jaw and a string at the back to work it, and many were the hours I had passed in private with my wooden friend on my knee, drawing oracular utterance and slavish praise from him whilst struggling to keep my lips still.

How painful on the night of my battle with the fat boy to hear my mother and Don Diego discussing the removal of Pedrito from my acquaintance.

"He talks to it, I tell you, and makes it talk back. He carries it with him everywhere, even out in the street. No wonder the Gomez boy had the effrontery to attack him. I tell you, Isabel, we are the laughingstock of the neighborhood."

"I admit there are prettier sights, husband, but the boy must have toys."

"Toy soldiers, a wooden sword, but not a doll. Dolls are for girls."

"But it is a boy doll, husband."

"So much the worse. Isn't it a doll of that notorious macaroon Pedrito? And the way he fought, biting like a girl. Do you want your son to become a poof, Isabel?"

From my place of concealment in the carriage loft I could not see them, but I had no trouble recognizing the guttural burst of my mother's chuckle, quickly swallowed. "No, I suppose not. And we must keep him from reading in bed by candlelight; they say it elongates the eyeballs."

That afternoon I took Pedrito on my knee for the last time, and both our voices trembled as I struggled to keep my lips from moving.

"Who will one day be the most feared swordsman in Spain?"

"Juanito Lucero de Sevilla."

"And what will he do to all those who would come between friends?"

"Toy with them until they beg forgiveness, and then run them through."

"Farewell, Pedrito, we are alike, you and I. Neither of us has a father."

So long as memory calls the tune, the dead will dance, says the proverb.

"Dear Yum Yum, you look just like your papa, in the eyes and around the mouth," my grandmama whispers in my ear. "Just like dear Angel come back to be with us."

And my mother stares; and with every year that I grow toward manhood, she seems that much more at a wary remove, as though I might be a ghost that haunts her. And Don Diego strives to be honorable and kind, yet eyes me nervously and askance. "Isabel, tell the boy to stop, he is looking through me again."

"Oh, certainly it is nice to have a new little brother," my grandmama persists. "But they couldn't possibly love you as much as your grandmama does, for they have Paco now, and he has both their hearts."

Several weeks after Pedrito was removed from my acquaintance, my grandmama came in her painted caravan to take me away for a day and a night, and again my mother made no resistance nor waved good-by, but only turned mournfully back into Don Diego's house.

I remember little of the trip to the gypsy camp and the longer journey from there to our destination, nor did I then know the celebrated name of the place: the Camposanto de Los Illustrios de la Confraternidad de Nuestra Señora del Cuerpo Inviolable y Eterno, known to the indelicate as Sevilla's boneyard.

But I will never forget the smell and look and feel of the place: the white walls as thick as a man is long; the huge gates, each with its black iron cross; the dark-jawed gatekeeper who accepted my grandmama's bribe and turned quickly away; the crunch of broken seashells underfoot as we made our way down the long double row of cypress trees; the pale mausoleums staring from all sides; the cold, shimmering moonlight giving the empty shadows life.

The gypsy scryer was a broad-shouldered woman with one eye missing. In its place was a silver ball which she several times removed and reflectively washed in her mouth, then replaced in its socket, whence it now and then caught the light and glimmered it back.

We went to a large crypt made of bluish marble, its low door barred by wrought-iron gates, with stairs leading down into sepuchral blackness. The scryer thrice circled the crypt, muttering to herself in a light, musical tongue and sprinkling what looked to be white ash from a pouch carried beneath her many skirts. Then she bent to remove the large bolt securing the iron doors. While the clashing of metal reverberated below, I craned to read the letters cut into the marble overhead, and recognized my father's family name: TENORIO.

I turned to flee, but too late; the scryer's husband clamped his rough hand about mine and drew me in and down, lighting the way with a candle. The smell was like no other; the stairs gritted underfoot; the clammy cold embraced us. As my eyes became accustomed, I could make out the pale sarcophagi on their shelves, each with a carved stone figure on top, lying on its back, hands crossed on chest and grasping roses or sword; and worse: the gaping empty spaces, waiting.

The scryer drew us closer to a figure at the back, handsome and young in ghastly granite, the cordage of the law at its shoulder, its hands crossed on the hilt of a sword, and on the craven face, a faint and arrogant smile.

"Close the circle," intoned the scryer, and my grandmama's claw closed on my left hand and the man secured me on the right. The scryer began to sway and babble in her strange tongue, calling my father's name. I was tugged to the left, then to the right, and soon we were swaying, and my grandmama was babbling too.

"Angel, we are calling you, Angel, give us a sign, kiss your loving Mama and kiss dear little Juanito, let us know you are here."

The scryer began to tremble and jerk, and my grandmama's hand tightened like a vise. "Angel, come to us and tell us why your bride neglected you and you died. Rise up, dear one. Touch us. Kiss your beloved Juanito."

The scryer's head jerked back; her eyes rolled in the candlelight, one milky white, the other silver, and her mouth popped open to let go a sawing moan.

"Angel, my son!" cried my grandmama. "You are coming, I can feel you! You are coming!"

I whimpered, the circle swayed, the stone eyes opened.

Was it a wraith or only an image on the inner slope of my eye? I

31

hadn't time to wonder. I saw it. Gray as dust, solid yet glimmering, it sat slowly up. It turned its head. The smile was now sad and imploring. It reached out a hand toward me.

"No!" It was a banshee shriek to raise hair on stone, and it was me. With sudden strength, I tore free of the circle and flung myself straight over backward to the stone floor, and there I thrashed and gnashed my teeth and howled, until finally a great white light rose up, then leaned upon my brain like a lowering sun, crushing me into darkness.

I shortly opened my eyes and looked up to find that they had made a new circle above me, and the gypsy scryer was allowing, narrow-eyed, that my grandmama could be right, yes, the child might have a certain talent for tongues, but in one so young, immediate application of the stick followed by a hearty dose of the salts was the only practical way to test the gift for permanency.

But my grandmama waved her away and bent closer, her voice a wistful wheedling in my ear. "What did you see, Juanito? Tell your grandmama. What did you see!"

How does one describe grisly nemesis and its blessed complement, surcease? "I saw a ghost," I offered faintly. "And then I saw the Grail."

child in his asleep father's house in a small town

3

Just as sure as we have all had a childhood, so each remembers a garden. Mine was the half hectare of rampant growth behind Don Diego's house in Barrio San Marco, Sevilla. The neighborhood, once the best in the city, had lost much of its elegance since the fifth Count Lucero had built there. Successful merchants and lawyers now occupied the disused villas of failed grandees; Dutchmen and Jews hurried along neglected streets where once only blooded Spaniards had strolled.

The reign of Philip the Prudent had lately been beset with wars and tumults, soon to culminate in those Netherland adventures that would cost him an Armada and the function of his vital member. With the ascent of Achmet the Venal to the sultanate of Tunis, there had been a renewal of the depredations of the Barbary corsairs, and the Englishman, Drake, was taking bullion from the galleons. The result was that the Indies trade was uncertain, the royal fifth diminished, and Don Diego was compelled to lean upon his meager inheritance for a living. Although he took care to keep the front of his house in repair, and had the coat of arms rechiseled once every two years, he could not afford to tend so carefully to the back side. The gardener had been sent on to other employment, and the garden had gone wild.

Thus I remember it, and thus I loved it: rampant, unpeopled, and vast, so that if one ignored the single neighboring house whose windows looked over our shrubbery, the place seemed all one world and all the world, with no beginning and no end, only moist gestation, pungent

33

decay, and the ceaseless hum and chatter of primal interchange. To all sides the vines and creepers thickened the shrubbery and spilled up the walls, reaching tangled fingers into the lower branches of the trees. Birds and grasshoppers chittered and whirred in the leaning grasses, rank weed sprang from the tiles of forgotten paths, and blood poppies were sudden in the greenery. At the very center stood a little sunhouse called the glorieta, its latticework rotting, its roof engulfed by honeysuckle.

I need only drop the damper between my innocence and my maturity to be young again in the grass, with the humus seething under my feet and life springing green between my toes, the first and only man, crawling on hands and knees through the leaf mold, lying on my back and watching the giant clouds of summer trundle the sky. It seemed to me that I would surely stay as I was, as the living garden was itself eternal, and that no ghost would ever hazard that sun, no death ever part me from that seething earth; and there would be no fall of faith or descent of testicles, only innocent sufficiency of self and the sweet delusion of a personal forever.

I was wrong, of course, for eventually I reached my thirteenth year, the age at which the boy Knights of Santiago were dubbed, girded, and sent to the Crusades; also, the age of Adam.

I knew next to nothing about girls, but I already had reason to be wary of approaching them wrongly. Once when I had been younger and attending the carnival with my grandmama, I had wandered away from her skirts, attracted by a muttering crowd gathered near the plaza fountain. Worming my way through, I had come suddenly upon the object of their attention, a copper basin containing a display the likes of which I had never seen before, yet which I knew immediately and with a certainty profound as the toothache to be the severed yard and codlings of a man no longer in the vicinity.

Unbelieving, I glanced desperately about for their owner, but saw instead the public hangman, standing on the rim of the fountain in his black mask, a bloody knife in one hand, and on his lips an expression that can only be described as ruttish. He must have sensed me there; perhaps he did not care to be stared at, or perhaps he only saw an opportunity to extend his afternoon's entertainment. He turned, and

34

the red-shot eyes looked left behind the eyeholes of the mask, then right, then fixed on me.

I ran, my hand clutched to my small cod, from which I would decline to remove it for two days. Once buried in the welcome stiflement of my grandmama's skirts, I found the breath to ask a most pressing question: What had the man done that he should be so cruelly separated from his parts?

"Why, no doubt because he was a constuprationist," she said with a judicious nod of her orange head. "No man has a right to construe ardor into violence upon a woman's person. Yes, a rapist. Or perhaps a pederast." Her painted lips curled, and she snorted indignantly. "Poofs! How dare they dally with one another and rob decent women of their attendance!"

"But, grandmama," I said, "are they both the same crime then?"

Considering this, she was suddenly seized with a fit of sniggering that shook her wig askew. "Well now, I suppose you might say that they are the two extremities of the same error, Yum Yum. At any rate, they have the same punishment, now don't they?"

The house that overlooked our garden had once been the winter retreat of an Aragonese nobleman whose other properties had been sequestered by the Holy Office as punishment for illuminism and book smuggling. It was a moderate-sized stone shambles roofed with slabs of Andorran slate. Time and the wind had loosened many of the roof tiles, and now and then one would slip off without warning and fall like a scimitar. Indeed, it was muttered amongst the servants of the barrio that on one particularly stormy night a falling tile had decapitated the nobleman whilst he was pursuing a housemaid into the garden, his naked body being later discovered just outside the scullery, his head several paces away in the compost pit, and the girl never seen again. Which event was said by the pious to have been a clear act of Providence designed as punishment for the old rake's licentious habits. One wonders what they might have said had he lost his noggin whilst on the way to Mass.

But the point is that there was a grisly air of amputation about the place, the which was not lessened by the presence of the new tenant, a retired military surgeon whose right arm was a quarter larger than his left, the result, the servants said, of his having sawed off so many mutilated limbs.

This menacing individual had two daughters, one of sixteen years, the other of nine or ten. The older girl went off to the nuns each day and soon took her vows, and so I never met her.

Quite another kettle of fish was the younger daughter, a narrow-headed creature, skinny like myself, and dull of hair, but with lively eyes and an air of voracious insistence rare in one so young. Perhaps too intimate a familiarity with her father's vocation had prematurely enflamed her. While her sister went to school, she was kept home and each afternoon put in her room to say her beads and do embroidery; and it was from such cloistering that she took to tormenting me from her window, which looked out over the hedge and down into my garden retreat.

Crouched in the grass and setting my rabbit snare, I would hear her laughter and look up to find her peering down at me, her face pressed to the bars.

> "Catch a rabbit,
> Catch a hare,
> Catch the housemaid on the stair."

Staining my cheeks with berry juice, I would hear her snigger and find myself no longer a painted Nubian warrior, but only a daubed and ludicrous pretender. Examining my private parts in the presumed seclusion of the glorieta, I heeded a crawling at the back of my neck and turned to discover her penetrating gaze fixed on my naked posteriors.

> "Bird in the bush,
> Bird in the hand,
> Hide rubbed wrong,
> Too soon tanned."

Still, I might have succeeded in ignoring her, had she not taken to accompanying her nagging with careless display of her limbs. Sequestered behind a palisade of branches built expressly to exclude her, I

36

heard her reedy cry, "Oh, nasty boy, I have a treat for you," and against my better judgment raised my head. She stood full length in her window with her skirts up over her head. "There, you nasty boy, what do you think of that?"

I was interested. But the moment I stood up, she dropped her skirts with a triumphant cackle, and I turned bitterly away.

On the next occasion, she announced herself dressed only in her shift and even wriggled a bit before snatching the curtain across herself and giving way to laughter. Finally she presented herself dressed only in her bloomers, and this time I found myself crossing the garden to glare upward from just below her window.

"What do you want?"

"Why nothing," she murmured, her manner suddenly aimless. "Only to talk." Striking a scrawny pose, she rolled her eyes. "Don't you think I am rather beautiful?"

I removed my gaze from her face and its unpleasant expression and fixed it on her bloomers. "Take your pants down." She said

"Everybody thinks my sister is pretty," she mused. "But that's because she is filling out. When I fill out I will be prettier, don't you think?"

"Take your pants down," I replied.

"I have my mother's eyes, but I have my father's chin, but thank goodness I don't have my father's nose, although I do have my mother's skin. Don't you think it smooth and nice?"

"Take your pants down!" I shouted.

Her eyes flew wide. "Oh!" She snatched the curtain across herself. "Lecher, how dare you!"

The furia rose hot in my throat, nearly choking me, and in an instant I was *el hombre a secas:* the elemental man, separated from everything that is not strictly himself or his own. I had just enough left of nurtured caution to ask if her parents were home. She shook her head, then put her hand to her mouth, but too late, for I was already rounding the far end of the hedge, racing the length of their garden, then up the steps and through the back door, down a short corridor, and into her room. "Kiss me!" I shouted.

She peered over the edge of her curtain, her eyes wide with delight. "You are too sudden. First you must send your father around to my father, then you must talk to my mother, then you must take me on paseo and buy me sweets—"

"Your bloomers!" I howled. "You showed them to me!" I clenched my fists and stamped my feet in a circle. "Take them down, take them down!"

"Never!" She drew the curtain tighter and looked down her bony cheeks. "You are wicked and I am not. You are a nasty boy, but I will be a lady—"

I flung myself upon her, tooth and nail. She bucked and shrieked like a rabbit, and the curtain tore down the middle; but after a minute I staggered back with her bloomers in my hand. She crouched with her small buttocks pressed tightly into the corner and both hands clamped to her hairless little coony, but not so effectively as to hide the small rosette of rusty discoloration just above it: a strawberry mark, like a rose grown from the magic hole.

As I bent my hot stare upon her, I became aware of her vivid radiance: the neck and shoulders flushed, the mouth gone moist and swollen open, the eyes wide and gleaming, stunned, mercurial: as pretty a picture as I had ever seen, and one that I would learn in time to recognize and love.

But my wondering study was cut short by the grind of a heavy tread at the front of the house; and I turned to see the surgeon coming down the corridor toward us, a limb not his own on his shoulder.

The doctor chose his surgery for my trial, explaining that it was the only place in the house where a man might be free of feminine intrusion. No doubt he was a kind enough man behind his frowns; more weary than mean, dulled by the revelations of his profession. I seem to recall him saying that what I had done had been regrettable but understandable, for he had heard his daughter nagging at me from her window on previous occasions and had asked his wife to chide her for it. Nonetheless, he cautioned, one could never be sure of women and should stay as clear of them as possible, no matter how inviting they might make themselves. He therefore advised me to ignore his daughter when I was in the garden, and he in turn would instruct her to cease tormenting me. Because he was confident that I would take his advice to heart, he would refrain from discussing the matter with Don Diego, unless, of course, I suffered a relapse. I should, of course, keep in mind that there were cruel punishments for entering a private house and forcibly divesting a lady of her undergarments.

And while he said this, he rested his outsized arm next to a bloody haunch of ox, and beside that was a copper basin. And as he smiled reassuringly, his hand played with a life of its own, hefting and trying the toothed edge of a gore-encrusted bone saw.

Scarcely a week later, as great caravels of cumulus sailed serenely down the sky, and I huddled down in my bower, pretending to be Orlando Furioso spying on Ali Jusef and his heathen encampment, familiar laughter rang out, and I turned to see my nemesis there again, standing full length behind the bars, her skirts over her head, the bloody bone saw in her hand.

The furia gripped me again, this time in double force. How can I describe these seizures of mingled rage, despair, and desire? The great Crusaders and some of the saints of old were said to have had a duende inside of them, driving them on to impress and remake and assault. This demon took me by the nape of the soul and shook me, rattling my bones and shaking tears from my eyes. I bent over, spewing curses, and peeled down my muslin trousers, then straightened with a howl, exposing all.

But my tormentor was gone from the window, and in her place now stood the imposing figure of her mother, peering uncertainly at first, then spotting me and pointing a finger. It would not have been so bad if first shock had been replaced by horror or even disgust. But she laughed, her rosy cheeks fattening, her tongue whipping the air. She laughed and rocked and pointed, and she was still roaring as I covered myself and went floundering away into the shrubbery, to come finally up against the high wall at the back of our garden. And there, cowering and grinding my teeth, I decided to go, if not at once, then the soonest possible, over east of Eden.

One afternoon some weeks later, I did climb the wall, and found myself gazing out across a ramshackle chaos of crumbling wattle and rotting thatch, threaded through with serpentine alleys, running with offal and teeming with life. And as I was staring, a coarse and lisping voice addressed me in bastard language from just below.

39

"M'lord, you perfumed snot, I am giving lessons in grinding, and for one copper marivedí you can attend. You look as though you might profit from some skill with the gristle."

He grinned boldly up: a large, bony boy festooned in dingy rags, his face and hands black with soot. As I studied him, several other tattered creatures shuffled forward to his side.

"Are you afraid, m'lord?" he challenged. "Or are you perchance a maricón?"

I hung myself over the edge and let go, landing in a heap and rolling down the rubble. Before I reached the bottom they had turned my pockets out, confiscating a pewter penknife and a copper sample of the king's debased coinage.

"Paid in full, m'lord. Now come and see a show." So urged the smut-faced king of the ragamuffins, placing a filthy hand on my shoulder and urging me toward a pig shed, while the others crowded along with us, excitedly picking vermin from their persons.

We gathered in the tumbledown stink of the sty, and our leader, who explained to me that he was apprenticed to the neighborhood charcoal seller, assumed the lectureship, sitting with dangling legs atop a broken box, with the top of a barrel for his lectern. There were perhaps a dozen of us in a circle at his feet, all younger than our mentor, but surely none so innocent as I.

"They'll tell you that it warps the knob and drains the cask," began the charcoal boy in pedantic tones. "But I say to you that no cask can be filled without it first be drained, and there never was a muscle that was not the better for exercise. And more, that it is God's gift to the poor man and the only honorable hedge against the slavery that awaits us all at the hands of the wenches, whose satisfaction does not come so cheap nor so easily to hand."

I did not comprehend all of it, but I could not mistake the drift. Grinding the gristle, he called it: jerking the gherkin, flogging, brandling. He described the technique, then waxed ecstatic over its refreshing effect, his eyes bright in their pallid sockets, his rags flapping as he spread his arms, pantomiming ecstasy.

I was fascinated, yet I found it difficult to believe that one might be able, first, to induce the organ to swell all out of proportion to itself without permanent distortion, and second, to coax it further by a process that sounded more like strangulation than anything else to spout a bodily product which was purportedly expendable yet at the same time precious in a most marvelous way.

The charcoal boy was openly proud of the stuff he claimed to produce with his arcane endeavor. It was, he declared, the grapeshot of every worthy warrior's cannon, the very milk and living substance of manhood. It contained, he claimed, minute homunculi or nascent human beings, capable of growing into full-size infants when deposited in the appropriate place. He further claimed that producing the stuff was a very pleasurable process available to the devoted practitioner several times a day, between which times the organ was busy manufacturing its homunculi and declined to either extend or extrude. One had only to be patient, however, before one might again have proof of one's manhood standing before one, ready to spout more of life's marrow pudding.

I had, of course, long been interested in the baubles of skin dangling from the bottom of my belly, which interest had deepened to fascination upon my being forbidden to do what was called "toying with myself"; and by reason of that tantalizing expression I had many times engrossed myself in secret manipulation, stretching it and pulling it, putting curtain rings on it, and even attempting to tie a knot in it. But, while I found these experiments to be mildly diverting, they were curiously unrewarding for a supposed sin.

Now, however, it seemed that my ignorance of the exercise's proper goal, together with my lack of training and practice in the correct technique, had kept me from full enjoyment. Or so our mentor told us, loosening his breeches and preparing to give a demonstration.

"All right, lads, if there be doubters among you still, let me show you how to work up a proper stand and when it pleases you to cast your rubric upon the ceiling."

I experienced a chill of unease, for the lesson was too suddenly intimate. And yet I could not move, but remained locked in the circle of my own fascination, my gaze fixed on the ragged crotch of the charcoal boy, whence his hands now brought forth his organ and tenderly displayed it, lying languid across his sooted palm. Its entire length was stained a smutty black, the color of his profession and mark of his addiction.

"There you are, lads," he announced. "The dragon of Misery Meadow," which name I later learned was that of the slum where we were. His eyes lost focus and a compliant smile wreathed his face as his hand closed upon it and began its masterful kneading. For a time there was only the urgent swilling of nearby pigs, the sodden flapping of his sleeve, and the whisk and slap of flesh on flesh.

Then his breath began to come short, his eyes closed, and his lips peeled back to reveal clenched brown teeth. I could not take my gaze from the organ. From the beginning it had seemed hose-huge to my enflamed imagination, and now it seemed to grow fat as a turnip, raising its sooty head free of mortal hand to tower over us all, even its spasmed owner.

Moisture bubbled from his clenched teeth, his eyes popped open and started from their sockets, and with one last series of furious strokes, he spent.

"Ah! Ahh! Ahhh!"

I began my experiments that night in the security of my bed. But before the bastonero had cried out midnight on our street, my worst fears had been confirmed. No matter how long or how vigorously or how gently I pulled, squeezed, stroked, and twisted, I could not get that small, infuriatingly indifferent appendage to do more than smart and flush an angry red. There was no heartening enlargement, delicious spasm, or glorious gouting. Instead, the thing seemed to shrink from my ministrations, as if in cowardly retreat from its proper function. But I could not allow it to get away, not on that night or any other. For the charcoal boy's lesson had been one of highest hope, and I had carried a new and exalting ambition away from the pigsty: to somehow induce my organ, this diminutive representative of myself as creator, to stand up and trumpet; for would not such an event proclaim me once and for all to be a man; and more, had not the charcoal boy promised a spasm so sweet and delicious as to take me right out of this world?

And so night after night I labored, coaxing it, cursing it, flailing it, and flattering it, always without the slightest sign beyond the burning of chafed skin and the ache of affronted gristle. It was a nightmare of diminishment and failure. But the longer it went on, the deeper became my conviction that I must succeed or die in the trying. I had no way of knowing that I was as yet a cryptorchid; that success was being delayed by the tardy descent of late-ripening stones. I knew only that I was in terrible danger and had to save myself, yet was constantly failing and did not know why.

Finally, when summer had gone and gray winter was in Sevilla, I took recourse in metaphysics, concluding that God the Rock had ordained my failure as punishment for my myriad sins. I picked my nose, squirmed at Mass, neglected my rosary, bearded my little brother, resisted labor, disappointed the high expectations of chivalry, harbored untold heresies, made an occasional clumsy attempt to secure advantage to myself by surreptitious means, and, of course, toyed with myself. Obviously I was a budding viper and out of favor in high circles, and was therefore being deprived of natural function until such time as I begged for forgiveness and earned it through renunciation, contrition, suffering, and prayer.

Thus I reasoned in the fever of my need, and thus it came to pass that, nightly beneath my blankets, ancient priapic ceremony enjoyed a curious revival. Head bowed, teeth grinding, recalcitrant organ in one hand and the other raised in supplication toward the tortured figure pinned to crossed sticks above my bed, I prayed to the Almighty, His Son, His Virgin, and various ordained associates, for success in my chosen endeavor.

For forty days before Christ's birthday and forty nights afterward, I ground my gristle and prayed to God; three and even four times a day. But the deluge was withheld. Not a dollop. Not a drop. It was obvious that the Lord didn't have the ravening need for my soul that I had for the spasm. And that is how I lost my faith in my thirteenth year and decided to save my breath for the essential effort.

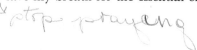

43

4

WHAT is life? the electors of Cordoba once asked Abd al Rahman II, the Aware; and the emir replied, "Dreams, awakening, and death." In childhood our dreams and nightmares germinate and sprout; in youth they wrap their roots around our souls. By my fourteenth year, I had come to dream of women through every third moment of my waking life.

Custom told me that my secret exercise had eventually to lead me to a female, but I feared the creatures. And so, if I could not manage at first on my own, and God declined to help me, then I would have to risk His wrath by invoking craven images of the imagination.

At first I took my models only from life, starting with the oldest of the sisters next door. Several times I had spied at her through the hedge as she drew water from the well, and on one occasion had glimpsed a swollen, pink-tipped breast as it swung briefly free of her jerkin. This sight had so awed me that I had immediately conceived a distant admiration for her: this plump marvel who already exhibited the formidable swellings of authority.

And so I prayed, in my way, to her breast, brandling away night after night, concentrating on the furtive pink wink of the nipple. But she inspired no result, and soon I grew discouraged and fickle, and abandoned her for the baker's daughter, glimpsed occasionally in the shadows at the back of the bakeshop, white to the elbows with flour and swollen ahead of her years. For a time I imagined that she had an eye for me as well, and in my fevered fancy she sprinkled powdered sugar

44

on her buns and warmly invited me in. But nothing came of her either, and in the end I became resentful and had to move on to another, and then to another.

How long would this go on? I asked myself. How many times would I have to try and fail before I finally came alive as a man? Were there men who tried all their lives and never managed to stiffen and spend? Were there a specific number of attempts required of each individual? If so, then it was only a matter of getting those preliminaries out of the way as quickly as possible. Desperately I stepped up the pace, taking every opportunity to seclude myself for a brisk rub: four, five, as many as ten times a day. And still: nothing.

Shortly after my fifteenth birthday, Don Diego sent my tutors away and placed my further education in the hands of the Black Monks. The Benedictines had never been much in the favor of the Crown, being principally Italian and infamous for moderation. But it was thanks to their policy of suffering nuns to come amongst them as teachers in the lighter disciplines that I found reassurance that I was not entirely alone in my obsession with female flesh.

Sister Alma de Flora was a Carmelite, originally from Rousillon, who spoke Catalan as well as she did Castellano and came twice a week from the nearby convent to recommend lyric verse and pencil drawing to the rowdy boys. Large-eyed, small-mouthed, and tiny in her red-crossed habit, she could be hard as iron in the name of discipline and kept a willow switch always close at hand.

And yet her face would soften as she read to us the old Galician lament of the locked-up maiden, and sweet melancholy would invade her eyes, revealing the girl she had left behind with her vows.

> "Badly wounded flies the heron,
> Struck with love;
> Alone it goes, uttering its cries."

Of course her charges had little sympathy with the plight of love-struck herons, and, anxious to be counted manly and among them, I would join them in their sniggering as she read from one of her less elevated favorites:

> "Three Moorish girls so fair
> Went to pick apples
> And found none there
>   in Jaen:
> Axa, Fatima, and Marien."

Her glance would sharpen at the telltale sounds of our prurience, and her dark eyes would flash and the willow cut the air above our heads, compelling silence but incurring resistance to the charms of poesy. I mimicked the resentment of my fellows, but I also faithfully copied out my verses and committed them to memory, for there was an ache in the words that echoed my own yearnings, and what was more, I was falling in love with Sister Alma, with both the susceptible maiden she had left behind and the stern mother she had become. Of course I knew nothing about women and was unaware that there was a third and more remote estate to which she aspired:

> "Mother, these mountains
> Are full of flowers;
> On their summit
> I hoard my love."

She must have detected the adoration behind my frowns, and certainly she could not help noticing that I was the only one who retained my couplets beyond recitation day and faithfully traced the Arcadian landscapes she gave us as models. She took me as her pet, retaining me after class and bidding me stand by her side while she cleaned slates and spoke with musing admiration of the travail of certain saintly searchers after Transcendent Beauty.

While I thrilled to the muted passion of her voice and the tintinnabulating click of her beads, she showed me engravings and apprentice copies of the toy angels of Fra Angelico and the quaint Annunciations of Filipili, and explained to me that these were works of men of true talent and great exaltation, but as simple in their faith as they were in their use of perspective, and as blind to the good in nature as they were immune to its temptations.

While I drank in the musky smells of her, the oily tang of tallow and the spicy tickle of incense, she showed me the spindle-legged Adam and Eve of Palladina and the heavily draped Virgin of Anonimo Castellano, and explained that while these artists did reveal an appreciation of the vegetable glories of nature, there remained a crippling fear of the flesh.

And then one day she drew from its paper wallet a small copy in oil of a picture that was my most ardent dream brought to life: the garden and the flesh made one. I had to bite my lip to prevent a spontaneous oath of appreciation from sullying Sister Alma's ear.

Six half-naked women stood and danced about in an Arcadian grove carpeted with flowers and overhung with a canopy of green leaves and oranges. There were two male deities, one at either end of the panel, and a fat cherub overhead amongst the fruit, but these scarcely interested me. The original was from the brush of a dead Florentine named Botticelli, Sister Alma told me, and it was commonly called *Primavera* or *Spring*, but she preferred to think of it as the Annunciation, not only of the Blessed Virgin's legendary achievement, but of the triumphant marriage of truth with faith. Here, in the rampant abundance of flowers and fruit, was nature accepted. Here, in the exposed limbs and frank postures of attendant ladies, was the flesh unashamed.

But it was to the central figure that I must look for the final triumph of Ideal Beauty, Sister Alma assured me. Correctly called Venus, she was nonetheless much more than a mere representation of fleshly beauty. It was no mistake that she stood at the center of the composition, for she was its heart and the artist's supreme achievement. There she was, her head haloed by a lacy bower of leaves, her expression open yet pensive, her pose graceful but not wanton, the lines of her body frankly revealed beneath the filmy pleats of her white chiton, yet with its lower reaches covered, not by the blue veil of chastity, but by the casually gathered folds of a mantle the color of an opened pomegranate.

Was this not the scarlet of passion honestly recognized but calmly assimilated? Sister Alma murmured, her habit rustling softly as she bent her head close to mine. Was not this eminently human yet utterly tranquil figure the picture of woman carnate, yet transcendent? she inquired, her quickened breath puffing hot little blasts of cinnamon-

47

scented air against my cheek. Clearly, to look upon this vision was to comprehend the Blessed Virgin anew as she who had known the sundering insistence of the flesh yet remained essentially immaculate through her undying aspiration to that higher invasion by the Father, Son, and/or Holy Ghost, as extolled in the verses of Fra Louis de León:

O Sound, O Voice!
Surely some small portion of you
Could descend upon my senses
And drive my soul beyond itself
And convert all of it into Thee, O Love!

"Oh, isn't it glorious!" Sister Alma cried, clutching me to her. "Aren't we blessed to be given this vision of True Beauty as our guide?" she gasped, her fulsome bosom knocking on my cheeks. "Oh, surely art is the Grace of God and an exalted calling! Go, my child, take this painting and copy it reverently, as you would the map of heaven, and learn the road to ecstasy."

I did so, carrying away the panel and a lingering redolence of candle wax, cinnamon, and something infinitely richer. And yet, eager as I was to please Sister Alma, I found it difficult to fix upon the figure she recommended, since it seemed only a pale cutout when compared to the lusty ladies on either side.

On the far right, a delectable creature in a transparent shift coyly evaded the gropings of some admirer, while at her side a handsome amazon scattered blossoms, her flowery gown clinging to one round thigh. Even the cupid overhead was of a more appealing mold than the pallid Virgin-Venus.

But it was to the three targets of Cupid's arrows that my gaze was drawn and helplessly fixed as I labored with my pencil. They were on the left of the Virgin and unnoticed by her, but were nonetheless the largest and closest to the viewer and certainly the objects of the painter's most ardent, if oblique, attention.

How eagerly must the Signore Botticelli have waited for the chill Virgin to vacate his studio, so that he might turn his attention to her naked attendants. What a time he and his three bulging models must have had, with Ideal Beauty and other grave ideals put aside, and the afternoon left free for mundane romping. Or so it seemed to me, gazing upon the prodigal three.

Clothed only in clinging swirls of ethereal gauze, they danced hand in hand in a closed circle of abundance and exposure: the three Graces, Verdure, Gladness, and Splendor. They were one creature, really. Thanks to the painter's ingenuity, one was given a triad view of the same sumptuous object seen from three strategic angles.

Now here was transcendence, it seemed to me; here was a truly artful extension of the mortal view. I had never seen such an undulating medley of flesh, such languid limbs, such softly sloping shoulders, such muscled buttocks and swollen thighs and rounded bellies sloping down to those deepest recesses where folds of gauze congregated in tantalizing shadow, encouraging my ogling eye to a desperate delving and my pencil hand to furious activity.

Closeted in my room and scribbling by candlelight, I had neither time nor thought for my secret exercise and so passed it up for the first time in many months, bedazzled as I was by high artifice, so eager to please Sister Alma. I did not neglect the Virgin, but dutifully sought to reproduce her polite pose and placid outlines. However, in my haste, I made her even stiffer and blander than she was, while in the fever of the early morning hours I failed to notice that I had made the Graces twice her size and lavished far more loving care upon them, down to the last detail of flirtatious invitation, the most suggestive crease of flesh. In the end, she came out a prim midget, while they were glorified giants.

Reeling with exhaustion and aflame with achievement, I breakfasted with the rolled drawing clenched between my knees, rushed to school, and found Sister Alma alone in the lecture room, just finishing her morning prayers.

With what sweet and maidenly bemusement she murmured her last Hail Mary and let go her beads. With what warm and motherly expectancy she smiled upon me as the foolscap unrolled before her. With what womanly outrage she gazed upon the evidence of my enchantment. With what a shriek of hellish fury she rose up, wild and witchlike, to bring her willow switch down again and again upon the careless buttocks and easy thighs of Verdure, Gladness, and Splendor.

"Foolish girls, wanton wenches, strumpets!" she cried, scourging my exposed instincts and her own bitter memories. "Little pagan, lost soul, lewd-minded boy!" she wailed, collapsing into her chair and reeling in her beads. "O treachery, O heartbreak!" she wept, clasping her hands in prayer. "Oh, where did I fail, how have I led this child astray from Thee, Blessed Mother, Bleeding Son, Almighty God? O Sound, O Voice, O Mystery, descend upon his senses and drive his soul beyond itself! . . ."

First came shock, then shame and regret. For, be assured, I wanted as much as any man to see Venus transcendent, and I too longed to have the Mystery descend upon my senses. But something told me that for the moment my best chance lay with the sisterly Graces; that it was one thing to cultivate celestial appetites with Sister Alma, and quite another to pick juicy apples with three Moorish girls from Jaen: Axa, Fatima, and Marien.

Aghast and ashamed, I mumbled my farewells and fled. But I did not forget to take my drawing, and that very night lay down with it in the seclusion of my room and enlisted the Graces in my own search for transcendence. But it did not come. Again, failure. All that flesh deployed before me, and still my traitor worm would not respond.

In the meantime, I sometimes had company in the garden in the person of my half brother, Francisco. Poor Paco, the more I was balked in my secret endeavor, the more I was inclined to take a big brother's advantage. When we played at Roman wrestling, I appointed him the villain and the vanquished, flinging him over my shoulder and into the bramble bush. When we reenacted the funeral of Charles V in the stable, it was he who was required to play the corpse, lying rigid on a catafalque of bundled hay, while I indulged in elaborate grief as the orphaned infante. I even employed him as replacement for the long-gone Pedrito, perching him on my knee and teaching him to waggle his jaw in response to jabs in the small of the back.

"What is your name, little one?"

"I am Cupid, love's messenger."

"And who am I, upon whose knee you sit?"

"Juanito Lucero, soon to be the greatest lover in all of Christendom."

But Paco did not long remain my obedient lickspittle. Very like a cherub with his sweet face and pale curls, he too had a demon in him. Moreover, he had become committed to disability as a source of power;

he had learned to stutter. One afternoon he asserted himself whilst seated on my knee, suddenly defying the first law of ventriloquism: that the dummy should speak only when spoken for.

"Who are you, little one?"

"Cupid, your obedient servant."

"And who am I?"

"Juanito Lucero, who tuh-tuh-toys with himself."

Instantly my duende went hot with fear and furia, and I dumped him off my knee. "If you tell," I said, aiming my toy crossbow, "you will get a bolt through your breast."

But the furia is not exclusive. His small face went a startling crimson and he opened his mouth to shout for all the neighbors to hear. "Juanito tuh-tuh-tuh-tuh—"

Perhaps it would not have happened if his impediment had not drawn the betrayal out so. I pulled the trigger, embedding a blunt arrow in the flesh of his upper arm.

"Toys with himself!" he screamed, and fell thrashing to the ground. Then how he did howl, and how the blood oozed from the puncture, blacker to my horrified gaze than all the seven wounds of San Sebastian. And how my heart wallowed and sank, for never in my worst nightmares had I come this close to the final dismissal.

We gather for domestic tribunal in the shuttered shade of the sala, Don Diego presiding in a high-backed chair, my mother with her head bent and her hands motionless on a heap of embroidery. Wooden-faced and of a ghastly hue, Don Diego interrogates the victim, his agonized gaze fixed upon the gigantic bandage at Paco's shoulder.

"Were you teasing him, Paco? Did you taunt him?"

"I duh-duh-didn't tuh-tuh-tuh—"

"You must have said something. What did you say?"

"I suh-suh-said that Juanito tuh-tuh-tuh—"

"Come now, speak up, there is no honor in lying."

"I'm nuh-nuh-not luh-luh-luh—"

"Calm down, you have only to tell the truth."

"I am tuh-tuh-telling the tuh-tuh-tuh—"

"That's enough, stop that, you know it makes me nervous. You have made your denial."

"He aimed the cuh-cuh-crossbow at me and puh-puh-pulled the tuh-tuh-tuh—"

"What do you say to all this, Juanito?"

"Puh-puh-pulled the tuh-tuh-trigger and shuh-shuh-shuh—"

"Enough, I say. Juanito—"

"Shot me in the arm and I was *bleeding!*"

The unstuttering cry of high dudgeon and heartfelt pain shrills off into silence, and blood suddenly does tell; moral dilemma loosens its enfeebling hold upon Don Diego's face, and his eyes fix on me, each a lance point of rage.

"Well, Juanito?"

I know that I am lost; there is no way to tell, nor any profit in it. I turn to my mother, but she turns her gaze away, her eyes dark with indecipherable gloom. Leaving me no recourse but to desperate deflection, no defense but suicidal attack.

"I don't care! You are not my real father! You don't love me! I don't care what you think!"

The words lash Don Diego's face. And then the tide of hapless comprehension, then the chill ebbing of blood from the cheeks. He sighs, his face gone to wood again, his voice droning wearied reason.

"We will forget that you said that. You will go to your room and have no dinner but bread and watered wine, and you will not be allowed to play in the garden for two months. God knows I have tried. Good night, Juanito."

Shame, sorrow, and guilt dogged me to my lonely room. No furia now; my duende had deserted me, leaving only the dread, the ache, the longing. Hidden away in the darkest recess of my mind there was always the one recourse and ready cry: "Papa, help me, teach me, touch me!" But I dared bring it to thought no more than I did any other prayer, for with the memory of his face also came the chilling threat of the tomb.

My gaze fell upon the three Graces, but I looked away; no surcease there, only empty promise and the dry grind of futility. I lay upon my bed and let the tears run into my ears. My hand made its way beneath my nightshirt and began to stroke soothingly, while I gave my mind over to dull worry and despair. And then it began.

At first I couldn't believe it and had to relinquish my grip and hoist my nightshirt to look, only to grab on again. It had fattened, it grew, it was rising! O, mighty muscle, O gorging veins of glory!

No guilt now, only the vision blurring and the mind lost to the urgency of the glands. All of me gathered, as it were, somewhere just below the coddling sack: a red-hot, swelling lodestone of insistence, shut of past and free of future, heeding only the devastating demand of now.

> O Sound, O Voice!
> Descend upon my senses
> And drive my soul beyond itself!

And now it was, like the violently precipitous yet excruciatingly slow, laudanum-numbed yet utterly engrossing pulling of a tooth, while somewhere the surgeon curses and the patient groans and the pincers draw ecstasy on to eternity, pulling not a mere tooth now, but the entire jaw, not merely the jaw, but the whole head, creaking and twisted on its roots and finally wrenching loose in a cataclysmic parting of all consciousness from the body practical; while the blinding white light wavers and leans, and the throbbing plug of the soul spouts and flops forth from the severed neck in curdled hot gobs of jittering protoplasm.

O proud and yeasty issue, O wrenching triumph, O sweet relief!

If I had not been before, I was surely now at the beginning of my tether. *he became a man*

53

5

How easeful to know that it could be done. Now, should the public executioner creep up behind me and snip off my apparatus, I could die secure in the knowledge that I had been capable of fundamental function. If my scepter yet lacked a subject, at least it no longer lacked the royal pearl. And whenever I suffered a momentary lapse of confidence, all I had to do was retire to seclusion somewhere, perform a simple manipulation and be reassured of rudimentary manhood.

Once I had absorbed the shock of discovery and assured myself that during climax I was experiencing rapture and not rupture, I set out to devote my fifteenth year to onanistic experiment, bringing to the study all the passionate relish of a lunatic prodigy teaching himself to saw the fiddle.

In a short time, I was a virtuoso. Of course my performances were essentially solo. Without a partner, I was entirely in control. However, I soon discovered that the more tension I created as I approached the climax, the more delicious would be the spasm, the more dazzling the nimbus.

But I was still mortifyingly ignorant of the subtler shapes and shadings of my target. I had glimpsed the surgeon's eldest daughter's breast only fleetingly, and now I was given another look at that organ, but this time in entirely too much detail.

54

My Grandmama Trotaconventos des Puig-Tenorio inveigled me to her house on the banks of the Guadalquivir, to meet her new husband, Don Cuero de Tortuga. But I had scarcely been there an hour when she whisked me into her dressing chamber, and there leaned forward with burning gaze, fumbling at the front of her blouse. "You are old enough now to know, Juanito. I want you to see the terrible suffering your poor grandmama must endure."

The silk fell aside, and there it was: a hanging puddle of bluish dough, with its broad, dark nipple, and close beside that, another eye, a charred crater the size of a doubloon, black as cinder and moistly fuming. "The surgeons want to cut away the whole tit, but I tell them, no, you plow but you do not sow. Never!"

She smiled tenderly upon the cindered flesh, and a tear formed in her eye. "It was your father's favorite. Dear, sweet Angel, how he would cry out for it, his tiny hands squeezing, his little teeth nibbling so hungrily, just here."

She touched a crimson-tipped finger to the crusty rim and muttered, "Hard as burned cake and won't go away. No salves, no creams, no magic potions will soften it." She raised her orange head, and her little black eyes glittered. "But I will not let them cut it off! And I will live ten years more to spite them. Twenty, longer! And when I die, I shall be buried whole, and not here and there!"

Nausea interfered with my attempts to admire her defiance, and the exhibition added a certain grisly bonus to my private ambition.

Inspired by my introduction to the gorgeous Graces, I took to augmenting my fancies by making drawings. How my hand trembled each time I took up my crayon to draw the first long curve of hip and thigh. How my heart began to trot and skip as I outlined one breast, then the other, traced the curve of the belly, then added a smudged dot for the navel. What a miracle it was to look upon the finished cartoon, this enticing beauty, forever mine, this maja desnuda, conjured up and stripped naked by my hand. I drew crudely at first, but eventually with some finesse, even adding variations of configuration, pose, and drapery.

There were not many representations of the uncovered body

available for guidance. In the churches there were only the thickly draped virgins and saints, and the life-size Christ that hung on nails over every altar, in such excruciating pain that He had to be undergoing punishment for nothing less than His nakedness. However, there were certain crude cartoons in circulation amongst the rabble, usually depicting peasants coupling with their animals and priests with one another, and one day as I was making my way home from school, a diseased mendicant accosted me from an alley, holding out such a drawing with one hand and his poxy organ with the other. I got a good look at the picture before fleeing, and carried away the boggling image of a soldier servicing a naked woman with his stave, which concept I later transformed into a drawing of Amadis slaying the winged serpent, the same causing some uneasiness amongst the monks at school, although none of them seemed quite able to bring to open declaration the fact that my dragon was quite voluptuous and graced with two scaly breasts.

This particular image stuck in my mind, and I found myself making variations, finally producing a sketch of a vegetable hawker servicing a lady customer with his prize gourd, the which work turned out to be quite vivid and grotesque. It was my custom when I was finished with a cartoon to hold a corner of the paper over the hot coals of my charcoal brazier until it was aflame, then to drop it out my back window. Usually it had turned to ashes by the time it reached the ground, but this time the wind blew out the flames without my noticing, allowing the partly charred paper to fall to the earth, where Don Diego discovered it on one of his periodic prowls of the grounds.

His knock on my door was deliberate and ominous, and when I opened it and laid eyes on his face, I thought surely the plague was in the town. He did not say why he took me to the stables for our conference, but he seemed quite certain that that was the place for it. There, he drew the drawing from his tunic with all the solemn relish with which the Inquisitor-General might produce a pact with the Devil.

"I found this on the ground below your window," he announced gravely. "It is yours, I presume."

I knew that he knew the color of my crayon. "Yes."

"I am surprised." He shook his head, his expression of saddened disgust meant to indicate that he was no such thing. "Disappointed as well. Oh, I'm not going to punish you. This is, well, beyond punishment. But I want you to be honest with me. We must get to the bottom of this if you are to be saved. Do you . . ."

He peered intently at me, then looked away and cleared his throat. "Do you toy with yourself?"

With a certain sly, sidelong curiosity, I answered, "Yes."

A sickly smile came and went under his mustache. "Yes." He looked away and studied the mule in the next stall, then nodded and began tumbling words like a priest rattling off the last rites over the victims of some incidental disaster among the poor.

"Of course you do, yes, boys will be boys, but you should restrain yourself, excessive self-pollution leads to arefaction and eventually tabefaction of the privy member, thickens the palm, and is likely to drive you mad and make you a poof as well. But the real danger lies in filthy thinking. Coupling is only filthy when it is done as the animals do it, purely for physical pleasure. We are not animals, we are better than that. We know that a hard yard has no soul, a stiff prick no conscience. But we also know that union between men and women can be beautiful and clean when it has a pure and exalted purpose. It must be so, for otherwise life would have no meaning, now would it? Surely our destiny is not to, excuse me, spend into one another through endless time like a string of apes. No, we are rising, generation after generation, mounting closer and closer to perfection. Does not the fact that we can conceive of something superior to physical gratification prove that higher goal to be a possibility, more, a promise? Oh, certainly, one falters occasionally and backslides. We all have a go in the cribs now and then, and I want you to come to me if you need protection. The peckernoose is painful, and using a gutsheath is like washing your feet with your hose on, but it is better to be safe than sorry. As for the spilling of seed, it may be a torment and seem a waste, but as my father the count used to say, God rest his soul, there is a time and a place for everything, and a wise woman will advise you as to the first and offer you the last. As for the real thing, well, someday you will meet the girl you want to marry. Don't abuse yourself with overindulgence and ruin your member and your mind. Save yourself for the maiden who is waiting for you somewhere now, keeping herself wholesome and complete for you alone."

He came up short, still staring at the mule's glossy hinderlings. "Do you have any questions?"

I peered at him in dismay, reeling from this flood of suggestion. "Did you say, was it, arefaction?"

"Of the privy member," he confirmed briskly. "Arefaction: drying up. Tabefaction: wasting away. But, as I have said, the greatest danger is spiritual, and in that regard I would mention this drawing of yours."

He allowed his glance to fall to the paper, then managed to hoist it away on a wince of disapproval. "Listen to me, son, and I call you that because, although you are not my son, I think of you as my solemn charge and obligation. You appear to have talent. But I hope to God you can find a better use for it than this. Think, Juanito. Use your head. A woman's body is a temple, not a tavern." His voice deepened in passionate entreaty, and his ring finger stabbed at the drawing. "What if this were your mother? Think about that."

It happened that very night. Snug beneath my blanket, I was brandling away whilst contemplating the phantom of Verdure, when I glimpsed, around the corner of my mind, so to speak, a fugitive and tantalizing image. Even as I recognized my danger and strove to turn my mind away, a fatal compulsion demanded that I face the phantom. And even as I saw my mother, nude and grinning upon the vegetable hawker's gourd, I felt my stomach turn with jealous rage, and at this, the first vision was promptly replaced by a second, in which I saw the gourd become my own organ, and saw that organ fatten and shudder, and then begin to spout, not creation's proud pudding, but dark-red life's blood, fonting with each lustful heave of my heart.

With a yell I leaped from my bed and flung my organ from me as the traveler flings the scorpion from his boot. Only after I had stopped trembling could I bring myself to climb back into bed, gingerly take up my gristle and submit it to a cursory grind, taking care to think only upon the bodies of strangers.

Thus I came to yearn all the more desperately for the moment when I might close with a woman. Pursuing me were the threats of arrefaction, tabefaction, hoof on the palm, and poofery. Beyond was that other dream of sweet surcease. Even Don Diego had said that there was a maiden waiting somewhere for me, and had not the mooning reverence of his tone implied a consummation more fine and beautiful than any I had heretofore enjoyed?

By now I had lost my baby fat and got my height. Although my voice still now and then went acroak, I had nearly got control of it. I knew that I had pretty curls, for I had been told so by my nurse and my grandmama, and my eyes were big, I could see that in the mirror. Sometimes when I looked there, I seemed most ungainly and epicene to my uncertain study, but at other times I gave the mirror a careful pose and could almost see the gallant I wanted to be, and at such times it seemed to me that surely if I were a wench I would want me to swive me.

It was a difficult and dangerous undertaking to get next to most girls of my age and class. But not all girls were so jealously protected by the community, since not all were held in equal esteem. Carolina Entremeses-Lopez lived at the edge of our Old Christian enclave in a plain house which her parents were allowed to rent but not to buy, although the gossips claimed that her father had enough gold slung behind his beard to buy the place ten times over. He was a *converso*, that is, a former Jew who had taken to nibbling the Host rather than biting the Inquisition's iron; and who enjoyed the tolerance of the neighborhood because he served as public scribe, the majority of his fine neighbors being unacquainted with letters. He took his family to Mass, where they were given a special place behind a pillar and watched closely for sprouting horns. His daughter went to lessons with the nuns, most of whom treated her with equal superstition, particularly since she was quite pretty.

As my mother was dark, so Carolina was too, with glossy black hair, light to lift yet weighty and slithering in the hand, and a hint of swarthiness in the flesh, a trace of smut beneath the scrubbed, translucent skin. Brown eyes, blood-dark lips around rueful laughter, buttocks and breasts that were never quite lost to the drapery but strained against restriction, refusing all fashion but their own. And what is more, certain young officers of the Catalan Academy had let it be known that she could be persuaded to lift her skirts.

My miracle occurred during the fiesta of San Juan, originally a pagan celebration, since imperfectly converted to the Church's use.

Father Nuncacura, a cropsick fanatic who went about with penitential psalms on his lips and caked spunk on the front of his cassock, had chosen the Temptations of Saint Anthony for that year's tableau, and had chosen me to play Anthony, Carolina to impersonate the saint's chief temptation.

Thus it came to pass that every afternoon for one glorious week I sat bolted by furtive lust and longing to the saint's rustic stool, rehearsing a face of pious resistance, as prescribed by old Crusty-cassock, while the Dominicans' paper harpies and masked demons clacked and capered about me, screeching for a soul publicly armored but secretly yearning for capitulation. At a command from Nuncacura, the lesser demons dispersed, and upon the sweetest of lute glissendos, Carolina appeared wrapped in gauze: Verdure, Gladness, and Splendor all rolled into one.

I scarcely remember the climax of the little drama, involving the use of a mirrored spirit lamp supposed to represent the blinding white light of the Supreme Father; I remember only that each time I tried to speak, I could not, and that the merciless light then drove the beautiful wraith away.

It might have ended thus in unspent mummery, had not Carolina herself made the crucial gesture, reaching out on the very last day of rehearsal and, in defiance of Nuncacura's jealous glance and even the forbidding glare of God's white light, touched me. To this day I can recall the dove-soft press of her breast to my shoulder, neither incidental nor accidental, but a deliberate, artful invitation. More than that, she laughed softly, acknowledging the wantonness of her gesture; and whispered something, it does not matter what, and her mouth opened in a blood-dark circle, and for the first time I saw the quicksilver worm coiling in her eyes.

O my God, to be warmed like that and still not burn! On the instant it became the dream of my life. The nuns and monks were to shepherd their charges to the seaside for a picnic the next day. Still in monkscloth and with the saint's anguish upon me, I edged up to Carolina after rehearsal and gave my longing voice. Yes, she whispered, and she was smiling, yes, she would be there tomorrow, yes, and she was gone.

I remember almost nothing of the performance that night in the plaza, only that this time she did not touch me, but gave way before the glaring eye of God, that Nuncacura smirked, while the Dominicans frowned and took recourse to their bottles; and that the parents and neighbors politely applauded their little saint's triumph over the flesh, then hurried off to douse their own with wine and put the torch to paper devils.

Later, while the fires blazed at every crossing and the reeling faithful passed in procession before our house, I lay wide awake in my bed, struggling to keep my hand from its usual occupation. Although I had not yet pushed my organ to the limit, it did seem that it must be close to dread arefaction. If it did not fall off from overwork, surely it would soon dry up at the source, like some holy spring overworked for miracles.

But whence came the quivering conviction that on the morrow we would lie together? Perhaps the past two years of compulsive grinding had already done their work, and my conviction was only the crazed delusion of an apprentice maniac. She had not touched me tonight; was I sure she had touched me earlier? And what had she actually said except that, yes, she would be at the picnic? How could I be sure that this raving need of my heart and flesh was equaled in hers and had not been merely echoed back, as from a mirror? How could I know that she loved me and I did not merely love myself?

By midnight, mingled anticipation and apprehension had me so agitated that I found I could no longer resist, and once started, found it impossible to stop until exhaustion overtook me. With my hand on my organ, I fell into sleep as a grave-digger might swoon into his own dreadful ditch, taking his shovel with him.

And yet, at the first crack of dawn, I bounded from my bed with the eagerness of an infante on coronation day, and had been a full hour on the curb before the coach full of sleepy youngsters, cupshot monks, and sharp-eyed nuns finally appeared and swept me up. The finches shook themselves awake in the shrubbery and the grass lay down with dew. We rattled along the streets and turned up hers, and the doors opened and she backed out on tiptoe and then came running. She climbed the step, and I could smell the wet cobbles of morning, the unseen fuming of the Universal Alkahest. Ablaze with the same but politically wise, she smiled and greeted each and every one, then settled herself beside me, leaning away to chatter of the weather, while her hand sought mine amongst the folds of her skirts; and from that moment on, all was delirium.

We rode with the chattering world but were alone in giddy conspiracy, hearing nothing the others said, nothing we said ourselves. Spilling from the carriage with the horde, we joined and jostled with them on the river bank, but company was only context, time only until.

Nuncacura was watching, but the Dominican abbot engaged him in scientific discussion and suggested a botanical tour, and soon the company had flocked to the water's edge to scry the river's castoff weeds. We backed away and fled. Climbing the bank, we darted into the underbrush, hand in hand and breathless, fainting now and blind. There was pause for the wonder to grow in me, the difference and the sameness, her face so close to mine, the smile that made me smile. I could not believe it, and yet here were my hungry lips finding an equal hunger in hers, and here was my hand at her tunic, fumbling the lacing away and drawing the cloth aside; and here was a breast, the nipple dark and jiggering upon the swollen crest. I stared, I gasped, I whimpered with dawning recognition. But before I could fall upon it, the motley shouted below.

There was nowhere to go but up the narrow path through the leaning cathedral of trees, pausing at the switchbacks to cling together and kiss, then wrench ourselves apart and struggle onward. Up and up, while the clamor of the mob pursued us, and still the top of the hill was an ever-receding glint of light and far, too far, away.

Halfway, we lay down on the precipitous path, and again I had time for wonder and giddy unbelief, and again the mouths and tongues, the stewy rehearsal of thrust and enclosure, my hand under her head in the soft astonishment of her hair, my other hand fumbling at her tunic, then her skirts, then her bloomers, sending them spinning off down the slope of leaves.

Still the wonder and unbelief, but now the scaly rustle of leaves as she lay back, and the incredible black bush below her belly, surging with her laughter. I moved a trembling hand toward it, pressed the heel against the wiry hump, and moved a finger in.

She moaned; and I snatched my hand back. Too fast, it was going too fast. In her eyes, the bright worm had spread into the milky, mercurial gaze of the deaf, dumb, blind, and abandoned. What was happening? Who was I? Who was she? She moaned again, clutching at me, her breasts wallowing. I sought to quiet her torment, but she shook her head impatiently and muttered through clenched teeth, "For God's sake, hurry!"

Hurry, yes, hurry. Each button of my codpiece was like ice as I unlimbered, and still the giddy desperation to comprehend, to slow this lunatic rush. It was happening, was it not? We were about to do it, were we not? Bracing my foot against a root, I rolled myself against her. Her mouth sawed out another moan, her knees shot up, and her legs fell open.

I gawked, struggling to believe the incredible wound, frilled and moistly ingesting beneath the mocking goatee.

"Put it in," she gasped. "Put it in!"

In. Yes, of course, in. I clambered between her legs and reached down, only to have her push my hand away, grasp my organ around its middle and, with a whistling little shriek, impale herself upon it.

It was happening. Surely we were doing it now. She span, her eyes closed, and her head tipped back, the cords of her neck swollen like hawsers, her mouth releasing little gasps and moans. And I delved, propped on stiffened arms and staring down at the ghastly marvel of it all. Yes, it was true, no doubt about it, I was doing it, she was doing it, we were doing it. And yet . . .

It did not come to me at once, but in a kind of slow and awful dawning, as it comes upon the staggered ass that he is running nowhere on the ice; as it comes upon the unbelieving communicant that he is only prating words and is alone and lost entirely where others claim to see God.

Was it something missing or something there? Did I hear Nuncacura ranting from his pulpit in the blackberries? At first I knew only the awful sense of suspension and helplessness, and then, as if through a hole in the back of my mind, I sensed a dark and ghastly figure stepping out from the trees just above, drifting soundlessly down the slope of leaves, hovering in awful reproval above us, then reaching in behind to close an icy claw upon the source of my seed.

At first she gave no sign, and so I kept doggedly on, nursing a vain hope that she would not notice the fruitless lurch and heave of my body, the adamant rigidity of my privy part, our colding sweat and the slap, slap, slap of our bellies. But soon enough she sensed it. Her moans ceased and her eyes unhooded, and the quicksilver flowed away.

As I saw the knowledge enter her eyes, I slowed atop her, and even as I knew that she knew, I ground to a halt. We stared at one another across the terrible gulf, no longer smiling, no longer dreaming, no longer beautiful. "Oh, no!" she said. "Oh, no!"

Her lament cut me through to the heart. "Yes, oh, yes!" I cried, but too late. Even as I resumed my pumping, my foot slipped off the root and we began to move, slowly at first, sliding sideways down the slope, faster and faster, the force of our rush drawing us inexorably apart, my organ pulling from her as I clutched and lost her and she fell away from my reach. And we each tumbled on alone, finally rolling to a stop on a leafy shelf below the path, she with her face turned away, I with my prick in the rubble.

> O Sound, O Voice, O Carolina!
> Free my bankrupt soul
> From this foreclosure of the senses
> And let me spend it all in Thee, O Love!

But it was too late for prayer or poesy. I could not bear to face her again, and one month after the debacle, I received word that I had been accepted to study civil and canon law at Osuna.

6

O<small>SUNA</small> was somewhat less than a distinguished institution, being known in loftier parts and even among its own professors as Clodpate College, committed as it was to the inflation of privileged bobos and the birthing of endless warrant officers, pocket lawyers, and abbey-lubbers. Don Diego had encouraged me thence because it was far away from home and it was cheap, the better part of his heart and purse being determined to see Paco elevated at Salamanca. He had, however, presented me with a letter of introduction from his confraternity, which sponsored a faction house at Osuna. There, he assured me, I would get lessons in that rewarding affectation known as philadelphy, or brotherly love.

The Adamant Brotherhood of the Sons of the Silver Oar, or the Stuffed Cods, as they were known to their rival confraternities, had originally been a secret society formed by certain fishermen of San Sebastián in order to better enable them to burn the boats and cut the nets of rivals and otherwise make advantage exclusive to themselves so as to rise above the common net-puller. Now, generations later, the Sons of the Oar included as many members of unrelated callings as it did fish dealers and fleet owners, all well fixed enough to send first and second sons off to the universities to study means of remaining well fixed and safely ashore. However, just as the Sons of Santiago clung to the quaint irrationalities of Crusade and tournament, so the sons of the Sons of the Oar affected a lugubrious fondness for the mystique of

65

the sea. Only dead soldiers tell the truth, as they say in Asturias, and the same may be said for sailors.

The Osuna chapter house was a disused villa with a ship's crosstrees on the roof and over the door a stuffed codfish held in place by crossed oars, with the motto below: SEMPER IN MER. It was there that I went to live and suffer initiation into their number, the which included two weeks of assorted tortures at the hands of the older Oars, ending in a particularly ingenious ordeal which required all of us neophytes to stand together in a small room, blindfolded and stark naked, while our superiors reminded us of our fraternal obligations to one another, then warned that there was a traitor among us inclined to befoul his fellows. "You are Christians and brothers in the same boat," a voice intoned, "and must learn to pull together. But beware. Satan the Black Mariner is among you and would scuttle your most earnest intentions."

Whereupon, while we milled about blindly, struggling to avoid intimate contact, one of our tormentors took up a wine bag and squirted tepid chicken broth upon my left buttock. Ignorant of the source of this affront, I felt my furia rise like hot gall in my throat, but swallowed it down in the name of philadelphy and that scriptural command regarding the other cheek. But even as I stood there like a proper martyr, with somebody else's soup running down my leg, the wine bag was squirted at a fellow neophyte nearby, and with a roar of rage he turned and blindly voided in my direction, wetting my other buttock. In no time at all, we were all pissing one upon the other, like young vipers gone amuck in the nest.

If education be of any value at all, it was there in that moment. But I chose to ignore the kernel of the lesson and even failed to ask myself how I had come to be naked and blind in such a trap. As we had all pissed in the end, I told myself, so we were all equally guilty and therefore must needs seek a common solution and be equally good and brothers all together, as at the millennium.

I found a broader species of enchantment in the person of my first tutor in the faculty of arts, Brother Gabriel Tellez, known to his students as Gabriel the Bawdy, to his fellow Mercedenian Friars as the Abbot's Maniac. He was more or less my height, which is to say somewhat above average, but was big chested and spindly legged, with most of his bulk squeezed topside, so that when he walked he gave the impression of a bloated insect moving on stilts. And when he sat in a chair with arms, he often stuck, if he did not break it down entirely. His eyes were large and heavy lidded, his chin jutted, and his nose looked to have been stepped on, which, indeed, it had, he claimed, as a result of a drunken brawl in his younger days over the proper wording of a lewd couplet which he claimed to have written himself, while his antagonists, two burly mussel farmers, had insisted that the ditty was the inspiration of a fellow fisherman, who had taught it to them one wave-lapped evening on the Bay of Cádiz, thus:

> When Adam delved and Eve span
> Who then was the gentleman? (Señorito)

It was further rumored that he wrote plays under another name and had already seen several dozens of his works put on the boards. He was fond of claiming that he had been a musician and buffoon to the defunct court of Sancho the Slack, pretender to the throne of Aragon, but that he had given up the cap and bells and taken to monkscloth and Matins out of unemployment and disgust with the world, and had chosen to throw his lot in with the Brothers of Mercy because of their liberal leanings and the sweet cordial which they keep in abundance against those times when faith falters and a stronger sacrament is required.

He was no more than ten years my senior, but they were those years through which one reaches manhood, and to my inexperienced study, he seemed a veritable patriarch. It took me only a few days in his lecture room to notice that his bawdy capering was only shrewd enticement to political and religious novelty of a rare and thrilling kind. Hidden amongst the customary wads of dogma which he carried about were certain red-hot volumes such as Cicero's *De Legibus* and the *Folly* of Erasmus, together with some voluptuous engravings by Marcantonio, after Raphael; all forbidden fruit and any one enough to bring him to the attention of the Holy Office, even to the fire. However, he was reported to enjoy the indulgence of his abbot, a Florentine, who frequently enlisted his aid in the crucial testing of a batch of cordial destined for the court at Madrid.

He was adept at insinuating his arcane beliefs into his lectures, pleading the habit of digression. Analyzing the structure of a patriotic ballad, he would stray to a discussion of the Reconquest, passing lightly over the finer hours of the Visigothic knights, to lavish considerable attention on the poverty of the people under Peter the Cruel, who was said to have butchered thousands of peasants, two of his half brothers, several cousins, an archbishop or two, and finally his own queen. With a glance at the door to make sure we were unobserved, Brother Gabriel would conclude the lesson by quoting a mysterious heresiarch whom he dared not name. "The Prince exists for the sake of the State, not the State for the sake of the Prince."

Outlining for us the procedures of the Mass, he might wander into a discussion of the Great Catholics, Ferdinand and Isabella, and they would subtly change from divinely appointed defenders of the faith into those astute politicians who had enlisted certain financial aid for the completion of the Reconquest, and also for the dispatching of the Genoan entrepreneur, Columbus, and then at the end of that same year, had decided to complete their cleansing of the peninsula by expelling the Jews, among them the very bankers to whom they were in such monumental debt. "Attendance at Mass doesn't necessarily make one a Christian any more than going to the bullfight makes one a matador," the monk would conclude with a wink.

But it was out in the cloisters after his lecture, beyond the sharp ears of the proctors, that he was at his best. With his back against the pillar and a ring of students before him, he could better gauge the degree of his risk, inviting challenge and flinging his answers back, while keeping a sharp eye out for informers.

He was not, however, always quick enough to avoid attention, and one afternoon, just as he was concluding a description of the citizen's republic with the words of Marsiglio of Padua, "To the people alone belongs the authority to make laws and elect their civil rulers," who should step briskly from behind the pillar but the rector himself, Don Gaspar Nieto Sinhuevos Rancheros.

Don Gaspar was the first son of the second minister to the Third Philip, and scion of that family which owns the smaller half of Andalucía, together with its waterways, mines, and inhabitants. He had been elected rector thanks to the loftiness of his character, the luster of his birth, and the liberal distribution of solid-silver medallions stamped with his profile on one side and the king's on the other.

Lean, febrile, and epicene, he nonetheless had a terrible temper and could without doubt have hoisted a full-grown stoat when in a rage, as he was now, turning upon Brother Gabriel in a flourish of silks, his face the color of raw suet. "Do I hear sedition, Master Tellez? Do you name an authority higher than the king?"

All eyes turned to the monk. It was a deadly game, Brother Gabriel being obliged to make his points without overstepping himself into unemployment, or worse.

"Come now, Gaspar, surely the king keeps foremost in his mind the good of his subjects. Do I hear you suggest otherwise?"

"You do not," grumbled the rector.

"Then you acknowledge what the king himself has acknowledged, that the good of the people comes first."

The rector's narrow face paled, and he made an effort to turn his head aside, but could not seem to free himself from the monk's steady stare. "I am the king's loyal knight and subject," he said through clenched teeth. "And as such, I acknowledge the king as the first authority in civil matters, the Church the highest authority in religion. Do you do the same?"

"I hold with Christ that a man should love his neighbor as himself."

"And God?" The rector's voice had begun to quaver and rise. "Do you acknowledge that a man must love and obey God above all else, and therefore his Holy Church and his supreme defender, the king?"

"I believe that a man should first love his king before bowing to his authority and must first love himself to properly love God."

"You deny the royal succession!" Don Gaspar cried triumphantly.

"I claim the rights of man."

"You would encourage anarchy!"

"I would dream of panarchy."

The rector propped himself upright with his jeweled sword. "And the kingdom of Heaven, would you deny men that?"

"I would see it created here on earth."

"And confession?"

"A man's first priest is the voice of his own soul."

"And penitence?"

"Natural remorse is the strongest candle of all."

"And absolution?"

"A man must forgive himself to be forgiven by God."

"You claim the divinity of man!"

"I claim his improvability."

"You deny original sin!"

"I claim original virtue."

"Is man wholly good, then?" the rector howled. "You would have him be his own constable and confessor, his own bishop and sovereign. Is he then above authority and in no need of grace?"

"He is neither wholly good nor wholly bad," Brother Gabriel said. "But he might be great, after the manner of Aristotle's great-souled man. Not a hidalgo made such by birth and fancy clothing, but the true gentleman: he who claims much and deserves much, who is justified in despising others, is fond of conferring benefits but ashamed to receive them, who refuses to ask for special consideration and is haughty toward men of position and fortune, who cares more for the truth than for what people will think, who is outspoken and frank, who is good without being vain, kind without being cowardly, who is firm when reminding others of their offenses to him, as at this moment, when I note that this baubled prop with which you seek to prevent yourself from falling on your face offends my shoe."

Don Gaspar looked down, as did we all, to see that the point of his sword stuck between the first and second toes of the monk's foot and pinned his sandal to the flagstones.

But Brother Gabriel was not finished. He leaned closer to the rector, and his voice dropped a tone toward intimacy. "But I do not expect you to understand, Gaspar. For all men are not the same, are they? Some court authority, do they not? Some secretly long to submit. Isn't that correct?"

The silence was long. They crouched like cocks at a standoff, except that the monk's spurs had already done their work.

"Now please unpin my foot, Your Honor the Rector, and take your poor tool away."

Don Gaspar's delicate mouth trembled and a tear parted company from his eye. For a moment it seemed that he might fall to the ground in one of his famous fits. But he tore his gaze away, pulled his sword free, and with a petulant toss of his head and a black look at us, stalked away down the arcade.

Our murmurs of congratulation were cut short by a nervous gesture from the monk. "Enough. Excuse me, I must try to beat him to the abbot." And with a gloomy grimace by way of farewell, he pulled his cowl over his head and went away through the shadows.

Surely here I had a hero at last. Not only had I been thrilled by his performance under fire, but his bold homilies rang a new angelus on my heart. Here were thoughts capable of reconciling the powerful conflicts and cruel divorces of my mind. Oh, to be something other than a graceless mortal; oh, to be great-souled!

I at once determined to dedicate myself to the study of egalitarian utopias, the great-souled way, and other liberated fancies. Like many another floundering apostate before me, I sought to steady myself with the sweet wines of Humanism, and would be some time taking up hard bitters with honest men. In no time at all I had become addicted to elucubration, that is, studying by candlelight, and was become notorious as a compulsive scholar and candlewaster.

But books cannot educate the huevos. The failure with Carolina was still a fox in my scrotum, and in that matter it seemed to me that I must look to my peers for guidance.

What a gaggle of coxcombs lived under the sign of the stuffed cod. When they were not mumming in fishnets and prating salt-sea mumbo jumbo, they were strutting abroad and tootling the tin horn. When they weren't drumming their bellies, they were fabricating pranks; and when they weren't doing that, they were drunk, their highest ideal of baccination being the communal consumption of a barrel of beer, the objective being to ascertain who could guzzle the largest amount and the most blithely cast it up again.

But they were most devoted to barborology, that is, the fulmination of filthy talk. There was even a closet under the stair, where they kept a fetid collection of aromatic talismans. Mostly this cubby contained strips of falbala torn from petticoats, by far the easiest trophy to come by. But there were also entire skirts and a few pairs of bloomers. One determined amoroso had even brought back a wedge of bloodied rag with which to verify his boast of having swived some doxy in the midst of her menses.

Seldom a week went by that the brothers did not gather around the door of the closet to hail a new rag and hear the tale of its capture. "Salute, my hearties, I have the ensign of the plump sloop, Maxima Ruiz, barmaid at the Green Rooster!"

"Barge is the better description, if it's the Maxima I know."

"I see that her colors are the same as the king's: yellow and red."

"Never mind, she struck them, and they are mine!"

Cuckle-mouthed chatrakes they surely were, and yet the half of them were older than I, and they seemed to know what they were talking about. I was as eager as any to get my oar in; more so, since I had reason to fear that I could not row. So I was there and all attention on the night when the most storied Oar of all brought home a garment that looked like nothing less than a jerkin for a camelopard.

His name was Elogio Ramires, called the Ram, and he was three years senior to me, tall and luridly handsome, with a rutting eye and a reputation for the most capacious bladder, loudest voice, and foulest mouth at Osuna; in short, the ideal Oar. The garment which he triumphantly waved under our noses was, he said, the bodice of the famous Pechita, said to have the largest breasts for her age in Osuna.

"Here is where she kept them," he declared, thrusting a fist into one of the bulges at the front. "And here is where I held them," he boasted, cupping his hairy paws before him. "Shitfire, I haven't seen such shitfire boobs since I last sucked on my shitfire mother."

"No news," drawled a doubter. "We've half of us hefted them." And he pointed to a heap of similar bodices in the closet. "The question is, did you put a ducat in her clapdish."

"Exactly," said another. "Many have bundled her, but did you get her to span?"

"Shitfire, yes, I spread her and gave her the ram."

"Prove it!" came the chorus.

The Ram drew himself up with a most episcopal dignity and extended his ring finger beneath the other's nose.

"Whew! No doubt about that."

That very night I began my investigations, discreetly taking each brother aside to find out what he knew. Her full name, I discovered, was Gabriela Maria Conhielo, and she did not care for her nickname. She was an only child and half an orphan, her mother having died of broach wounds as a result of bringing her forth. Her father kept a sausage shop, and it was there that she was to be found at any hour of the day or night, but it was unwise to approach her until the early evening, by which time her father, a notorious tosspot, would have his bottle down to the spider and would be snoring in the back room. I was recommended to extreme caution, since the father did not always sleep soundly, was a dangerous religionist, and had been known to rise up suddenly with his sausage knife. Finally, I was told not to bother bringing back another of her bodices; it was her bloomers they wanted to see.

Late the next afternoon I set out, rattling with apprehension, but embravoed by half a flagon of Indies rum. My directions led me around to the back of the town and into a slum the likes of which I had not seen since my lesson in brandling from the charcoal boy.

Here was the same tumble of rotting huts and river of mire, the same raggle-taggle furor and grubby vivacity, but this time poverty's circus brought a different thrill, for with each bandy limb, swollen belly, and running sore that I saw, I remembered Brother Gabriel's fervid injunction: "Blessed are the rich and cursed are the poor, and the great-souled know their duty: while there is one man hungry, all other flesh should fast."

Thus did my fevers multiply as I made my way, and arrival afforded small relief, for the sausage store was a mud hut next to an empty field full of bones, which was next to an abattoir; and on the doorsill of the sausage shop sat a ragged ancient, weeping steadily upon a loaf of horsebread, as if to soften it up for his toothless gums.

Then I saw Pechita, and all my fevers gathered into the one. She stood behind a rickety counter, pensively kneading paprika into a vast lump of minced pigmeat, the light from the door rousing darts of dull flame in her russet hair. She had a pert nose and rosy mouth, and her arms were slim and her shoulders delicate and sprinkled lightly with freckles and paprika. But it was upon the fabled bosom that my gaze quickly fixed.

73

They hung inside the loose front of her shirt like lungs from a butcher's hook, swinging with each thrust of her fists into the meat. In response to a reflex installed by the Dominicans, who had taught me thus to honor the great, the good, and the sacred, I doffed my cap. I did not realize that I had also allowed my mouth to fall open, until the breasts suddenly ceased their gyrations, and I looked up to find her unwelcoming gaze upon me.

Her narrowed eye measured my frazzled cloak, darned hose, baggy cod, and scuffed boots, and then I remembered what they had told me: "She will have nothing to do with the neighborhood crambos; it's education that turns her head." Hastily I replaced my four-cornered cap and mustered a scholarly smile. "I hope I didn't startle you, señorita. I was just on my way to a lecture on moral logic and thought I would stop in to pick up a little peppered meat."

It was not the most gainly sally ever to grease the rails, but it worked; her scowl came unstuck, and in no time we were chatting away about some popular romance which she had managed to read. I hardly knew what we were saying; within minutes I was helplessly enmeshed in the wistful, sidelong anxiety of her smile, and touched by the pride she took in the small knowledge of letters she had got from the nuns. But most of all, I was struck by the way she held her chin high and thrust out the gigantic buttress of her bosom, as if to confirm the callow slanders from which I drew my courage. It did not occur to me that, since she could not escape her tits, she thus sought to transcend them.

It was she who first noted that it was growing dark outside, and moved to close the shop door. Her evenings were long and her cloistering a burden, she sighed, and made a wry gesture toward the darkened cubby at the back. Through a low door behind the counter, I could now make out the figure of her father, sprawled on a sagging cot, one hairy hand dangling to the floor, where an earthenware jug lay overturned, and beside it, a long pigknife, stuck upright in the mud. Even as I stared, he rolled onto his back, his dark jaw fell open, and he began to snore. And as she lit a grease lamp and led me aside to a low bench against the wall, the resonant rattling of his membranes pursued us.

I had brought some wine, and she drank reluctantly at first, but once started, went at it with a will. As we chattered away, about, as I recall, some verses of Gil Robles which had been pervulgated for public consumption, I murmured appropriate encouragement and gazed hungrily upon her, and as my sympathy deepened, my lust mounted. She was so eager, so touchingly in need, yet so abundant, so lavishly endowed. She hardly seemed to notice as I edged closer, she scarcely paused as I took her hand, and she leaned her head backward for a moment so that she might complete her sentence, before allowing me to find her lips with mine.

It was not that she turned me away; in fact, she soon taught me a thing or two about kissing, and so vigorously that there were moments when I feared my tongue might come out by its roots. Yet there was an air of dolorous indifference in her performance; she was almost too compliant. When I groped for her bosom, she made no move to defend them, but only leaned back with a sigh and turned her head away, almost as though she were bored by the incredible event.

The bodice was so impacted that I could not get my hand between the two hot swellings. Hooking a thumb over the rim of the garment, I gave a tug downward, but the flesh only wallowed. Grunting, I put my shoulder into it, and with a rasping sigh, the entire contraption crumpled into her lap, and, suddenly, there they were.

O my God, what moonly monuments, fugitive in my hands, first one, then both, weighty as water, soft as velvet, powdery and resilient against my cheek, recalling wide welcome and warmth and long-lost dairy dream.

Yet still she sat rigid and unmoved, her eyes fixed in melancholy unfocus upon the sausages that hung overhead. I hesitated, while they flowed in my hands. Was it the veins, the freckles, the recollection of raucous post-coitums in the bloomer closet, the pitiable narrowness of her shoulders, so frail a rack for all that meat? Was it the stuttering of the oil wick, the steady saw of her father's snores?

She closed her eyes and her joints went loose, and it seemed she fled from her fleshly dilemma, choosing a surrender that was strategic retreat: go ahead, do what you will, just do not ask my full attendance. Was this how such a multitude of her bodices had turned up in the bloomer closet, scraped off and stolen away whilst she was in her desultory trance?

Out of breath and chilled, I nonetheless pressed on, getting a hand under her skirts and working a finger under her bloomers and stirring it around until it gathered enough faint effluvium of urine and low-grade lubrication to serve as aromatic talisman at bloomer-closet muster. Groping for my cod and shaking like a leaf, I prepared to unlimber. And then she gave a loose and vinous moan and let her legs fall open.

In an instant, I was back on the leafy slope in the dark cathedral of trees, with the tribes clamoring below, Nuncacura ranting from his pulpit in the trees, the specter gliding closer.

I froze to her like a jack to his steeple, ashamed to back away, afraid to go on. I might well have stayed thus forever had she not begun to shudder quietly. And I looked and found her gazing down upon the tits as a man with a clubfoot must gaze upon his malformity, with utter hatred and loathing.

"As long as they are there, nobody will ever love me for myself," she said bitterly. "Oh, sometimes I wish they would just dry up and drop off!"

"No!" I cried, gathering up the poor orphans. "Don't say that!"

"I mean it," she murmured ruefully. But my displaced passion had turned her head. She looked at me, the smear of her mouth trembling, and suddenly her eyes were wet.

All in all, it was too rich and convenient to let pass. "Oh, Pechita," I murmured, but she stiffened. "Maria," I amended, drawing her gently to me and wiping her tears away with a thumb. "You must learn to respect yourself. Trust me, I will help you. I will respect you. You will see." And I cupped protective hands to her breasts, while tears of respective relief rolled down our cheeks.

My own relief was somewhat short of complete, however. For when we finally whispered our tender farewells and she let me out into the night, I made my way along the mired alleys bent over, my lips raw and swollen, my neck aflame with paprika and mottled by bites, but most of all, my groin aching and my codlings bleating for relief. It was as though some hot hand had reached in and closed on my engorged huevos and was squeezing them like grapes. Any minute now they would jelly under the unmerciful pressure and splatter to all four corners of Spain.

This condition was more prevalent among the Oars than they cared to admit, and was called by them, the Flaming Stones. They had a ritual remedy for it, known as "lifting the corner of the house." But a mere house was not enough for me. Pausing now and then to double over and indulge in a groan, I made my wincing way toward the center of town.

Above the plaza, clouds raced against the face of a full moon, and the twin towers of the cathedral leaned against the traveling sky. Groaning, I found the corner of the cathedral, and there I bent, as Oar lore would have me do, and fitted my fingers under the cornerstone. Planting my feet wide, I bowed my back and began to lift.

The moon raced, the towers leaned, and I strained upward, teeth clenched, eyes watering, brow bursting beads of sweat. Spittle bubbled on my lips, the sharp edge of the stone cut my fingers, my boot soles squeaked on the slippery stones.

And still the cathedral did not budge. More to the point, the ache did not go away. The harder I strained, the worse it got. The hotter the fire in my groin, the louder grew the thunder in my brain. Blinding red-and-white darts of light shot this way and that behind my clenched eyes, and suddenly I knew that I was on the verge of a visitation, a revelation beyond the flesh: the word, the vision that would reveal all at last, the whole source of the ache and the whole reason for it, and the whole comprehension that might relieve me of it.

The fact is, of course, that I was on the verge of a hernia. But my foot slipped and the lesson was lost. I crashed to one knee, nearly breaking my fingers off, then staggered back to my feet. Reeling in place, I lifted my eyes to the moon and looked to my aching heart for a cure. I gasped, tears splashing down my cheeks, and my greedy heart reached down and took all the lust from the groin below, and reached up and took all the sense from the brain above. I would save Pechita from her tits and rout this suicidal desire for self-mutilation. I would show the world, and the Oars in particular, that stinkfinger gave no man license, that the scarlet letter had never been knitted that could not be erased with a little human saintliness.

Grasping my aching huevos in one hand, I put the other to my heart, raised my streaming face to the moon and cried out, "O Sound, O Voice, let me be great-souled and good!"

With the dawn behind me and the fever of makeshift religion upon me, I staggered in under the stuffed cod to find a welcoming party of Oars awaiting my news. Their grins faded when they saw that I brought neither bodice nor bloomers; gathering anger darkened their faces as I received their questions with aloof and stony mien.

"What, no rag, no trophy? Was some other jack there before you, then?"

"There was no other. We had a pleasant talk."

"You begabbed her, of course. A tit for a tattle is her bargain. And then?"

"Then nothing. I bade her good night and came home."

"Nothing? You go to the public fountain and come back with a dry bucket? Do you mean to tell us you didn't juggle her bubbles?"

"I mean to tell you nothing."

"Then it must be nothing you have to tell."

"What happened between us shall remain between us."

"And that which stands between you, shall it remain standing?" It was the Ram, lounging against the wall in his drawers and fixing me with a scornful gaze whilst diligently digging at his cod. "Shitfire, I wonder if it stands at all."

They laughed. But the great-souled man is above the mockery of others and holds tight to his virtue. "However I might burn my candles, I have no need to burn them in the marketplace." And with that, I turned on my heel and left them for my books.

But I soon found that I could no longer confine my candlewasting to my study room, now that lofty endeavor had found its laboratory. I became a habitué of the sausage shop and was soon spending my evenings in fevered alternation between text and tit.

I met Pechita's father only once, for I usually contrived to arrive after that hour at which he relinquished his black choler to the stunning power of the grape. On the one occasion that we did come face to face, he took me for a customer, informed me that he did not like students and considered letters to be the peckertracks of the Devil, and abruptly retired to his bottle. He was, she explained, a species of self-made illuminist and claimed to have been instructed by the angel Ariel to atone for the death of his wife by devoting the remainder of his life to seeing that his daughter died a virgin. She once showed me a scissor with which he intended to alter her private parts, should she ever allow herself to be got with child. Although he never woke up, he was always there in the back room, blue-gilled and black-roached, snoring like a horse.

Pechita herself wrote poetry that was surprisingly spare and without conventional sentiment, being mostly about an imaginary place which she called Ultimacopla, where men and women looked and dressed exactly alike, and there was neither paprika nor sausage, but all foods were odorless pebbles and taken by ear. She had a dread of the flies which were all about the place, and often wore a net over her head, claiming that should one of the little animals get into her ear, it would inflict an incurable buzzing, lay eggs, and adversely affect her intellect. On the other hand, she was entirely unafraid of the stunted red rats which populated the neighborhood and, should one of them scuttle past while we were bundling on the bench, was likely to break its back with one practiced stamp of her pretty foot, and that without taking her lips from mine.

I remember little else about her, and virtually nothing of what we talked about through those many hours that I sat gazing hungrily at her swinging breasts while she ground pigmeat and stuffed gut, and the many hours more that we passed together on the bench under the sausages, breathlessly rubbing one against the other, somewhat as they say the savages of the Indies rub sticks to make fire, except that we only rubbed ourselves raw, and kept our separate flames each to himself.

Always it was the same. First, my fervid pledging and pleading, followed by the unveiling of the speckled glands; and always she stiffened as they came forth, and even as I fondled and nuzzled them, sneezing with paprika and stifled passion, she looked on in bitter silence; and all that peppered meat, however prodigal and entrancing, became melancholy rebuke. I sometimes wondered if her father, in youthful fever to locate heaven, had become unduly enlarged with religion one night and reached right through his pregnant wife and touched his unborn daughter, once, twice, with the red-hot sword of Zion, raising those two pale and damning blisters.

Always the bittersweet thrill of mingled rut and remorse, so like my lovelorn memory of Carolina, which until only a month before had been lingering on like a septic condition. Always, following the ritual of adoration and contrition, the fumbling return of her double-bellied dilemma to its casing, then the desperate farewell kisses and gasping renewal of my pledge to guard her good name. And finally, the reeling, ecstatic journey home astride my flaming stones.

Thus I came to spend many a late night with a tit in my mouth, and early morning with my cock in my hand. The perfect picture of the plaster saint, if you ask me. And so thought the Oars, and said so, with increasing ire, since by then, Pechita had taken to turning them away from her bulbous hearth and would suffer only me to suckle and sizzle there.

"What have you done to her? She even sent the Ram packing. She threatened to wake up her shitfire father!"

"Nothing, I have done nothing."

"Then you have said something. She will have none of us now. Nary a foot in the door, nary a bundle on the bench. What did you tell her?"

"Nothing, only that I respect her rights."

"Pizzlepudding! You have spoiled the mule! Since when does laced mutton have rights? You have betrayed your brothers. Cormorant! You want it all for yourself!"

"I have betrayed nobody and have taken nothing."

"What? Do you claim that you don't play rollmelon all night long under the sausages? We have seen you through the shutter."

"That is between myself and the lady."

"Lady, my breach! And do you claim that you don't concupie her?"

"Never mind."

"All that hawking, and you haven't put a bird in her bush?"

"She is a good creature, and I am fond of her."

"Ah, but fond enough to fuck her?"

Even the greatest of great-souled men sometimes loses the reins of his furia. My sense of philadelphy came to sudden alchemic boil. "Are you fond enough of your teeth to shut your mouth?"

But my tormentors found the shrewder part of valor in derision. "Well, well, such fire from a cold stove. But perhaps you are telling the truth. Perhaps you like to be different. Has it occurred to you that you might be just about the only one who hasn't swived Our Lady of the Mincemeat? One of these nights we will see the rest of the brothers between her legs, and then you will have gained your goal, candle-waster. You will be different, all right. You will be alone."

Alone I did not want to be, but there was a certain safety in the difference, and like Simeon on his pillar, I preferred not to think of myself as in vertical retreat from horizontal dilemma, but rather as closer to God, or in this case, to Aristotle. Such exalted position placed me that much farther away from another goal, to be sure, and the conflict began to take its toll. Pimples began to bloom amongst the sparse hairs of my new beard and between my shoulder blades. My nose began to take on a rosy hue, thanks to my nightly snootful of paprika, and my lips to crack and pucker from too much tugging on dry dugs. And I was increasingly beset by novel and discomforting visions, as when I dreamed I was a fly fresh from the bloomer closet and drunk with effluvium of underparts, hurling myself into Pechita's ear.

Examination week did afford some relief, and I stayed with my books for ten whole days before returning to Pechita's bathykolpian hearth. Only to find that there had been a change.

At first all seemed the same: the flies buzzing and the sausages hanging, the father sawing his sinuses in the back room. She seemed at once paler and more feverish, but the freckled lungs still swung from her ribs. While I was able to coax neither smile nor welcoming kiss from her, I did finally convince her to close the doors and sit beside me on the bench. But she remained curiously indifferent to my chatter. When a rat passed close by our feet and she made no attempt to stamp on it, I knew that something was amiss. Sure enough, when I reached for her shoulders, she shrank back and began to shudder and sob, waving me away, then holding me transfixed with her tale.

It seems that she had become lonely while I had been at my studies. Her cloistering was painful, she reminded me. So, when a boy unfamiliar to her had come late one afternoon with a bottle of expensive Jerez and an academic air, she had allowed him to coax her from counter to bench and from bench to bottle with a dissertation on the art of astrology. Plied with erudition and strong drink, she had reached that state of stunned compliance of which I had once nearly taken advantage, and had allowed him to lead her out into the yard beside the slaughterhouse, whence, he had assured her, she would be able to see the constellation of which he spoke, Virgo, her very own sign, from which he promised to read her a rosy future.

Magic and women: ink and blotting paper. Stargazing and drunk, she had let him draw her down amongst the ribs and weeds, only dimly aware of the other Oars gathering in an expectant circle, drawing straws to determine precedence, loosening their codflaps and forming an orderly line opposite the loosened gate of her thighs.

Number One's first thrust brought her fly-flocked nightmares to life, and his second thrust split the drum to the sound of her shriek. Surprise, the Ram was a fraud as a cod. Ergo: this Virgo had been intacto.

But no longer was. And then Numero Dos, and then Numero Tres, and then Numero Cuatro, and after that, all count was lost to consciousness, for she was passing onward and all alone into a state of consummate office that would have struck Sister Alma blue with envy.

With what a confusion of fascinations I received this lurid picture of her Annunciation. Horror and shame pulled me one way as she talked, mounting excitement another. Uncharitable jealousies fumed from the vision; now I cringed back in shame, now I circled closer to join the hyenas. Even as she was finishing, a hand was reaching out of the turbulent lake in my breast, bearing neither cross nor blade, but only anxious vacuosity and five clutching fingers.

"Aieee!" she shrieked, striking the twitching spider from her lap. "You mustn't, don't, I cannot," she gasped, her eyes wide, the freckles black upon her cheeks.

I gaped, incredulous; I swore, dumbfounded. I flung myself upon her, grubbing in her bodice. "Pechita, Maria, please . . ."

"Don't touch me!" With astonishing strength she thrust me away and shrank back into her shadow, a gleam of sweat on her upper lip. "Please, Juanito," she whispered. "You must understand, you must."

But I still could not bear what I knew. Not quite. I stretched out the tip of a finger and touched the heaving swell of one breast. The flesh was cold as clay; the goose was plucked and dead.

"You see now, don't you, Juanito?" She straightened from her shadow, and the breasts came ponderously into the light, too large to be real, too heavy to bear. And yet she thrust them out before her with a calmer, deeper passion than before. Chin up, cheeks vivid with color, she looked beyond me with exalted eyes. "Something happened to me that night," she murmured. "I cannot stand to be touched now. Not anywhere, not at all. I am different now, Juanito, truly different."

There was no denying it. She was radiant with a new and terrible grace. She had come through. Dragged on by her enormous glands and dogged on all sides by scorn and rut, she had fled it all and in one lunatic leap had passed back through her ruptured hymen into the underworld of herself, pulling her sex closed behind her.

"Yes, different," she murmured again, and the smile trembled on her lips. "Just as you are different, Juanito. Afterward, for a week, locked in the back room, with my father outside the door, praying for the curse, I kept thinking of you. And when I did begin to bleed, and my father touched my arm, and I found out how much I had changed, I thought of you. You were never like the others, you never wanted what they wanted. You were always good to me. And you'll be good to me now, won't you, Juanito, even though I have changed, even though I am different?"

Some say that in the end Simeon flung himself headlong from his pillar, others that he arose thence straight to Heaven. I rather think that late one evening he took a look about him, had a brief but clear-eyed view of his position, and simply slithered down, likely on the far side, away from the demanding stares of the faithful.

I backed to the door, ducking the dangling sausages; and she leaned after me, her eyes imploring, her need plainer and more poignant than ever, the freckled orbs hanging hugely in their hammock. And I ended it as I had begun it, doffing my four-cornered cap and fabricating a scholarly smile. "We must talk again sometime. But just now I must get back to my studies in moral logic."

Once again the stones of the plaza gritted underfoot, the cathedral towers leaned against the rushing sky, and I clutched one hand to my heart, the other to my aching groin. But this time I did not beseech the heavens, for I could not bear the news, yet neither could I escape it. I still wanted to be good. But, God forgive me, not that good.

And so I unlimbered with one hand and raised the other in a fist and shook it at the sky, and at Him who had created heaven and earth, big tits, hyenas, and me; and simultaneously let go the contents of my bladder square upon the corner of His temple.

83

7

CLEARLY I needed advice. But the Osuna curriculum included no symposium on girl husbandry, and I had lost trust in my fellow Oars. So it was with a certain hopeful anticipation that I greeted the end of my first year at Clodpate College and headed north to visit my Uncle Adan in Old Castile, where my mother had many years ago stood under the hot sun with her father, studying the jiggling pizzles of the bulls.

Adan kept no bulls himself, but only docile Lybian oxen. But he had run bulls in his youth and had even killed a few from horseback. He was the eldest of my mother's five brothers and the first son of Don Salvador, and was said to bear the closest resemblance to the old knight, even to being mildly warped from much horseback riding. Indeed, when the family had gathered to divide Don Salvador's possessions, all the brothers had tried on the armor, but only Adan had been able to fit the curved cuisses to his bandy legs.

As the first son, he had inherited the estates, but also the debts and taxes. The stone château and the best of the land had quickly fallen into other hands, compelling him to seek his fortune elsewhere. In the Pyrenées, he sieved gold from the gravel of icy Andorran streams, then glimpsed giant nuggets gleaming in deeper waters, invested his gold dust in the casting of a clay diving bell, and nearly drowned when it broke on the rocks. In the Moroccos, he chased camels in from the Sahara, but when the only buyers proved to be Arab slavers, insisted that no wild creature should be haltered for the purpose of enslaving men, and let his herd and profit melt back into the blowing sands. In the Indies, he nearly cornered the parrot-feather trade, only to have the governor-general confiscate his shipment, and when the price of the required bribe proved to be the removal of an emerald earring along with its red owner's ear, flung his knife from him and with it all hope of regaining his feathers.

Returning with small profit beyond memories and his maturity, he married and settled on the barren parcel of land left to him, and devoted the remainder of his life to restoring the ditches, nurturing the alien crabapple, and building a house that was no castle, but had walls tight and dry enough to keep his family and solid enough to bear the weight of his father's shield and girdings.

Here, it seemed to me, was a man who had followed his own lead, yet had been able to come back home; who had abjured the crueler sciences of life, yet had pursued success as heartily as any man; who had his feet on the ground, yet still retained a zest for flight.

He had gone half the world round and had known all manner of men and women. Surely he was familiar with those feverish cross-currents in the Montesa blood which had driven his father to keep two families and breed six times as many children, to say nothing of uncounted by-blows. Surely he could help me to correct my faltering steps and get me back on the proper road to manhood.

I finally got around to it one afternoon as we stood on a hill overlooking his orchard. Just there, beyond the farthest slope, he was saying, were the estates of the House of Lanza, from whence he had stolen away the duke's pretty ward, his own beloved Costanza. "Across the saddle," he assured me with some relish. "Lanza was a passionate man, but portly. He rode after us as far as yonder wall, but no farther, for he was afraid to jump his horse lest his heart jump farther."

"Then you had a way with women, uncle?" I suggested hopefully.

"The same way as other men, I suppose." He shrugged.

"I mean to say," I persisted, "that in your courting years you must have learned much in the matter of their beguilement, and no doubt still remember the more effective methods."

His glance was mild and absent. "Well, now, I wouldn't say that. For beguilement I told her I wanted her, and for method I took her away and married her."

85

"I see," I said. "But beyond plain courting, I mean, in the more intimate matters, would you recommend—"

"And as for love-making," he put in briskly, turning his attention back to the landscape, "I find that it is simple enough once you've got well into it. Now, just down there is where I will dig my new well. . . ."

Perhaps it is as they say, that in that stern northern region, the qualities of the grape and the humours of the blood come full only every other season.

But I did not pass my holiday without a certain progress, thanks to the rough men who worked for my uncle, in particular, his foreman, Pep Riera Zarapets, known to friends and enemies alike as Muchomacho, the which meant to the former, "a man's man," and to the latter, "a fool's fool," when, in truth, if it meant the one, it meant both.

Sprung from the stony slopes of Cantabria, he was short in stature and had wide shoulders, atop which his small head sat like a mossy river stone of the sort used to hold down the tops of pickling barrels. With his loud voice, prodigious swagger, and dread of being alone, he was a natural leader of men and might have risen above his station, had it not been for his double addiction to bulls and whores.

For he was an expert castrator and much sought after by neighboring breeders. But he claimed to detest the making of oxen from bulls, and each time that he was asked to do the job, protested so vehemently and at such length that his price had doubled by the time he condescended, with the consequence that he might have become moderately rich at it, had it not been for the fact that each and every time he completed the operation, he was seized by that expensive compulsion which my Aunt Costanza referred to scathingly as his "weakness."

I was aware of Muchomacho's affliction, but did not have occasion to witness its effects until my last week there. One afternoon I rode up on my cousin's mare to find the foreman and his crew of tree-skinners gathered about a trussed black yearling bull, Pep standing spraddle-legged over the beast, his eyes red-shot and glassy, a wine bag in one hand, a knife in the other. Suddenly he fell to his knees, crossed himself, uttered a tremendous oath concerning the milk of the Virgin, slit open the bollock sack, got hold of the slippery eggs and pulled them out, first one, then the other, then snipped the cords and flung them from him. Even as the codlings rolled in the dust and were gathered up, he was spreading the emptied sack with his fingers and tipping the wine bag above the opening, his face all anguish above the silent animal; and there was no doubt about it, I could see them glisten in the sun: two tears rolled down the foreman's leathered cheeks and fell, plink, plink, to add their salty tang to the healing fire of the aguardiente.

I sat pegged to the mare, my huevos tight to my belly, while the sack was sewed up and the stunned ox released. The foreman put the wineskin to his face and drank deep, then the bottle went round the circle, then around again.

Suddenly they were looking at me. They ducked their dusty heads together, and then the foreman came swaggering toward me, wine bag extended, eyes agleam with a furia which I knew by the ache of my eyeballs was mirrored in my own gaze.

"Wet your teeth, young master," he commanded. "Then come with us to the nunnery, I am paying the bill. Unless, of course, you prefer to say your prayers alone."

His grin was terrible to behold, but even as I lifted the bag and poured aguardiente on my own codfright, I felt a similar smirk spread my cheeks, and a bitter tang, as of a blade between my teeth.

Away we went after sundown, in an ox cart stacked with cider, sprawled atop the kegs and bawling what have you, just so long as it was ripe and assertive. I had left a note attached to the butter churn: "Dear Aunt, gone to see the Three Kings." (We were just five days from Christ's birthday.)

"A star in the east draws us on!" bawled a bumpkin, pointing toward the dim twinkle of light across the dark plain. And another brayed in crapulous baritone:

> "O, the notch house lights are bright tonight,
> And the plackets all so gay,
> And the only way to quiet the fire,
> Is to blow the coals away."

"I say Rosita for you, young donjon," declared the nearest rustic, locking a foul armpit to my shoulder. "She cherishes a pull on the pillicock and shags like a viper."

"Let him choose," protested another. "Let water find its level."

"Or piss its proper pot," drawled a voice, and it was Muchomacho, enthroned atop the highest barrel with the reins in one hand and his wine bag in the other, grinning down his shoulder at me. "Perhaps the young master is shy of snake. Cow may be his meat: Madam Gorda, the Hippopotopussy. Or Bocabruta, God's other mouth. She'd draw damp out of a pumice stone. But you must mind the glass, young master, for time runs ahead of the best of us. Or are you, perchance, quick to pop?"

They were all watching me now, the swart and wily villeins atop their lurching kegs, and I remembered another such moment in the slum behind the garden, and another such foxy cryptarch, grinning from his barrel. But I had no clue, only an uncertain crawling in the spine, and so could only smirk and toast the puzzle with my wine bag, whereupon they turned their attention again to the small glitter that lay low in the east and drew our lumbering wagon on.

And then, so suddenly, we were there.

The brothel stood alone one long cannonshot from the nearest village wall, a large and colorless hulk, save for the flicker of its lamps, one behind the bars of each front window, three upstairs and three down.

"Halloo the chinchery, Muchomacho is here!" bawled the foreman, and on the instant was down from the wagon and reeling before the great doors, each with its iron ring gripped in the jaws of a brass Medusa.

"Mother Leech, let us in, your sons are here to bleed!" He set one of the knockers to pounding, then staggered back. The doors swung wide, and against the light loomed a great pearly hogshead of a woman, her bare shoulders like oiled pudding, her hair a congerie of eels.

"Pepito!" she cried in the voice of a rusty drawbridge. "How many are you?"

"Myself, the King of Staves," he grinned, assaying a buffoon's bow and pointing a splintered clog before him. "Plus two pair of knaves and one greengroin, unless he be the Fool. We are fresh from the oyster harvest, mother, and each has a wolf in him. Let us in."

"Welcome, wolves," she said, her smile a spreading stain of crimson.

She stepped aside, and as I passed, she leaned close to murmur, "You too, my lamb," and I knew that she saw through to the wobble of my heart and the jelly in my knees.

Inside, gleaming brocades festooned shrouds of shadow, tassels danced in the doorways, and above the rosy braziers, the green-limbed girls moved and smiled, pale blooms amongst the weedy drunkards, doggedly breeding choice.

Stunned upon my pillow in a corner, I watched, growing groggy with miasmic allure. I could not quite believe that actuality could have a mind so fevered as my own. The actors had stepped across the footlights, the wild phantoms had escaped the zoo, and I was as enraptured as I was quite incapable of election.

But soon enough Muchomacho came reeling, drawing a creature by the hand. "The swollen bud I told you about," he said into her ear as he pressed her down into my lap. Then to me with a leer: "Her name is Ceresa. Ripe fruit prepared especially for you."

I opened my mouth to make fuddled protest, but he held up a hand. "No, no, don't thank me now, young master." A gargling chuckle escaped him, and there was an odd glint in his eye as he turned away. "Later, should you still feel so inclined."

She wore the short red cape of her profession and in that uncertain light looked to be as plump and juicy as the cherry of her name, with a round and vacant face only slightly sprung to one side and topped with a helmet of reddish curls that held their shape like metalwork.

"Whatcher name, honey?" she inquired, grinding her buttocks into my lap and gazing off across the room.

I said my name and laid a hand on one leg, only to snatch it back quickly. The knee was thick with callus.

"What a nice name," she said, turning to run the blunt fingers of one hand down my cheek and reach under with the other to locate my privy parts. "How's about you and me going somewhere?"

"Where?" I asked, alarmed at the thought of leaving my companions.

She laughed, diligently rubbing my yard and codlings. "Around the world?"

I knew the expression from the Oars, who claimed it had originated with an ancestral brother who had sailed with Columbus of the Indies. But it seemed an excessive exercise, considering my uncertain record. "No, I don't think so . . . ."

"Arse over teakettle?"

"No, I can't. I mean, I couldn't. That is, I don't require anything beyond the usual plain bacon. . . . ." I heard my own lame laughter rattle into silence and realized that they were all listening: the bony green girls and their grinning swains, the great pearly mother, and especially Muchomacho, lurking beneath the billowing mass of Hippopotopussy like some banty rooster beneath a giant hen. He put his hand to his mouth, imperfectly smothering a mocking cucucucuroo.

If that sound was not the inspiration, it was certainly the goad. "Lead the way," I muttered, slipping her from my lap and following after her, through the archway, down a dark and heavy-scented corridor, into a small and plain apartment. The bed was narrow, the window shuttered, and a wedge of brown soap floated motionless in a basin. Gone was the undulating mantle of Oriental mystery, fallen away as swiftly as the red cape which she now shed and hung behind the door. I experienced a sudden desire for conversation.

Because she had grown weary of giving it away, was her reply to my first question, delivered crisply as she shrugged free of her chiton and let it fall, scooped it up with her toe, and hung it with the cape.

Because of her devotion to religion, she replied to my second query, crossing herself with one hand and setting the soap to sloshing with the other. Since women of her class were not allowed hassocks in church, the geniculation of constant prayer was bound to thicken the knee. And as she worked up a lather, a dim blue cipher jiggled upon one buttock: DZ.

Diazinsiper, was her third reply: the nickname of her first and last love, the Morisco gallant who had tattooed it there whilst she had been in a hemp sopor; and it stood for ginger, having the larger sense of the Essential Spice of Life, although an alternative meaning was lingum fever, or plain prick itch, if you liked, the which at this late date she was bitterly inclined to think was the more pointed interpretation.

"So put half a silver real on the table, get your clothes off, and bring yours here," she concluded briskly. "Enough of instruction, time for communion."

I hesitated over which to shed first, money or trousers, but found that the act of placing the coin on the table lent a definite ease to the removal of the pants and hose. Despite the fact that Muchomacho had given it to me, some of my fear left me with that bit of silver. But not all.

"Over here, my angel, and let me swab off that giant cucumber I notice between your legs."

The flattery was pleasant, the water tepid, and her touch vigorous and sure; and I was soon absorbed in the soothing slide of the soap and the reassuring fattening of my yard. As on another long-ago occasion, she hummed a washerwoman's ditty as she scrubbed, and my gaze shifted sidelong to the wide and winsome vacancy of her face.

What was she thinking? Was she dreaming of mighty Baltazar Bedpresser, with his thick shoulders and hambone tool? Of prick-me-daintie Pietro Preencod, with his knowing manipulations and fingerly beard? Of callow Carlos Greengroin and his shamefaced spurts? Of deliquient Sancho Senile and the long, limp grind? Of furtive Casado Bedswerver, bearing wife slander in his heart and garters in his pocket? Was she thinking that she had had better or worrying that she might get worse? Did her mind seethe like mine, with venereal apparitions and orgiastic tableaux; was it one vast carnival of carnal abandon and ever-living museum of the eternal fever?

"Whistle while you scrub," she hummed.
"Put it in a tub,
Wish it in,
And wash it out,
And rub-a-dub-a-dub."

"There," she said briskly, "he's ready." Leaving me to gaze in rapt appreciation upon the pink log afloat in the sudsy shallows, she gave her hands a shake and turned to pull something from beneath the bed and place it on the table. At the sight of it my heart paused and my flesh began to shrink.

It was an hourglass, but of no species known to me, with two glass bulbs, one containing pea-sized pebbles, the pair set horizontally upon a set of scales; behind the scales a mechanism of cogs and pulleys, and atop that, a jar-sized brass bell. And, poised on tiny cloven feet beside the bell, hammer at the ready: a delicately carved and leering little satyr.

91

It was obviously some modern form of horologue, or perhaps, whorologue, or, better, or should that be worse: horrorlogue? I gaped, dripping and atremble, recalling Muchomacho's warning: *Mind the glass, young master, time runs ahead of the best of us.*

She gave me no time for questions. Kneeling on the bed, she performed some manipulation upon the mechanism, setting the pebbles to tumbling from the full bulb to the empty, then fell straightway upon her back and opened her legs with the purposeful determination with which most women close theirs. "Come my lamb," she commanded briskly, holding her arms out to me. "And hurry, for time's a-wasting."

Time was the gallop of my heart, the running rattle of the pebbles; and all the confusions whirled like flotsam down the drain toward the one contusion. I stumbled to the bed and fell groaning upon her.

Now. Or at least soon, my besmirched escutcheon was to be wiped clean and a new era begun, here in this homely room, between these pale thighs, with the aid of this rubbery vulva which I was now probing with blunt diligence and a purchased assurance. If, that is, I could just get things properly started. . . .

"Here, honey, let baby help you. There, he's home!" she cried with professional enthusiasm. "Oh, darling, that's good. Oh, baby, you could be arrested for carrying that cannon. Oh, sweetie, oh, lamb, oh, do, do, do."

I did, did, did, with a certain tentative serenity and grim determination, push, pull, push, pull, in the warm and affable convenience of her coony, and slowly, it seemed, there was a steady acceleration toward what promised to be a perfunctory and painless consummation.

And then I felt the first tug of the leash, struggled not to recognize it, fell back, conjured a silver coin, pushed ahead, and felt the tug of the reins again. Who, what, held them? A watching tomb, Nuncacura, Aristotle? My reeling gaze caught on the pinpoint eye of the little satyr atop the horologue and held, transfixed. But the glint was too tiny, too far for understanding. Push followed pull, followed push, and the tumble of the pebbles slowed, then suddenly ceased. And, I swear, the little bastard winked, there was a grinding from the mechanism, he swung his hammer: BWANG!

"Time's up!" The vacuum pump serving me abruptly withdrew and

I flopped moistly free and fell back, throbbing with rut and sick with shame, yet somehow unsurprised.

She sat up beside me, and I closed my eyes, avoiding the glance of the grinning capripede atop the clock, giving myself over to the bittersweet suck of the leech beneath my ribs. There was money in my purse, but what could be the use? There was something wrong with me; I was born to fail. This was punishment for some unknown and monstrous sin, and although I could not name it, I had long known it was mine.

I opened a cautious eye to test the satyr's gimlet stare, but found her smiling down upon me. "Did you lose it, lamb? And do you fear that it is lost forever?"

"Lose?" I mumbled, trying to hide the shamed face of Pocomacho.

"The diazinsiper," she said soothingly. "Never mind, you will find it again. You must never stop searching for it. In the meantime, don't lose heart in the moment." And then, miracle of miracles, she reached across me and again readied her infernal machine. "Mother will never know if we don't tell her," she confided as the pebbles began to roll again. "Besides, Ceresa is nobody's chattel." So saying, she put her mouth to mine, pressed upon me, and reached down for my ever-ready yard.

If my mind could not quite believe it, my flesh could, and in no time at all, I was between her thighs and we were off again, at a Tartar gallop now, for if I could not foil the satyr, I would beat the clock. In close to the saddle, I was riding hard, down the back stretch and rounding toward home, lathered and leaning, stretched out and nearly there, then suddenly down and rolling, felled by a wink and a: BWANG!

"O God," I moaned, my head in my hands and my face to the wall. "Oh, to the Devil with it, let's call it a day."

But she had gone mad, for she was setting the clock again, her eyes fixed upon me in a curious heat of fascination, and it dawned on me through the fog of my ennui that she was looking at me in a certain sense for the very first time.

"You know," she murmured, gripping me by my adamant gristle, "you are something, you are."

I hadn't the slightest idea what she meant. What I wanted was simple enough to my mind, and with that as focus for my fever, off I went again, riding the slippery mound of her stalwart insistence, hellbent forevermore and nearly there, and then the wink of doom, the hammer, and the bell.

"Why?" I moaned. "What is wrong with me? Why is it taking so long?"

"Retardismo," she said, staring at me in open wonder now. Her flesh was no longer cool to my touch, and her lips seemed swollen. "Men tend toward two extremes, you see, although half are merely in between. Of the rest, there are the rapidos and there are the retardos." She gave a rueful little laugh. "And you, my tender parts tell me, are a retardo to beat all retardos."

"I am sorry." I reached for my trousers. "I certainly did not want to cause you discomfort—"

"Now, now, do not be hasty," she said, hurriedly drawing me back against her. "It only smarts a little, and we should not give up now and waste all that work. You are not the quitting kind, are you?"

"No," I said, "but . . ."

But she had already set the clock, and off we went again, myself up on stiffened arms now, so as to lean more into it, heaving against the icy tug of the leash, dimly aware that she had begun to moan and turn her head from side to side. I looked away. How lonely to be here in chill remove, while she labored at her most intense and private business. And then again: BWANG. And then again: "Do not despair, my lamb. You must never stop trying!" And again into the insatiable breach.

Twelve times. Thrice times four I did all the work and the satyr and his sibyl had all the fun. And then, as I lay face down and weeping hot brine from every pore, and she lay quietly beside me, apparently having come to some conclusion of her own, she murmured again, "You know, you really are something."

And as if to second this incomprehensible opinion, there came as from another world the sound of agitated muttering. Then muffled laughter. I looked to the shuttered window and caught the glint of a rolling eye between the blinds and saw the slats twitch. Chilled to my root, I leaped from the bed and threw the shutters open.

There they were, most of them still crouched below the window: the four bumpkins, several of the girls, and Muchomacho. He held back, looking glum. As I was soon to discover, he had just lost the equivalent in silver of his fee for one castration. But to my astonishment, the others gazed respectfully up at me, and as I stepped full into the light, they clapped their hands together in admiring applause.

It seemed that I had been the subject of a kind of venal sweepstakes. Each gambler had speculated as to what would be the exact point in the whorologue marathon when I would capitulate to nature. There were customarily ten units to the marathon, although thus far no subject of less than fifty years had lasted that long, at least not with Ceresa. Muchomacho, as banker and promoter of the outrage, had held for the first run of the pebbles against all bets, having been convinced that I would be a rapido, which, to the sports of the region, was tantamount to being an amateur at the game and without a worldly sense of time and money.

In fact, as Ceresa soon informed me, Muchomacho himself was a notorious rapido, making him all the more popular in that house. The doxies had agreed to guard his secret from the rest of the world on the condition that he be just as rapido a rapido as possible each time, with the result that after some years of training, he could be very nearly induced to spend at the mere sight of the soap in the basin, and, who could tell, might one day succeed in transferring consummation all the way back to the gelding pen, saving himself much expense at the brothel and eventually becoming rich enough to own his own bulls, which is what he really wanted.

No wonder that he was reluctant to join the others in hailing my peculiar achievement. Since they were unaware that my resistance to nature had been so complete, and Ceresa had the decency not to tell them, they had decided that the winner was the bumpkin who had figured me for the tenth tumble. But if he was anything, Muchomacho was a sporting man, and once the celebration was underway inside, he came across the room with a brave smile on his shattered face and holding out his hand. "Congratulations, young master. You are something, you are."

How I longed to clutch both hands to my flaming stones and cry out that if I was something, it was something I did not care to be: not this tortured puppet strung between will he and won't he. How I would have liked to ask him, as an old and experienced hand at the matter, what it all meant.

But what can a rapido tell a retardo, after all?

And so I offered instead a champion's smile of benign good cheer. "Thanks, Pep, it was nothing."

And the soonest possible, let myself out into the dark night, there to strain, without success, to lift the corner of the leaping house.

8

I HAD LONG suspected that there was something amiss with me, and now I knew its name: retardismo. Clearly I was still sorely in need of advice. On the last day but one before I was to return to the university, I went to my Grandmama Celestina des Puig-Tenorio. Surely a woman could tell me something about women.

Her hair was all gray now, and she seemed considerably diminished, but she still painted her face and enjoyed glee and mourning with equal relish. "Oh, I am increasingly filled with dark bodements, Yum Yum, for the five years of grace allowed me by the surgeons have passed twice over, and the black canker has nibbled me down to the ribs. I want to rehearse my funeral for you, and demonstrate certain precautions I have arranged against grisly error, for after all, it will be your tomb as well someday."

I shuddered, remembering the gypsy scryer, the stone specter, and the tomb. But I went along with her, waiting my chance to speak about what I still thought was a quite separate matter.

As we neared the Camposanto de Los Illustrios & Etc., she began to assume a festive and informative air, confessing that she had taken to visiting the place frequently. "So that I will know my way when the time comes."

The coach put us down just inside the gates, at what she said was the Chapel of Celestial Readiness. "Here I will be received with all due reverence," she assured me. "They will dress me in a plain smock of the purest linen; the contract demands it. And they must provide me with my personal page, young and comely, to brush the flies away and see that my skirts do not show too much ankle."

Next, the Hospital of the Bleeding Heart, but we did not go in, for here certain things would be done to her that she did not care to see demonstrated. "But they claim to do it with only two strokes of the knife, and promise to sew everything up neatly and even take a few extra stitches where they might be needed to make my parts tidy."

Next, the Paradisal Perfumery, where those oddments which she had left behind in the hospital would be replaced with stuffing. "I have chosen angelica water and the very same Sacred Fleece that packs the cavities of the late king; and best of all, they have pledged to fill me out to fit my wedding dress. Mind you, I ask no more than what I was granted by God, and only so that dear Angel might know me when I arrive."

Then the Salon of Eternal Beauty, where she showed me a gilt cabinet with her personal paints and powders, a bright new orange wig, a mirror. "They have promised to paint my cinder to resemble a full-blown rose come to rest by chance on my bosom. Notice the velvet cushions; they guarantee that at no time shall I be uncomfortable."

On to the Beatific Botanical Gardens, from which she had selected for her bier sops-in-wine, gillyflower, sweet eglantine, and roses. Then to a round room at the top of the tower, the Chamber of Divine Intervention, where she would lie in waiting for a week in case of a reprieve. "They say that Saint Elmo wanders these hills on turbulent nights and sometimes sends down a bolt that raises the virtuous right up again, in which case they promise to reduce all charges by half out of respect for the miracle."

Then the Chamber of Celestial Harmony, where she had decided on the harmonium, a kind of giant mouth harp worked by bellows. Then the Everlasting Aviary, from which she had chosen a yellow canary, guaranteed to sing outside her tomb for eternity.

At last the church, and here she called for her coffin to be placed on its catafalque before the altar, draped in blood-red velvet, and flanked by tall brass candlesticks. We climbed the stairs, and she bent to rap the wood of the coffin, and the sound echoed into the vaulted gloom. "Edenwood, from the Archipelago of the Amaranthines, where, they say, the Garden yet abides. Its sap bears a poison offensive to worms, and it has no pores. All joints are sealed with lead and calked with tar, so that a rabbit placed inside dies for lack of air within a day."

Stepping briskly into the coffin, she lay herself down, then reached up a claw and tugged me closer. "But I will not suffocate, Yum Yum, for there is a secret lever which I need only press to be free, and in addition I will be provided with a hammer, an awl, a small spade, four lengths of wooden pipe, and a hand bell."

She lay back in the satin. "See what pretty colors I have chosen: spring peach and rose, to go with my complexion." She crossed her spindly arms on her chest and closed her eyes. "Once a week I come here to rest like this. It is the only place I can sleep properly these days. I hear the harmonium and the chanting. The canary sings, and I smell the flowers and incense. I hear the weeping of the mourners as they pass and look down upon me, showering me with their tears. Poor dear Celestina, she was so clever, so sweet, so fatally attractive to men." She spied up a hopeful eye. "How do I look?"

Finally, the remembered journey out through the graveyard to the tombs, down the lane of leaning cypress. And although it was the full light of day, my being tightened with dread. We halted before the great chunk of marble, with its blank maw and my father's name cut into the stone: TENORIO. She bade me light a candle and bent to throw the bolt, then prepared to draw me with her down into the dark hole.

"Grandmama!" I cried. "I do not understand women!"

She paused and gave a birdlike twist of her head to peer up at me, and her eyes were bright with pert flirtation. "I know, Yum Yum, I know. Your old grandmama can read your pimples as clearly as any book. We will talk about it." She patted my sweating hand. "But first lessons first. Come," and she clutched my hand and drew me after her into dank gloom.

My stomach cringed at the odor; once you know it, you never forget it until you are, yourself, forgotten. In the guttering light I saw the pale sarcophagi, and the one at the back, the handsome granite face, the smug smile. Then the candle went out.

"Quickly, the air is bad!" she cried, and hurled herself into the darkness. I could not move; something had me by the throat, iron

99

bands clamped my chest, my huevos were beads of ice tight up against my belly. "Help me, Yum Yum, push!"

I found her scrambling at the stone wall at the back. I put my shoulder to the wall and heaved, and, lo, one small stone moved, then the larger one beside it swung ponderously out of the way, and my cheek thrilled to the kiss of sweet fresh air.

In an instant we were stumbling down a long, narrow passage, then making a turn, glimpsing a wedge of light ahead, finally clambering up a set of steps to where an iron grille fell across the sunshine.

She had what looked to be a small gold crucifix hanging on a fine chain from around her neck, but proved to be also the key with which she unlocked this final barrier. Then we were out into the sunshine of a pretty hillside just outside the walls of the Camposanto de Los Illustrios & Etc.

"You see, Yum Yum," she beamed, stepping nimbly over a golden heap of defunct eternal canaries. "There is a way back to life again, if you know the route and understand the reason."

Her groom was the same Catalinon who had served her during my childhood. He was one of those wily pícaros who spring from our city slums like mushrooms from the rubbish: plain as a mud wall and squat as an andiron, built to bear the weight and take the heat, but spry as a spider and shrewd when he had to be. He looked to have reached about one score and ten years.

"I wonder, young Master Juan," he said as I got down from the coach and prepared to follow my grandmama into her house, "if you remember a night when you were just a tyke and your nurse and me was sitting in the entrada, and you came to us all afright and saucer-eyed from something you'd heard in Don Diego's bedroom."

"No, I can't say that I do, Catalinon," I lied, and quickly showed him my back so as not to see his grin as he led the horses away.

At dinner, the old lady must needs confide to me certain details of her personal life, in the belief, she said, "that a view of the worst side of love might be instructive in your present puzzlement."

Her marriage to Don Cuero de Tortuga had recently come to a sordid end, she told me. It seems that they had each married out of the mutual misapprehension that the other was both rich and careless. Things had come to climax one night when a copper marivedí of no established ownership had got loose in their bed. In the resultant struggle, each had got hold of it with his teeth, bringing them together in as passionate an embrace as they had ever shared, but resulting in the fracture of three of her ceramic teeth, and finally, in his gulping down the coin and thereafter refusing to discuss its possible recovery and division, but instead moving his bowels at a remove and in penurious secrecy, eventually, she did not doubt, recovering the coin and placing it in one of the half-dozen safe-deposit chests which he maintained in various cities under assorted names not his own.

"So you see, Yum Yum, love is not often a dependable thing, even when it is inspired by such solid stuff as money."

During the divorce proceedings before the bishop's secretary, she had accused Don Tortuga of eating her housekeeping money, whereupon he had charged her with the ownership of vanities in excess, including no less than seventeen crinoline falbalas, twenty-four tapada veils, and thirty pairs of silk shoes; and of consorting with wizards and cumberworlds.

She had countercharged that after each meal, Don Tortuga crept out behind the house, snatched the garbage from under the snouts of the swine and sorted through it to see if she had wasted any small cheeseparing which might be considered by the average destitute leper to be edible. This being verified through examination of their hogs, razor-backed and spavined from hunger, and by witness as well, finally won her the bishop's dispensation to part company from her husband, Don Tortuga being commanded to pay an amount in silver every second month until such time as the divorce petition was reviewed by Rome. The restoration of her dentures was to be undertaken by herself, which suited her just fine, she declared with a bawdy sneer.

"I'll put my teeth back in and be pleased to keep them there, believe me. God only knows how many times I offered the old gundyguts my bare gums, and still he couldn't get it up. Oh, I tell you, Yum Yum, the love of a good woman is a powerful thing, but there is no love so mighty as to raise sap in a dead tree."

I was astonished at her language, for she had never spoken so colorfully or on such subjects before. But the wine had loosened us both, and when she suggested that we get into her bed for a while, I did it with trepidation, but I did it.

"There, it is more comfortable here, since we have no wood fire. I hope you are not embarrassed." She sniggered, and her frail little body quivered beside me. "Oh, yes, your poor old grandmama has had her troubles with men. If it isn't feast, it's famine, and the more you give them of pudding, the more they want of raisins. Why, I was even the victim of a venereal miracle once. I am sure that God meant well, but He certainly can be curious in His designs."

The miracle had occurred in response to prayer, she claimed, when, some two years after my father's death, followed by her husband's sudden demise, she, being still a vigorous woman and not without natural passion, had found herself attracted to a stoutly built wagoner of Hunnish origin, whom she had taken as her lover, only to discover that the lout was a secret tosspot and apt to become so cupshot by bedtime that his organ, while large enough to her experience in its essential bulk, was wont to become deliquescent, which was not to say that he was afflicted by entire apandry, only that, often as not, he was unable or unwilling to rise entirely to the occasion and certainly not to her expectations, with the result that, after several such disappoint-ments, love and pity, as well as a certain modicum of natural impatience, had compelled her to burn innumerable candles and go down on her knees in church without benefit of hassock, petitioning God, the Virgin, and Saint Pituitary to fortify her husband's flesh, the which prayers had not been as carefully worded as they might have been, for the final result had been that her request had been granted, but with unexpected and rare, not to say horrifying embellishment; that is, that one morning the wagoner, having been even more drunk than usual the previous night, had awakened in a crapulous stupor, stumbled out into the yard, let his trousers down, and pissed into his own face.

"Oh, it was hard all right," she giggled. "Hard as a rock, but curled like a hook and pointing upward. A stricture, the doctors called it. The demon of drink had made the muscle seize up into a knot, and no amount of love, warm water, or cold could soften it, and a mixed blessing it was. We tried, and there was plenty of time, God knows, for the thing was never soft. But because of the bent of it, we could only just manage toe to snozzle, and if one of us wasn't losing his direction, the other was, so that in the end it was just too much for me, with that thing churning around like a shepherd's crook. So that finally I just had to send him on his way. I am told that he eventually found a place in a traveling troupe of mixed jugglers and curiosities, lifting light weights with it, pulling a small wagon up an incline, swinging a censer from it on holy days, and otherwise displaying himself for a price. And I suppose that if the poor yellow-haired dear is still alive, it is still hard and pointing the way to Heaven, although to no heaven of my liking, I'm afraid. Why, once we became so entangled it took us an hour to separate ourselves, and then I was sure he had snagged my liver. Oh, I tell you, Yum Yum, your poor old grandmama has suffered much from love and good intention, and it is not entirely a blessing to be fatally attractive to men. Now do you see why I have chosen to tell you of the dangers of love before I teach you its tricks?"

What could I say? I was sixteen. The only danger I saw was that of my huevos exploding, my manhood remaining unproved, my dreams untried. And besides, she was a woman, was she not? I saw little trouble in her tales for a man. "I suppose I do, grandmama."

She peered at me. In the flickering light her orange wig rode her skull side-saddle, her arms and shoulders seemed bundled sticks of chalk, and beneath the flimsy front of her shift her bosom was nonexistent; the terrible cinder had finally consumed all the fat of her chest. And yet from deep in their sockets her eyes still burned, each with its spark of unquenchable desire, and as she spoke, her hand plucked and scrabbled at the muslin beside my thigh, and now and then a cracked nail reached out to snag my hose.

"Very well, then, open your ears, and I will tell you what any woman can, but only a loving grandmama will: how to find your way through the pickets and over the moat to castle keep and honeypot. And the first lesson is this, that we are all the same at center, lady and chambermaid, and whether the way be through patched petticoats or ribboned farthingale, the lodestone draws to the same power. Although the route can be various, the way is the same. Like the rope dancer, you must be nimble and quick of foot, yet not look down, and keep your eye always on the knot at the far end of the wire and never lose heart for your goal, no matter how whimsically the small winds may whistle and shift."

In order to avoid wasting time, she said, I must learn to recognize the proper type of woman, which she described as *"en cama loca, en casa cuerda,"* that is, prudent in public, but wild in bed. I would do best to begin with a woman less pretty than myself, for women tended to overvalue appearance, mainly because the world judged them by that measure. Therefore, to an ugly woman, my callow good looks were likely to seem a bonus.

It sometimes helped, she said, to procure the services of a good bawd to act as go-between, one of those canny old callets who hang about churches and convents, festooned in beads and selling aromatic powders and carnal introduction, but who often overcharged, she warned, and could never be fully trusted, for weren't they women themselves?

Most difficult and galling of all her advice was that I must accustom myself to a fundamental contradiction in women: that they were led to the greatest abandon by the daintiest deceit. The more indirect, polite, and mannered the suit, the lewder and looser the final reception. I must learn good customs, avoid public drunkenness and bad company, and always assume an air of confidence, good cheer, and discretion. "Be like a pigeon, sedate and well preened," she advised, sniggering and squirming at my side. "Be like a peacock, gallant and assured. Be discreet, not violent, neither gloomy nor enraged."

The problem was not so much to get around a woman, she said, as to help her to get around herself; and to do this, I must nurse her from her natural wariness by polite and delicate pretense, reassuring her up to the very last moment that the world was pretty, polite, and eternally joyous, and, in fact, that there was neither need nor intention for us to enter into that turbulent engagement that waited at the end of our tiddly exchange.

"You must not tell her what it is you really want, although, of course, she knows. She does not want to believe that you wish to merely make use of a part of her, but must be led to believe that you want all, and particularly that you recognize those qualities which she believes make her unique among women, and by means of which she might prevent you from going on to another woman. Does that make sense to you, Yum Yum?"

"No, grandmama."

"Ah, but it does, from her point of view. And so that is why I say: there are various keys to a woman's heart and body, but there is one passkey, and that is deceit."

Finally, and above all, she said, while her little claw danced beside my thigh, the successful lover was the one who persisted to the end, no matter how clever, contrary, and adamant the resistance. "Never take no to be the answer, Yum Yum," she whispered, and her voice was a frail and throbbing insistence in my ear, and my nostrils flared to an effluvium as elusive and poignant as a whiff of pollen blown across desert sands from some dying flower. "For to a woman, no is yes, sooner or later, and always will be."

She cackled, thrashing beside me, then suddenly her voice dwindled, drained of all jape; her breath fluttered at my ear and she trembled beside me like some young girl gone suddenly shy, or a yearling hind poised in dappled light; ears up, eyes wide, heart thumping beneath the tender hide. "Just like Angel," she whispered, touching a trembling claw to my cheek. "In the eyes and around the mouth, just like my dear dead son . . ."

I remembered the narrow-headed girl of the garden, her wide eyes and flushed cheeks, and somewhere deep inside me stirred the hunter's compulsion, the ogling lean against the drawn bow, the command to pounce. On the instant a snug skein of sweat covered me. But before I could begin to comprehend the moment, she let go a spasmed gasp. "Oh, Angel!" And it was she who lost her grip on her arrow; it was her twitching claw that pounced.

"Grandmama!" The next feeling admitted to sensation was the cold of the floor tiles against the bottoms of my burning feet. "Oh, please do not do that!"

She stared, clutching the sheet to her nonexistent bosom. A convulsive snigger seized her, but she mastered it. "I don't know what came over me," she said primly. "Perhaps a touch of the Saint Vitus."

"Yes," I eagerly agreed. "It must have been that. Well, grandmama, I think I should go to my bed now."

"By all means," she said, looking away and giving a fretful toss of her head. "And send Catalinon in here, I want him to stoke up my bedwarmer."

As I let myself out, she was muttering to herself and primping at her wig. To my surprise, I found the groom already there beside the door. "The mistress needs you to blow her coals," I told him.

"I daresay she does," he said with a sly and sidelong grin. "And if I may add a bit of advice of my own on the matter of love, young master." Damned if the rascal didn't clap a hand to his codflap by way of demonstration, and double damned if he wasn't unbuttoning as he pushed into my grandmama's bedroom. "When in doubt, out."

9

I HAD BEEN back at Osuna for a fortnight when I found myself out swilling with the Oars. As I recall it, we were swaying on the curb all in a clamoring huddle, the Green Rooster having closed half an hour before, when one of our number pointed out a large woman moving past the end of the alley alone.

"There she blows! The great sperm whale, all blubber and six cubits wide!"

It was Maxima Ruiz, she of the royally colored undergunnies. I had not forgotten that first bloomer-closet symposium in which the Oars had gloated upon her bad name, and I had seen her since through the tallow smoke of the Rooster, like some barnacled caravel at anchor behind the plank and kegs, or wallowing through the roisterers, beer jugs in her fists and a painted smile flapping at her masthead.

Now all hailed her bawdily, yet no man made a move to pursue. This tendency of the Oars to mistake horseplay for dressage and demonstration for consummation had an agitating effect on my demon. Why were we shouting so loud as we roamed the unpeopled streets, why reeling into the brothel parlor to grope the girls and dicker, only to reel right out again in the same nervous gather? Why reciting bawdy stories when there was no one among us to be scandalized?

Clearly the matter was not so important to them. But, by God's nose, it was to me. My furia boiled up, stirred by the stiffening stick of rut. One of them struck up a ballad, and in an instant all were caterwauling and reeling in place, with one exception: myself.

"And now we're out to sea, my boys,
And the wind comes on to blow,
One half the watch is sick on deck,
The other half below."

As I rounded the far corner, I heard their song break off and someone call my name, but only once, and then I was alone, speeding to intercept my quarry. Peeking around the wall, I held to the shadows and saw her coming ponderously on, head down and skirts lifted to avoid the puddles, one sock halfway down and the clay pellets of her beaded bag pattering a faint, dying rain behind her.

O my God, to distribute oneself like that in a meandering, purposeless trail across the face of the earth; and to find one's substance spent at the end of the task, with nothing behind and nothing before, at one with the dust all the way. I shuddered for her and simultaneously felt the lift of my cod. Poor, damned, susceptible creature, I thought, poor overripe and easy fruit.

As she passed, I leaped from my shadow and placed myself before her, doffed my cap, and made a small but elegant bow. *Be polite, careful, and mannered; assume an air of confidence, good cheer, and discretion.*

"Good evening, Doniña Ruiz. You do not know me, but I saw you passing and felt compelled to introduce myself."

She laughed crisply, but not without a certain stirring in her flesh-enfolded eyes. "It is not evening but past midnight, I am no doniña but a barmaid, and I already know of you. You are Lucero, the famous tit-sucker."

I was taken aback. Apparently the tale of my long bundle with Pechita was loose in the town. But I managed to hide my fluster with a smile and an even deeper bow. *Be like a peacock, gallant and assured; like a pigeon, sedate and well preened.* "I am honored that my name has known your lips, even though it be by means of vicious slander, the which I am sure by your fine carriage and gracious manner you would scorn as far beneath you, did you but know the truth."

She curled a lip and laughed again, and yet she seemed to love it, beginning to wallow opposite me now, shifting her shawl and slithering a glance at my cod. "Is it slander then that you find your pleasure only above the waist?" she asked with a grin. "Is it wrong rumor that you love virtue more than meat and can only couple with the corners of cathedrals?"

Again I was shaken, recognizing the twist of some Oar's dagger, no doubt that of the Ram himself. But still I managed to muster a smile of dismissal, braced by my grandmama's advice. *Be discreet, not violent, neither gloomy nor enraged.* "Slander all and cowardly as well, dear lady. As dark and nefarious as this thin-mooned night, in which I fear to see you wend your way thus, like some precious jewel going carelessly unguarded."

"Jewel?" She snorted and tossed her heavy head, but showed delight as well. "An old ruby perhaps," she muttered, giving my cod another measuring glance. "Cracked, but still on fire."

"I see the flame," I confided. "And I am warmed."

Sniggering, she eased her bulk closer. "All right then, guard me from crime, if you insist, only excepting rape." And, grasping my hand so firmly that the knuckles cracked, she turned and towed me a few paces down the cobbles, past the windows of a shabby inn, and into a low doorway.

Clammy dank of wattle and chitter of my heart, faint glimmerings of light, and ahoy the whale: the spread of her hinderlings rising ahead of my nose and luring me on, the vast rump bumping side to side as we climbed, two flights, four, to her narrow closet at the top of the house, the cramped home port of her dim sorrows and sodden secrets.

With the door closed, the cubby was so crowded with my bones and her abundance that she had to ease herself onto her narrow cot to give me room, and there she lay, beached and wheezing, while I teetered above her, hunched beneath the beams and whiffing in the rich redolence of her storied rags, so close to high heaven and its dizzying stink, yet still doggedly cleaving to my grandmama's recommendations. *There are various keys to a woman's heart, but there is one passkey, and that is deceit.*

"You will excuse me, Maxima, if I may be so familiar with your name, but the climb has momentarily fuddled me and I feel I must lay down. There being but little space in your charming apartment, I wonder if . . ."

Behemoth's booming grunt cut me short; she lurched upright and wrapped her arms about me, and I was sinking into ripe and steaming flesh, like the baker's thumb in the uncooked loaf. And still I clung to the illusion of deliberate endeavor. *Never take no to be the answer.* Squirming, I managed to free an arm and groped for her thighs, only to discover that those two sweltering hams were already spread wide, and what was more, that she wore no bloomers. Some marauding Oar must have made off with the poor creature's last pair.

At my first tentative touch upon the hairy conjunction, the thighs swung firmly shut again, clamping hot jaws upon my wrist and beginning moistly to grind. And still my mind struggled to retain the illusion of command. *When in doubt, out!* Twisting in her embrace, I freed my other hand, fumbled for my codflap and stiffly unlimbered. From that touch she did recoil, but only briefly, reaching down to pluck something from under the bed and offering it, her instructions brisk and clear between gasped punctuation. "We must take precautions (*grunt*), the gutsheath (*groan*), quickly, put it on (*moan*)."

It looked to be a length of pig gut, knotted at one end, soft and powdered, and rolled into a collar. I had, of course, heard of the contrivance, but had only a vague idea of how to don it. Struggling to sit up, I cracked my head on an overhead beam. Rotting thatch rained down and the husks of dead woodworms pattered upon us. She wallowed close against me, sneezed, and moaned again, while in the small window at the end of the attic, the crescent moon was the night's crooked grin.

Positioning the little collar atop my yard, I attempted to roll it down. But I had got it wrong side up and it resisted; and when I pressed with both hands, it escaped my grip, catapulting straight for the moon and out the window.

My yard began to waver and lean. "Gone," I muttered, my melancholy not entirely unsweetened by a certain furtive relief. "Gone forever."

"No!" she cried out in alarm. "They are expensive!" Floundering upright, she flung herself at the window and wedged tight, and her voice came in a muffled wail from the far side. "There it is, I see it. Just out of reach. Push me out. The roof is not steep, push me!"

I applied my shoulder to the bulging plug of flesh and heaved once, tentatively, then with vigor. "Ouch!" she cried, but then: "Harder!" and I heaved again: "Ouch!" but yet again: "Don't stop!"

And the harder I shoved, the louder were her complaints. The more desperate were her cries, the more insistent her commands. "Harder, more, ouch, harder, oh yeoww, don't stop, harder!"

And so I shoved and she yowled and the window frame creaked, and the sweat gathered in the roots of my hair and rolled down my nose, and it was a touch of the past and a glimpse of the future as well. I was on the threshold of a revelation, some vision that would reveal all, the whole source of the ache and the whole reason for it.

But once again fate and failing fibers intervened, and the lesson was lost. The window frame parted company from its parent masonry, and with a shriek of wrenched pegs and a howl from her, she went tumbling onto the adjoining roof, landing boobs over bunghole, her legs pedaling the air, her great bottom still stuck fast in the frame.

Yet she had not lost heart for the joust, far from it. Floundering in the moonlight, she plucked the gutsheath from the thatch and held it aloft triumphantly. "I have found it! Hurry, but take care, for the beams are sound but the thatch rotten."

There was more than thatch on the rot thereabouts; the roof was littered with cabbage leaves and orange peels, and slick with the fruit of the cuckstool. The straw itself was firm enough beneath my feet, but I could see that the binding strings had rotted through here and there, and the pitch of the roof, while not extreme, was steep enough to suggest that I go on all fours to her side, there to be welcomed with renewed moans interspersed with brisk injunction. "Put it on (*gasp*), we must take care (*groan*), oh, hurry (*moan*)."

I braced myself upright and tried again. The moon grinned, the cobbles gleamed far below, and the street was a dark cleft between the rooftops, reaching out to the winding high road beyond the town. As I fumbled the gut at my rigid yard, my eyes were drawn helplessly to the black bush snouting out between her thighs, and even as I gaped, sweat dripping past my eyes, she moaned again and let her thighs fall open, and there it was: the many-lipped portal and gaping maw, vaster and more vivid than I had ever seen it, and steaming.

I gawked, conjuring rich and deadly stiflement, longing to tumble in, afraid I might not get out. Then she reached up and wrapped her huge arms around me and rolled me astride her. Holding myself upright on my arms, I cast a nervous glance down at my yard; I had succeeded in rolling the gut down its full length, but an equal excess hung off the end and swung fitfully, like some flabby extension of the organ, and even as I stared, it caught on the end of a splintered window peg and tore.

For one awful moment I thought I had decapitated myself, but immediately as I realized that I had instead rent the veil of caution, I experienced a sudden sense of hurry and furtively stuffed the offensive rupture out of sight inside her. She squealed, and I began dutifully to pump.

We lay midway upon the slope of garbaged thatch, the eaves a few rods below our feet, the peak an equal distance above, the moon riding low over the folded straw at the top. She moaned and humped beneath me, and I propped myself up on my arms, gripping the edge of the window frame and holding her dead center and spit upon my spindle; and now it was night's mummery again, Our Lady of the Brown Soap and her tattooed cipher; the gimlet eye of the satyr and time running away in the glass. I groaned, grinding my teeth, and raised my sweating face to the moon. Now I lay me down to swive, and pray my yard to come alive . . .

They say in Burgos that God eventually answers every prayer, but does it in His own way. I first became aware of my delicate situation at the sound of a distant pattering behind. A rotten cabbage head went tumbling past. Twisting my head to look back down the roof, I saw bits of thatch and offal tumbling over the eaves and falling to the cobbles below. This unsettling revelation was followed by recognition of another sound: the clatter of wheels coming down the high road toward town.

Next came a truly alarming discovery. As I jabbed diligently away at my companion, it seemed to my startled glance that the moon was no longer setting above the peak, but was rising instead, and not at the traditional pace, but in rhythmic jerks, like a paper fish on a string, and in intimate association with my own movements, as though I somehow controlled the toy fishing pole that pulled the string that jerked the moon. Grotesque as this conception was, what followed was even more horrific. It came to me that it was not the moon that was moving after all, but the entire roof. That is, each time that I thrust into my moaning partner, the mass of thatch moved, taking us with it, closer and closer to the crumbling edge.

And as if that weren't enough, the clatter of wheels came closer. They say that in certain states of ecstasy the yellow wizards of magic's capital develop a third eye in the forehead for the glimpsing of the deeper truths. Mine was at the back and lower down, and through it, in a fever of fancy, I thought I could see the morning coach, as I had seen it many times before, knifing through the narrow alley, glossy black of body and Chinese red of wheel, its muscled nags foaming green at the mouth and galloping straight for the pile of trash which awaited our bodies below. And in the same fevered fancy, I saw the driver of the coach as I remembered the phantom of the nursery, all in drifting black, rising up with her whip, or was it with the clyster pipe, her hair in glossy black ringlets, as though she had just emerged from a bath of warm oil, her throat swollen with a low and gloating chuckle.

My third eye winked shut. Oh, I came, be assured, I spent. As the bull comes to the cape, as the torero spends in the tavern, both. With headlong lurch and spasmed spouting, heave and howl and grateful gouting.

Then came hastily back to the moment, to realize first that our feet rested scarcely half a pace from the edge of the roof; second, that we hung like sacks across the ceiling beam; third, that the heads of irate tenants were popping into view from windows all around.

"I did it! I did it!" I cried out exultantly, but only to look down through the torn roofing and into bright candlelight, to see, just below on the tiles of the inn's topmost apartment, what looked at first to be a nun and a soldier interrupted at leapfrog, but which subsequently proved to be not a nun at all, but the rector, Don Gaspar Born Without Ranch Eggs, and not a soldier at all, but Brother Gabriel Tellez, in the position of advantage.

It was only a matter of time, and before the week was out, I got word to meet with the monk, not out in the cloisters, where our tutorial sessions had always taken place, but in his apartments at the back of the abbot's house.

I had always expected a plain cell furnished only with books and perhaps a bust of Aristotle, but he received me in the first of several rooms which were not only large but decorated with brocades and padded chairs, foreign rugs, and even a set of stuffed songbirds under glass. Aristotle was nowhere in sight, but the books were there, displayed in orderly prominence, as a knight might display his letters patent, a banker his ledgers, a bishop his papal bulls.

He did not greet me with the usual bawdy jocularity, but held his face in such an expression of pained solemnity that I suspected with a foolish lift of the heart that at any moment he might burst into laughter. But he did not.

The rector, he straightway informed me, had ordered my tuition suspended and had directed that I leave the university at once, expelled for venal excess and public fornication.

"Excess! Me!" I had expected a reprimand, but not expulsion; my duende gnashed its teeth and furia brought me right up off my chair. "But what about him. Venal excess? That silly goose—"

But a fretful snap of his bulging eyes warned me, and I stopped myself. "That is, I mean to say," I mumbled, "if it is about what happened the other night when the roof fell in, be assured that my lips are sealed and that I harbor no prejudice, for the great-souled man judges others only when they intend him harm, and steadfastly refuses to broadcast hateful rumor—"

But too late. He shook his head, chewing on an anise cigar. Was there a trace of regret as he informed me that there was no appeal? I must leave at once, he told me, and should I try to go over the rector's head, there were further punishments possible. "You would be wise to remember that Gaspar's father is the Duke of Antiquera, and Gaspar is aware that your stepfather has ambitions to go to court—"

"But the Prince exists for the good of the people!" I shouted.

He cut me off with a sour smile and wave of his cigar. "The Prince exists."

"But the great-souled man is haughty toward men of position . . ."

". . . but can't expect to get away with it every time."

". . . claims much and deserves much . . ."

". . . but doesn't often get it . . ."

". . . cares more for the truth than for what people think . . ."

". . . but is wiser not to care too much either way . . ."

". . . speaks ill of his enemies only when he intends to give offense, as now, when I ask my mentor by way of farewell . . ."

I was shouting now and very near to foaming at the mouth, yet was not too far gone to miss his weary amusement as I backed to the door, howling as only youth can howl, ". . . when the monk delved and the rector span, who then was the gentleman!"

10

HE WHO HAS not seen Sevilla has not seen a wonder, everybody says so. It was a joy once again to see the handsome Giralda standing tall above the red roofs, and to smell the sweet breeze from the Court of Oranges. But it was small fun to face Don Diego's measured anger at the news that I had lost my chance at the Law, even less to see the mournful disgust in my mother's eyes as she learned that I had been disembogued from the university.

"O my God, Juanito, you have done it again!"

What, then, were my plans, Don Diego wanted to know, and hastened to suggest: there was the army. The Crown was once again soliciting recruits to go off to Flanders and trade atrocities with the Dutch. He might be persuaded to use his influence to wrangle me a commission, providing I promised to conduct myself like a proper Lucero. By which he meant, of course, keeping wrinkles from my uniform, currying the favor of my superiors, and at the earliest opportunity, shouting *Santiago y cerra España!* and sticking my head in a cannon.

Otherwise, there was always the Church. Only the other day, Father Nuncacura, who was miraculously alive after a surgical operation to replace his grommet with a leather valve, had mentioned that he had always thought that I had dodged my destiny. Finally, should I feel prepared to revise my previously warped and arrogant view of Don Diego's own work, he might be persuaded to find me a place in the upper reaches of the king's civil service.

Well? A man was not a man without a vocation and a goal. What was my choice to be?

I needed time to think it over, I told them. Meanwhile, if Don Diego could see his way clear to make me a small loan of pocket money?

He thought he could, on condition that I devote myself to the problem at hand and endeavor to stay clear of bad company and out of the taverns. "You have three months to get your horse under you, Juan. There must be something you want to do."

Indeed there was. And once I had the price of a jar of wine, I sought out one who might help me. For a most distressing question pressed: could I only spend under threat of imminent death?

Some years before, Estebanillo Guzman had been the outstanding amoroso and venereal prodigy of Barrio San Marco, and my secret idol. Three years older and rich to boot, he was reported to have lifted the skirts of his first scullery maid at the age of fifteen.

It required only a quick tour of Calle Sierpes to find him, throwing dice with other plumed bravos in a small bodega next to the shop where Pierre Pepin sells playing cards. Exceedingly tall, loose of movement, and bland of feature, he dressed in fashion, but never flamboyantly, carried a sword, but treated it absently; and his manner was quietly assured, suaveloquent, satinosco.

"Juanito, isn't it? Lucero, of course, the one with the talking doll. Well, well, welcome to Snake Street. Join the fallen angels and have a glass of wine."

We took our jars to a table apart from the others, and there he propped his long bones opposite and showed me a solicitous face, at the same time endeavoring to follow the dice game over my shoulder. The news that I had been expelled from Osuna brought a chuckle of comroguery from him, and he confided that he also had been thrown out of the university, Salamanca in his case, and not just once, but three times in all, twice for gaming, and finally for spoiling the rector's mutton.

"The old man had hired a new housemaid, a lusty little bellybumper from the countryside, but old enough to know fresh sausage from moldy, and we had a glad time of it until we got caught. But I daresay you could tell a saltier tale, Juanito. How were the girls at Osuna?"

117

"That's just it," I said. "You see, I didn't, that is, I don't—"

"Wait," he said with sudden enthusiasm, snapping his long fingers. "We have something else in common. Do you remember Carolina?"

Numbed to my root, I managed to shrug. "I suppose I do. . . ."

"Suppose!" He leaned closer, a little smile curling his lips, his tongue darting out to moisten them. "Come now, I remember a tale about a picnic. As for myself, I believe I took her to the woods in my mother's coach. Ah, what a juicy pomegranate she was, and how the seeds did fly. O my God, yes, I remember now. I had to let her walk ahead into the boscage, while I got behind the coach and had it off by hand for fear I would be too quick when the time came. The choicest ones have that effect on me."

His eye caught the fall of dice beyond my shoulder, and with the same loose, hot look in his eye, he licked his lips. "Double zero, a difficult point to make. But you did not come here to reminisce, Juan. Perhaps there is something I can do for you?"

I was no longer sure. Too many embarrassing admissions stood between me and the knowledge I sought. "Nothing in particular," I said. "Only that I have been a year away from Sevilla and am somewhat out of touch—"

"Say no more." He put a hand on my arm. "I know what it is to come home with a wolf in you and the lambs scattered. Why, you probably haven't had a good tumble for a week, poor fellow. I know a good clean leaping house just down the street. Do you have money?"

"Yes, but to pay is not to know."

"I beg your pardon, know what?"

How could I tell this most suave and accomplished amorist that I feared that I was a chronic retardo and had never yet spent without benefit of either silver or threat of death? I looked away. "I have forgotten."

"You are strange, Lucero." He twiddled his fingers at his chin, watching the dice fly. "But let me think, surely we can find something for you. God knows, I myself have plenty to spare these days, and scarcely a moment free for cards. I have it!" He gave a snap of his lanky fingers. "When all else fails, a widow!"

"A widow? Oh, I don't know, Esteban. . . ."

"Come now, you can't lose with a widow: already broken to saddle, and nobody to guard the stirrup. And this one a devil's mule at that. You know what they say: once the priest is through the door, the whole parish follows. Let me explain."

For several years now, he said, he had enjoyed the confidence of a certain priest of San Detras de la Frontera, south of the city, and it happened that this very week, the priest, a scrofulous man in his middle years, wished to make pilgrimage to San Juan Compostella, a miracle being expected and therefore trade likely to be brisk in the lead medallions which he was in the habit of striking off, blessing with holy water, and giving a semblance of bronzing by sprinkling them with his own urine, or, that not always available whilst the lead was hot, the void of his housekeeper, which had equally ennobling properties.

There was, however, the problem of hearing the daily confessions of his parish while he was gone, the which duty he was not prepared to trust to a fellow priest, due to certain confidences between himself and various lambs of his flock, all women, and there already being much jealous gossip at large in the town, to the detriment of civil peace and the Lord's work. He was therefore prepared to invite Esteban to sit in the confessional of his small church twice a day while he was gone and hearken to the labored regrets of the sinners of San Detras. There was little chance of discovery, the confessional being of the modern kind, with a wooden lattice separating confessor and sinner, and a private tunnel leading from the confessional to the Curia, the only key of which the priest was prepared to hand over when he set off for Compostella.

"You can do it for me," Esteban assured me. "All you have to do is get into a cassock and shovel hat and go in my place. Nobody will know the difference."

"But my voice."

"Lower it, oil it with solemnity and pious intent; all voices echo the same in that place."

"But the words."

"Surely you remember enough of Dominican jabber, and besides, it is all the same sauce to a sore soul. When you fear to fumble, mumble. Indulgentiam, absolutionem, et remissionem peccatorum, and all that. Fill all awkward pauses with twelve candles and a hundred Hail Marys. And when in doubt, shout, 'Dominus vobiscum! Gloria tibi Domine!' "

"But my figure. I am too young."

"Nonsense, none will see you but the widow. And to her, you are just another priest, a replacement while His Celsitude turns lead to gold at Compostella. To some a young priest is closer to God than an old one, be sure of that."

"But this widow. What if I hazard the wrong creature?"

He smiled his confiding smile and wet his lips. "Believe me, you will know her by her voice. Just bide your time. There will be no mistake once you have heard her speak." He got to his feet. "Come then, let us make haste. I will borrow a horse for you, and we can gather up your costume at my house, then on to your rendezvous."

Still I hesitated. He frowned, watching the dice and drumming the table with his long fingers. "Have I read you wrong, then? Have the monks taught you unmanly tricks at Osuna? No, I do not believe it. You are a Spaniard and a hidalgo and always ready for adventure. We are men, are we not, and made for the chase?"

That is how, a scant two hours later, I found myself in place behind a wooden screen, harkening to the mumbled confessions of the plain people of San Detras, who, I must say, are virtuous to a fault, if one is to believe them, their venial sins having to do mostly with chick-peas, the principal fruit of the region, and their mortal sins most often involving sheep, in which the district abounds. Which is not to say that I was unmoved by what I heard, for who could remain indifferent to those abject voices begging absolution from a latticework: that fuddled rustic who gruffly confessed to green jealousy and scarlet rage at the neighbor who had coveted and conspurcated his favorite and most juicy ewe, the contrite sharecrop who begged forgiveness for having laced the landlord's nine-tenths share of the pea crop with a handful of gravel from his wife's bleeding kidneys, or that unmarried cowmaid and mother of five dwarfish children who insisted that the father of her brood was a visitor from another star and feared that God was shrinking her children as punishment for her lack of matrimony?

And then, all of a sudden, the widow was there. She was neither more nor less a presence than any of the other dim shadows that had slipped into place on the far side of the screen, until she spoke. But then, O my

God, I have never heard a voice so lubricious and warmly intimate with itself, except perhaps from an oboe. Woody yet moist, languid and lewd, it trembled the fibers of the screen and oozed exploratory tendrils in through the latticework to where I sat.

"It is me, Torito," it murmured, fluid and fruity, lingering and low. "I have sinned again. Oh, how I have sinned! And I have rushed over here to tell you about it, with my bed still warm and Don Gonzales' shirttails scarce tucked in against his wife's inspection, so eager am I to confess to you once again, so much in need of your guiding hand. Oh, how wicked I have been, and with the king's own postal clerk at that, although he is neither so aloof nor so sluggish as his official demeanor and personal corpulence might suggest. But he does not love me as Jesus loves me, as you love me, sweet Torito. So let me confess down to the last disgusting detail, and quickly. And then you must give me penance and administer it to me this very day, for I have been so wicked and it has been so humid this week, I am simply steaming. Why do you not answer? Do you hear me? I have sinned with the Devil's own goat; you called him that yourself last week when he lost your letter. Torito, are you there? Doesn't my confession enflame you? Speak!"

How could I? Until her arrival, I had bent my voice low and oiled it with that droning solemnity reassuring to men, or piped it high enough to convince the most prudent matron that I was at the worst a seminarian, if not an outright cliptnuts. But clearly this one was too intimately familiar with her Torito; she was sure to find me out the moment I opened my mouth. And there was more to my preoccupation, for I stared down in helpless fascination at a restive stirring in my cassocked lap, conjured entirely by the caress of her irresistible voice.

"Torito, my little bull," she crooned, and the sound flowed yet had the substance of nuzzling flesh; and I gazed, rapt, upon the little tent readying itself in my lap.

"It is me, your own dear Parnella," she whispered. "Ah, Torito, you are angry with me, and rightly so. Oh, the dance that devil led me to, the sinful acrobatics!" Her shadow pressed closer to the screen; I quaffed a heavy scent and felt the heat of her breath; and my tent pole stiffened in the masterful grip of her voice.

"Torito, O my God, speak, I cannot wait! Shame cakes my thighs and guilt itches in my veins. I am on fire with the need for absolution!''

Her groaning stroked, root to head, and obediently, majestically, the black tent arose between my legs.

"Dominus vobiscum! Gloria tibi Domine!" I cried.

The silence was chaste yet pregnant. Did I hear the rattle of her beads as she fled, or did they rub the screen as she sought to spy in upon me?

When she finally spoke, it was in the same caressing tones, lent a new vibrancy by curiosity. "What a fine, plangent voice you have," she murmured. "And who are you?"

There was nothing for it now but to put the first half of the pretense aside. "I am your priest, my child."

"But not my Torito. His voice is pretty, but not the same. You are young. How young?"

"Young enough to know that I am old enough." But surely I overplayed my hand! My throat closed on this burst of audacity. "Come, let us to business, madam, there are other sinners waiting. You will say one hundred Hail Marys and burn twelve tapers before the shrine of San Juan Climax—"

"Not until I have seen his ladder and known his miracle," she murmured, and before I could protest, her voice was in full flow again, fiddling and feeling, stoking and stroking. "Each thing to its proper place, first confession, then penance, then absolution, that is the way my Torito taught it to me, and I have much to confess, if only it weren't so warm, I must slip this cloak off, some say black wool guards against the sun, others that it sucks it in, there, that is better, you have such a sweet voice, like a young prince of the Church, but then I suppose I am hopelessly romantic, a lady should keep her skin white, but there is no sun here, only heat, this collar chokes me, I've known all our priests, but you sound the sweetest so far. Let me tell you my life's sad tale, for I would have you know that I have not always had the habit of excitement in the confessional."

What could I do? I was her priest; I listened. She had once been a lady of substantial dignity and few sins worthy of expeccation, she assured me. Unfortunately, her husband had died, and her young son shortly afterward. She had thought to go on the stage to ease her broken heart, but had been unable to find a place, for what reason she could not fathom, since she had been willing to play opposite any leading man, only requiring that he be sufficiently handsome to make a balanced match. For those few years that her house had been in good repair, she had not lacked for suitors, but something had always driven them away, more than one gone hastily into the night without his boots.

"I believe myself to be guarded by the ghost of my husband, who always was jealous of my good looks," she said. "This blouse is so tight, there, it is open and I can breathe, so cooling to feel the air upon one's bosom, oh, the way that devil of a postman did nibble at me. But I was not always wanton; it takes bereavement as well as bad weather to bring on the prickly itch, believe me."

With each suitor who had abandoned her, and each shot fallen short of matrimony, she had found herself drawn more and more to religion, and had been considering withdrawing into a nunnery, there to hide her light under a bushel in order to teach malekind a lesson, when she had fallen precipitously into love with a young priest of the neighboring village, who, after addicting her to the smell of candlewax and the habit of confession, had proceeded to cart away the more valuable parts of her house one by one, telling her that they were for the furnishing of a new shrine to Eulalia, the which she had foolishly believed, until, thanks to a brief interlude with a highwayman, since hanged, she had discovered that her priest was actually equipping a new and lavish brothel in Sevilla; but when she had so accused him, asking why he robbed the lily to gild the wormwort, her confessor had flown into a rage, cursing her in a language known only to the Devil, and had mockingly held up her most precious crystal mirror, subsequently claiming that it was confrontation with her face that had cracked it and not the spiteful blow of his knuckles, the which cruel and incomprehensible insult had so unsettled her that she had since found it impossible to pursue religious intercourse except with the screen between herself and her confessor, while on the other hand, since she had become even more wary of secular men, and besides, was firmly conditioned by habit as well as her spiritual nature to the homey odor of cassock cloth and the reassuring exchange of the confessional, she could not find it in herself to seek satisfaction elsewhere either.

"So now you know my painful history and have some idea of my dilemma," she breathed, at once plaintively and suggestively, against the screen. "My sins and my salvation have taken a common house, and only God's sacred sifter prevents them from mixing the deadly brew of lunacy. Ever since that beautiful but villainous capon cracked my heart and my looking glass, my soul has wept and my loins been a sponge for sin. For once I loved him as I love God, and called him Torito, as I have called all the others since. Cursed is woman, who must have both bull and cowherd, devil and priest in one man. Let me get these skirts off, there, now my knees can breathe. Thank God I found you, for you are a priest and privileged to complete me. That postal clerk could offer me only plain sin without savory, leaving my poor soul half satisfied, for he proved to be devoid of Latin. Give me penance now; Latin is best, talk to me, speak, or I shall scream."

There was an insinuating rustle of petticoats close against the screen. I began to fling broken Latin, as the nervous jackdaw scatters straw, to no clear purpose, but with a lunatic will. "Indulgentiam, absolutionem, et remissionem preccatorum, Ave Maria, semper fidelis, ex cathedra, pro re nata . . ."

"Yes, oh, that's good, that's good, I am the widow Cabeza de Vaca, but you may call me Parnella, oh, don't stop, let me get these bloomers off. . . ."

Now there were ruffles and lace, now doughy flesh pressed in pillowed squares against the screen. "Six semper tyrannus, ceteris paribus, aut Caesar aut nullus, post hoc, ergo propter, pro patria . . ."

"Oh, yes, yes, don't stop, come closer to the screen, as I do, for I am the petitioner and you the priest, and this sieve between us is the Veil, the septum of the sacrament, filtering the dross from the pure, the peccable from the impeccable. Yes, yes, come closer, come closer. Take my voice into your ear and my sins into your soul, as I shall take in your Godly heat and blessing. I am ready, Torito. Extend so that we might be at once One and Trinity, sinner, saint, and separation, Mother, Son, and Holy Ghost. Extend yourself, pierce me with your angelic sword and free me!"

I tried, God knows, I did my best. Dizzied by her hot babble and gusty breath and a rising pungency of overwrought glands, I lifted my cassock and pressed close to the screen, taking aim at the vivid target between the waffled press of her buttocks. But when I attempted to

124

poke through one of the diamond-shaped openings in the latticework, I found that it would not go.

"Hurry, oh, hurry!" she gasped. "Speak Latin and hurry!"

"Aut Caesar aut nullus," I said, trying another opening, then another. But the edges of the slats only bit and turned me back.

"Talk to me, extend to me!" she cried, and the screen rattled and jumped between us as she whacked it with her buttocks. "Give me penance, give it to me, give it to me!"

"Contineutor remedium, crambe repetita," I muttered, poking and recoiling, poking again, again wincing back. "Trahit sua quemque voluptas, principia non homines, latet anguis en herba, sic transit gloria mundi . . ."

"Hurry, O God, hurry . . ."

It was too much: her groaning enticements, my throbbing gristle, the stubborn resistance of the latticework. With a curse, I whirled from the screen and raced back through the Curia, my skirts lifted, my tent bobbing before me, out of the sacristy and around the farthest buttress, into the church and down the aisle, headfirst through the door of the confessional, scraping to a stop before the figure that crouched against the screen.

"Sic itur ad astra!" I thundered, lifting my skirts shoulder high.

She stood against the screen, bent at the waist, head and shoulders obscured by the fall of turned out petticoats. At the sound of my shout, she slowly unbent to face me.

She looked like a horse. I mean a horse, with the narrow brow, the bulging eyes to either side of the long, ungainly snout, the rubbery mauve lips and random whiskers above the bucking thrust of the long yellow teeth.

But I was too far into rut for the sight to halt me at once. In a flash I was on her, pressing her down to the bench, pulling her skirts up and getting between her legs.

"But what kind of a priest are you!" she cried. "O my God, what are you doing!"

"Sending the pope to Rome," I said, and stuck it in her.

O salted earth, O bitter victory. Her small bones jangled, her flesh was piebald with imperfect passion, her teeth thrust up like a graveyard. I discovered, first with my mouth, then with an astonished glance, hairs sprouting from her teats, several so long that I conjectured that they perhaps went in at another place. There was a hole in her: a small, rusty fold inside a little bun of orange hair; and I had fumbled myself in past the dry flaps of this sorry envelope. Now she went suddenly limp beneath me and murmured with the weary abandon of a martyr who has been many times to the block but never beyond, "Oh, all right, go ahead, you needn't wait for me. I haven't spent in fifteen years."

My mind gawked, my body boggled. Many a time I would take my lessons thus, frozen in mid-stroke and pinched between the thighs of yet another paradox. "You?" I gasped, "spend?"

"Not since my husband died of a cracked heart between these very thighs," she sighed, turning her long head to the bench. "God is punishing my flesh for that murder. And for seeking to cuckold him these many times since, I am sure of it. That is why the screen tightens each time, the bull becomes impatient and leaps the barrera, and time after time I am robbed of my relief. For I cannot enjoy it without the sacred separation, and God has not seen fit to send a torito adroit and delicate enough to slide his awl through the net."

She sighed again, and her rusty bun gummed my yard with lips of clay. "So you had just as well go ahead and get it over with. Don't worry about me. They say the Son of God will come a second time. I have waited this long, I can wait a little longer."

Female spending, a distaff spasm? I had never heard of such a thing. What was more, I did not wish to hear of it. But the sight of her equine face and the thought of her unkind fate were quite something else and inescapable. How could I possibly take my pleasure from this spavined hack, in this terrible chapel of confused intention, where disappointment was become devotion, and satisfaction was doomed always to have a shorter reach than sorrow?

For one fatal moment more I hovered between her legs like a small boy poised before the door of the root cellar, chilled by the mournful darkness, inclined just to fling his stone and flee.

I drew back, no doubt to do the last. But too far, for hesitation can be critical at the mouth of a coony, and friction will serve its function, regardless of direction. Before I could push in again, a dim and sickly

126

sensation reached me, a sense of cold and nerveless draining. And even as I glanced down in dread, I saw the swollen worm pop free, drooling the last watery dregs along her thigh.

I had come, but going away.

11

G͟OD'S NOSE, was this the glorious chase to which the trumpets of my manhood called me? At every hedge my horse stumbled over some new stump or stone. I wet the saddle and went flying over the horn. I began to wish there was some other study to which I might less painfully apply myself.

One afternoon whilst avoiding regular employment and fretting over my secret disability, I found myself strolling down the Arenal, amongst piles of timber, tobacco, and raw bullion, through hordes of sailors, pícaros, and trulls, most drunk, for the Indies fleet was in. A brightly colored broadside drew me away from the river and up an alley, and there, to my great delight, I discovered a theater.

It seems that the Third Philip, quite a different cut of goods than the Second, had recently lifted his father's ban on theatrical performances. All over the peninsula there had been a sudden reduction in the numbers of pedlars, ring-piggers, and pickpockets, and the players and jugglers had reemerged in their draggled silks and feathers, like a horde of tawdry phoenixes risen from the ashes of the Second Philip's decree. The pious could now lament the presence of several theaters in Sevilla, and one of them was here on the Calle del Pollo Punzando and bore the same name.

The play of the afternoon was a wearisome tragedy concerning the struggles of some virgin saint to avoid the attentions of a venal and elderly king, but I was well diverted by the spectacular groaning and flailing of the players, particularly the stout individual who played the tyrant, rolling his strange yellow eyes and reciting in a voice so rich and effusive that one suspected that one was privy to some species of oral evacuation; while at the same time he tirelessly embroidered his actions with inventive business, as when, each time that he spoke the name of his intended, he clapped one hand to his heart and the other to his cod, and touched the end of his considerable nose with the tip of his long red tongue.

In addition, there were the interludes, including a clown pantomime in the Italian manner, and the presentation of three large and downcast turkey fowl which, at a command from their master, proceeded to dance a stately gavotte.

I was much struck by these novelties. But I admit that my attention was also drawn upward and backward. Like all the common corrales, the Theater of the Jittering Chicken was not a building, but a short length of street, closed off at one end by the stage and its draperies, at the other by the house which terminated the alley. The pit was the street itself, where some few sat, but most shuffled their feet and spat upon the cobbles. At the back of this makeshift court and facing the stage, there was a closed benchery, raised well above the pit on wooden stilts, and it was toward this beribboned box that I often found myself staring, for it was called the *cazuela*, or hen basket, and it was a-brim with women.

As I recall, the performance concluded with an amusing graveyard satire in which the stout actor impersonated a royal tax farmer attempting to extract blood from the corpse of a bankrupt peasant who had committed suicide by opening his veins with the sharpened edge of his last copper marivedí.

Soon enough it was done, but I lingered on, watching the hen basket empty in a flurry of giggles and flying ribbons. And when the candles had all been snuffed and the truncheoned ushers had herded the last blowze and yahoo from the pit, I clung at the entrance to the alley, studying a large paper broadside affixed to the wall and featuring the master thespian, posturing in the robes of a Roman senator, his mouth opened wide to issue a thunderclap, his name emblazoned in thick red letters five palms high: DON RIPIO DE REBOMBAR.

Now here was glory, to own the name on every lip and pasted to every wall, to spout fangled words and spew fulminated passion, to drown all din but one's own, and be the dazzle of every eye. Oh, to be deafened by the clamorous praise of the multitude and blinded by the dazzling light of all those attentive candles! To say nothing of playing the cock to all those hens in the basket.

And then my eager eye lit on a scrawled announcement affixed to the bottom of the broadside: the management of the Theater of the Jittering Chicken would be pleased to allow amateurs upon their boards, providing that the volunteer be deeply devoted to the theatrical arts, and owned his own face paints and costume.

The next day, following a performance of *Amadis of Gaul*, I introduced myself to the clown and was taken straightway into the presence of the director, Ripio de Rebombar. He was no giant after all, except for his very large head, but his eyes were even more fearful seen close-up, for that quality which lent them the lion's burning gaze could now be seen as a narrow ring of sulphurous tint around each black iris.

Still clad in the tin armor of Amadis, he lounged between two large barrels, his helmet upside down in his hand. As he studied me, he moved this makeshift flagon in a circle, and I saw that it was a-slosh with liquid of the same bilious color as his eyes.

"So you want to be an actor," he thundered, yet seemingly without effort, for his plump lips barely moved.

"I am without experience, but I am willing to try."

He nodded, drinking and drawing a tin sleeve across his mouth. "I see that you are gifted with modesty, a quality I find becoming." He chuckled. "In others." Lifting his helmet to his lips, he watched over its rim with his fuming yellow eyes. "Not a bad-looking piece of goods either, and your voice is tolerable."

"Thank you."

"And appreciative, not like some I could mention." He glared around at the gathered players. "Very well, you will do for stage dressing and stand-by, perhaps even to spout a couplet or two. Mind you, we usually charge for lessons in stagecraft, the state of the coinage being what it is and expenses rising daily. However, I am prepared to make an exception, provided you are punctual and never drink before the second-act curtain. Come tomorrow at six, and we'll start you in the pantomime."

"I will, and thank you."

He cocked a canny yellow eye. "As for any attendant motive which you might be entertaining, think well on this, that love and the theater have much in common. Hence the player's first commandment: Never mistake the play for the game, nor the hen basket for heaven."

And with that, he waved a hand in dismissal, drank again, and began to lay about him with his tin sword. "Ungird me, you scullions, I am not yet rich enough to sleep in my armor!"

Thus I became an apprentice upon the boards of the Jittering Chicken, learning to strut the buskin, toot the swazzle, and lust for the approval of the faceless multitude. In the beginning, I played dumb buckler to the clown's foil, the which consisted mainly in submitting my fundament to the poke of his canvas phallus and subsequently, with the tug of a hidden string, voiding a liter and a half of soured white wine into the pit. The first time this vulgar demonstration brought laughter from the audience, I suffered a moment of sanity, that is, I was fleetingly unsure as to just who was making whom do what.

But the glare of the candlelight was so near to Climax's blinding nimbus; the heat of all that attention so close to taking me out of the world. And when they applauded at the end of the interlude, my doubts vanished and my hopes soared, hitched to the winged wagon of Thespis, who surely would tow me aloft to fame, glory, and the hen basket.

Soon I wrangled brief appearances in sword-and-cape plays, religious autos, and romantic idyls, most often dressed as a page, a shepherd boy, or a faun, and responsible for such striking announcements as, "My liege, there is an ogre loose in the land," "Behold, there is a star in the East," and, "I am sent to bid you frolic beneath the mistletoe."

I had my reasons for preferring sword and cape to phallus and bladder, well-fitting hose to baggy. Surely one could not be too elegant if one hoped to catch the eye of one of the choicer ladies. I had lately taken to books for help in my search, eagerly studying the adventures of such colorful pícaros as Lazarillo, Guzman de Alfarache, and Marcos de Obregon. Here I was assured that only rich and restless women attended the theater, and of these some were maidens on the lookout for husbands, some elderly widows, but many were neglected wives: the pretty property of rich and thin-blooded old men who failed to warm their beds adequately, leaving them dissatisfied and receptive to the attentions of any young jack bold enough to find his way to them. These poor creatures were often to be seen in the balconies of the theaters and in their coaches, stuffing rich cakes between their famished lips, but it was really the love of a virile youth they hungered for. How foolish their husbands were to think they might buy off natural need with fancy pastries and clammy gold. Or so my books assured me.

Also, I was still deep harbor to the dream of perfect beauty. Somewhere the ideal woman waited for me. Hadn't Don Diego said as much? It followed, then, that I did myself wrong to be content with less than a perfect prize. I would have been hard pressed to describe this creature, but convention had established certain standards for me: eyes not too narrow, brow not too low, neck not too short, chin not too sharp, etcetera not too etcetera. In my dreams this fabulous homogenine had everlasting life as the ephemeral focus of my nightly conjurations, now drifting tantalizingly away, now glowing closer, as I taught my body the games of my yearning mind. In fact, with my usual inclination to excess, I soon fixed upon one particular occupant of the hen basket, convincing myself that she was the ideal creature, when, in fact, all that I could see of her beyond gold threads and expensive lace was her right eye.

She rarely missed a performance and always sat in the same shadowed corner of the basket. Others were inclined to shift about, fluffing their feathers and fluttering their fans in competition with the players on the stage. Clearly these were the virgins, hoping to catch the eye of some promising swain in the boxes at the side of the street, but well guarded by their duenas. There were others as sedate as she, but most were wrinkled and all wore black: the weedy widows and old wives.

What was more, of all the hens in that basket, she was always the most completely *tapado*, that is, veiled. She not only covered her head and the lower part of her face with lace, but went *tapado de medio ojo* as well, drawing her veil up across the whole left side of her face, so that only her right eye showed.

This, it seemed to my fevered reason, was a clear indication that she sought to hide her need. And yet she came into public three and four times a week. Poor thing, nagged by yearning, she clung to the wrappings of chastity, even as her flesh itched.

It was even possible that she already strayed from the conjugal fold. It was not yet against the king's will to go about so completely shrouded, but a growing proportion of polite society deemed the custom suspect, since certain of the bolder ladies had been known to employ the veil as convenient disguise whilst shuttling to and fro twixt home and lover; and what was more, their counterparts of the streets had taken to brazenly posing as ladies themselves and offending the sensibilities of passers-by by soliciting from behind the veil. The which only made her all that more inviting to my imagination, for what could be more enticing than a decent but neglected wife partly veiled, than a possibly indecent neglected wife wrapped up to the tear ducts?

Not one of my fellow players knew her name or anything else beyond the obvious fact that she was not poor. Twice I sent a note to her, but received no answer. Once I stationed myself in a doorway after the performance and watched her descend to her coach from the hen basket, attended by a large black slave dressed à la Turque and wielding an ebony staff with a feathered fan at one end and a velvet claw at the other. With this appliance he lifted her skirts clear of puddles and guided her petticoats over snags, turning his head away as she descended the ladder. I never got more than a glimpse of one silken heel nor saw more of her face than that one eye, but how I longed to be that slave, that staff, that claw, that ladder, even one of those puddles. For beneath the cloak and veils and high-necked bodice there had to be the elaborately worked undergarments, the cork-heeled clogs that made a lady lofty, the fabled whalebone corset, and beneath the petticoats, the struts and tapes of the guardinfante, belling out her skirts and surely providing accommodation for such an ambitious invader as myself.

And yet I delayed making any forceful move to close with her. For one thing, I hesitated to risk my dream of perfect beauty. Also, in teaching my body the games of my mind, I had learned the habit of yearning only when and as I saw fit, and satisfying myself the same.

I had long since decided that I was not nightly gouting bits of my brain onto my mother's sheets. In fact, as I had once taken the doll Pedrito into my confidence, I had recently found a friendly conversant in my gristle, and had invented a method of manipulating the organ so as to cause its mouth to open and close in a manner which could be synchronized with projected speech. Thus:

MYSELF: Good morning, Corporal. At ease.

ITSELF: I am at ease, sir.

MYSELF: Not entirely, old fellow, by the look of you. Full of vim and vinegar, are you?

ITSELF: Full enough of the last, sir. We had wine last evening, and have been the whole night abed.

MYSELF: Yes of course, and a bit stiff and swollen from sleep, I daresay. We'll see to that in a moment, but first let's have a look at you. All parts in place and looking in good color. No wounds from last night's artillery practice?

ITSELF: Well, I am a bit raw here on the shoulder.

MYSELF: Steady now, I thought so, only a light abrasion. Toughen you up.

ITSELF: Yes, sir. Thank you, sir.

MYSELF: Oh, we had a hearty good time, didn't we, Corporal? I saw you there, tall and ready in the thick of the fight.

ITSELF: Thank you, sir. I do my best.

MYSELF: And the enemy deployed before us, pale and trembling in her corsets. A lovely sight.

ITSELF: If you say so, sir.

MYSELF: Our steadfast line, your burnished blade, my shrewd and subtle tactics.

ITSELF: Very clever you are, sir, I'm sure, although I must admit I am sometimes confused.

MYSELF: Never mind, Corporal, yours is not to reason why. Strategy is an exercise of the intellect and imagination. Press forward here, fall back there. Eager eyes follow our feint, we close the jaws of the trap, and up go the skirts! Then the flash of your blade, the moans of their wounded, and I call for the final charge. *Santiago y arriba Juan!* The gaping thighs and admiring eyes of the enemy, the last dazzling cannonade. Victory! Oh, is it not glorious, Corporal?

ITSELF: I suppose so, sir. But it isn't as though it was a real engagement.

MYSELF: Ah, but how is a victorious army forged but through trial and practice?

ITSELF: Perhaps you are right.

MYSELF: And you are right to leave tactics and poetry to the officers. Yours is the more prosaic calling, to be sure. And yet, without you there could be no victory. I would like you to know that I am recommending you for the Loyal Order of the Stout Stave, which brings with it promotion to sergeant and will no doubt eventually lead you to a private audience with the queen, or at the very least a famous actress.

ITSELF: I'm grateful, sir. But I do not care to be a sergeant. In fact, I wish we might eschew military games and give me a proper name.

MYSELF: Then how would you have me call you?

ITSELF: Less often, if that could be arranged.

MYSELF: Come now, I did not hear that. You are my slave, so Esclavo shall be your name. Now stop skulking in that codflap like a worm. Join me in recalling our prize, that poor neglected wife of the hen basket: the rustle of her petticoats as she descends the ladder, the silken shimmer of that pretty heel. I tell you, I am on fire with the memory!

ITSELF: The fire must be on the roof, then, for it is cold enough down here.

MYSELF: Then I will chaff you warm again. Come forth, I say. Must I whip you?

ITSELF: You will anyway, but start slowly, master, for I am still half asleep.

MYSELF: I know, I understand. You would prefer the real thing. And it shall be yours soon, I promise you. But for now, imagine that corset, its ribbons, its delicate bonery; the provocative lift of those cork heels . . .

So it might well have come to nothing, had she not suddenly taken to acknowledging my posturings in a most provocative manner.

It first happened during a performance of a comedy by old Cervantes. Doubtless my speech of the moment was something like, "Command me, my queen, I am your footstool," the which I delivered with an appealing roll of my eye in the direction of the hen basket. Whereupon and immediately, I was struck in the center of the forehead by some small projectile which was hard enough and fired with enough force to wrench an involuntary yelp from me, much to the amusement of the pit. It was later brought to me by the clown and proved to be a small ball of aromatic bucaro, a kind of potter's clay imported from the Indies and chewed by certain ladies for purposes of keeping their nerves calm and their mouths occupied until such time as discretion and convenience might allow them more direct release for their cloistered energies. The habit was not as approved of as confession, embroidery, and other conventional cathartics, since the stuff was said to bestow an undue feeling of well-being upon the user, and was therefore chewed by only the more reckless, since others could tell by the movements of the cheeks above the veil whether or not the lady was an addict.

A sidelong perusal of the basket's occupants during the next night's performance confirmed that none of them was chewing and therefore likely to be the culprit, save only the one. My suspicions were confirmed at the end of the performance, as I was joining the others for the final bow, contriving to keep one eye cocked upward on the hen basket and thereby able to see a slender white hand reach in under a veil, and even to note the excruciatingly suggestive pucker of ruby-red lips as the chewing wax was removed and wadded into a ball. And then the projectile came whistling, catching me smartly above the eye with which I ogled. Again I failed to suppress a wince and a yelp, and again the audience responded with delight, more boisterous this time, for they perceived in the exchange the makings of a diversion not normally included in the price of admission. They roared with glee and threw trash.

As for me, I was thrilled as I fled the stage, but in a somewhat contradictory way, with mixed delight and loathing, much as the Moorish camel drover is moved by success in locating a prize camel in the bush through certain suggestive sounds and gestures which provoke the concealed beast to conspute great gobs of phlegm upon its suitor.

Though love and hate spring from different seeds, they thrive on the same manure, as they say in Pongalo en Supipa. For six nights running I thrilled and smarted beneath her masticated grapeshot. On the seventh, a Friday, I found the director in good spirits, a rare attitude for those tense hours before the second-act curtain and his first dose of absinthe. His sulphurous eyes started agreeably from their sockets, the grog-blossom of his nose shone like a rose.

"Congratulations, young fellow, your apprenticeship is at an end. You have learned your catechism well: Once on, do not leave the stage until you have done your part. Never give them all you've got. Always leave them asking for more. When in doubt, shout!"

He put a finger below one mustard-ringed eye. "But it is something more that has impressed me. It is the way you have comprehended the last commandment: Never mind which cheek you turn, just so long as the stile keeps turning and the pit stays full. Why, any common apprentice might have lost his temper after the second or third barrage of bucaro, but your performance under fire, at once poignantly pathetic and eloquently ludicrous, equals the highest of tragio-comic attainment, and what is more, and certainly of equal value in this difficult world, it brings them in!"

Bending to a rent in the curtain, he looked through at the audience. "Attendance has improved ever since the lady first spat upon you, increasing the more rapidly as it became public gossip that you seemed prepared, even eager to take all the abuse she could dole out. Why, they are even taking bets in the bodegas as to how long you will manage to hold fast. And tonight, I doubt if we could cram one more dandy into the boxes, one more bumpkin into the pit. Why, if it goes on like this, you will be famous. And I will be rich enough to drink before the second-act curtain!"

He drew me over to the wall and a newly printed broadside nailed there. "You may now consider yourself a journeyman player, and any day now we will begin to pay you for your services. Until then, however, and in lieu of cash . . ."

The poster featured my name in letters nearly as large as his, although still brown to his crimson, and featured a representation of myself as the clown's foil, chin high and paper sword in hand, standing firm against a hail of chewing wax, whilst voiding in my boots.

Ah, fame, thy kiss be clapt.

And, as if my furia needed further stoking, as I was donning my costume beside the paint box, I happened to notice for the first time that a ragged assistant crouched beneath the little stage of the waltzing turkeys, and that he pumped a bellows, that blew some coals, that made of their stage the red-hot skillet by dint of which they were inspired to do their famous dance.

The play of the evening was an eminently forgettable allegory by Gil Vincente about the Greek aeronaughts, Daedalus and son. Old Ripio was to play the father, and I was expected to enjoy my first leading role as his son, Icarus, an assignment which required the wearing of a heavy leather girdle beneath my chiton and a pair of wings made of wire, wax, and goosefeathers.

As I stepped out onto the boards, there arose that same buzz of hungry expectancy with which the arena greets the bull. And yet they held back through the whole first act, their glances drawn, like mine, to the hen basket, where the veiled maja sat silent and serene, as the king sits in the royal box, biding his time before calling for the kill.

The second act passed away in equally tense but unmolested dullness, but this time as I left the stage I deliberately measured the distance from the outermost board of the stage to the railing of the benchery, and thence to the corner of the hen basket. For I knew, just as the bull must know after the preliminary capework and light barbing, that one way or the other, my time had come.

"I've never known them to be so quiet," marveled the director at his kegs. Drawing a flagon for himself, he handed one to me. "It is time we received due respect. Drink, my friend. Tonight the theater enters a new era of dignity and dedication. Why, I may even give up absinthe and take elocution lessons."

I took a second portion when he had turned away, and choked down a third as he headed back onto the boards, so that when I once again faced the arena, I had spirits in me to more than double the fever and was as full of furia as ever was the mighty Cid before the walls of Mensador.

It happened midway through the third act, shortly after the lanterns had been lit behind the false sun that hung above the thatched roof of the hen basket. I had my wings on and was attached by my leather truss to a wire than ran over a set of pulleys affixed to the highest balcony and terminating in the hands of two young boys who poised on the balcony at the far side of the house, ready to fling themselves off and thus provide the counterforce required to get me aloft and send me sailing up over the pit toward the paper sun.

"Behold, my well-waxed son, the witching sun; my Grail, your destiny!" thundered Ripio, or something to that effect, thrashing in his toga and pointing upward toward the glowing disc above the hen basket.

"I go, father, further and better feathered than I have ever flown before," I declared. "And furthermore—"

"Every gander needs a goose," rang out a voice, fresh as a new bell, clear and terrible; and it was hers, for I saw the veils stir and the white hand lifted. "Or is this only a giddy goose at which we gander; let us see if it flees or flies!"

And with that, the first pellet came flying to strike me square on the cod. This time I did not yelp; I swore; but it was signal enough to the others, and all heads turned toward me, the first patter of pellets became a stinging shower, then a veritable barrage of chewing wax and chick-peas, beads and pebbles, a variety of rotten fruits, and a good deal of just plain spittle.

I saw her veils shake and her shoulders clench with laughter. I looked to the enflamed faces of the pit and saw all those gaping mouths and mocking grins.

"Out, out!" bellowed the director, expertly ducking the flying cabbages and heading for sanctuary.

"Up! Up!" I howled, for once more plangently than he. "Up, and away!" and, although it was not the accustomed cue, it was close enough and rose forcibly enough above the uproar to reach the ears of the two boys, who forthwith hurled themselves headlong from their balcony, causing our pulleys to sing and myself to part company from the stage, slowly at first, my wings flapping sluggishly, then picking up speed, sailing out over the swarming pit to alight on the corner of the benchery, trip along the railing, then vault upward to the corner of the hen basket, there to crash over the railing in a flurry of feathers, sending the hens screeching in all directions.

Only my one-eyed maja held to her seat, suddenly small despite her veils and load of gold, but upright and unflinching.

Jerking free of my wire, I faced her, but the only sign was a warning rattle from the fan in her lap. I hesitated, remembering the player's first commandment: *Never mistake the play for the game, nor the hen basket for heaven,* and suddenly my knees trembled and my duende seemed about to abandon me. Then I remembered: *Once on, do not leave the stage until you have done your part.*

My attempt at a courtly bow was made somewhat clumsy by my drooping wings. "Señorita, I have long looked forward to this meeting, as you have surely surmised, and I am honored—"

"You are a flying ass and a bad actor," came the crisp rejoinder, and her single eye glared. "Get out of my presence."

There were shouts from below and feet crashing up the stairs. I decided to go straight to the heart of the matter. "Mademoiselle, it is my guess that you have an elderly husband. Am I right?"

Was the defiant eye abruptly stricken? She gave the faintest of nods.

"I thought so. Poor creature, you married, and now you are mummified. But you must not despair; it is never too late for love. Do not let the frosts of winter kill the flameflower in the bud. That is the only true sin, to knot the veins with wrong-minded chastity, to strangle natural and God-meant need. Hesitation is as deadly as the cold hands of an old man, denial sours the blood as swiftly as does the failing flesh of an unwanted husband. O my God, revive yourself, poor cloistered creature, and let me help you. . . ."

It came to me, even through the turmoil rapidly closing in around us, that she was laughing. It began as a choking, then was a giggling, then a strangling cough become a guffaw, blowing her veils out before her face.

"My husband," she gasped, "is in his late years, but he is far from inactive. In fact, he is so damned ardent, that when I was with the nuns to have my babies, I asked to stay a few extra days so as to avoid his embraces, and that is why I come so frequently to the theater, while he goes off to the brothel. Even then, he wants me at crack of dawn, and then after breakfast, and then just before he leaves for the ministry, and then when he comes home for lunch, and then after siesta, and then before dinner, and then . . ."

I could not bear it. I lurched forward and snatched the veils from her face. She was perfect, dark, as my mother was dark, eyes not too narrow, brow not too low, etcetera not too etcetera.

She regarded me with her great round eyes, and a chuckle rattled the swan-white throat. "You are mildly amusing. But you had better go. The aguaciles will be here in a moment, and my husband has an unforgiving nature in addition to being a nympholeptic."

It was true, they were banging on the door with their truncheons, and one was just clambering over the far rail, sword in hand. And yet for one long moment more I could not move. Her beauty blinded me, her smile mocked, and my furia underwent a startling change of direction; had I had a sword with me, I surely would have drawn it, just as my grandfather had drawn his on the steps of the Burgos cathedral, and run her through then and there.

But this horror was a fleeting thing, a reversal for the future and the makings of a madness still young and all unwitting. The constable's blade went through my sleeve, bringing me back to the moment, and I kicked free and jumped to the railing and hauled myself up, then plunged through the false sun, struggled to my feet in a tangle of lanterns, and set off full tilt across the rooftops, my wings on fire.

12

I⊤ SEEMS that a thatch fire had consumed certain buildings on the Calle del Pollo Picando, and the magistrate of Sevilla had ordered his police to find and punish the culprit, the usual punishment for arson requiring that the criminal be broken on the wheel.

The Spinola brothers were once again getting up an army to secure Flanders for Philip, and I experienced a sudden surge of patriotism. Inciting myself with visions of rapine and loot, I took myself to the open pasture outside the city where the recruiters were selecting from an assortment of lacklinens, cumberworlds, and civil fugitives. My first urge to turn about came at the sight of the sagging tents and tiny fires, the piles of cannonshot and mule dung, the stink of cabbage soup and the shrieks of enraged corporals. But I was already in the line of shuffling volunteers, all of them more gaunt and ragged than me, so that as my turn came and I stepped up to the table, the broken-faced individual there surveyed me with unconcealed disdain.

"Well well, look what we have here, a young gentleman. And has your father cut you from his will or your veiled lady spurned you, or do you come to us warped by ideas of some unnatural bedrite you intend to practice upon your inferiors?"

"I am here to do my duty to God, king, and country," I declared without much conviction. "And with no other profit in mind but honor."

"If that is true, you will be history's first," muttered the sergeant, but he had me write my name on a piece of paper and handed it to the next table. "Pass on, then, and if you are sound in mind and body, we will have you."

The tables were set in a row at the edge of the muddy parade ground, and as I moved to the next, a squad of new soldiers marched into the quagmire just beyond. How assured and secure they seemed, all their eyes to the front, all their limbs moving briskly in unison.

"Do you believe in the king as divinely appointed, Mary as immaculately conceived, and this war as a beneficent crusade for the restoration of the True Faith?" inquired my next questioner, a chaplain by the purple ophreys around his neck, a Dominican by the pierce of his eye.

"Yes," I said, a certain absence lending grace to the lie, for I was watching the soldiers over his shoulder. How colorful they were in their ill-fitting tunics, their sleeves slashed with yellow and black, their helmets burnished, as they wheeled to their corporal's shouted commands and stood all in a row like painted ninepins.

"Have you ever coughed blood, voided tar, or had the pox?" inquired the doctor, holding a mirror before my mouth and pressing an ear to my chest.

"No," I said, my gaze aimed over his shoulder, for the corporal had barked again, and now all the soldiers crouched as one, their pikes thrust out before them.

"Show me your yard," said the doctor. "Come come, a clapt soldier cannot march."

While he looked, I watched the corporal shout out numbers, and with each one, a soldier went charging out across the field, with another close behind, then another; all in the strictest order, yet each with his face twisted in a grimace and his mouth wide open to emit a bellow of thrilled and bloodthirsty intent. How satisfying thus to scream and plunge by the numbers, licensed to murder by another's command.

"Have you ever pissed your bed, lain with a sheep, or coveted the parts of other than woman?" inquired my next questioner.

I shook my head, still craning, for I could not see the target of the soldiers' charge. Then I did: a modern version of the tilting post, that same quintain at which plumed bluebloods had tested their lances in the mock tournaments of my childhood, except that here the two wooden effigies were of foot soldiers, one at each end of a long pole that swiveled on a post set into the ground. Each dummy faced in an opposite direction, each with sharpened pike extended. A solid blow struck at one brought the other around to face the next attacker.

"Which is your left foot?" inquired my questioner.

I pointed vaguely downward, struck by a hideous scream. The first soldier had laid such a fierce blow upon his stuffed adversary that the second effigy had swung past too swiftly, allowing the first to come around and strike back to back against the second soldier, knocking him down, whereupon the first soldier had whirled and struck this wooden offender in the middle of the back, then bent to the aid of his fallen companion, only to take the pike of the second dummy straight up his hinderlings.

And the more viciously he struck out at the one, the deeper the other penetrated, and the more desperately he raged.

"Which is your right foot?"

Again I pointed numbly downward, made absent by the confusions of war. I moved on to my last questioner, a young officer with waxed mustaches and a plumed helmet. Over his shoulder I could see the corporal cursing and belaboring the two tangled soldiers with his shortsword, while a third soldier, still in a murderous ecstasy and denied his turn at the dummies, ran around in a circle, chasing himself with his own pike.

"It says here that you claim to have two left feet," observed the officer with a frown.

"Yes, indeed," I said, mustering up a mincing little snigger. How it turned my stomach to do it, yet how easily it came! "I have always had trouble telling left from right. In fact, my life is all one pretty turmoil of ambidextrous confusions," and by way of demonstration, I made as if to plant a kiss on his cheek.

As I hurried away, pursued by the lieutenant's curses, they were just carrying the wounded from the field, and as I passed, the corporal bent solicitously over one broken and bleeding stalwart, looking for a place on the battered chest to pin a bit of hero's braid.

As it turned out, the police had been unable to trace the arsonist of the Calle Pollo Picando, reported to be a young actor of unknown name and address.

"Whoever he was," Don Diego said after he had announced that my period of grace had passed and my allowance been suspended, "he is the sort of scurvy scoundrel you have been associating with. But that is now at an end. Your mother and I have decided to remove you from bad influence. You cannot go on avoiding decent employment forever. If you cannot give your life some semblance of propriety and purpose, then I will. You will give up this foolish play-acting. I have found you a position as clerk to the quartermaster-general of militia."

"Yes, and it is high time you met some girls of the proper age and class," my mother added. "After your work, you will join us for paseo."

That is how I came to sort cannonballs all day and march in circles every other evening. Out of dull disheartenment and the lack of any better prospect whatsoever, and because the purse and roof most convenient to me belonged to Don Diego.

This paseo business was a most rarefied torment. Each evening after dinner, in the plazas of the city's more polite neighborhoods, indeed, in such plazas over most of Spain, the well-to-do and the ambitious emerged in their best clothes and walked up and down for hours, peering at one another. Some of the men did business, an occasional mendicant tootled the flute or played the fool for the children. But mostly, the gentry strolled in family groups, up the long side of the plaza to the church, there to cross themselves, all in a chorus, like so many monkeys picking fleas, then wheeling solemnly and starting back down the other side, passing other families coming up, finally reaching the bottom, only to turn solemnly about and start back up, the men glaring at business competitors, the women eying one another's jewelery, the old people estimating the hours of life left to their contemporaries, and all smiling, nodding, and greeting one another in the very best Castellano.

Now I joined in this dismal pageant at least thrice weekly, sometimes more, linked to my mother, with Don Diego on the other side. (Paco was seldom with us, having been put out to the Dominicans, who did nothing to remedy his impediment, but instead taught him what he

145

might and might not stutter.) Up and down and around and around we went, always in the same direction over the same course at the same deadly pace, locked to the groaning wheel of society.

"Smile, here comes Palita Torres," my mother would mutter behind her veil, digging an elbow into my ribs. And I would manage a thin wince as Palita drifted past on her mother's arm, falling swiftly astern, too plain of sail and narrow in the beam to draw my fire, even had I been free to indulge the piratanical promptings of my loins, which I was not.

Careful calculation had long ago informed me that flirting on the hoof was a most uneconomical way to go about getting close to a girl. I had watched other young men suffer the tedious ritual, the smiling and nodding going on for weeks, even months; then an equal period of spoken greetings, followed by another long period of conversations held in the center of the plaza under the watchful eyes of all; then first touch, and she takes his arm, and now they are formally courting, promenading together for weeks, months, years.

Even if I were to go after so plain a prize as Palita, it would cost me two hundred trips around the plaza to engage her in private conversation, an additional eight hundred to win her hand on my arm, another two thousand to get her into the alley behind the church or to climb her balcony, at least a thousand more to coax a tit into the open air, and certainly no less than another four thousand to get between her legs. In all, no less than fifteen months and eight thousand circumambulations of that dreary arena, watching and watched by those terrible faces, and obliged to pause each and every time before the steps of the church and make as if to pick one flea from each: right shoulder, left shoulder, forehead, breast. If I was an ape, I would be damned before I would be that species.

In the meantime, I could see no recourse but to my nightly conversation with Esclavo.

ITSELF: Oh no, not again.
MYSELF: Come forth, I say. Hide your head, will you. Then I will take you by the neck—
ITSELF: Ouch. All right, what is it you want, as if I didn't know.
MYSELF: To see you stand proud and know we aren't going soft. To feel

146

the blood drain from my aching brain and fatten you with purpose. To feel the sweet wrench of your spouting and know that I am myself.

ITSELF: Yourself?

MYSELF: All right, ourselves. But come, you are my slave and I am your master.

ITSELF: So you insist, but are you sure this is nature's way, beating me silly night after night? My God, I have bile in my veins, my head is pounding, and all I can cough up is watery spittle.

MYSELF: Nonsense, I am sure we can manage one more.

ITSELF: But why? At it night and day, and neglecting to change your drawers as well. One of these days I will break out in blisters. Sometimes I think your real aim is to destroy me.

MYSELF: Don't say that, it is not true. I only want us to learn, to improve. I admit I do not understand it all yet. But surely you dream of the perfect coony, as I dream of the perfect creature, the perfect union.

ITSELF: I've told you, they are all the same to me.

MYSELF: Oaf, you are without poetry. Come now, just once more. And I promise you, one day soon we will find you the real thing, and then we will be able to enjoy her just as often and heartily as we now enjoy one another. Five, seven, ten times a day. I can hardly wait!

ITSELF: I can. But you never listen to me.

And then one evening, after I had been paseando for a month or more, I set eyes on Dorita Nieves Gracias de Nada, and dull propriety suddenly had new promise. She came out of that gray circus between two others in black: round face, pale hair, pink cheeks: all china blue stare and watercolor blushes: the perfect peach.

My mother was immediately aware of my interest, no doubt alerted by the fact that I had suddenly stepped up the pace, hurrying to make the circle and study this prize again. No doubt about it, here was a marvel of another and safer sort. For I also honored a different convention: voice not too loud, experience not too broad, imagination not too vivid, etcetera not too etcetera. If I could not have dark and worldly beauty, I would prefer this winsome innocent: pristine and discreet, pale and delicate, tidy and tight.

"Her family has only just moved here from the Levant," my mother said into my ear as we passed on for the third time. "I suppose she may have Gallic failings, but I am told the father is an importer of velvets, and it is said they have bought a nice enough house. Isn't she a pretty little thing, and well scrubbed, I notice. I'll have Don Diego make inquiries."

But I could not wait out the slow grinding of the cogs of protocol. How could I doubt the invitation as we drifted lingeringly past one another for the next four evenings in a row, the unblinking blue of her eyes transfixing me, her pink and protean lip curling a tremulous smile? What did that glance say but: Now, come hither, now!

I decided to by-pass the first and most dreary stage of courtship, thus avoiding two thousand circumambulations of the plaza and a like number of genuflections. Following her family's coach home one evening, I located their house, narrow but well made, on the Calle Coronado. The next evening I watched for my chance, and when my mother was looking elsewhere, I gave the peach a bold wink, and a twitch of her fan assured me that she had caught my plea and invited me in return. Response!

At midnight, I stood before her house with a borrowed gittern, my fingers already shredded, for I had been practicing at the unfamiliar art for hours. It was moonless midnight on the street, and no bastonero's lantern visible in either direction, only the faintest glimmer of candlelight through the shutters of the balcony above. Putting a foot on the curb, I plucked at random, threw back my head, and prepared to bray. I heard the shutter creak and a watery swish and ducked my head in time to take the turds on my hat, but not in time to escape the full and pungent drench of the criticism.

Once again my duende took me by the nape and rattled me, shaking hot tears from my eyes. Perhaps it was that I had not even been given a chance to sing before cuckstool judgment had been passed. Perhaps it was all those weeks of tedious paseando. My furia rose as gall in my throat, and I kicked out at the entrada doors, intending only to vent my rage and flee, vowed never again to condescend to propriety's mince-me-daintie ways.

But, lo, one door croaked ponderously open, and I took a quick glance up and down the street and darted in. Moonless night was nothing to the blackness inside. There were the smells of horse sweat and geraniums, but the coach and horses had been taken to the stables. My toe nudged a flowerpot, my hand found an ironwork post. It seemed I stood under one of the balconies that ran around the central courtyard. Somewhere above in the impenetrable darkness was her bedroom. But also her parents, countless servants, a bloodthirsty doorkeeper. Sweating, I turned to go. But a sudden vision pulled me up short: she sprawled in my fancy, white breast billowing, pink lips swollen and needy. Something rubbed against my boot, going away, then coming back. I plucked it up, located the well at the center of the patio, stepped four paces back, and tossed my captive underhand.

Such an uproar. Then: two, four, six, eight doors burst open, and the entire household appeared all around the balconies above, and in the light of their candles a very damp cat could be seen climbing pertly up the well rope, spitting like a consumptive.

But I directed my attention elsewhere, and soon I found her, wide-eyed at the top of the house, sweet as sherbet behind her candle and shimmering like an angel. "Oh, poor pussums!" she cried. And in my protecting shadow I trembled and softly purred.

When all was quiet again, I took boots in hand and mounted the stairs, thanking God they were new. Outside her door I paused and heard nothing. To my surprise it was not latched; I pushed in, and there she was, propped against her pillows, wide-eyed and expectant.

"Get out." She drew the blanket up to her neck.

"You are not surprised to see me."

"Cats do not fall down wells. But do not deceive yourself, I am a lady."

"Ladies do not leave their doors unlatched."

"I wanted to see what kind of fool you are."

"A fool for love, a victim of your eyes."

"You read it in a book."

"I read it in your face last Wednesday eve, and the next, and the next. You invited me here."

"Perhaps. But you are too sudden. First you must talk to my father and take me on paseo and buy me sweets. . . ."

How frail and delicate her voice, yet also insufferably arch. I remembered the surgeon's daughter, and a spurt of furia came up my gullet. "But you ogled me!" I stepped to the side of her bed. "Let me see you!"

She cringed, clutching the blanket to her, her eyes widened in a winsome semblance of terror. Yet she did not cry out. Why not? Surely, because she wanted me to give rein to the fire she fanned. My quickening heart gave me no time for any other explanation. I sat down on the edge of her couch. The bed ropes rattled with her trembling. I reached out to tug the blanket from her breast.

"No, don't!"

But I did, then gawked. She appeared to be encased in a sack of heavy canvas, drawn snug up around her neck, allowing only her arms outside. "My God, what is it?"

Her cheeks went a darker pink and she looked away. "It is called the chemise cagoule, and my parents require that I wear it to bed."

"You poor cloistered thing," I murmured, but even as I was offering sympathy, the sight of such tight packaging set my blood to rushing in quite another vein. With a will of its own, my hand snatched the blanket entirely away.

"Please, you must go now!" she cried, but it was too late. My eyes had discovered the suede vent, located in an appropriate place and no doubt meant for her convenience and not mine, but so strikingly suggestive that I could no longer contain myself. I fell upon her tooth and nail.

"Oh, please do not do that!" she whimpered, but not loudly, and even as I crawled atop her, a part of me wished that she would prompt me to flight with a hearty scream, but she did not; and so I continued at her in a fumbling fury, making her black and blue with my sucking kiss, muttering every fuddled blandishment that came to mind.

And gradually her protests became less adamant and her thrashing less resistant. "You mustn't," she said, pressing gobbling lips to mine. "Oh, don't," she whimpered, squirming against my groping hand.

"Oh, please do not."

"Oh, please."

"Oh!"

I had found the straps and buckles at the side of her chemise. "No!"

she cried with sudden and quite a frantic firmness. "I must wear it until I am married. You will have to make do this way."

And with that, she went briskly onto her back, reached down and opened wide the leather lips of her vent. It was a most boggling sight. There she lay, all trussed up and helpless, eyes clenched shut, head thrown back, leather hatch gaping. Like a corpse awaiting the surgeons, indeed. Ah, but my corpse.

In an instant, I was on her, then in, then off at a spastic gallop; and that tidal wave of desperation which had been so long a-building finally carried me, this flotsam clot of fused fevers, beyond myself. And this time, when sparks flew from my coals and Esclavo pumped pudding, I knew it. And as the tongs let go my eyeballs and I fell back, congratulations wafted up to my nostrils in the form of a nosegay of aromas which I had never known before, but recognized at once as the rich savory of venal achievement. How quick and neat; how easeful, how relieving at last. I did it, I moaned inside myself. I did it!

Ah, but was it done?

A short time later, as I lay awake in my bed in Don Diego's house, musing upon my accomplishment and flooded with tender gratitude to her who had allowed it, I became aware of renewed heat behind my eyes and a slowly hardening urgency in my loins; and suddenly there came upon me a revelation which four years of obsession had failed to anticipate. I had finally swived a girl without suffering retardismo and without threat of imminent death. It would seem that I had at long last won respite from myriad terror and nagging need. Yet now, scarcely an hour later, and as desperately as ever, nay, even more so, I wanted to swive her again!

Love, some jaded Roman has said, is but an alternation of the agrodulce, a one-sided view of the turning coin. Ah, but in the beginning, how sweet it is, all dulce and no agro. Before I knew it, I was spending half my waking hours next to her. Most nights I came to her street late, to find her household snugly abed, and that she had contrived to leave the entrada doors open. With my heart in my throat, I crept up to her chamber, and there we lay down to our business, she in her canvas sack, I in my suit of rutsweat. Again we confricated and I laved her with endearment, and she lay back and spread her vent, and I humped, headlong and perfuncturate; and again the swift and giddy passage from here to there, followed by the gratifying glaze of aftermath. Oh, to go so pleasantly out of this world and come so blithely back again. More, I wanted more!

When she could get away during the day, I took her on my horse into the countryside, the chemise folded and jouncing behind us; and we sought out the prettiest meadow and the merriest stream, there to dally for so long as the shrubbery should hide us and our hearts desire, exchanging delicate confidences and fornicating.

How delightful to lie with our heads together on the tender grass, or in the snug of the linen, exchanging histories and dispelling doubts, sharing old dreams and creating new. How delicious to fit our bodies together and do what is essentially the same. What a wonder to gaze upon that pert and peachy prettiness and imagine the slender body inside the canvas casing. How handy to have her there and to know that whenever I wished, I might reach out, and she would be mine. How strange and suspenseful to stroke a hand down the rough fabric to the inviting vent and slide a finger in, digging for the warm and ready oyster that lived in her considerable bush. How delirious to give way to sudden hurry and the bludgeoning of my blood, pushing blindly into her and crashing out of this world. How sweet to lie in pungent aftermath, savoring the last tumble, sniffing ahead to the next. How simple life had suddenly become, with time reduced to only two kinds: during and until.

For the first time, I was swiving regularly and at a rate approaching my need. And yet there was one nagging flaw to keep it from perfection: she steadfastly refused to allow me between her legs without the separation of the chemise cagoule. However, as we told each other our little histories, I did learn how she had come to be so tightly wrapped.

It seems she had been courted before by a young Catalan nobleman named Vittorio, about whom she would tell me no more, except that she had reluctantly allowed him onto her balcony and finally into her bed, where he had devirginated her, afterward telling her, "Not bad, but I prefer boys." What is more, this villain had then broadcast news of his conquest to all of Barcelona, with the result that her parents had been forced to take her away from scandal in hopes of salvaging her virtue. That is how they had come to Sevilla, where her father had ordered her to cloister herself in canvas, swearing that should she ever sleep without the chemise before marriage, he would put her straight-away into a nunnery.

"Nor do I protest," she murmured against my chest. "For if it is only symbolic protection, it is all I have to keep my pride against the depredations of such as Vittorio. Men! Runagate rabiators and faithless breakpromises! They are all beasts!"

A venerable complaint, and it was a knife in my heart, wrenching forth an equally venerable response: "Not I, Dorita, not I!"

"Oh, I pray not," she sighed. "In the name of the Virgin, I do."

And surely it was that evening that she suggested we begin strolling together on paseo, and I agreed.

When I was not with her or tallying pikes for the militia, I more and more found myself wandering down to the river and strolling the Arenal. Yet even as I mingled with the low life there, I found myself mooning back to her and the bland but assured welcome of her arms. One such afternoon, as I dawdled at the wharfside, watching red sleeves unloading caged popinjays from an Indies caravel, I felt a hand pluck at my sleeve and turned to find a two-legged macaw there: a most gaunt and tattered slattern, pointing a bony hand.

"Yes, I thought so, it is you!"

"I beg your pardon," I said. "I do not know you."

"But I know you. You are Lucero, the one who had poor Maxima and left her paggled."

Furia's opposite, cold dread, embraced me. Even as I recognized her as one of Maxima's fellow grog-floggers at the Green Rooster, I remembered that the gutsheath had not come forth after our collapse upon the rooftree, and I had a vivid vision of it wadded in the whale's moist interior and swarming with ready homunculi.

"Oh, no, not pregnant," I groaned.

But yes, she told me. A month or more after my disappearance from Osuna, poor Maxima had discovered that she was swollen from my recklessness. No, I needn't make the usual objection. It was true that Maxima was much in the company of men due to her calling, but she was not often given to their private entertainment, due to her chaste character and concern with personal hygiene, and despite all that cruel rumor might suggest. Certainly the poor dear was positive that she had seen nobody but myself to her room during that crucial week, and besides, her woman's intuition coupled with a certain disgusting discovery made shortly after my departure convinced her that I was the father.

"The father!"

Exactly so. Because of the failure of any known herb or cathartic to relieve her condition, coupled with an understandable fear of gypsies, cottage witches, and other baby-wrenchers, Maxima had refused help to the end and had had the child alive.

"Alive!"

That was correct, and the poor dear had even laid eyes upon the newborn and kissed it once before it was taken away to be bound over to the Carmelites.

The gaunt sibyl peered; a savoring smile pulled her lips one way, disgust another. "By my bum, I don't see what she saw in you. What she sees in any of them, for that matter."

Then her face turned to stone again, and she thrust out a ruddy claw. "All your kind are rich, or should be if they intend to carry on slighting the poor during the day and acting like goats at night. Pay me for my silence or hear me broadcast. I know where to find your father."

I put all my coins in her hand and numbly watched as she turned and shuffled away through the rowt; and turned and shuddered with nausea as her rusty voice drifted back for one last twist of the blade:

"No doubt like all men, you would prefer a son. Well, it was a boy."

How much more precious Dorita seemed that night, as I feverishly confided that there were certain cruel losses and unspeakable sins in my past, and she assured me that the only way to make up for wronging someone in the past was to do right by someone in the future.

How winsome and wise she seemed, musing in my arms that, "Life has its ups and arounds." How touching her confession that there had been times during her ill-fated love for Vittorio when she had wandered the fields, "during the more lurid phrases of the moon."

I too had been a waif dismayed by the waywardness of life; I too had

154

been an outcast yearning under the moon. We had both been guilty but could both be good again, one to the other. What mattered her scrambled homilies; the heart speaks its own language, and should it have doubts, the loins are ever ready to amend. Just as sure as my yard fitted her coony, so it seemed to me that we were alike at heart as two peas in a pod; more than merely lovers, more even than brother and sister. At long last I had found philadelphy: she was my soul's hermana.

Yes, I had been thinking upon it gingerly, but with increasing abandon. Oh, to never again suffer these doubts, that guilt. No more furtive brandling, no more nightmares of orphaned eyes, no more maddening veils and taunting majas. Oh, to end once and for all the time-consuming, often hurtful, and always uncertain pursuit of women, and then be free to turn my energies to making my mark on the world. There was a way to be good and get on to being great, and still continue to swive regularly.

Still I might never have said it, had I not felt compelled to nag her out of the chemise cagoule. It was a pall upon our love, I told her. It was the image of hateful repression and prudish fear. As it always divided us, so it stood between us and the perfection of our love.

"What I see of you is so good-looking that I must see the rest. As we touch so deeply, let us touch all over!"

"But if I give you that as well, then I will have given you everything, and you will no longer love me."

"Not so! I will only love you the more, for by your gift you will have proved that you love only me."

She finally agreed to try, but when we rode into the country, she took along the chemise, rolled and ready behind her. We went across the bridge to Triana and were scarce off the horse and into the bushes before it began suddenly to rain. She gladsomely prepared to flee homeward, but I could not let my chance pass.

"Dorita, you promised."

"Oh, very well, I will try."

We made our way to the nearest inn. It stood dark in the squeeze of a filthy alley, swine roaming its cobbled yard. Nor was the postern pretty: a lardish brute with the neck and shoulders of a headsman and much hair on the backs of his hands. He grinned as I asked for a room. "And will you be with us the night, m'lord?"

Dorita's face flushed beneath the insinuating gaze, and I stepped briskly forward to shield her. "Not if we can help it. Here is the money, give me the key."

His grin tightened a notch toward menace. "The last duke what was here run off with it. But don't worry, ain't been nobody but fine gentlemen like yourself up there in that pesthole in years."

Dorita seemed fevered as we mounted the crumbling stairs, her hands nervous, her gaze distracted. Poor thing, I thought, her timid nature was offended by the sordid surroundings. I led the way down the hall and into a room at the back. There were a splintered cot, mildewed plaster, trash in the corners.

Pulling the door shut, I turned solicitously. "I am sorry it is so unpretty," only to find that she had wandered to the window. Following her, I found myself looking over her shoulder and down upon the heavy shoulders of the postern. One sleeve was rolled to the shoulder, and the muscles of his back squirmed as he bent above the nether end of a large spotted sow, diligently performing that operation known amongst country folk as reaming the bacon, that is, relieving the beast of a plugged bowel.

Hastily I put a hand on Dorita's shoulder to draw her away from this repugnant sight. Yet she seemed prone to linger, doubtlessly putting off impending nudity. Gently I pried the rolled chemise from her grip and laid it on the floor beside the cot, then drew her down to sit beside me. She had never looked more delicate, enticing, and tight: pale hair, flushed cheeks, blue eyes wide and rapt upon the window.

She remained thus as I disrobed her, plucking away veil, cloak, and hood with trembling hands, then the shawl, then the blouse, then peeling down the beribboned undertunic. The breasts were small and soft, helpless as doves. Jittering with joy, I pressed her onto her back and tugged off her little boots, the skirts, the petticoats, the bloomers.

Finally she lay before me, my mild diet and tidy delight, exactly as I had imagined her, no less sweet and acquiescent, except that now not even cruel canvas separated me from a hearty banquet, to be taken at my leisure and to my taste.

And then, just as I was settling myself between her legs and preparing to fondly perfuncturate, the pig gave out an ecstatic shriek below the window, the shriek became a duet, and my compliant peach became something else again.

Gasping and howling, she sank her fingers into my hair. Groaning, she thrashed beneath me. Grunting and grinding her teeth, she cranked her narrow hips left, then right, then in a circle, twice nearly tossing me clear. I clung on in astonishment and dawning horror, remembering other sawing moans and gnashing thighs, another mad and mercurial gaze. On the instant, all my terrors came flocking: toilet, tomb, morning coach, clock, and clyster bag.

"Harder!" she cried.

"Dorita," I gasped.

"Come on!" she shouted.

"I love you," I cried.

"Use the spurs!" she urged.

"Dorita!" I howled, raising up on stiffened arms and screaming down the siren song of the swine. "Put it back on. And marry me!"

13

I HAD LONG cherished a fanciful picture of the wedding of my mother and Don Angel: the cathedral hung with garlands and echoing to the joyous songs of cherubim and seraphim, the bride and groom kneeling side by side before the great altar, the bishop all gold-encrusted and kindly, his voice a sure and true-cast clarion, proclaiming, "Pax Domini sit semper vobiscum! Peace be with you, and may God bless this union."

And afterward, the feast at my grandmama's house on the banks of the Guadalquivir: the steam and dazzle of the board, the bright mingle of the gentry, the bumpkins dancing the sardana, the groom proud and handsome in brown velvet; and the virgin-mother-bride, embowered prize of every Spaniard's deepest dream.

How sweet the picture, how full of promise. They had been young, good-looking, and in love. Surely they would have been happy, had not the septic lobster intervened.

Now, nineteen years later, my childhood fancy was brought to life, first in the Sevilla cathedral, later at the country house of Don Benino Gracias de Nada. Here were the garden, the feast, the dancing rustics. Here was I in a new starched ruff and velvet breeches, and there was Dorita in her ribboned chair beneath arches of flowers, a bouquet of thyme in her lap and all the dower loot and votive gain of her victory marshaled at her feet: silver candlesticks and pewter cooking pots, a chest white to the gunwales with linen, and on each and every rag, our initials entwined in a flowery Gordian knot.

What matter that in my new ruff I looked painfully like the Baptist served up on Salome's platter. Never mind that the bishop's droning voice had put me uncomfortably in mind of that famous prelate said to have administered the last rites to the drowning population of his flooded parish from atop the cathedral tower.

Never mind that after we had climbed into our carriage and been wished well by all and sundry, and I had touched the whip to the mules, I bent my glance backward and saw the mob make room for a hairy bumpkin who stumbled into view in castoff skirts, with a swatch of thistle in his fist and a veil of dingled cheesecloth before his face, to meet another stumbling clodpate who aped the groom in threadshot hose and crusty goosefeather. A third put a black cloak on backward to make a cassock, and solemnly received the reeling couple before the barrels, made over them a cross of sprinkled wine, pressed their hands together, and invited them to kiss. And they did, obscenely, whereupon the false groom proceeded to pursue his bride with a wine bag spouting soured goats' milk from between his legs, and shortly afterward, she chased him with a broom, shouting wifely invective, while all the gay and swillbowl company reeled and roared with glee, and the benches groaned with convulsions of fat women.

Cynics! No, I would not let their mockery or my fears injure sweet expectation. For with all my heart I wanted to believe what had long been bandied to me by advocates of the conjugal contract: that what God hath joined, God will neither sour nor put asunder; that there is an everlasting joy and an imperishable sanctity in the twain, that two make a perfection and share a faith denied to one. The onrushing road, the wheeling sky, Dorita's giddy radiance beside me, even the jumble of domestic baggage in the back of our hack: all were omens and talismen of promised bliss ahead. I took her hand in mine and squeezed until she cried out. We would have a happy life together, or I would know the reason why.

We went to Madrid, where I was to become third squire and privy lestrado to Don Marco Lucero, the duke himself. I had satisfied Don Diego that I had the makings of a bureaucrat by counting the militia's cannonballs no less than four hundred and forty-four times, once on my feet and henceforth on my back; and always faithfully declaring whenever the quartermaster-captain required it, that if there was anything the kingdom needed beyond the blessing of God, it was a few thousand more cannonballs.

My marriage had further convinced Don Diego that my errant nature had been properly brought to the domestic block. And so he had agreed with my mother that I should be got started in a career at court, and had even arranged a small allowance until such time as I might catch the eye of the king and get my thumb into the national calamity. I should keep in mind, of course, that should I offend my uncle or otherwise waste the advantage of nepotismo, I would be damaging Don Diego's own hopes for a high place at court, and could expect to lose his favor, this time forever.

We took a little house that floated on logs at the edge of the Manzanares. In one direction we could see the Alcazar and the city walls, in the other a grassy beach. The house was plain, in keeping with our income, but we were not dismayed, for sweet infatuation made of it a castle.

In fact, it had a gatekeeper, one of the dozens of swans which infested our part of the shore. How pretty they seemed, sailing serenely by as we stood arm in arm on our small porch, rosy with the lingering flush of conjugal elation. Indeed, a swan upon smooth water is a dream of tranquility and grace, but out of it it is something else again. One morning I stepped upon the plank that led to our house to the shore, to find myself confronted by one of these beasts, handsome enough in its upper markings, but distinguished by a crusty coagulation befouling its underfeathers. It was a cob, a macho.

At my second step upon the plank, it began to hiss like an uncorked alembic. At my third, it cracked its sinuous neck like a whip and drove its beak at my coddlings. Leaping back just in time and overcome by furia, I went for my sword. But Dorita held me back, subscribing to that superstition which holds that to kill a swan is to ensure your death by drowning. In the end, we were left with no choice but bribery. It shared our breakfast, for how else could I win a way across the moat, except to cast bread upon the waters? It shared our dinner, for how else could Dorita have me back except by coaxing it aside with a slice of her liver paste?

Yet even this was fun, for we were fresh from the game of love, and now we played the game of marriage. When we went out in public, she put her hand on my arm, and we let it be known by our serious demeanor and deliberate pace that we were not mere frivolous sweethearts. She made curtains for our windows, and I sat on the porch and smoked my pipe. Through many a long evening we elaborated the future and made plans for the use of impending wealth. She giggled above her pen, learning to write my name with hers, and I learned to say most casually, "My wife, you know. She won't let me out without my cloak in this inclement weather."

And yet, incredibly, the game played out, the past grew more and more dim, the future more and more distant; and the present was too much with us and painfully plain: each of us facing the other across the dinner table with nothing to say that the other had not already heard.

So it seemed. Or was it only that we were getting acquainted?

Dorita, my delicate peach, now I began to know her. Not that she became some other fruit or suddenly cruel. Unlike the rose, the peach does not harbor thorns. But its velvet does shed a subtle fuzz which can stick in the throat and stifle.

Day by day, month by month, and despite my nervous resistance, I began to see through her, and what I saw was not nearly so pleasingly simple as what I had been shown before. It was as though the perfumed show of spring slowly ceased, the blossoms began to fade and fall, and I saw the starker landscape beyond. On the one hand she was a dim silhouette hung upon the crisscrossed tree of my own confusions; my shadow and my puppet, my token helpmeet and conjugal convenience: she who had plighted her troth to my ambitions and never found me wanting. On the other hand, I came to perceive that this obliging package was wrapped in armor worthy of an armadillo, and enclosed the will of a mule.

She could be chillingly lofty and demanding with tradesmen, or any person over whom she had circumstantial advantage. She was capable of furtive scheming and refined duplicity of the sort I had always associated with servants and felons. She sometimes suffered the most bleak and withdrawn sorrows; her face became a stone slope down which the tears rolled like icy pebbles, wrenching me with guilt and sickening me with my own furia.

Her concern with the petty details of life annoyed me, and when we argued, she often changed weapons or rules of conduct in mid-sentence, utterly baffling and enraging me. Her moods were uneven; one day she would be clinging, the next cool, the next snapping like a viper. She loved gossip and seemed more and more to talk merely to hear her tongue rattle; many a time I reeled from her babble, and still she poured it into my ear. For her part, she had little patience with my abstractions, my delicate compunctions, my concern for such intangibles as honor, art, poverty, consistency, politics. Whatever she did not personally know, whatever she could not reach out and touch, that seemed to have little or no meaning for her. But if it did affect her, she saw the reality of it with an accuracy that often surprised and even shocked me; and whenever she was thus touched, she could be fearlessly assertive, loving, possessive, tender, murderous.

I had never had a sister. All I knew was that this creature, whom I had thought was my hermana, was quite the contrary: of another and alien breed, not like me, after all.

Most baffling of all was the oblique but iron grip of her will. As patience was her virtue, so stubbornness seemed her most annoying vice. She who had seemed so reassuringly helpless could be astonishingly strong. Her wrists were thin as sticks, her hands fragile and inept, laboring over so simple a maneuver as the threading of a needle, yet capable of persisting for an hour and against all odds, until the thread was through. As a girl she had found it difficult to learn to write under the stern eyes of the nuns, and so had taken to practicing at home in her sleep, scratching at the sheet with her fingernail until she had finally got it right; and she was still given to scribbling thus at the mattress while she slept, most often following an unhappy day.

And then there was the matter of the almond trifle. During the wedding preparations, my mother had confided to Dorita that I had always hungered after her almond cake, a dark, strong-tasting concoction normally made round, but which for some reason she had always produced in triangular form, roughly in the shape of a heart. It is true that this particular delicacy had always aroused strong feelings in me, so much so that as a boy I had been in the habit of bribing or otherwise coercing Paco into consuming my share, or, that failing, would manage to gag it down, excuse myself at the earliest opportunity, and rush out behind the house to throw it up.

No doubt the stuff had become controversial as a result of some unremembered dispute between my mother and me, and I admit that to this day I am not so sure that it disagrees with me as I am that I disagree with it. Perhaps it seemed a chip off the black rock of God, perhaps something else. At any rate, I did not like it, my mother deceived herself in that. Or was it only Dorita whom she deceived? The old resentment impinges, even here as I wait to be hanged; the guttural chuckle sounds in my cell as I write, and I see the dark nemesis of the nursery gliding closer and bending over my bassinet to stuff her trifle in my mouth.

Dorita was not a cook nor ever would be, but she was determined to make me into a happy husband, after the conventional model. The first trifle appeared without warning at the beginning of our second week in Madrid. Returning from the palace, I dodged the swan and stepped into the house to find my wife seated at the table with a nervous smile on her face and a dark, triangular object before her.

I recognized it at once, despite the fact that its center was a bubble and the whole was black as the plague. For a moment I could not unglue my hand from the door latch. Then Dorita's smile, by now my heart's home tether and weathervane, began to waver, and I hastened to bend and kiss her. "Well, well," I said, forcing myself to sit. "What is it?" Oh, why, even when the intent was good, did the words so often come out with an alternative bias, as it were?

"It is a cake," she said with muffled dignity, while the swan tapped menacingly at the bottom of the door.

"I meant, what do you call it?" I amended, hastily taking up my spoon. "My mother used to call it Almond Delight, but I called it Isabel's Revenge. . . ."

She stiffened, and the first glass tear rolled down the stony slope. "You don't like it."

"No, that is, I do!" I protested, cramming it in. "I love it. And I love you. I am eating it, am I not?"

One of the disadvantages of life on a houseboat is the ever-present danger of mal de mer; and the river was running rough that night.

Nonetheless, I managed to get the whole portion down, and even had the presence of mind to brush away the crumbs in a manner so calm and decorous as to conceal all signs of revulsion. Or so I thought. But it was not so easy, nor ever would be.

"You look ill," she observed accusingly.

"Not at all, I feel fine. How delicious it was."

"Have more."

"More?" I made an attempt to conceal my condition with my napkin. "I am full just now. Perhaps later."

"You didn't like it."

"But I did!"

"It was your mother's recipe."

"I thought I recognized a certain—"

"Is it because it is burned?"

"That's it, yes!"

"Then you didn't like it."

"No, yes! Please, my darling, it is delicious, a bit browned perhaps, a bit swollen in the middle—"

"Tomorrow I will use less of fire and more of milk," she muttered, and there came across her pretty face that fixed and gimlet-eyed look that I would learn to know and dread.

The next evening's offering was pale as buttermilk, sunken in the middle and no less loathesome to my palate. I ate it, but despite my efforts, her narrow eye detected signs of nausea.

"You didn't like it."

"I did."

"Have more."

"Not now."

"It made you ill."

"The weather, my love, a tempest! See how the floor dips and slides. . . ."

And so, night after night, I do followed you don't, and again and again I found myself assuring her that I loved her trifle as I loved herself, even as my gorge churned denial.

And then suddenly, after a month of it, I returned home to find no menacing wedge on my plate. Concealing my relief, I congratulated myself that the crisis had passed. But the next evening, as I was returning along the shore, I noticed a suggestive object bobbing sluggishly in the shallows, and, coming closer, discovered a dark and soggy wedge of trifle. She had taken to making the things in secret and donating her failures to the river until such time as she might achieve perfection. It was typical of her in small matters as large: she was prone to accept too readily that the fault lay with her, but was equally convinced that if she persisted long and stubbornly enough, she could make it right on her own.

From that day on, on any random day of the week, I might come unexpectedly upon forlorn evidence of her secret campaign: a burnt fragment hidden in the garbage, a telltale scatter of almond skins on the porch, a sodden wedge bobbing in the shadowy waves beneath our house. I came to live in abiding dread of these discoveries, for each one pierced me with a pang of guilty remorse. And yet, should I bring the matter to words again, I ran the risk of no longer having my circumstantial protectors, the river and the garbage pail, standing between me and cruel indigestion.

And so I said nothing, and she said nothing. And thus it was that the mute and accusing specter of the imperfect almond cake came to haunt our marriage. For, although it was a trifle, it was one of those trifles that bear a world of meaning.

Big woman, big coony; little woman, all coony. I had heard it said, but I did not want to think about it. In response to my shouted proposal in the Triana cuckle house, Dorita had held a moment like a strung bow, then had gone abruptly limp beneath me, sighed, and raised up obediently to buckle herself back into the chemise cagoule. Whereupon I had concluded gratefully that she was herself again, and had proceeded to go ahead and finish in my usual manner: poke, gasp, groan, squirt. Done.

Thus it had been ever since, and why not, it was all that I knew. I had taken a wife, and now, whenever the shade of my former terror threatened, all I need do was ask Dorita to get into her sack, climb on top, and perform a simple exercise, to be once again reassured of manhood, and husbandhood as well. I had been taught that no wife should ever, except she be mortally ill or her legs broken, deny her husband his bedright, and she honored this convention, and I accepted her compliance as my due. It is true that she often seemed stolid and distant there beneath me, but I did my best not to notice. For I was the man and she was the woman, and it was her obligation to be swived, and my duty to swive her.

And that I did, with determined regularity, once a night and twice on Saturdays, doggedly accruing spasms with the nervous absence of a military man saluting the flag, the superstitious man knocking on wood. For it had to be done, to confirm our love, to claim her and keep her, and to ensure against arrefaction, retardismo, the clyster, and the tomb.

Thus I struggled to retain in our marriage the glancing bliss that had made our courtship charming to me. There was, however, an occasional lapse. As on the evening of the day that I brought home a cork for her coony.

I had noticed a gaunt barmaid some days previous and had been sharply reminded of Maxima and my nameless by-blow, that orphaned child who sat somewhere at the back of my mind, wide-eyed and stunned and forever lost. Dorita had already begun to murmur of children, but I could not bring myself to respond nor even to consider the thought. So I went straight to a Morisco wizard and amethodist who sold me an appliance which he guaranteed would prevent any homunculi from swimming up her ducts. She accepted the cork and its knotted string without argument, but with a dark and rueful glance; and as I showed her how to fit it into place, her face turned stony slope, and a single icy pebble rolled down it.

That night, the river had drawn away from its banks and left our house aground on black and odorous mud flats. She had span beneath the canvas, and I was preparing to delve, when suddenly her center began to buck beneath me, and I looked to find her head twisted aside, her eyes running to silver, and her lips preparing to let go the first sawing moan. Ice formed on my buttocks, my heart sank, and I pulled out and rolled away to face the wall.

The silence was long; the stink of sewage wafted up between the floor boards; somewhere a swan was hissing. Finally I felt the timid touch of her hand at my shoulder. "You didn't finish it."

"I am suddenly drowsy."

"You didn't like it."

"No, I mean, yes, I did."

"But it made you ill."

"No, never!"

"I had fits as a child. Something comes over me."

"The mud flats, my love, the stink. Smell how it seeps up through the floor. No doubt it crazed you."

"Yes, I suppose so. But please, Juanito, you mustn't turn away from me like that. I'm all right now. Come here and have some more."

Thus, and thanks to her stubborn compliance, my faith in the chemise chagoule remained intact, and the moment passed on into perfunctory poke and grateful squirt. But with each such glimpse beyond the pretty blossoms, the dread more and more returned. And even as I learned to fear her, I found my head increasingly twisted elsewhere, almost as though marriage had not changed me after all.

I first thought my uncle, the count, to be something of a fop, for he wore a powdered wig in public, and although his figure was good and he was tall, he pinched his waist with a doublet of hidden quilting, wore false sleeves which suggested he might be smuggling pumpkins, and tied false calves to his legs. I soon discovered, however, that this was only the uniform of the expert courtier, and in this as in most everything, Don Pedro was most astute and practical.

As a youth at Salamanca, he had won honors in tournament and lecture room, and, if rumor was right, in the leaping house as well. In Flanders with the Spinola brothers he had put a great number of Dutchmen under the tulips and had been rewarded with marriage to the second richest and fourth-best-looking maiden at court, getting two brilliant children by her. Most recently, he had commanded one of the few military successes of the decade, sacking Ottoman Zante, Patmos, and Duruzzo, and delivering to the king five three-masted jabaques, ten dozen silk rugs, any number of meershaum pipes, and the right ears of forty Turks.

"Unless it was both the right and left of only twenty," he told me with his very knowing and urbane smile.

It was the day that I first reported for service, and he had brought me straightaway to the Alcazar, doubtless to study my behavior in hectic company. To three sides of the vast courtyard, the palace walls rose a full three stories high, and all around the vast plaza there gathered and hurried a bright swarm of beribboned belswaggers, clerks, pettifoggers, tax farmers, merchants, priests, and ladies.

While I gazed about me, struggling to maintain an air of studious calm, the count talked and watched me closely.

"The twelve royal councils are here, and the ministries. The Council of the Indies there, Portugal across the way, Naples over there. The first and second stories are reserved for the royal household. The queen sometimes comes out on that balcony, looking like green pudding, for it is said that her uterus is out of place, though certainly through no fault of her husband, for he has not been in its vicinity since he brought her from Austria."

He paused, noting that my heated gaze had fixed upon a nearby carriage and its pretty occupant. "Juana Godoy, keeper of the queen's stool," he said. "Do you like her?"

"Excuse me," I said, hastily putting my gaze elsewhere.

He chuckled, leaning closer. "She is available, or was last week. But never mind, these things change so rapidly here. Once we have you properly trigged out and you learn your way about the palace, you will have no lack of ladies to flatter. All squires try, as the wise knight must do. For there is no minister so powerful at this court that there is not some wench even more so."

"I am sure that what you say is true, uncle, but I will not be able, that is, I cannot—"

"Are you telling me that you are married?"

I nodded.

He chewed his mustaches. "Diego did not tell me in his letter."

"It happened last year," I said, stealing another glance at the good-looking Godoy.

"But you are so young. You married too soon, nephew."

"But no, uncle!" I protested, prying my gaze from her. "I am quite happy with it, I am!"

He stared at me for a long moment, then shrugged. "Of course you are, nephew." He smiled and put his arm across my shoulders. "As I am the same."

A doe-eyed Galiciano named Ruben was his first squire and most often with him. He had another man, a veteran, who carried his weapons in tournament and in the field, and who was usually at the stables or the armory. I was mostly required to stay at a table in a little room across from the palace, taking messages and writing letters. Out through the narrow doorway I could watch the Alcazar courtyard and see all the way down the Calle Mayor. What a carnival. And most giddifying of all: the women. Beauty always gathers near to the treasury, of course, but I had never seen so much of it, nor so openly displayed. Twice-painted and -powdered ladies and strumpets of high degree rode up and down in carriages, accompanied by squadrons of pages, lackeys, and plumed paramours. Even the common wenches seemed to saunter with a special carelessness, balancing light bundles on their heads, the which added a beguiling severity of posture to that sway and twitch of the hinderlings which is woman's involuntary semaphore.

How it maddened me, and still I struggled not to care, concentrating instead on the mannered movements of those courtiers I deemed to be the best at it; and I even bought a wig toward that day when the work might become more lively.

It came sooner than I expected. My uncle called me to his villa in Aranjuez one afternoon and sat me down for solemn instruction. It seemed we were going to hornswaggle the king.

"As you know, nephew, when the Second Philip died and this one took the throne, he made his valet chief minister and named him Duke of Lerma. Since that time, Lerma's wife has become chief lady-in-waiting to the queen, his uncle is Archbishop of Toledo, another uncle is the President of the Council of Portugal, his brother is Viceroy of Valencia, a brother-in-law is Viceroy of Naples, and so on."

Despite his serious expression, his gray and steely eye twinkled. "It has even been suggested that our Lord Lerma might one day put all persons unrelated to him out of the country so that his family might more conveniently enjoy Spain."

He frowned. "At any rate, you get my drift. He is powerful, and therefore our respected ally. Now, you know about the king's love for public spectacle, his addiction to trap-ball and cudgel-play. Perhaps you have also heard that he is deathly afraid of all contagion, particularly the mumps. But mostly he preoccupies himself with the delicate balancing of his attentions between the brothel and the confessional. He has his father's pious bent, but not his joy in self-denial. He prefers to order the two hundred nuns of the Abbey of Our Lady of Infinite Sorrows to pray around the clock for the sins of his insatiable venality, whilst he diligently gives them reason to do so at another nunnery over the hill. All of which Lerma has thus far considered to be to his convenience, since it keeps the king from meddling in affairs of state."

Again his eye gleamed, again he was serious. "However, the king has lately become enamored of one particular creature, a nun at Calatrava. The which fixation is bad enough and food for scandal, but she is also the daughter of Gil Robles, Conde de Castillo Real, recently discredited by Lerma and jailed for sedition. It is feared that she might turn the king's heart as she has turned his head, and manage her father's freedom."

He got to his feet, and I got to mine. "So the king must be convinced to come unstuck from her. In fact, dissuaded from ever visiting her again. I have been selected for the job, doubtless because of my reputation in such matters." Again his eye gleamed, and now he smiled. "And so I have concocted a neat scheme, and have selected you to attend as my squire, so that your education might be advanced."

He leaned closer. "You are wondering why Ruben stays behind." His smile went odd and enigmatic. "The sight of a naked woman is repugnant to him. Whereas I am sure the same cannot be said of you, nephew."

Pausing to enjoy my reception of this, he then laughed heartily, thrust his sword and scabbard into my hands, and headed for the door. "So come on. This promises to be a diverting evening, or I do not know fun when I see it coming."

The ruse was simple but ingenious. It had been secretly arranged with the abbess of Calatrava, through the intervention of the Bishop of Almaden, a cousin of Lerma, that the nun in question should be fed a certain drug without her knowledge, the which perpotation soon caused her to abandon her senses and slip into a deep sopor exactly resembling death. She was then placed upon a catafalque in her chambers and surrounded by prayer and candles, and it was at my uncle's insistence that she was bereft of all but the barest covering, for he wanted, he said, the impression to be strong and lasting when the king came at his usual hour to exercise the royal privilege.

That is how I came to don monkish robe and hood and stand with my uncle and others equally disguised, behind the bier, so as to make the masquerade more solemn, and to witness its effect.

We had been there scarcely half an hour when there was the approach of boots and high-heeled shoes, a fretful voice ordered the guards to stand by, the door opened, and the king let himself in.

Thus far I had seen him only once at a tournament and distantly: a tinsel doll on a tiny balcony. But up close, what a marvel: that pallid and womanly coloring, no eyebrows above the large and lacrymose blue of the mooning eyes, the mouth like a ruptured tomato. Now it pursed as he glanced coyly about in the flickering gloom, now it ran with anticipatory juices as he approached the place where his nun's bed was supposed to be. Playfully, he snatched the curtain aside.

The heavy Hapsburg jaw fell, threatening to break the Hapsburg collarbone. He gawked, he gurgled; he reached out a hand, shuddered, and snatched it back. Imperious anger struggled with horror as he searched the shadowed faces beyond the light.

"What is it!"

"We fear it is the plague that took her off, m'lord. Unless it was the mumps."

Now the last vestiges of desire peeled from the great blue eyes, and they went bald with terror. He groaned, and then his face went soft with quite another kind of amour. He fell to the tiles and clasped his hands and beseeched the Holy Mother for forgiveness and protection. And then: I had never seen a man go backward on his knees, and so rapidly! In an instant he was gone.

There was a long silence, and my uncle said, "All of the worst of Spain was in that face, that moment."

But I heard him not, for the moment was something other for me, and not so easily over. I could not take my eyes from the nun. Here again was perfect beauty: neck not too short, breast not too shallow,

171

hips not too wide, etcetera not too etcetera. And more: the suggestive smell of candle wax, the muttering of prayer, the dark velvet beneath the pale form . . .

My uncle had to pull me backward by the sleeve. "Nympholepsy is what you have, nephew. I say it again, you married too soon."

It happened that very night. I had just fitted myself between my wife's legs and was preparing to perfuncturate, when I glimpsed around the corner of my mind a tantalizing image. Even as I strove to turn away, I smelled the candles and detected priestly muttering. Desperately I sought to chill the betrayal with memories of retardismo, but wild fancy had run away with my mind; the creature beneath me became the nun, lambent and blue in beauteous death, and in record time I spent. Hail Mary, full of spunk. Amen.

Dorita glanced at me in dim but not ungrateful surprise as I rolled my face to the wall. I had told her about a nun, but not a naked one. Could she guess? But no, in a short time I heard steady breathing, then the twitch and scrape of her fingernail on the sheet as she practiced writing in her sleep.

I myself could not sleep for shame. Married scarcely a year, and was this the way I fulfilled my pledge to love, honor, and cherish one woman alone?

Until death do you part.

The phrase was itself enough to hold me awake and staring into the darkness beside my lifetime's partner. Her nail scribbled on beside my ear. I decided to dull myself into slumber by tallying sheep in my head. But before the second woolly ewe had run the counting gate, the third had become a doxy glimpsed on the Calle Mayor the day before, her round hams gleaming as she sailed over the bar.

Once started, I could not stop, and from that night on, the only way I could sleep was to conjure and count them. For it eased me to dream that they also were mine and I theirs, until death did us part. But the ease was short of perfect, for I could not get it out of my mind that I was missing something.

Thus a new bad habit daily doubled my shame and growing dread. Clearly my uncle was right and I was cursed with nympholepsy. To swive regularly was not enough after all. The heaven I had thought to make mine by saying I do was no more than that same and ever-receding vagary at the top of Climax's ladder.

14

THERE IS no capital but Madrid,
they say, by which is meant that Madrid is the court and the court,
Madrid. The life of the city centers around the palace and its ministries,
and the Madridleños even cack to the king's command. Every night at
ten o'clock, by royal decree, the cuckstools are emptied and ten
thousand turds hit the street.

The court had been away for six years, so distressing the city fathers
that they had offered Philip a bribe of 250,000 ducats, together with
one-sixth of all house rents over the next ten years, to bring his
household back from Valladolid. The which blithe extortion and casual
rackrentry he then invited the populace to celebrate, and they did.

Every other day was a fiesta, it seemed. There were military parades
in the Puerta del Sol, bull-baitings in the Plaza Mayor, theatrical
performances at the Corral Pacheco, masked balls and fireworks at the
palace. Mountebanks and strolling players trooped the gutters, bears
did tricks while gypsies picked pockets, trying, as is their nature, to keep
up with the king. And every few months, the Holy Office staged a
solemn auto-da-fé, and the night was lit up with pious good fellowship
and burning heretics.

While the rest of the kingdom pinched and winced, there was only
revelry in Madrid. Even the turds thumping the cobbles seemed to
drum out an accolade to good times, for the municipality now paid the
unemployed a few coppers to roll them away to the river.

174

One way and another, I soon found myself drawn into this meretricious roundelay. Lingering in the Alcazar courtyard after my work, I chatted with other young bloods upon such matters as most concerned them: how to climb a balcony without tearing one's hose, where to get boxed chocolates cheap, and how best to challenge a dishonor and still not come to an actual duel.

Among the squires there was a loose confraternity of bravos who called themselves Los Gamberos de Castizo. These high-born shrimpfishers had much in common with the Oars, in that they were most fond of large talk and busy nonsense, and I soon found myself in their company every Wednesday to drink and make noise, to break lances and rupture horses in tournament, and to otherwise help satisfy the king's passion for expensive play.

I did not like it so much as they, and unlike the most of them, I was married. But I found myself increasingly reluctant to go home and face my domestic castle's hissing gatekeeper and perhaps glimpse another menacing trifle soaking up the moat. Besides, Dorita accepted my hobbies with a most goodwifely patience, so long as they were kept to a schedule and I was home in bed at night. Dear Dorita, she still believed that she held my vital ends in her hands, as she held her apron strings, and that the cure for my knot was to loosen it just a little.

In my nervous wanderings, I soon discovered another fascination more to my taste, and that was the world of the artistas. Like beauty, the inventive knack also gathers close to the treasury, for how can the aspiring dauber, scribbler, or playwreck pay for his pencils without patrons? Such persons could be found at the various mentideros about town, my favorite such lie parlor being a small bodega on Lion Street, where Lope and Calderón were said to drink sometimes. There, at any hour of the day, the tousled artistas could be seen lounging at deal benches, jars of wine at their elbows, new crayons behind their ears, and on their brows that look of meditative arrestment which denotes lofty intent ill acquainted with action.

No doubt it was a similar motley of lesser libertines and kill-cow thinkers who vapored about the marketplace at Athens, every man his own Aristotle, including the same. Still, I found them fascinating, for I was new to the game, and many were the clever deviations and rare heresies to bewilder and thrill me. Perhaps my most rattling moments came amongst that group of jaded scramblers who called themselves the Regular Renegades and Actual Artistas.

Harken to one of them, Salto Cuidado, dour-faced scribbler of political lampoons, assuring his fellows with the satisfaction of a leper noting the prevalence of the privy pox, that: "Man has not made a moral step forward in five thousand years."

Myself, shaken by this news: "But how can you say that? Not a step? The Romans threw Christians to the lions."

"And we strap Lutherans to the stake."

"Before that, then, the Hottentots cooked and devoured their enemies."

"We roast heretics. And do you know why we do not eat them? Morality, or rather the lack of it, does not change, but tastes do. We have got used to mutton and are afraid we will vomit."

"But what of the triumph of science, the new inventions?"

"Which do you mean? The harquebus, the cannon? Have you ever seen a flying ball take a man's head off, or angel shot distribute him? Perhaps you mean that ingenious device, the printing press, which has enabled the Holy Office to publish the Index and circulate long lists of Moriscos and Jews destined to suffer moral improvement at the hands of those other charming inventions, the pulley and the rack."

"But the compass and the sextant, the new navigation, the discovery of the Indies, the spread of civilization, trade!"

"Civilization? We discovered the red king with his foot on the neck of a million slaves, and what did we do? We killed the king and branded a million red buttocks with the Cross. We tumbled their idols and smashed their stone calendars and raised up statues of the Virgin and taught them to count their days of toil and misery in the Gregorian manner. Trade? We took them wine and the plague and brought back tobacco and the clap. No, my friend, man has not changed and never shall. His true god, first and foremost, is himself. His primary objective, after sheltering and feeding himself, is now and always has been: to spend."

"I'm for that!" This from the Marquis Mendo de la Mota, beaming through the blear of the day's drink with that naughty grin with which he claimed to have conquered the wives and mistresses of the great and famous. "Where the gristle stands, that is home!"

This Mendo was a rare charmer, at once obnoxious and attractive. By his own account, he had always been pretty and spoiled. High-browed and bow-lipped, with reckless curls and dimpled, he had much of the grown-up baby about him, and so was the darling of such women as knew the perfect plaything when they saw it. The second son of an archbishop of Leon, he had compromised his father once too often and been sent away to the capital, and here he had stayed into his middle years, receiving a small stipend each month, in exchange for which his family asked only that he stay away from Asturias.

"I tell you, I am more dreaded in my home city than a thousand Jews!" he was fond of announcing, always gilding the cupshout with an impish smile. "Put your hand in a Spaniard's pocket, and he will disdain you, but lay a finger on his lady, and he will kill. Be assured that what I do not know about women could be printed on your thumbnail. I have learned it all, only excepting one thing, and that is why God made them."

This line of talk was more to my bent, and I increasingly found myself taking a seat beside him in hopes of getting something useful from his ravings.

"Treat the chambermaid like a duchess, the duchess like a chamber-maid, is my motto," he said one afternoon. "You've got to keep them off your toes and on their backsides, or they'll think you lax and not worthy of their intentions. For it is your huevos they want, and never forget it. Every woman's principal intent is to persuade a man that he does not want to do what in fact he does want to do, and that is to swive the nearest female each time he is blessed, or cursed, depending on your life's view, with a hard yard."

"But must it always be deceit?" I complained. "Does one always have to demean oneself by lying and cheating?"

"Unless you want to be demeaned and cheated yourself. No man ever seduces a woman except by deceiving her or raping her. If he thinks so, he only deceives himself; it is he who has been seduced by her."

Now he gave me amused and mocking study. "Tuerto is what I shall call you, Lucero, for you are decidedly a deadeye on the one side, while the other reveals the ardent sparkle of the innocent. It is true, you need both for success with women, the one to heat up the blood lust of the huntress, the other to know her intention for what it is."

He shook his head and chuckled. "But God help such as yourself when you fall in love and your heart goes cross-eye. Now loan me some silver and go away, for a poem has just come half-made to me, and I must drink on it:

> "They say that in the spring in Lapland,
> On the banks of the Lemonjoke,
> The river of long-lost love . . ."

But all my lessons were not so cynical and detractive, for there is another sort of artista. Pasmo Cristad was half Norseman, with pale hair and a bland and sagging face that might have been made of iced pudding; as though one might poke a finger through the halfmoon maw of the mouth and get frostbit. He was not often at the bodegas, but one afternoon he appeared displaying a small book which was handwritten on skin and looked to be an original. I could just make out the title from where I sat against the wall: *Secrets of Carnal Contentment.*

"This is a very interesting book, very delicate and informative," the painter allowed, pulling a stool up beside the Regular Renegades and Actual Artistas. But they were deep in argument as to whether Caravaggio had died of cauliflower liver or knotted rimroids, and so they shifted their backs to him and went on arguing.

But in his diffident and feverish way, Pasmo was a driven man. Among such as the Real Renegades, he seemed always to provoke profound revulsion. It must have given him a tempting sense of power to be able to stir up such intense emotion with a mere wave of the tragic wand of his personality, so to speak. He humped his stool closer and thrust his fiberless face into the charmed circle. "Do you realize," he said, "that ninety percent of men and women never have a real spasm?"

They took pause. Caravaggio was returned to the crypt, and as one man, they turned on the Norseman.

"By my beard, Pasmo. A real spasm, you say."

178

"That's right. Oh, everybody has spasms, or almost everybody, but very few have the real thing."

"Is that so? The real thing, you say."

"That's right. A consummate release and at the same time a true coming together."

"Fusion, you mean. Alchemic explosion. Greek fire, perhaps?"

"Oh, no. Violent in a way, yes, but not destructive."

"Ah. Something from Galen, perhaps. The blood and the membrane. Rapture born of near rupture."

"Well, yes, but not so extreme."

"Perhaps something from the horticultural poet al-Haquim. Mandrake the Root plows Fati Mama, and up sprout the daisies in the spring."

"Well, he had the idea."

"He was a lucky bugger, eh?"

"I'm afraid I don't know the man—"

"But what does it feel like, Pasmo, a real one? You've had a few yourself, we gather."

"I, well . . ."

"It's like Solomon's Sonnets, I'll wager. The honeycomb breaks and the earth moves."

"Well . . ."

"And then the earth settles down and your bowels move. Or does your grommet just sort of slide up the length of your yard and go shooting off the end like a quoit?"

"Not so crude as that—"

"Not crude. Sweet. You font marmalade and she makes rose water."

"Not sickening, not sensuality for its own sake. There is a spiritual—"

"Oh, holy is it? All those angels dancing on the head of your prick. But how many angels for a real one, Pasmo? Ten, a thousand, ten thousand?"

"I didn't say religious. Certainly the command to reproduce is sacred to nature, but—"

"Ah, so secular orifice has sacred office? But what about the spilling of seed, Pasmo, or for that matter, the Greek pastime of spitting it up the nether hole? Are you one of those who believe such measures stand in the way of the Second Coming? If so, then what about the

Annunciation? Are you sure you can wait nine months for the final benediction? I mean, aren't you likely to get the itch for a little profane stuff in the meantime?"

"It doesn't matter, it's in the giving—"

"Oh, you give her a dildo on her saint's day."

"No, the sharing—"

"On All Saints Day, then, and you both use the dildo."

"No, damn, you've got it all wrong."

"Well, I suppose we have. It appears that all of us here are among the unfortunate ninety percentum. But frankly, Pasmo, you seem to be a bit hazy on the subject yourself. Are you sure you have had a real one?"

"Of course. But for some it is not so easily recognized."

"But there must be some criterion. Give us a sign, Pasmo. We would like to be prepared in case it happens to us. We don't want to have a real one and let it go by as just another counterfeit."

"You know when it happens, that is all I can say. You just know, you both know. It is like, it is like—"

"Popping your cork, name of Christ!" howled Uncle Lazarillo Blas, bringing a fist down on the barrelhead. "Blowing your wad, getting your stones off, spending plain and simple!"

"No, you do not understand," Pasmo protested. "It is not just that. It is something more. It is something, well, transcendental."

But Uncle Lazarillo had cut purses and pimped from Lisboa's bloody wharfs to the bawd pits of Vera Cruz of the Indies and had left more than one fellow ruffian to soak the cobbles with his blood; and had escaped wife, children, and the galleys to become a successful portraitist and blackmailer at the age of sixty-two, thereby earning his spurs as Intrepid Elder of the Regular Renegades and Actual Artistas. When he had fallen into the hands of the surgeons in Napoli on what was agreed by medical and ecclesiastical consensus to be his deathbed, with a sweat tent over his head and lengths of gut dripping balsam down his throat, a priest had come by to give him the last rites, and old Lazarillo had seen the black cassock through the iron ache of his own expiration, and had raised up from his bed and wrenched out the tubes in a bloody fistful and flailed Death from the room. He lurched to his feet now, eager to do the same with the Prophet of the Perfect Spasm.

"Listen, you Icelandic whelp, I've had more spasms than you've got shit for brains. All you need to get one is a wench, and all you do is take her somewhere and get her skirts over her head, and she spreads her legs, and you get in between them and stick it in, and you bang away, and when you are ready, you either spend or you don't. And if she don't want to come, well then . . ." His voice rose to a howl of exasperation. "Fuck her!"

All roared with laughter, and I could not help but join in from my seat against the wall. But I did not follow the others as they moved off in search of other entertainment, leaving Pasmo behind with his book dog-eared in his lap, and a thin smile upon his face. I waited until they were gone around the corner, then sidled closer along the bench.

"Did you say," I inquired, "carnal contentment?"

He turned his face to me, and each eye was a small blue pool beneath its sloping lid, and far down in the icy deeps of each there burned a needlepoint flame. "More than mere contentment," he murmured. "Have you heard of the Golden Mean?"

"No," I said. "Tell me about it."

It took him some time. He had a way of affixing himself to his listener like a mollusk, propped on an elbow and ladling minutiae into the other's ear with a wheedling urgency that was mostly deaf and blind to its reception. But I stuck it out, hoping for some real answers.

The Golden Mean, he explained, was sometimes called the Golden Section, and was the cipher at the heart of the works of such as Giorgione and Titian, who had made it their custom to lay out their compositions with geometry before putting on the paint. He showed me copies of their cartoons, crisscrossed with lines and triangles, arranged, he said, by means of Golden Mathematics. Whether the Golden Section was the length of the lute string plus a third, or the whole plus half of the two-thirds part, or the length of the pig's gut minus the length of the musician's yard, I disremember just now, but it was held to account for the pleasant tone of music and the look of good painting, and was the essence of harmony and the secret of true beauty. I did wonder how it was that when he used the selfsame triangles and lines, his paintings did not come out so good as Giorgione's, but he was a brilliant talker and convinced me that he had something.

When I had assured him that I had the idea, he proposed to take me to his house on the Street of the Bent Scissor to offer further proof by way of example, and as we walked along, he continued to bend my ear.

Since the Golden Mean was the essence of harmony and beauty, he told me, it followed that it should have its counterpart in all substances and all creatures, as well as in every intricacy of their relations, including the various forms of amatory commerce, wherein the attainment of perfection was known as the Golden Moment.

"The Golden Moment!" I cried, quite excited, for we had been a week getting to it. "This moment, does it come two-thirds of the way through, or is it the whole plus a third, or might it be governed by some other proportion?"

"It is not easy to say," he said shortly. "However, as I was saying of the harmonic ideal in painting, music, and love-making, the first is in the geometrical mode, while the second is in the tonic, the last in the sensual realm. All require skill and understanding, but most of all, the devotion and faith of the adept. In the end, as in every search for perfection, both search and reward are spiritual."

"Then it does come at the end! And you say there is peace, no lingering itch springing up afterward, no more of this blasted nympholepsy—"

"It is utterly beautiful," he droned earnestly, and far down in the little fjords of his eyes a humpback blacksmith pumped tepid mists from a bellows made of ice. "For you and for her."

"Her?"

He nodded. "The coming together of two souls as one."

"I see," I said, unsettled by this unwelcome insinuation of the distaff spasm. "Well, and I presume that once you have the hang of it you can manage it with any woman?"

His were not the sort of eyes to widen; rather, they grew blander, bluer. "You cannot make the noble from the dross. I told you, the achievement is spiritual, and so must be the means. Its ideal is harmony, its key is the desire to make it so. We do not speak here of *pandemos eros,* or common love, but of *ouranius eros,* heavenly love. I can give you no more specifics, except that the seekers must be close in every sense, and without inhibition. The Golden Means to the Golden Moment is a species of faith, a kind of prayer, given grace by devotion, constancy, love."

"It is not necessary to lay it on so thickly," I said. "I am only asking after the method, and how it feels so that I might know it when it happens. . . ."

But we had already entered his house and come to the door of his studio. "I had forgotten," he said, inviting me in. "Today is my day to paint my wife."

I already knew her name was Belica. She posed all in purple velvet on a platform at the end of the room, long-necked and perfectly made, with large and staring eyes: stunning and stunned, one of those beauties about whom one constantly wonders, "What is she thinking?"

Pasmo led me to his easel, murmuring that the carved and gilded chair upon which his beloved sat was the work of his own hands. A throne it was, and she sat it like a queen, or better, an empress, for her suzerainty extended beyond the domestic borders; there was another devoted subject in attendance, two easels before her, two portraits in the making.

While Pasmo daubed delicately at one canvas, another jumped nearby under the fierce strokes of a short, wiry young man, all red curls, green eyes, and goat beard. Tomas was his name, and he was bright-colored where Pasmo was pale, sharp where Pasmo was round, quick where Pasmo was slow. His best friend, Pasmo explained, and the one with whom he shared study of the Golden Mean and other devotions, including reverence for Transcendental Harmony in its fleshly manifestation, that is, in the person of his wife.

What a strange atmosphere: both the chapel's hush and the brothel's seethe, and all with the stunned statue for its fulcrum and focus. So delicate was the balance of their triangle that my presence soon became an intrusion. The beauty broke her pose and announced that she wished to refresh herself at the well, and I was given a fleeting glimpse of quite another Belica as she stood up and threw her hair into wild disarray, then came over to look at Tomas's picture, cried out coyly, "Oh, can that be me?" and went rushing from the room.

Pasmo came with me as far as the door. "About this Golden Moment," I said. "Are you sure? I mean, it has happened to you?"

"Oh, yes," he said most earnestly. "But then I am in love with my wife."

Over his shoulder I could see both pictures, and his was all tender caress, while the one by Tomas was something else; the husband was faithfully painting the one Belica, but his friend was hard at work on the other.

"You must be," I said, and left him.

Nonetheless, his words had rung a new angelus on the rusty bells in my heart. All was not lost, there was still hope at the top of the ladder. True, I was short of specifics in the matter, but Pasmo had said that the seekers must be close and all inhibition removed. Surely if that could be arranged, I might then discover the Golden Moment on or about the person of my wife, and from that day on we would swive happily ever after.

That Saturday I was the whole afternoon with the Gamberos, playing at juego de cañas for the entertainment of the king and his cronies. Javelin jousting had much in common with the old tournament à la Française. The balconies of the Plaza Mayor were draped in costly tapestries, special lists had been made of wood, and all around the lower levels there were beautiful women and pretty girls eager to offer gloves for their champions to carry in their belts, and colored scarfs with which they might bind up their heads when they got them cracked.

Although I had left Dorita at home, I carried her colors, and a dim and dreary rag it seemed, while I held to the shadows and the others gaily made the circle, collecting gloves and flirting with the jilts. How enticing all that forbidden fruit seemed in the corner of my jealous eye, each and every one a toothsome beauty. And here was I, already an ancient married man, with no prize to win, nothing to fight for.

And yet, when the drums and trumpets sounded, I was the first one into the arena, leading my uncle's quadrille headlong at the foursome galloping toward us; and what a delicious sight it was to see my wooden javelin go through the leather shield of the most famous bachelor of all, hopefully to pin the lecher's huevos to the saddle. With each clattering turn and charge, my furia came up the thicker in my throat, and it was not until far too late that I realized that I had cleared the field with my ravings and was now breaking every rule of tournament decorum by chasing my last opponent straight across the plaza and up the Calle Mayor, with every intention of putting my pike up his horse's posticum.

I did not bother to go back to hear the major domo's censure and learn my fine, then to watch the other lucky devils lean upon the parapet and cozen up to their sweethearts, later to bundle them or climb their balconies, or, that lacking, to reel away to the leaping house, there to vent the bloodheat roused by our violent games. Instead, I turned about and took mine home.

Was it only chance that the moon was full that night and our house once again aground on the pungent mud? My marrow still seethed with unspent furia, but I ignored it, determined to carry out my plan. Finding my wife already in her canvas bed garb, I bent down to kiss her, took a deep breath, and said, "Take it off, my darling, and let us get close again."

"Off?" Her eyes beamed. "You mean it? Oh yes!"

It had been a long time since I had seen such a pretty flush on her cheeks. And yet, with what ferocious energy she clawed at the buckles and shucked the chemise from her, and were those bubbles at the corners of her muttering mouth?

"Close, oh yes, close!" She clamped a hand to either side of my face and drew me fiercely down, and despite myself, as her tongue wrestled a way in and proceeded to whip my gums, I was put in mind of that ugsome sea worm said to seal itself to its victim with a powerful sucking kiss, then to mine for its meal with a tongue like a thorny piston. I wanted to be close, but not that close!

With a grunt I wrenched myself free, tumbled from the bed, and yet again found myself in retreat at the window, there to gloom and wait.

This time the silence was longer than ever before. But finally the voice came, faint and weary, dutifully beseeching. "You didn't finish it."

"I got a cramp."

"You didn't like it."

"No, I did. I do. It is just that—"

"I know," she drawled, and suddenly it was the voice of another

Dorita, finally out of patience and devoid of gravy, scalding: "I know the recipe: less of fire, more of milk. All right then, come here and let's get it over with."

Oh what a chill from such bald authenticity; a maelstrom of fevers whirled in my breast, while below, in the dim light from the quarter moon, the beast with the dingle-berried bottom waddled in the shallows, hunting a dark and suggestive wedge upon the water.

The swan arched its neck toward the moon and hooted, spread long-feathered sleeves and pranced, courting the bobbing cake. Closer and closer, hissing and hooting; then the neck coiled, stiffened, and thrust. The clacking beak caught a corner of trifle; the long muscle shuddered and squirmed, drew quivering back and stabbed, then stabbed again, and again.

I was on her like a pot-furied sweep upon his chimney, and had I had a broom to hand, I surely would have used it. But I did have my yard, and this I jammed through the stork's nest and into the sooty hole, braced myself with stiffened arms against the rooftree of her knees, and proceeded furiously to scour her.

In quick time, she began to arch and flail, the first moan sawed the air, and all the masks of nemesis came flocking. But this time, charging furia carried me beyond old battlegrounds.

At first I told myself that I was faced with a runaway coony that had to be brought to the stick, and the only way that I could think to quiet it was to pummel it to death. As before, if fear of failure froze me, it also kept me stiff. All hot paralysis and battering ram, I had little more feeling in my flesh than an oaken log. All clenched fist, I pounded at her gate: silence within, silence!

However, once started, I could not help but know that I was becoming something more than the retardo I had once been. Now I was a retardo malavencio. I mean there was forbidden fruit overhanging these lists as well, pretty flirts in the balconies, their maddening glances and laughing mouths too much to bear; and I still raved and rode my lathered nag, a-boil with envy and rage, hurling my javelin again and again: you keep me from all the others, it is your fault, yours!

How long did it go on? How long is it from fevered sunset to stunning light? How did it end? How does the fever finally crack and the black swoon begin? I recall floating back to awareness on a wave of afterstink, feeling her hand pluck at my thigh, and turning to see her mouth making words. But does the man who beats his wife want to hear her commentary?

Overcome by a dull nausea of satiation and shame, I turned my back on her. "I do not wish to talk about it." And from that night on, we never did.

15

LATE ONE night my uncle sent word
that the king had found out the ruse that had separated him from his
favorite nun. The conspirators were scattering until such time as some
new liaison mighty modify the royal anger by way of the royal
contrition. The count had left for Valencia in such a hurry that he had
left his wife and children behind, but not in so much of a hurry as to
leave Ruben. I was relieved of my duties and advised to stay away from
court.

Nepotismo was a double-edged blade after all, and had a treacherous
backswing.

Once I had got over the disappointment, I announced to Dorita that
I would become a painter. As ever, she showed me only sweet
sufferance, but this time she did ask me why.

I was ready, for I had been imbibing heady apologiae from books and
such devotees as Pasmo Cristad: Art is not a pastime, but a priesthood.
A work of art is a shadow of divine perfection. The bust outlasts the
throne, the coin Tiberius; all passes, but art alone endures.

From this store of sophistries I selected a favorite. "Why, in order to
forge a loftier reality, my dear." Then I bought some paints and a large
brush and headed straight for Belica Cristad.

She met me at the door of the studio, blocking it with her velvet
purple presence, all handsome skull and staring eyes. Her husband, she
told me, was out at the moment, burying a caudel of lime and mule

urine in a dung heap in hopes of discovering the lost formula for the Golden Gesso, the perfect paint that had made Leonardo great. I should come back later.

"But you are the one I come to petition," I said, showing her my paints. "I had thought that since you already serve two, you might welcome a third. I would like to join in painting you."

A smile frescoed the blank wall of her beauty. "How flattering of you to ask. But no." She shook her head most solemnly, while somewhere in the room behind her, a canvas jumped and trembled under the thrusts of the goatish Tomas, and as he went at it, he fired off a hearty grunt.

"It would not be fair to Dorita," she said.

"But," I said, pointing indignantly toward the studio behind her. "Your husband's best friend!"

Her demon briefly showed itself in that inane giggle, but she got hold of herself. "Yes, but he is not married, you see," and with a prim and regretful smile, she firmly closed the door.

"The true artista," Cennino Cennini had written, "must spare his precious hand, preserving it from such strains as heaving crowbars and other things which might weary it or make it unsteady, such as indulging too much in the company of women."

I decided to avoid the society of others, including the Gamberos, and took to daubing paint on pine shingles at home. In this way, an unexpected reversal began to show itself in our marriage. Even as I took to hiding in my room, Dorita took to wandering.

She let our scullery maid go and began to do her own shopping, arguing that the loss of my uncle's support made servants beyond our means. She had a cousin who waited on some lesser lady at court, and began to spend much time there, doing embroidery, she said. Her ramblings also took her past certain mentideros, and soon titillating tales concerning the activities of various sybarites of the town became regular fare at our table.

It did not help to have it on my mind as I retired after lunch to my portrait of the Cobbler at his Last, after Zurabin, that some Gallego dauber named Jorge, known in the bodegas as the Cob, had discovered that the Romans had long ago kept a temble to Apollo outside the city, and was at that moment reviving ancient ritual in the ruins with the well-preserved and quite intelligent, Dorita assured me, Contessa Mumia de Medinaceli, known to gossip as Lady Cuspidor.

Such considerations tended to cause my mind to wander and my brush to stray from those portraits of humble artisans through which I was then attempting to forge a loftier reality. Alone in my room, I would become aware that my hand strayed to my huevos, and would the more fiercely lock it to my brush. Sitting on the porch waiting for my wife to return, I would realize that I was neglecting the swift passage of time and letting immortalidad get away from me; and what was more, that my pencil had scribbled a slender limb, a pretty face; and I would crumple the paper and fling it into the river and force myself back to my sketch of the venerable torture of the olive tree, the stalwart lean of the plowman.

My hermitic mood annoyed the new Dorita. She suggested that I was getting sour for lack of social intercourse. And when I steadfastly declined to accompany her on her daily gambols amongst the Lotophagi, she began to bring them home.

First came Felicio, last name Mariposa-Cid, wearing a blue cotton toga and a straw hat woven round with rosemary, and holding a cucumber aloft.

"Always in season!" he whooped, and I cringed from the tone, the mannered imitation of matronly hysteria, and decided it was liquor he was drunk with. Dorita seemed to have had her nose in the bowl herself, waving Moorish lettuce in each fist and informing me with a suggestion of bleary defiance that she had brought him home to liven up our afternoon with his Tenerife salad.

"If you can tear yourself away from your Cobbler," he added, leaning in the window to cast a pink-rimmed eye upon my painting. "My goodness, isn't he a grim study. And that shoe between his knees, it has no tongue. Has he cut it out for fear of the tales it might tell?"

Yellow-haired and boyish, he might have been any young man of refined lineage and delicate make, and yet there was a difference, a certain pinch of feature and expression, as though he might have been squeezed askew in the womb. Even the thread of a scar running diagonally down one cheek seemed less an accident than a part of the design that drew his face forward in a ferrety thrust, suggesting the tilted eyes, pointed ears, and moist muzzle of the faun.

But most distressing was the compulsive ambiloquence, the double-tongued flood of shrewd and arcane insinuation, much of which glanced off, yet still stirred certain tender regions of my mind with which I did not care to become acquainted.

"I love a houseboat, it is like an island," he declared, tossing lettuce leaves on our porch, his toga slung about his waist. "And islands part men from the mainlands of their nurture and cast them adrift on turbulent seas. If some Greek did not say it, then it must have been me. I was born on an island myself: Tenerife in the Canaries, to eight interlocking generations of Old Christian nobility. All that close breeding had watered the blood to pale blue, and so my parents dedicated their lives to bringing it to the proper purple by the infusion of much red wine. And when my mother drowned in her own bile in Algeceris, and my father died of a poisoned tooth from pulling one cork too many, I took my inheritance and sailed with the hairy Portugee to an island beyond the Indian Sea, where children dance all their lives, the young men walk naked and cocoa-colored on the beach, expectantly. And there is always a cozy bush near to hand. Will you take ginger in your salad, my dear Juan, or do you fear that it might unduly enflame your brush and cause you to spoil the shoe?"

"You worry about the salad, I will worry about the shoe," was typical of my testy response; and he whooped with glee, while I glowered, impatient with myself for playing his game, waiting for him to go so that I might get back to my easel tree, my palette of blood and vinegar.

But once with us, he seemed forever there. He arrived in the afternoons with Dorita, their arms full of salad greens, their faces bright with drink. He dragged his groaning wine fits to our porch while we slept, and was there in the morning, holding his head and eager for more wine, ready to recite more scandal.

"The Conde Camillo's spotted hound has a tumor of the posticum and will die; what will the old fellow do now for carnal entertainment? I saw Lady Cuspidor with no less than four of the palace guard last night; she must stuff them in all in a gather and go off like a roman candle. Do you mind if I take your wife to the rocks for a swim, Juan, since you are so shy yourself of appearing in your drawers?"

191

He hailed and whooped from the bodega terraces as I hurried past with fresh paints and rolls of paper. He brought handfuls of artichokes to boil, and when we ate them, made ribald comparisons regarding their hairy centers. He showed me his drawings: red-lipped harlequins and capering fauns. He presented us with a beautiful waxprint toga from that mystic isle where he had dispensed with his inheritance. He whispered to Dorita on the porch, while I struggled to fix my mind on my Cobbler. He stayed late into the night, agitating with his impudent wit, reaching out with veiled tales of his tortured youth. And finally he reeled to his feet, his face squeezed with drink and his scar vivid, smiled at Dorita, gave me a look of painted intensity, then went plunging across the plank and down the moonlit beach. And before his parting whoop had faded, I had my pants off and Dorita on the bed.

Did they not giggle together, swim together, meet in the town? Clearly they had something in common, some elusive understanding that excluded me. As for his epicene posturings, I preferred to discount them in favor of a simpler distress. He had codlings and a yard, did he not? The rascal was after my wife!

Stab, stab, stab, you are mine, mine, mine.

Our bed was the invention of some misguided carpenter, many-jointed and designed to fold up during the day, and as we bounced upon it, its bolts jumped in their holes, its joints creaked and howled, and there were times when I thought, indeed moments when I wished, that it might close upon us like a crocodile's jaws. Or was it the Inquisition's catasta, its creaking that of the windlass, Dorita's groans those of the stretched heretic, my grunts those of some diligent familiar at the wheel of the rack?

She had ceased trying to produce an acceptable trifle and had thrown her bake pans into the river along with the chemise cagoule. And now she closed her eyes and sought what she sought elsewhere, even as I banged her, doing the same.

Bit by bit, I was teaching myself the habit of raging delay, or cunctation: the nightmare of retardismo in harness, but still uncured. Day by day, inch by inch, I had begun to lean farther and farther away from her, even as I clung and pummeled, propped on stiffened arms; my body shrinking back from the splayed sacrifice of hers, as my throbbing yard reached out, stretching desperately for the necessary contact, just kissing the mouth of her coony. Somewhere back along the line we had passed like ships in an Arctic night, and now we wallowed and heaved at either end of my frozen boom, the husband grinding his gristle at one extremity, the wife twiddling hers at the other.

You are my wife, wife, wife; I am a man, man, man.

But my new nemesis knew my strings. Was I a coward, afraid a shark might nip off my jewels? Or was I afraid of some other unnamed marauder? Thus he challenged me, day after day for a week, and I finally agreed to go swimming. But I took my fish spear to give the outing purpose beyond getting wet, and strode, oh so vigorously, across the rocks, never thinking that my mannered swagger was flirtation to his split eye. And made certain I killed the first fish, nearly drowning myself in the effort, for he was the better swimmer, if the truth be told. I dragged my trophy from the water at the foot of a red cliff and proceeded to stick my spear into it again, once, twice, while he lay back on his elbows and watched. "It is dead fore and aft, or do you seek to prod it alive again? Come and lie down, the stones are warm."

I frowned and ground my teeth. He had left his confession, and two nights before I had surrendered to fascination and read it: brashly titled with a boy's name, an attempt to make conventional romance of an unconventional love, with not a single venereal detail to reward my ogling eye, yet with all the strain showing through the stitching, and one line that stuck: says the diarist as he lies in the arms of his seducer: "I felt such relief; at last it was over."

Tumbling rubble announced a small boy scrambling down the far path, with a priest close behind, holding his black hat to his head, the bat-wings of his skirts flapping in the wind; and they disappeared around the rocks to a pealing whoop from Felicio. "My goodness, this must be the day, everybody's doing it!"

Still, I thought it better to sit down than to stand there in pimpled display. But I took my fish with me and lay it down between us, glittering green and bleeding black on the round white stones.

"Do you really like fish so much?" He rolled to face me, and as I looked, his face seemed to narrow upon its wan and watchful smile, and the two biased halves to slip slightly askance along the line of the scar. Dorita had asked him where he had got it, and he had replied that he

193

had never been sure whether he had been born with it or it had just appeared one day. Was this the sign of the relief he had found; this fine fracture that divided him, hair-thin, yet deep to the heart of the marble? "Really," he said, wrinkling his nose above my trophy. "It does stink, you know. Whereas this . . ." He took up one of the stones and rubbed it lingeringly. "Smells only of the salt sweat of the manly sea. Warm yet cool, smooth yet firm . . ."

"About your paintings," I said.

". . . white as the limb of a young boy . . ."

"About your gesso," I shouted. "Have you thought of using something other than egg yolk!"

He stared, glee convulsed him, and he whooped. "Have I!" He thrashed on the rattling stones, then was suddenly still, looking at me. Hilarity became something else in his eyes, the stone slipped from his fingers, and he swayed toward me, reaching out a hand. "Blessed be the virgin."

"God be damned, oh, Jesus shitfire!" Had I been a rocket, I would have shot straight up the cliff behind us. Had I had a sword, I likely would have pinked him. As it was, I landed on my feet some distance from him, found my cod to be still intact, cast a few more obscene epithets his way, and took my fish and went into the river and towed it ruefully home, occasionally casting a disgusted glance back over my shoulder, to find him following at a distance, stopping when I stopped and gaily waving, his eye teeth glinting in the foam.

The next day I announced to Dorita that I had rented a disused tower at the corner of the old city walls. I had to have a more secluded place to work, I explained. Salads and afternoon swims were not for the dedicated artista. And for my authority I quoted Leonardo: "The painter ought to be solitary, in order that the well-being of the body may not sap the vigor of the mind."

Unfortunately, I soon discovered that the washermaids of the town gathered daily on the rocks just below my tower, chattering of the doings of high-born ladies and pounding their linen, naked to the waist and sometimes more so, their round buttocks twitching as they kneeled to their work, their heavy breasts swinging.

Turning my back to them, I only discovered that out my other window I could see down through the rooftops toward Lion Street and just make out the terrace of my favorite mentidero: the sun-warmed benches, the jars of wine in the fists of the lucky layabouts.

Three weeks of this multiple torture, and I found myself on the bench beside the Marquis Mendo with a jar in my hand and deep furrows in my forehead.

"You seem bothered, Deadeye," observed the Marquis, not without a certain crapulous glee.

"What do you know about the distaff spasm?" I asked him.

"Oh, that." He stretched and let go a belch. "Well now, first consider that women are the wildlife of the country, and morality corresponds to the game laws. Which is not to say the laws always work. Sometimes they break down, and the game goes wild, and wild it is when it is set loose, believe me. Now some consider this distaff spasm to be the key to a woman's heart, but I am no such fool. Oh, it can be one amongst many ways to control one of the creatures, and works best on a young and inexperienced doxy. But it can be nettlesome too, one of those leashes that tug in both directions. A woman wants two things, you see."

He held up his fist and extended the first finger. "Power over a man." Now he let the little finger pop up. "And to be overpowered by a man." He waggled each of the horns, straining to make them touch, but failing. "As you can see, it is impossible for any merely mortal hand to get the two poles together."

He sighed and lifted his jar. "As for the effect of this spasm on the man, it all depends on how much in need is his vanity. But one thing always holds true, and is one of life's finer ironies: the better the swive has been, the more the flesh swells and sticks, and the harder it is to pull out again."

I drank, not satisfied, but leery of submitting the Golden Moment to his knowing scorn.

But he was canny, cocking an eye at me. "You seem troubled with the tentigo, Deadeye. I mean, aren't you lately suffering a hard spell of priapism?"

"It is those girls doing washing below my tower," I complained. "They uncover their breasts. There should be a law."

"There will never be a law to cure your affliction," he assured me with a hiccup. "I know because I share it. Abarcy: the state of always desiring more."

"But why!" I groaned. "There must be some way around it!"

He looked at me; how suddenly swazzled he could look. "No way over, under, around, or through." He shook his head, lifting his jar. "You simply take your choice of mistresses. Here is mine." He drank it down, then regarded me with a foxy eye. "Tell me, Deadeye, just exactly what is it that you want anyway? Do you know?"

In a seizure of confusions, I struggled against his knowing gaze. "I want . . ." I blushed. "Well, for one thing, to be good."

He snorted, blowing a fine spray of Jerez. "Well then, what do the doxies say? You look to have enough blood in you, and you are young. You can't be that bad at it."

I hid my cringe with a glare. "You know what I mean."

"All right, all right." He poured himself another jar. "Tell me, then, when your wife is eating, are you painfully aware of the sounds of her mastication?"

"Yes," I admitted. "And to touch her hair is to breed shivers between my shoulders. God's nose, what can I do!"

Again he studied me irritably. "Look, the trouble with marriage is that it forces two people into too prolonged and intimate an association. Nobody bears being known that well. So sooner or later you come to detest one another. And if something is not done, hatred soon overtakes habit. You are in trouble. I should know, I have been married three times."

"That makes you twice a bigamist."

"And three times a fool," he observed with another hiccup. "But I have bitter experience with which to assure you that if you wish to keep your marriage, you cannot bottle your tentigo up forever, but must pull the cork sometime, unless you would have the whole barrel burst. You must first commit a crime before you really begin to live. If you are bored by the one hole, try the other one."

"God's nose!" I said, making a face.

"All right, then, try another bed."

"But how cruel if Dorita finds out. And the other creature, I can promise her nothing, but will only exploit her and then cast her aside."

"Exploit, did you say?" He studied me with a new incredulity. "I

196

perceive that we are near to the heart of your confusions, Deadeye. By my bone, don't you think the women enjoy it as much as we?"

I stared, stunned by this reversal, remembering priestly condemnation of rapacious lust, and the chilling confirmation of the clyster. "I never thought of it that way."

He snorted and waved me away. "It is never too late. Pull the cork, you fool. Try the Red Cape District, there are trollops enough there to unconfuse the likes of you. Or find yourself a midwife, they are second best only to lady butchers. Now buy me a drink and leave me, for I have told you all that I know and more than you understand, and I have just thought of an end for my poem:

> "They say that in the spring in Lapland,
> On the banks of the Lemonjoke,
> The river of long-lost love,
> The women bite the balls off reindeer,
> And spit them out in the fall,
> If at all."

In fact, there was a midwife in our neighborhood, named Pandema Meraviglia-Gros, of Italian origin, and a truly boggling prodigy. She was married to the local blacksmith and boxing champion, said to be a tireless roisterer but no match for his wife. She was vast in her parts as she was prodigal in her spirit, with an abundance of black glossy hair, wide and generous cheeks, lavish lips, large eyes, and a fine, high-arched, and rapacious nose. When she walked, all the earth's largesse jounced upon her frame, the sun darted from rings and nose jewels, and there was a tinkling of ornaments; and she swept the world as she passed with her wise and hungry eyes, drugged as few women are by the steam of her own fissures and folds. From the first moment that I saw her, she had seemed the dark earth itself, and I sensed the moldering roots and leaves, the seething compost of her underside.

Her husband gave occasional rustic fetes, banchettos, they called them, for the scullions and domestics that lived in the hovels along the river bank. These fiestas took place in a disused orchard above our houseboat, and we could see their bonfires from our porch and hear the mouth harps and bagpipes going. One night, as Dorita slept like a log beside me, I crawled from my bed and scrambled up the river bank, nervous but intent upon testing the fruity invitation of those sleepy eyes.

I was in luck, her husband had been kicked whilst shoeing a stallion and lay propped on a cot beside the fire, poking with a hay rake at a huge pig turning on a spit. Pandema wore a great tent of white satin, within which her abundance jostled and undulated. There was a hint of warning in her welcoming smile, bidding me bide my time and wait. The locals were already well perpotated and in a festive mood, taking their food in the grass.

Fat gleamed on chins and ran down hairy chests and wallowing breasts; noisy chatter ebbed and flowed; and the slovenly evening evolved toward its appointed end: men arose and belched and women laughed; two by two and sometimes three, they wandered off amongst the trees.

I found her by some sense I would not have been able to name. She was a swamp in the darkness, her husky greeting the melodic croak of the bullfrog, and the whole vast morass of her seemed to fume and bubble, bidding me step off and wade in her warm bayou. Perhaps I blurted out some inept reference to her husband's injury, perhaps passed a remark on the necessity of keeping the chin up in the face of adversity.

"But, bambino," she crooned, "what does a girl do if her husband cannot get it up at all?"

I stepped closer. Now she jangled with welts and crescents of silver and gold, and her broad feet squished in the mud. Another step, and I was falling toward the operatic invitation of those slutty eyes. "Over there," I gasped, "where it is darker. Come!"

She ran, wallowing white and pearly. I leaped over the wall, sank to my knees in the clods, then went scrambling to intercept her. Crouching by a conglomeration of prickly pear, I waited, all thumping yard and racing heart, while she picked her way toward me, jiggling and bangled, all a-glow.

There is an ecstasy that is best nourished by danger, furtive duress, and secret places, preferably forbidden, best within hearing of some polite and restrictive ritual: a ladies' embroidery circle, a literary tertulia, the confirmation of some promising virgin. While the music played on and the celebrants chattered, we gasped and grappled, rolling in the clods, and I snorted, rooting in the mildewed Venus.

In fact, there were pigs somewhere nearby, and they snuffled excitedly, as though they had got wind of bucketsful of yesterday's cabbage, any moment to come dumping from the skies, to be trampled in the mud and marinated with dung and savored wetly, tusks sliding in the slime, bristles dingle-berried brown, eyes squeezed shut and heads thrusting, screwing through the fecal earth toward home. Nothing about her face, no heart-rending stare, no moans so strong as to drown my own, no remorse, no nemesis of nursery, tomb, or tit. Only the sensual savor, the membrionic slip and slide, and ancient memory of succor, of some sweet and mindless former life when we were snails. "Now, bambino, now!" And I was there, driving up the mountainside, Sisyphus with his organ in the humus and his eyes on the moon, yet all unaware of onerous labor. While in their pits nearby, the swine were suddenly attentive and silent, and from the fireside, the lutes plunked and plinkled on.

So simple, so neat, so easy. Scarcely a quarter of an hour later I was back in bed beside Dorita, cautiously parading the memory through my mind. I even imagined more such delights, and saw myself crouched beneath their table while she and her husband played at marital draughts, and I helped her to cheat by thrusting my hand up between her massive thighs: one finger for an ace, two for a deuce, five for a full frame, and up to the wrist for a royal flush.

A vague uneasiness did linger, an uneasy sense of incompletion. As though it had been too simple, too neat, too easy. Don Diego's voice wheedled in memory: "We were not meant to merely spend into one another through eternity, like a string of apes."

And yet the truth was that my partner had returned to her hearth unscathed, and I to mine. In the days to come, I would pass her in the alley, and she would smile warmly, but give no sign of either disappointment or further expectancy, and certainly none of the clinging common to most women. If she was a phenomenon, at least she proved such existed. No pain had been passed on in either direction; the only aftermath was silence. I had committed my small crime and was, by all good sense, only the better for it.

199

There had even been a sweet bonus to put the seal on my bewildered delight. Afterward she had pressed her lips to my ear and said: "I knew you would be good."

Now that good I did want to be.

By God, if it truly could be this neat and sweet, if men and women could simply meet and love as the spirit moved them, and afterward part in mutual respect and affection—then the dilemma of life was solved, my torture was at an end!

I enjoyed a fortnight of this blissful delusion, and then one night, responding to another kind of itch, I absently unbuttoned my codflap, only to cringe back in horror. Esclavo was weeping.

MYSELF: In God's name, stem that disgusting tide. You are making me ill!

ITSELF: I cannot, I tell you. O God, I knew you would get us into trouble with your interminable speculations, your infernal nympholepsy.

MYSELF: Me! I beg your pardon, it is you with your throbbing veins and perpetual erection. Beast! Tell me how it feels.

ITSELF: When you piss, I burn. Otherwise, a bit feverish, and this annoying cheese, how it stifles me.

MYSELF: Enough, you lascivious worm, I fear we have the Old Jose.

ITSELF: The clap?

MYSELF: Or worse.

ITSELF: The pox! Help, I feel faint. Get me to a doctor, quickly!

The Lesser Emerods was my affliction's name, according to the doctor I secretly sought out: a stunted Catalan amethodist by the name of Manolo Dedo de Fortuna, who claimed to have learned bleeding in the army and represented himself to me as a disabled war veteran and circumstantial eunuch, the last claim doubtlessly offered by way of reassurance in connection with my treatment, which was by herbs and bleeding, but also included examination and message of the penal gland, the which, he insisted, although I doubted him to the end, could be reached only through the nether orifice.

Four times was his prescription and four times I submitted myself to his attentions. Oh what a bitter mull of distaste and sickly furia seized me up each time that I faced him at his door, shook that hated hand, and followed him into his clinic. Why was he so thoughtful as he scrubbed his hands, gazing out the window? Why did I care? Was there the hint of a smile at the corner of his bloodless lips as he turned, a touch of anticipatory relish in that blank and narrow face as he bade me peel down my trousers and bend at his table? Now the banal exchange of words, his absent bumside manner:

"Lovely day today," he observes, as he greases his finger and poises it before my fundament.

"A bit chilly," I reply, as he gently probes, then sends it gliding in.

And even as the dreadful intruder pokes at the tender gland, and I wince and grit my teeth, my rattled mind rushes from one corner of memory to the other, furiously rehearsing all moments but the present one. So that afterward, as I hastily tug my drawers up against the chill vacancy of his withdrawal, and he inquires absently, scrubbing his hands, "I hope I did not hurt you," I am able to reply with equal unconcern and something quite close to honesty: "Not at all; in fact, I didn't feel a thing."

But now on the fourth and last day, I take a deep breath and lower my drawers and close a hand about each ankle. He makes his usual observation upon the weather, but I give no reply as he enters, for I am already elsewhere, clear of the moment and quite out of my mind. My brow bursts beads of sweat, my ankles turn white where I grip them, and my boot soles squeak on the slippery tiles. Blinding red-and-white darts of light shoot this way and that behind my clenched eyelids, and suddenly I know that I am on the verge of a revelation: the vision that will reveal all at last. But once again, my foot slips and the lesson is lost. Crashing forward onto one knee, I slide right off that accusing finger and come up running, in need of confession for the first time in years.

I found my wife in the market with Felicio. "Over there by the cucumbers!" I shouted at him, and he went.

Then to Dorita, trembling like a leaf and clutching for her hand: "I must tell you, for I am poisoned with shame. Forgive me, Dorita, you must forgive me!"

And there next to the cabbages, I solemnly told her all, from my nympholepsy to Pandema Meraviglia-Gros to the Old Jose. And the tears silently rolled down her face, and her hands flapped before her like those of a mute struggling to call attention to broken wrists.

And when it was done, and the tears had stopped rolling, she forgave me. And exactly three months later announced that she was with child.

So much for confession and other cathartics. I was not the only one who could pull the cork.

16

Dear Adan (the midwife had promised a boy), you have moved in your mother, meager blue convolution, leviathan, my son. I heard her gloating moan and turned to see her neck arched back against the pillow. "It moves, feel it, here!" And I reached to the taut hillock where you lived and felt the distant, fatted turn, then the quick thump, chilling me to the bone. What man will not be shaken to see his mortality step forth from the mirror in his woman's belly?

The closer the day came, the more Dorita dreamed apart, her hands upon the pearly globe. More and more I suffered a sense of dim estrangement, watching her. There was a lambency of contentment I had never seen, a drift of sweet mist behind her eyes, a cool quiet in her flesh. No matter how close I contrived to get, I still felt apart and without effect: an unemployed buffoon posting letters to the moon. And yet I had never seen her so beautiful, nor ever would again.

I began to paint at night. It was summer and the air was heavy with damp, so that all the sounds of the night came muted one by one, poignant accents to the dark and silent slide of time. Would someone out there hear my cry and be moved by my picture? I cared little. What mattered was the act itself, the snug distraction of trying, the elusive dream of synthesis. Below in our houseboat, Dorita glowed like an exalted orphan, her hands upon her belly. Alone in my tower, with my need at the tips of my fingers and my sorrow close at hand, I learned a separate contentment, as though through deliberate vacation of the world, I somehow purchased it; and of comprehension, as though the shared silence were all the understanding needed.

I did twelve paintings, and in each a pair of figures stood in pained opposition, yet reaching out, one to the other; and the best was the last. I had seen the blind man and his lead boy about the town, the man selling cartoons and gossip sheets, shouting his wares in his cracked and lightless voice as he shuffled along with his hand clamped to the boy's narrow shoulder. I had seen the man pay for a jar of wine and receive his change, and the boy reached slyly for a coin, but his master heard the telltale clink and caught a slender wrist in one hand and the boy's scrawny neck in the other and banged the wrist until the coins fell, and banged the head until it bled. And a day or two later, when the blind man asked the boy to take him to some secluded spot where he might relieve himself, the boy took him in circles and finally to a space before the bodega, and there the blind man unlimbered and proceeded to void, only to cringe and wither before the laughter of the bodega's patrons. And the sniggering boy dodged, but his shuffling feet betrayed him, and his master caught him by the neck and beat him, raging as he pummeled, yet holding his borrowed eyes close, cursing his need, yet helplessly tethered to it.

That is how I painted them: the blind man beating the ragged boy, each struggling to escape, each doomed to cling: reaching and unreached, divorced yet forever wed.

Who knows, I might even have become a great artista, given a longer pregnancy, say ten or fifteen years. But soon enough Pandema Meraviglia-Gros arrived.

"Come, wicked Juan," she said to me. "Your wife has begun her greatest labor. And you are about to learn why it is you suffer."

Dorita lay in state with her knees up and a cloth across them, glowing like a pearly moon, the blue-veined and quaking egg of the beginning. "Soon?" she murmured, "soon?"

Pandema nodded, mighty twigger herself and mother of four; and the old crone who assisted her waggled a hoary head. "Sooner than later, my child."

But soon can seem forever. Time, the expectant hush of the long night outside the shutters, the smell of rose water, aqua regis, candlewax, the little hourglass gleaming on the bedside shelf, the muttering of midwifery. Now she moaned softly with each deep breath, engrossed in the tremors, the distant, sudden gusts, the vast agitation growing in the earth of her. Time and more time, as the old crone tilted the glass, helping her to measure the pains, and her groans grew deeper, yet still distant and steady, patient and expectant. I watched from my shadowed corner, and as the drama grew in the room, so did my sense of separation from it. I choked, breathing with her, recoiling from my presumption.

It seemed forever. And then a groan started deep and held on, stretching into a long and thrilling shriek; and Dorita arched back and clenched the sheets.

"It is time," muttered Meraviglia-Gros, bending to look. "Now!"

"Now!" cried the wild creature in the Triana cuckle house, and I proposed marriage instead.

"Now!" howls the woman at nativity, and the bed ropes cry out as Dorita turns, gritting her teeth against the wild rhythm of her breathing, eyes turned to quicksilver, brow a knee of alabaster, turning left, right, left. . . .

"Now!" the hourglass falls to the floor, the old crone lowers her head to look. "Si!" she hisses. "Arra, arra!" and the two women heave while the third arches against their pushing, and the second great contraction strikes, tearing forth a groan like that which a great tree makes in falling, then another thrilling roar of exultant frenzy, then another, then another.

"Dorita!" I shout. "Arriba, Dorita!"

"Olé!" cries Pandema, her laces untied, her huge breasts swinging. "Lean into it, Dorita, bear down!"

"Arra, nadadora, arra!" howls the old crone.

Dorita screams again.

"Olé! Olé!"

She screams again, we scream with her, she roars and the plaza rocks, and I bend to peer through a maze of arms to the pale span of her thighs, the great purple eye opening, the earth splitting, giving birth to itself, opening, opening. . . .

Suddenly it stopped. Everything stopped. Black, black as obsidian, as sin, as the gate of my father's tomb; something crusty and adamant, a bulging eruption of volcanic sputum, a rock, a stone, arrested in the strained socket, unable to press on, unable to retreat.

"O my God, no, push it back, send it back!"

"Idiot!" The old crone thrusts me aside, muttering, wheeling in a dry rustle of weeds; a silver scissor glints, then, snip! pale-rose blood spurts, the cinder pinkens, pales, becomes a crown of dampened hair, pushing forth, followed swiftly, slickly by the rest, bursting through and slithering into Pandema's hands, a living tropic flower, blossoming in visceral blue and pink, folding out petals of arms and legs and showing a tiny face, a squeeze of eyes, a choking, bawling mouth, a trumpeting child! And we cheer with it: fingers and toes, and the cord looping heavily down; and Dorita lets out a pure, clear cry of utter joy, reaching up through the bloody cradle of her thighs to snatch her prize from the midwife's hands and fiercely press it to her breast.

I watch, trembling, admiring, mortified. The women press closer, the infant chokes, Dorita gazes upon it with adoring eyes. I am drifting backward, reeling in a slow dream away. In a moment I will be rushing forward to kiss her and clutch up the bloody sheet and rush with it into the street, waving my gory banner: "A girl! I am the father of a girl!"

But for this one terrible instant I am alone against the wall with the blades of my shoulders two knives turned against me, and more than the giddy puffing of pride, more than my joy at seeing Dorita at last herself, there is born a dim and mourning rue in me. Clearly Dorita has had her Golden Moment, but, God forgive me, what about mine?

Six months and seven passed, with me at my easel and Dorita at the river bank, shaking out the swaddling. She several times asked if I still loved her, and I replied each time that I cherished her exactly as I always had. In fact, I scarcely saw her now, but gazed upon that screaming lodestone, the infant, wondering that so helpless a creature could have such power to make me at once wild with dreams and sick with dread.

I had long had nightmares of crisis in which I saw my wife fallen in the path of the fearsome Morning Coach; and I hesitated for one long and shameful moment before casting myself under the wheels to save her. Another such nightmare had the two of us in a closed coach fallen into a deep and swift-running stream, the icy water spouting in through the leather windowshade. Dorita could not swim. I had to decide whether to save her, myself, or both of us. How my heart beat as I gasped for air in my sleep, how heavy my burden as I grasped her by the hair and crawled with bursting lungs toward that distant, sunburst surface.

Now the nightmare was the same, but the dilemma was multiplied, for I had to save not one, but two, and sometimes it seemed that in order to get the window open in time, I must make a choice between wife and daughter.

"No!" I sat upright, a cape of ice on my shoulders, my navel puddled with sweat.

"Are you all right?" asked the wide-eyed woman beside me. "You choke so and cry out. It is only the baby crying. Hold the candle while I feed her."

Yes, yes, light a candle and hold it near, while the child choops and gurgles at the breast. Yet I am half blind to this usually entrancing sight, shivering in an unseen draft, struggling to bury the horror.

"Before your nightmare, you were counting in your sleep," murmurs Dorita, and she interrupts her study of the creature at her breast to lift a measuring eye to my response. "What were you counting, Juan?"

"Counting? Was I? Why, sheep, I suppose. Or coins, money for the little one's future . . ."

"Clearly the birth of a child has not rescued you from the tentigo or cured your abarcy after all," observed the marquis, grinning mercilessly over the rim of his jar. "Perhaps you should try for two."

"My loins are filled with illusions," I groaned.

"I beg your pardon, you are dislocating again. It is lurch and spunk that your loins are full of. The illusions are in your noggin. If you fear getting clapt again, get a mistress. All married gentlemen do, it is the custom. Now buy me a drink and go away."

All very well, but where was I going to get a mistress? Even if I were to find her, how could I make the dalliance worth her while, since I was lately an artista and therefore patch poor? Besides, I still had that other itch to be good. Surely I had not tried enough to discover the antidote to abarcy on or about the person of my wife.

These days, she wandered less and had daily visits from Felicio and others of his friends. They sat on the porch and gossiped, eating salads and twining flowers in the baby's hair. I could see them from my tower window, and sometimes they ran down the beach like gamboling children and disappeared around a bend in the river. At dinner she told me aimless tales of her picnics, or we discussed household matters with the redundant attention to detail of two random companions on a cross-country coach, or perhaps in a dungeon.

It was the same in bed. More and more she put the child to bed early and then went there herself, while I dallied, most often contriving to arrive late, usually to find her snoring with great deliberation, whereupon I got carefully in beside her and proceeded to put myself into restive sleep by making restive tallies.

When I did claim my conjugal right, she still complied without protest, but with an increasing air of distraction and quiet distance. As on that night after my last conversation with Mendo, when I most fawningly solicited her, then got between her legs and began diligently to pump. No longer did she thrash and moan at her end of my spindle, while I leaned away in clenched cunctation. Now she only closed her eyes and lay without moving, hands loose and open upon the sheets. Horror of horrors: she was behaving as though she were in the chemise cagoule, but without the chemise!

I saw no choice but to proceed to lurch and squirt, then to roll off and lay there in cold turmoil, to suffer the final indignity: the restive scratching of her fingernail on the sheet, as though she were recording my failure to move her.

From that night on it was thus: I either avoided her and suffered endless nympholeptic fits, or I got between her legs and proceeded to beat her with dull news, while she took it like a newel post.

Where could I go from that cold rack but back to my easel? I set to work on a large equestrian portrait of my Uncle Adan, reasoning that such a heroic work would be well received at court and make that fortune whereby I might be relieved of a part of my paternal consternation. There rode the Knight of the Strong Arm and Open Heart, gleaming in his father's silver-chased armor, tall astride his

Arabian jaca, Sidi Habismilk, holding high his flawless blade, Don Carnal de Amor, hilt uppermost, so as to cast the beneficent and quieting sign of the Cross out across the troubled world. I had almost finished it when word came that my Grandmama Celestina Trotaconventos des Puig-Tenorio was dying and hankered to see me before she went.

"But you can't just fold up your cloak and stream away into the night like a Moor," my wife objected.

"But I owe it to the old one," I told her. And I added cannily: "Besides, there is her property."

She soon agreed to let me go, once I had promised that Felicio could keep her company. In his turn, he asked that he might have his boy friend of the moment, a slender and pretty page named Cristobal.

It seemed quite a handy arrangement. And as I stopped my horse at the top of the river bank and turned to wave farewell, I couldn't help smiling to myself to see the trio on the porch below, the two holding hands off to the side, Dorita in the doorway and well weighted down by the child on her hip.

17

I was three weeks getting to Málaga, whence my grandmama had removed herself in hopes that the hot air of the sirroco might cure her, and certain experiments in pneumology might enlist the aid of the spirits in restoring her once fabulous bosom. But the sea air had done her no good, and the best efforts of her present astrologaster, a Venetian hedgepriest whose claim to occult influence was founded on the fact that he had been born an atretus, that is, with an unperforated fundament, had only exhausted her.

Now she lay on a white bed in a white room under a tent of gauze, while in the corner a servant trod a foot bellows which pumped in a mist of balsam to keep her lungs from clogging. Her head had shrunk to a veritable caput mortem, and her body was scarcely there beneath the blankets. Yet her orange wig still flamed amidst the smothering white, there was a thumbprint of living pink upon each cheek, and as her eyes came open, I saw that deep in each there was still a spark of unquenchable desire.

"Juanito!" she cried, yet it could scarcely be heard above the wheezing of the bellows. "My grandson is here, why didn't somebody tell me? Quick, my lip rouge, and tell that fool to stop blowing evergreen at me. Oh, Yum Yum, your poor old grandmama is going over there to be with dear Angel again. He came to me in my tent last night, and he was holding the baby Jesus by the hand, and he bent down to kiss me and told me it would be all right. Kiss me, Juanito, and tell your old grandmama you love her."

I bent, and my lips brushed dry snow. I straightened, waggling the head of a stunned puppet. And two figures sidled up to either side of me, each feeling for my string. They had met me at the door and pegged themselves to me since, as though we might be some conspiring junta that dared not separate.

"Indeed, he does love you, Celestina, he told me so the moment his coach came in." This from a hefty sloven in her middle years, my grandmama's only niece, named Marta. "And he and I have determined to consult toward your betterment until you are well again."

"By God, the same and better here!" This from none other than Catalinon, our wily old groom, now near onto forty years, but still slyly grinning. "And don't you look like a young virgin this morning, Celestina. Take care you don't lose your cherry!"

She giggled and showed her gums, rustling like corn husks in the sheets. "Oh, you rascal, Catalinon!" Then, sobering herself, she lay back, her eyes shifting behind lids of onionskin. "You will both leave me alone with my grandson now."

The moment they were gone, she reached out from her tent, clamped hold of my arm as though it were the last hawser holding her to the quay of life, and began ferociously to reel it in. *You are coming with me. . . .*

It was all I could do not to strike out; I cringed back, ready to leave my outer covering in her fist, if she had to have it. "Grandmama, it is all right, let go!"

"You must not leave me!" she gasped, falling back with a small clatter of bones. "I can trust no one. Catalinon is desperately in love with me, as you can see. But he has taken to drink these past years, and the liquor diabolifies him and makes him another man. He has sworn to me that he has not touched rum these three months, and all I smell from him is cinnamon. But my nose is weak, and I fear his will is weaker. As for Marta, she is a woman and either fails to think what she says or declines to say what she thinks. Stay, Yum Yum, and keep carefully between them so that I might be free of treachery here at the last."

She clutched my shirt and drew me closer, whispering. "When I am gone, this house and lands will remain, as well as some property in Sevilla. I have changed my will, for your youth has made you neglect me these many years, but I have not left you out. You will receive three hundred ducats and my caravan as well. Oh, Yum Yum, what a sweet child you were, so like my dear Angel before . . ." She shuddered, gasping and reeling in again. "Say you will stay until it is over, Yum Yum, say it!"

I did so.

Between daily ordeal at the bedside, I languished down the road in the ill-kept house where Marta lived with her two dull children and husband. He was a small and fretful man, a fletcher by trade, disappointed in the middle of his career, he claimed, by the decline of the crossbow, and inclined to drink and loose talk.

"You are wasting your time, Marta," he assured her one afternoon, waving his wine bag and sneering. "It is all going into rum for Catalinon and balsam for the old crow. By the time she dies there will be nothing left."

"Mind your manners," she said, sliding a glance my way. "If you cannot be a gentleman in my presence, consider our guest."

"Ah, the young Don Juan." He offered a mock bow, an insinuating wink. "I certainly have no wish to offend you, sir. Only to warn you that your fat accomplice here can be a fair-weather friend." He glared at his wife and made for the door, musing aloud as he went out: "In fact, she is good for only one thing. No doubt that is why she is so good at it."

The large but handsome Marta bent a motherly smile upon me and came closer. "Pay no attention to him, Juan, the drink tends to make men worthless. I cannot imagine why our dear, sweet Celestina clings to that other swillbowl, Catalinon, except that he is a master liar. He got her to change her will in his favor by promising to give up the drink, but you and I know that he is a veritable slough of rum behind that cloud of pepsin and cinnamon. Why, do you know, once last year he knocked her on the head with a jar when he was swizzled, the old lady told me so herself. It doesn't seem right that such a man should deceive such a sweet soul as your grandmama, to say nothing of making off with that nice little house and all that money when the poor dear finally passes on. I have even considered snatching his cinnamon sticks away just as he goes into her room. But how wicked of me. Are you hungry, cousin, and I do hope you are comfortable these chilly nights. . . ."

Catalinon was no less eager that I have sympathy for his side, but his first effort was a sly and grinning attempt to set me back on my heels. "Do you recall, young master, when me and your nurse was sitting in the hallway, and you came to us all frightened by something you had heard in your mother's bedroom?"

"I do," I said, giving him a cold eye. "And that will be enough of that."

His face, already the color of raw mutton from the rum, went a darker red. But his eyes shifted and the grin dwindled. How the years had changed him; to look at him was to wince with apprehensions of drear middle age. His head still rode his broad shoulders like a river stone, but its moss had gone gray in patches; the shoulders were stooped, and he had gone thick in the middle. "You look weary," I said, relenting.

It was a mistake. His eye brightened with a kind of feverish drama, and his voice began to wheedle. "It's true, I'm a brokebone lacklinen now, young master. Were your Uncle Adan to see me, he would not recognize his old groom. But then, he never knew my life's tragic history."

And with that glooming introduction and a canny sidelong glance to measure for pity, he proceeded through the next days to tell me his miserable story. As a child in Malta, he had revered sundials and had dreamed of learning their manufacture, hoping someday to become a professor of sciatherics. But, alas, he had been born into abject poverty, his mother being a scullery maid, his father a passing gypsy, and there had been no money for bread, much less for his schooling. And so he had been obliged instead to take up the life of a strolling musician and occasional pickharness, the which had been so unbearably hard and lonely, he claimed, as to drive him early into the clutches of demon rum.

He had enjoyed a few good years as groom to Don Diego, he said, and an even better time as foreman on my Uncle Adan's land, but a certain revulsion for long hours together with his nemesis, strong drink, had lost him that employment, and his luck had only changed for the better when he had found work in the stables and bed of my grandmama.

He had been married once, he confessed, but his wife had left him for another, and he had fed and clothed his two daughters for twenty years off and on, working as a hostler and playing the gittern in peacetime, and robbing battlefields in wartime, until he was finally blown up whilst attempting to pry a gold-chased breastplate from a cadaver stuck beneath a cannon; and during the two years that he lay in the Benedictine hostel, waiting for his bones to knit, neither daughter had once come to visit him.

"See how I have suffered for love!" he cried, showing me one hand lacking in two fingers, the other missing a thumb. "See what cruel misfortune has left me to stand upon!" he croaked, rolling down patched hose to show me a shin like a toothpick. And now he leaned through his own rumish vapors and pressed his flaming face close to mine. "Then I found your sweet old grandmama, and she took me in. Why, even when I filched a cithern from a barber shop and they put me in the calabozo, she stood by me. It is not for her money that I cleave to her, no matter what that blowze, Marta, says. It is for love that I love her!"

And for emphasis, he hefted his favorite brass sundial in one hand and glared at me. "And nobody will be permitted to convince her otherwise, nobody!"

Meanwhile, I stood my daily vigil at the bedside, mostly propped in a chair against the wall and often dozing there. Now and then the frail wheedle of her voice would reach out and pull me from my stupor.

"Yum Yum, are you there?"

"Yes, grandmama."

"What is your age now?"

"I am nearly twenty-five."

"Your dear father died when he was twenty-five. Have you not feared that it might be the same for you?"

"Yes, I have, grandmama. I tell myself that it is superstition, but the premonition sticks."

"Do not think too much upon it. It may be, and then again, it may not. But it is quite true that we never know what the morrow will bring, and it is always possible that it will be death. Your marriage, Yum Yum, does it flourish or does it stifle you?"

"I fear it is the latter, grandmama."

"I am sorry for you, and for the child. I wish I might have seen her. I daresay you have tried trothbreach and found it wanting. Variety is the spice of life, but it can also burn. We are imperfect creatures, in that we have this mad desire for diversion on the one hand, perfection on the other. I wish that I could give you some word of guidance that would save you your pain, but I know of no such word. Only that youth is a bubble and stoop-gallant old age a host of grievance, and therefore that we must taste all of life that we can, while we can."

Yet another time I came suddenly out of my drowse and looked over to find her cackling feverishly. "Oh, I fooled them, didn't I? Five years they gave me, and I have taken fifteen!" Fairly foaming with glee, she let go a rattling cough, and her ceramic teeth fell onto the sheets. She fumbled them back in. "They wanted to cut me, but I would not let them. Beware of the surgeons, for they plow but do not sow. I taught your father that, but when he fell ill, your foolish mother brought a surgeon to the bedside. Had I been able to get my wizard to him in time, he surely would have been saved."

"But, grandmama," I said. "It was because he talked the surgeon into going away that he died. Now you say that you taught him to fear the knife. Grandmama, it could be that it was the fear of death that killed him!"

But even as I was protesting, her claws were letting go the sheets, and she slipped into a deep if convenient torpor. And I was left to remember the contentions of guilt and fear that went back. So far back.

That night, or the next, as I sat on my bed at the back of Marta's house, struggling to sort my confusions, my hostess came slippering in with a tray of cakes. Usually she left the tray, but this time she let down her weight on the bed, her broad lips freshly painted and unsmiling. Her husband was to be away for the night, she said. Her bed was empty and cold. Was mine?

I made a face, but I had been a month from home. She leaned against me, digging amongst the quilts that covered my legs.

215

"I have resisted telling you because it is too horrible to believe and quite beggers my poor powers of description," she said, groping between my thighs and finding me stiff. "It happened three months ago, shortly after your grandmama had changed her will in favor of Catalinon, when the Venetian first installed the bellows beside her bed, for she was having difficulty breathing."

Not bored by her tale, but embarrassed by her manipulations, I made an attempt to topple her and get aboard. But she was sturdy and shook her head. "No, we mustn't, we are cousins," and went on doing what she did. "One night Catalinon crept into her room and cut the hoses, shutting off the flow of life-giving vapors. Then he went down to the bodega to wait for the dear old lady to die. I know, because it was I who found her gasping and put the tubes back together so that she might get back her breath. He is a Maltese, you know, and exiled from Spain as well, for coining in a monastery. The only decent thing to do is knock him on the head and take him to Valencia, and there embark him for the Barbary Shore, later warning the king's customs agents should he try to return. Once your dear grandmama knew that he had abandoned her, she would be bound to recognize my devotion and yours, and would surely revise her will. But it would not be for money or lands that we would do our duty, but for the triumph of love over lust, truth over lies, right over wrong, good over evil. My goodness, wasn't that a rusty old load!"

By such shocks and shuckings I passed a most anguished fortnight, made dull and weak by dread, pushed and pulled by moral confusions and niggling avarice. In the end, I was ready to try anything, just so long as it might resolve the confusion and get me out of the philosophical diamerdes. I got a cudgel and a sack and went to my grandmama's house, determined to find out from the Venetian doctor if the old lady's hoses had been cut, and if there was proof of it, to knock Catalinon on the head, put him in the sack, and ship him to Barbary.

I found him waiting before her door, so perpotated that he could scarcely keep his feet and fairly bleeding from the eyes. He saw my weapon and leaned closer, enveloping me in his tremendous breath.

"Forget any plan to hurt me," he said. "I am what she needs, and if you do not believe me, shut your mouth and come in, for her time has come and she has sent for me." Stuffing a handful of cinnamon sticks into his mouth, he wrenched himself upright and went unsteadily into her room.

I paced, juggling hot coals in my mind, struggling to sort my rights from the world's wrongs. Finally I could stand it no longer. I pushed through the door and pulled up short, to crusade in that region no more.

A priest was praying in a corner, while the Venetian fingered his purple robes and gazed out the window. And there beside the bed, all stitching and mended bone, Catalinon stood like a burning martyr, his chin up, his eyes exalted, his hose down about his ankles. The bellows creaked and the steam sighed, and under the little tent of gauze, my grandmama lay with a faint smile upon her bloodless lips and one scrawny arm thrusting from the tent, its hand gripping the leathered coddlings and rubescent yard of her lover. And when she saw me, her smile became fleetingly a grin, she tugged upon her prize, and cried out in frail but fervent glee, "Take heed, Yum Yum. It is later than you think!"

As it happened, she did not die that afternoon, but was in a swoon for five days more and never did come all the way back again. Several times she said my father's name in a voice less loud than the bellows' breathing. I was alone with her on the evening of the fifth day, when she suddenly began to shudder, and I scrambled to my feet to see the last moisture leaving her flesh as tears.

"She is dead," came faintly from the puncture of her mouth. "Poor, dear Celestina is dead."

I rushed into the corridor and told the priest, then I went looking for Catalinon.

As we burst back into the room, the priest was bending over the bed. "Discover to her, O my God, the nothingness of this world, the greatness of Heaven, the shortness of time and the length of eternity . . ."

But we were too late. The last color had fled her cheek. There was nothing there, only her semblance in pale clay.

18

Catalinon being concerned to convert his inheritance into liquid form as rapidly as possible, it was left to me to see that my grandmama's body reached its appointed resting place in the Camposanto de Los Illustrios & Etc., outside Sevilla. We set sail from Valencia, bound for Cádiz aboard the Sicilian barque *La Ventura Folia*, my grandmama in a jar of aqua vitae in the hold, myself most often up on deck and biting at the wind.

The waves rolled implacably on before our plunging bow; the sun rose behind, blazed above our leaning masts, then slipped red into the sea: once, twice, three days, four; while the waves thumped, the timbers shuddered, the footings creaked, and the rigging rattled and sang, all sounds coming bit by bit into subtle tune, all vibrations becoming day by day the same pervasive tremble, so that finally every object and creature aboard seemed locked in rhythmic conjunction with another: the marlin spikes with the pinrail, the running lines with the blocks, the cook with the pork roast, the boatswain with the cabin boy.

The first day out I had noticed a most arresting deck cargo: two nuns, of some liberal order of Ursulines, and unattended, save for the captain, an elderly Neapolitan, whose principal effort toward their protection was to keep his crew of wild Sicilians forward of the poop, whence they watched, all oiled locks and blue lust, but dared come no farther for fear of the captain's ire and the first mate's harquebus. That left me as the only man unencumbered by either duty or fear of the lash, and on the fifth evening, the sirens of the eternal shiver hunted me down and found me out.

My first choice was by elimination: The mate was chatting to the one sister at the rail following the captain's retirement, and I drank wine from a bag and dimly attended their sprightly threesome. Of a sudden, the mate made off into the darkness with his choice, and I found myself provoked into a thin fever of competitive ambition. Allowing a temporary infiltration of the vibration, I conjured the resultant itch into a burst of attentiveness that was barely complimentary, but was enough to turn the head of the other nun and eventually to coax her into the shadows at the back of the poop. My grimaces and gestures soon ran short of variety, and she was a Portugee and spoke only that mewing tongue, so that in the end there was nothing to do but kiss her, the which she received without protest, but neither with much enthusiasm. Finally, with much urging, I got her into the captain's chair and prepared to cuckold her husband, Christ.

But it did not go well. Perhaps it was her pale and absent compliance, perhaps the lack of sufficient provocation, for I would have liked to hear her call out for the pope or otherwise offer titillation. Another trouble lay with the captain's lounging chair, adequate for one, impossible for two. I fumbled myself down beside her, kissing her blue lips and ferreting amongst the black folds of her habit, faintly thrilled by the starchy crackle of her hood as it bent beneath our twisting heads, but unable to fit myself between her thighs by virtue of the chair's unyielding arms. There was nothing for it in the end but to pull her toward me, so that she lay prone, and proceed to delve with my knees hanging in air and my feet treadmilling upon the dewy boards of the deck.

Was I in, had I invaded the sanctum, was I robbing the Church of a maidenhead? I could not tell. She was so mute, so dry and odorless; too bony and too soft, too much awake, too little awakened.

A nun, a nun, your first nun! I spurred myself, but still the reins of my reluctance held, and the chair creaked and wailed, reminding me of the catasta, and her teeth were too long, fencing off my flaccid tongue. What is more, the chair was moving, just as the roof thatch had done that other time, giving a little hop each time that I thrust my limp unlove into her clammy unwelcome, inching us closer and closer to what I now perceived to be a gap in the railing beneath the longboat. And as I cunctated and she perfuncturated and the chair perambulated, I glimpsed out of the corner of my eye, our luminescent wake fanning in ghostly rabble off into the black of the night, and found myself indulging in murder of the moment, not with the old vision of the coach and its chuckling rider, but of a motley host of sea monsters waiting below in the foam, some chuckling, some praying, some cursing, all waiting eagerly for me to finish at crackhalter pace and skid myself and my dim victim over the gunwale and into the waiting jaws of the sharks of righteous wrath and ruinous retribution.

Fortunately, at just about this time, my companion abandoned all hope for a conventional finish, unsheathed herself from me, and went for my yard with her mouth. Having but little experience with buccination, I could not imagine how she could get that gorged cucumber into her mouth together with all those teeth. Fretting about this and gazing unhappily up at the reeling stars, I finally spent, blandly disgorging a few grudging gobbets, which she had the delicacy to swallow without comment.

We then bade one another a nervous and melancholy good night. She murmured something in the Portugee tongue; was it her curse or her blessing? I didn't care. I went back to my cabin and spent the next hour mourning my double sin of spousebreach and nunswive. However, my senses having been so utterly indifferent to the event, I could not much interest my soul, and soon slipped off to sleep.

But morning brought renewed unease and much to think about, and so I returned to my coil of rope and clenched myself about melancholy puzzlement and stern abjuration. My wife was in Madrid, was she not, waiting for a good man to return to her. My infant daughter waited as well, for a great man to come and drive the dragons of uncertainty from her future. Five days at sea had convinced me that their salvation depended upon my ability to resist the idiorhythmic tremble of running lines, the fretful twitch of the belaying pin in its wicket. Locking myself about this conviction, I hugged myself against the wind and invited the narcoleptic impulse to sidle up, blow in my ear, and bid me sleep: in inaction lay the only innocence.

Nonetheless, I dreamed of nuns, pale and yielding, ribald and wild, and while the thrumming ropes searched me out in my dreams and the sun warmed my loins, an eminently reasonable voice argued that my mistake had been to confess to Dorita. If I truly loved her and the child, I would seek reasonable release by learning to commit trothbreach without guilt; and if it had to be, I should take a mistress, as the Marquis Mendo had prescribed. Anything but consider that ominous possibility increasingly pressing itself upon me, this terrible urge to step out upon the sea and just keep running.

Then I found myself awake and staring into the face of the other nun. She sat on a small barrel opposite my nest of rope, her stance at once careless and tense, her gaze both bold and hungering. Her knees were apart beneath her skirts, her elbows propped upon them. Wooden beads dangled from her hand and trailed a large carved crucifix along the deck. Her eyes were a most unusual deep-night blue, almost violet, and regarded me steadily from a face that was not unpretty, yet far from saccharine: virulent and fevered, rough-skinned, pocked, and bristled. The hair that showed beneath her starched blinders was blood-russet, strong in its color, thick at its roots; and her lips were heavy and muscular, bitten brown in places, gleaming with some winy lip rouge. She smiled, and behind her heavy teeth, her tongue curled, fat and purple against deep red gums. "Are you a hermit, then?" Her voice was equally sanguine, blood-thick, husky.

"After a fashion."

She laughed, and the sound had the fuming richness of decaying fruit, of tropic fermentation. "An unlikely hermit."

I indicated her careless posture, the neglected rosary, the lip rouge. "An unlikely nun."

Her stare was no less bright and bold, but there was a trace of solemnity to her reply. "Know me better before you judge, for I am as much God's servant as any other nun." And now she leaned forward until her face was only inches from mine, pairing us by her proximity. "As for your own pose as an angry anchorite, Sister Piacula tells me that you are slow."

I felt my cheeks darken and prepared to spit out some rebuff. But it came to me that there was neither distaste nor derision in her gaze, but only fascination. She swept a glance across the empty poop, then bent so close that the starched panels of her bonnet enclosed us both, and I could feel the furnace heat of her breath upon my lips.

"Do not understand me too quickly," she whispered. "I did not say that I was the common nun, nor even a normal woman. Cunctation suits my needs. Do you understand? Now come, the captain is below decks, and Piacula has promised to vacate our cabin until the sun drops below the yardarm. Hurry, I am on fire, and you are the same. Are we not God's creatures, as deserving of our pleasure as others of more common cut? Here," she said, swinging her rattling beads toward me. "Hold onto the Cross, if you must, and I will tow you to my bed."

My God, the fevers, the boilings, the boanthropic butt and gallop, ardor and ordure of our tumble, our toil, our tournament. At last, a venality mad enough to match my own, have at you!

At one point there came a pause. Propped back beneath me, her prickly thighs making a yoke for my shoulders, she asked me, "What is it you are trying to kill in there?"

Despite the hint of mockery, she knew the answer to her question, and she delighted in it, created it, and craved it; the hankering overflowed her, popped forth in postules on her cheeks, thrust up in feverish lumps and suppurated follicles upon her neck, sprouted stiff and black in the cleft of her upper lip, on her chin, from the curdled coronas of her nipples, from all around the mounded slopes of that fuming caldron between her legs.

Roaring, I drove her up against the end of the bunk until her head banged the wall and she groaned, her mouth aslant and drooling.

What was I trying to kill in there, indeed; and what was it that she wanted me to kill? What did she seek but the same giddy attenuation as I? What did she desire but to be all desire, kneading my raging fevers and scratching my deathless itch with her own.

It was love at first swive, no doubt about it. As romantic convention would have it, we were meant for one another: a pair of yearning stumblefeet seeking to assuage our uncertainties by massaging one another's aching parts in delicious concordance and on the presumption that if we went at hard enough and long enough, we might at some point exchange pains and, for that moment, each be freed of self.

Finally my brain cracked and I proceeded to spend, howling and humping, poleaxed and rigid above her, then crashing into the cheesy briarpatch of her thighs; like a rope dancer tumbling to the neck-cracking sawdust, not because his desire to dance is spent; only because the stretched cord can no longer hold against his strenuous flirtations with earth's relentless lease on floating bodies.

Thus it went for two swift weeks, for the *Ventura Folia* had the wind against her. Each afternoon in that humid little cubby at the front of the poop, and some days in the morning, we raged and burned together. After an engagement of two or three hours, we would lave ourselves in salt water, leaving the cabin still ripe with our aftermath, and go to find a place alone together behind a hatch or heap of barrels, there to touch hands and muster words with which to garnish the alliance of our lunacies.

Her name was Juanita. Her mother had been the daughter of a municipal official in Valencia, her father a captain in the episcopal guard. Encouraged by her mother, who had harbored deep regrets regarding her marriage and the captain's behavior in bed, she had wanted to be a nun since her fifth year. At first given a conventional education at the hands of the Carmelites, she had rebelled in her thirteenth year, at once resentful of their restrictions and outraged to learn that the mother superior had a taste for thirteen-year-old boys. After a few months of wandering, during which she received the rudiments of worldly knowledge and surrendered her maidenhead, she found a home with the Ursulines, who trained her as a nurse, then put her to work in one of their madhouses.

There, for four years of her young womanhood, she had gathered memories disturbing enough to turn any mind. She told me of the patients: the incontinent crone blaming her pollutions on the Christ of her crucifix: "Naughty boy, you've wet yourself and spoiled the floor again." The once famous and respected surgeon who had eventrated one belly too many and now plucked at imaginary buttons on his own, querulously dunning himself: "Come now, open your purse, sir, you have not paid your bill." The Aegean giant, once headsman for Pietro Medici, who had lost his nerve on the day that a condemned and beautiful young cutpurse had turned his head upon the block and smiled, saying, "God blesses the man who loves his work." After eleven swings of the axe had failed to sever that smile, the headsman had been led away screaming, and ever since had huddled his six cubits and fourteen-stone weight beneath the nearest bench, whimpering that he was only two palms high and afraid the cat might get him. Also: the once beautiful and popular courtesan, now crazed by the privy pox, writing letters to her lover, the Man in the Moon; and beseeching the Virgin: "Give me all the running sores that I deserve, only spare me above the collar."

"Tell me no more," I pleaded. "My God, what cruel work for a young girl."

Her color had deepened with the telling; now she turned her dark-blue gaze to me. "Yet no crueler than life. And it stirred me strangely. Just as it has stirred you."

I stared, my brain clenched against the admission, my heart racing in alarm, and as a consequence, there was nowhere for the stoked and pounding blood to go but into that tumor between my legs, rising and swelling, demanding the surcease of its mindless exercise; and I clutched at her hand, and we scuttled across the deck and into the little cabin, brought together by knowledge and fleeing from it, beating one another into sweet insensibility.

When she had suggested to the Ursuline Sisters that if she did not get out of the locoria she might become a permanent resident, they had given her new work which they promised would take her more often out-of-doors and into touch with normal creatures; they made her assistant to one of their midwives.

Still a girl, she had witnessed no less than seven hundred and fifty partitions in two years. Seven hundred and fifty times she had listened to the sawing groans of quake and breech, had watched the lurid incision swell and spread, had thrilled to the priapic reversal, the juggernaut exit of the thrusting head, the sluggish spilling of gray caul, the screeching miracle come forth upon a tide of blood.

Always the groans and tearing tissues, but not always the miracle. She was an aspiring watercolorist and had made drawings and showed them to me: here was a polliwog born lucky, pink and wriggling on a rag between its mother's bloody thighs; here one not so lucky, caught in the breech with frog legs kicking, but in the next picture: the troglodyte head pinched in the silver grip of the forceps and pulled forth and saved to dribble ten years onto a bib; and here yet another, as perfect as the first, as pink and sweetly formed, yet flat, motionless, like some tiny naked god, a nascent Odysseus, having swum a long and terrible way, washed up and collapsed upon the shore.

"It is dead," I whispered.

Her deep-blue eyes looked at me. "You are the first to know without being told."

And yet again I felt the sickly longing coiling about my heart, and her hand crawled on my thigh, and my yard thickened and quivered, and we clutched at one another and fell into the bed like twin cadavers into a single grave.

In the last months of her service as doorman to those thousand bloody portals, she had been courted by and had finally sought relief in the company of two young Franciscans, one watching while the other availed himself, sometimes all three coupling in assorted arrangement. And yet too seldom had she found escape from her memories, relief from her daily lesson. Finally, a sympathetic priest had recommended to her mother superior that she be sent away, and thus she was bound now for the Moroccos, to help convert and nurse the great number of lepers amongst the heathen.

"Perhaps it is out of purgatory and into hell for me," she murmured. "But even this respite is welcome, for my monks were better fitted to one another, the one being a pedipulator, the other a pedosculator."

"Toes?" I gasped.

She smiled. "You should try it sometime." And she leaned her blinders to shield us both and pressed her gorged lips to mine, heating me with the flaming shield of her face, the drilling blue of her gaze.

"Oh swive me!" she cried, and I beat her frozen flesh with my own.

While the dead homunculus slept on its piece of foolscap in the corner, and the unresting sea ebbed and flowed, and the gulls wheeled and flung themselves sideways, screaming.

One afternoon, while she slept below, I found myself on deck and alone with my fever and enough time to know how deep into my bones it had reached. Committing trothbreach was not so simple; having done it once, twice, four times, ten, I only wanted to do it again. But there was more to it than that. This was different. When Dorita had her fits, I only felt estranged, for she seemed to enjoy success all on her own. This nun and I shared a common duende and raged with the same never quite satisfied furia. The objective of our wrestling was not so much the end of desire as its refinement and attenuation; not to get out of the fever of abarcy, but to stay in it and at the eye of the storm.

There was a deep recognition I had not known before, and it shook me to the root and made me long to give it some kind of grace. Sometime in the tourbillon, twice, perhaps three times, I had choked out the words, and now I shuddered, remembering: "I love you!"

Yet I trembled faster, knowing that, like the navigator who sights the coastline and deceives himself that he is within reach of the passage, I longed to shout them again and again, as though mere enthusiasm might put wind in my sails and lead me to the prize. "I love you! Land ho! I love you!"

It happened that even as I was thus musing at the rail of the poop, a gaunt and red-eyed Morisco stood at the rail of the forecastle forward. This same sailor had become cupshot a week before and had attempted to ride one of the ship's cannons the length of the main deck during a storm, only to be knocked on the head by the boatswain, put in irons, and flung in the rope locker. Apparently he had just this day been released, for I had seen him that morning, pacing the main deck and gesticulating toward the empty horizon, insisting that he saw his homeland. In fact, we had long since passed through the Pillars of Hercules and were well out of sight of the shore, on a wide tack for Cádiz. But even now, this mournful creature leaned far out over his rail, pointing toward the blank sea and crying out that he had sighted the orange groves of Ceuta and wanted to be home.

I heard cursing beside me and turned to find our captain just opening his mouth to call for the boatswain, then subsiding with a gesture of despair. Following his gaze, I was in time to see the madman clamber over the railing, pause on the scupper ledge to adjust his neck scarf, and with a determined and confident air, step off the gunwale, tread twice upon the air, and, still in an erect and arrogant position, strike the water and sink like a stone.

"Calenture," sighed the captain. "The green sickness, a distemper which now and then strikes sailors long at sea, in which they mistake the water for green fields and attempt to run out and play. I have had it myself a time or two, but always just as we reach Cádiz and my wife heaves into view, and with the knowledge that she would only have me fished out. Marriage has its uses. As for that fellow, we have a following wind and all sails on, and besides, no boat could reach him now, he is with Neptune."

That night she and I stood at that same place at the rail. The starry black bowl wheeled overhead, and still the ship and all its fibers hummed and buzzed with the siren song.

"I am married," I told her.

"I had guessed as much," she murmured. "And children?"

"A daughter." Suddenly the breeze was cool; the night, the ship, its rigging and timbers abruptly lost their vibrancy. I turned, clutching for her heat. "Come ashore with me at Cádiz. You could find a living in Madrid, we could see each other, and you would be saved from the lepers."

Her hand was burning in mine, almost too hot to touch. And yet she shook her head, her blinders rattling softly in the dark. "I have taken vows, too, you know."

The stars wheeled, the rigging hummed again, and it seemed impossible that the heat of our hands could not make a lasting weld. "Have you heard of the Golden Moment?" I asked.

"Yes."

"Do you believe in it?"

She nodded and turned her face to me, and I marveled that the tears did not rise in a cloud of steam as they ran down her ravaged cheeks. "Is that what is wrong with us?" she cried softly. "Is that what brings us together and keeps us apart?"

I stared, and had no answer but to take her hand and tow her, the two of us weeping like babies, back to our sweltering stall and bucking catasta.

Two days later, we sailed into the Bay of Cádiz, and while the waiting longboat bumped against our hull, I bent above her cot to kiss her. "Sister Juanita," I whispered.

But she only squeezed my hand, staring upward, all the dislocated minds and dying babies in her deep-blue eyes. "You are married," she said. "Go back to your wife and child," and she turned her face to the wall.

I had brought with me the little golden crucifix that was a key, and held it in my hand as they put my grandmama's coffin in with that of my father. For an hour after the funeral party had left, I stood staring at that dark hole, its iron gate, and TENORIO chiseled into the stone. I risked to thought the old longing to go closer and cry out, "Dear papa, help me!" I even went close enough to throw the bolt on the gate. But, as always, the dread was more than equal to the yearning, and I could not go in.

And so I went out of the Camposanto de Los Illustrios & Etc. and around behind to the other little gate at the base of its wall. This I opened with the gold key, then wrapped myself in my cloak and sat down to wait, as I had promised my grandmama I would do. I was there all that night and all the next say. It was August and soon to be my birthday. My father had died in the same year of life which I was about to enter. If my lifelong apprehension did not prove true and I did not die this year, would we then pass one another at time's crossroads, each bound for his corner of eternity. And would I then be free?

Nobody came. I locked the little gate again, put the key around my neck, and went home.

19

WHO WAS this familiar stranger, my wife? Who this small, great force, my child? I struggled, but it was all up for me; I had the green sickness.

My portrait of my Uncle Adan had been declined by the king's critic with the comment that it was "neither novel nor morally ingenious enough to warrant purchase." Raging at my easel, I found myself painting a nun in a circle of flame, dead babies at her feet, a ladder leading upward to a golden glow with its heart outside the picture.

"Novel enough, but still lacking in moral ingenuity," I decided.

"Who is it?" Dorita wanted to know.

"No one we know," I said, and she knew that I lied.

I drank, she drank. On the first night that I was home, we finished two bottles of wine and went to bed. There, I got between her legs and prepared to cunctate drunkenly, but there was a sudden surge of activity beneath me, and before I knew it, I was on my back and she was astride me, posting like a cavalry officer, banging her knees at my ribs and shouting with an authority entirely unfamiliar to me, "Arre, arre! Gidyap!"

I quickly rolled her back into the proper position, but the picture of her haughty and dominating glare was not easily forgotten. Where had she learned these new tricks? I could guess, but I didn't want to think of it.

That night and the next, and the next, I walked the rim of the city wall above the river, all the way down and around the bend, back home more slowly, more reluctantly each time.

My birthday came and went, and I did not die. And yet I felt no elation, but only disappointment and deepened loneliness. Robbed of its event, the dread yet abided, and it seemed to my sweating mind that I now joined the living dead, and that my life was all the more empty, dull, and incomplete.

Two days with a rotted grinder, and I suddenly took Dorita to bed and began furiously to drill her, then as suddenly pulled free of her cold flesh and rolled away, aware that it had been my intention to give her my toothache. And more.

Returning from my journey a week before, I had looked down to discover her two friends still with her, but one on each side of her, and Felicio with the child in his arms. Now she was more and more with them, and finally she was out all night, leaving the child with me. Until morning, I walked up and down the room, holding the fretful creature to my chest with its chin on my shoulder, as Dorita had taught me to do, rhythmically patting the small back with my hand. And as I was thus cradling and patting, whilst gazing out the door at the tempting path of moonlight leading away across the river, I was brought back from my vagabond musings with a wrench that nearly twisted my heart from its socket. Even as I patted the child, a tiny hand was diligently thumping me in return.

Finally, through the mists of dawn, I saw her coming, hand in hand with the pretty Cristobal. At the bend he kissed her cheek and left her.

They had only been walking and talking through the night, she said, and dancing under the moon; if I doubted her, I should ask Felicio, for he had been there as well. I began to break crockery and shout. She would not argue back, but only wept and shook her wrists before her. I scattered my paints and took up my sword and stood trembling before the portrait of the Silver Knight. "Is he a better lover than I?" I demanded.

"Who?"

"Whomever."

"It is not fair of you to ask."

"It is less fair of you to keep the answer."

"Very well then, yes."

I roared, slashing, first down the length of the figure, then across. I whirled, flinging tears, and put the point of my sword at her throat.

"What do you have against me?" she wept.

I could not say it. *Only that I do not love you.* Instead: "Why, oh, why, have you never done me any wrong!"

She stared through the steadily rolling tears. "O God," she moaned, "you are rendering me inertless. If you are going to go——" She turned and flung herself into the bedroom— "then go!"

Still, I would not. That night as she lay asleep, she moaned softly, her nail scratched and scrabbled at the sheet. I went to get the ink pot and dipped her finger in, then slipped a sheet of foolscap beneath the jittering nail. And slowly, scrawlingly, it wrote:

CRISTOBAL, FELICIO, COME TO BED!

I finally fell into sleep as a man falls down a well, and dreamed that my wife reached out to me, and that I took her hand as gently as I could, and bent to kiss it, determined to deny all hateful feelings, yet grinding my teeth all the while; and saw too late that I had suddenly bit off one of her fingers. There it lay in her palm, kinking and wriggling, pale and helpless, yes, like a tiny homunculus, a cruelly severed infant.

Still I struggled. For a week I stuck to my easel, commanding myself to stay away from the window and its view of the houseboat and beach. Then they came to get me, all three, whooping and banging on my door. They had seen a pair of doves in a small cave in the cliff below my tower.

"Doves for peace, Juan!" Felicio shouted gleefully. "Squab for lunch! We decided that only one with your tremendous courage could help us."

Grimly I accepted the challenge, taking a coil of rope down with me and tying one end to a tree at the edge of the precipice. Dorita watched with the child on her hip and her lower lip in the grip of her teeth. And yet when I tossed the rope down the face of the cliff and prepared to let myself over its rim, and Felicio cried mockingly, "My goodness, aren't you afraid?" she only made a wry face and said, "Nonsense, he used to ride his rocking horse downstairs as a child, he loves it," and turned away.

231

"I suppose so," Felicio said. "Since he is such a chasmophile, I mean, being so in love with nooks and crannies."

But I was already out of sight, dangling four paces down from the top, clutching the rope with one hand and swinging in under the overhang to the crumbling mouth of the cave. Out of sight, but not out of earshot. I could hear them sniggering above. The dark cleft was deep in droppings, and in a nest of twigs, two small squabs silently held their mouths open. Holding on to the rope with one hand, I swung in, snatched up the birds, and swung out again, then climbed back up to find them huddled together and grinning.

I held my feathered prize out to Dorita, my face feeling like a board. Cristobal gazed solemnly, Felicio leered, and I felt the lurk and niggle of conspiracy.

"Oh, the poor little things!" said my wife. "We cannot take them away from their mother," and there was half of maternal sincerity in it, but half of something less pleasant as well. Her blue eyes were flat, her cheeks flushed. "You must take them back."

"Yes, Juan," Felicio put in, his face pinched to hold back the glee. "Unless wisdom came to you down there at rope's end, and you have finally learned the folly of machismo."

Spitting into the dust at his feet, I took the birds in hand and turned my back on them, and climbed back down. Once again out of sight below, I heard them whispering, then Felicio's hilarious whoop, Cristobal's quieter chuckle, Dorita's muted shushing, then her coughing laughter. Was there a sob in it as well?

I swung in and deposited the birds, then swung back to dangle. Out from my perch was the vast blue, indifferent sky. Below were jagged rocks littered with broken trash. Just down the beach, a dozen washermaids laughed and scrubbed, their brown breasts swinging, and beyond was the broad green road of the river.

For one long moment more I dangled by one hand, considering the third and final alternative. Then the giddy laughter of the washermaids reached me, and I made up my mind and began swiftly to lower myself the rest of the way down the rope.

And as I reached the bottom and scrambled across the rocks and through the screeching maids, I heard Felicio's whooping shout from high above: "You are not running to, Juan, you are running away!"

232

To which I replied, "It is not now, nor has it ever been a crime to live before you die!"

And with nary another glance backward, I fled down the river and away.

INTERLUDE

THE COURTIER closed the first volume and let his hand rest a moment on its title. "Dreams, indeed. Ah, the fevers of youth. I had half forgotten."

"And yet your smile is fond," observed the monk from his bench.

"Time gilds the memory, I suppose." He lifted the next volume to the top. "Of course, I was never such a bunglebundle as this fellow. I hope he sharpens up in the second book. But tell me, what do you think of the various portraits he paints here. Are they true to life?"

The monk's glance was cautious. "You tell me."

The courtier chuckled. "Still parrying, eh? Well, you have good reason to be wary. As I told you, the king is uncommonly curious about this play of yours. He does not usually maintain interest in anything for so long." He indicated the stage, where the actor who played the Rake was again seducing a virgin fishermaid. "But this is the third night running that he has come here, and still he has not had enough." He took a pinch from a jeweled snuff box and eyed the monk as he snorted. "As for these memoirs, I don't think you want His Majesty to read about a certain intimate liaison you maintained with the rector at Osuna, who is the son of one of the king's own knights."

The monk's nose drooped and his heavy lids lowered to shield his eyes. "I think we would all rather His Majesty never saw these books."

He exchanged a sorrowful glance with the little nun, who looked quickly down at her embroidery.

"In fact," the monk said, showing the courtier a dry smile, "neither would you care, I think, to have His Majesty read about a certain episode concerning a trusted member of his court and a deception involving an apparently dead nun."

The courtier's tonsured mustaches twitched. He gave a bow of his plumes. "It would seem that we have common cause here. However, there is still His Majesty's curiosity and his suspicion that the hero of your play might be alive somewhere."

He cut himself short at the unmistakable tattle of high-heeled clogs coming around the side of the stage. There was the suggestion of a very powerful perfume, and suddenly there appeared an elaborate construction of velvets, jewels, and laces, made roughly in the shape of a man, and with a living head atop it. The Third Philip's gingery mustaches bristled and his plump mouth made a simpering smile as he came closer, looking about him at the stage machinery, and taking very small steps so as to preserve a noble bearing. "So this is fancy's behind. How fascinating."

With a warning glance at the monk, the courtier made a practiced bow. "What a pleasant surprise, Your Majesty. So you have come to see for yourself."

"Yes, yes, for myself." The heavy jaw swiveled about atop the pleated ruff, and the large blue eyes gleamed with feverish intensity, yet seemed unable to light anywhere for long. They found the little nun, and the king halted suddenly, causing various attendants and sycophants to stumble into one another behind him.

"What pretty work you do, my dear," he said in his fluting voice, and with some effort managed to bend over far enough to study the nun's bosom. "And very devout too, hmmm?"

The little nun's large brown eyes lifted for one wide, bleak glance. The monk went noisily down onto his knees, and the king's gaze went thither.

"Ah," he said. "And this is the famous Tirso who writes plays? Please get up, I cannot see you."

The monk got to his feet. "Your Majesty."

"Also known as Fray Gabriel Tellez, eh?" A genial titter rattled the royal curls. "Never mind, despite what the Junta de Reformacion may say about you, I happen to be rather fond of your plays. Unlike certain more parochial natures."

236

He turned a contemptuous glance behind him to his bishop, and that individual found it convenient to look elsewhere. The king turned back to the monk and showed his large teeth. "Your plays have an amusing earthiness, if you know what I mean." Now he gave a lewd chuckle, now he looked pious. "But always with an uplifting conclusion, of course."

The monk's eyes seemed about to burst from their sockets, but his bow was humble. "I do my best to remain loyal to my deeper values, Your Majesty, while at the same time endeavoring to satisfy the public."

"Ah yes, it is the same with statesmanship," sighed the monarch. He looked petulant and made a snuffling sound through his nose. "But we are not here to complain." He gave a shake of his slashed sleeves and tilted the Hapsburg jaw. "We are here just now to learn the true name of the hero of your play, as I hope the count has informed you. We would ask this question of you: have I known the person who was the model for your Don Juan, and if so . . ."

Then a roaming blue eye fastened upon the three books at the edge of the stage. "But what is this?"

"Theater records," quickly said the monk.

"A novel," said the courtier. "A very boring one, I am afraid. . . ."

But it was too late. The king leaned and read the title of the topmost volume. "*Awakening.* Is it a dream book, then? Come now, Marco, why didn't you tell me? You know how fond I am of fanciful speculation. . . ."

And while the courtier, the monk, and the little nun watched unhappily, His Majesty affixed a pair of wooden spectacles to his nose, opened the second volume, and began to read.

AWAKENING

20

AH, THE heady joys and soaring expectancies of freedom. No crack-halter felon escaped from the galleys ever gulped in the open air more greedily than I, nor thrilled more to the vistas suddenly spread before him. At the edge of the capital, I stopped and bought a horse, a bay cob, strong-framed and two palms above the mark, described to me by its owner as the flower of Spain. Further equipping myself with a saddle and bags, I headed south for Toledo, where I hoped to complete my knightly mien with the purchase of a good blade.

But I had no fixed plan, nor did I want to interfere with this loose elation that had me so drunk. It was like being suddenly a boy again and giddy, as the young are, with every possibility the fancy can conjure, and more. Anything might happen at any moment. All the world lay before me, with all its marvels and secrets, and I wanted to keep it that way.

And yet, as I rode along, doffing my hat to the cattle and hailing the birds with careless song, I could feel the sense of random pleasure already beginning to fade from me, as though liquid freedom were not my natural medium. Less and less did the world stretch limitless, more and more it seemed to gather beneath me like sand in the hourglass, drawing me downward toward the running hole of time.

I remembered the ditty sung years before by my uncle's roustabouts, and by the third day it had got stuck in my mind:

Oh, the notch house lights are bright tonight,
And the plackets all so gay,
And the only way to quiet the fire,
Is to blow the coals away.

Very well then, why not? Certainly I could not expect to be cured of abarcy merely by separating myself from a wife, and it was quite natural for the body to hanker. As all the wonders of the world awaited discovery, so did all its women. Hadn't some Phoenician said it: Every man a mariner, every woman an island to be inhabited?

Or, to bring the metaphor ashore, did I not now ride in the company of the knight errants of my childhood tales: Amadis, Orlando, the noble Cid and the gentle Perceval, all of whom had gone in search of *hazañas,* which was to say, exploits and adventures with which to test their *almas,* which was to say, to make sure their souls stayed upright? Except that in my case, it was not my soul, in the usual sense of the word, with which I was most concerned. And, while the knight of old was dedicated to the defense of his lady's honor, I had something quite else in mind.

At any rate, I no longer need resist the promptings of my loins; that was one of the rewards of freedom.

Thus reassuring myself that I was equal to my new estate, I came to the Tagus, rode across the Puenta da Alcántara, and in under the walls of the ancient capital. Lingering in the thronged Zocodover, I deliberately took my time selecting a sword, and once I had that, wandered to the church of Santo Tomé to look at the latest saint painted by El Greco, who was reported to be on his deathbed outside the city. I must say, the Greek certainly could paint them skinny.

And then, lo and behold, where should I find myself just at sundown, but behind the house of Rabbi ben Ezra, on the Calle del Coño, Toledo's red-cape district. Downing two flagons of Indies rum, I was launched, cruising up and down the trolloped doorways, strolling with the throng of preencod catzos and other locals. What a joy to shake off the traces and spit out the bit without fear of another's ire or tears. What a pleasure to be slovenly and coarse, happy as a hog in swill. No veiled lady shopping the bright displays of the silk bazaar, nor any whetgut goodwife eying the treasures of the butcher's hook ever experienced a more delicious sensation of attenuated desire and giddy anticipation than I.

And what a variety! They came in all sizes, all colors, all shades of character, from languid to sprightly, dark to light, quiet to loud, fat to bony, retiring to ribald and rough. Returning to the top of the street, I fortified myself with another toddy, then went straight for the nearest red cape. She was red-haired, as I recall, rangy and sharp, but full of fun. The next was older, somewhat melancholy and forlorn, but gentle and kind. The third, as I remember, had long breasts that came to her waist, but didn't mind what we did, and had a sense of humor. The next I don't recall, and the rest were a pleasant blur of bright silks and strong perfumes.

The reason men get along passing well with whores is that once the price is set and the pact made, they seldom if ever seek further advantage or try to renege. A good whore is, in short, a gentleman. With her customers. It is, of course, quite another matter when it comes to the man in whom she chooses to invest her dreams.

At any rate, I was having a good time freebooting on the high seas of licentious abandon, even if I was sliding rapidly toward bankruptcy and apoplexy. Until, on the sixth, or perhaps it was the tenth night, I suddenly found myself surfacing into pungent and dense darkness, with no idea where I was or who owned the pillowed flesh I was clutching so desperately to me, nor how it was that these rummish tears ran down my cheeks, while my parched throat croaked, incredibly, "My heart is yours!"

Whoever she was, and I am fond of her to this day, she laughed and pushed me out of bed, saying, "Thank you, but I have one of my own." And as I stumbled from the place, brought somewhat to my senses by a dose of night air, I broke into a coursing sweat and felt my stomach knot with that sickly afterterror that comes to the man who has narrowly missed a deadfall.

There was a lesson in it, and I considered myself lucky to be thus warned against the dragon which lies in wait for the most determined knight venerrant. I mean that fever known to popular consensus as love.

243

Not entirely to my surprise, I found myself eleven days later in Sevilla, and there I hung about two more days before I could muster the nerve to confront my family.

My mother looked old beyond reason of time; there was a pall of tensions upon her face, a new complexity of unease. Worse than the discomfort of seeing her cheeks stream was the chilling realization that I had never before seen her weep. "My granddaughter!" she wailed. "I have not seen her nor held the creature in my arms!"

She glared at me, her face dark with a furia also startling to me, although I should have known it as mate to my own. "Selfish dupe, fool! You go back there before it is too late. Go back to your wife and child at once!" And then, pressing her veil to her face, she fled the room.

I was shaken enough, but most of all by how old she suddenly seemed, how unattractive. I could not explain it, but I felt a forlorn disappointment and deepened sense of the cruelty of time. Although I could not have said for what, I knew that it was suddenly, irrevocably, too late.

Don Diego sighed and shook his head. "Very well, I know how stubborn you can be. But I have a stake in this myself. I am about to be accepted at court, and I want no more scandal. I shall broadcast it that I have sent you about the country on secret and honorable business, and I will tell your mother the same, for she is lately afflicted with womb rage and the change of life. We move to the capital next month, and she will be able to see her grandchild. It will soothe her, and henceforth I will see to it that your wife and child are comfortably cared for. I will post you a small and regular stipend, providing that you remain away from Sevilla and Madrid and keep your activities from the king's attention. Do you accept?"

When I remained silent, he frowned. "There is no use asking for more than the sum I have named. I have considerable expense in making this move to Madrid."

Still I had trouble responding. His hair was going white and his beard as well. He had told me with poorly concealed anguish that Paco was having difficulty at Salamanca, his stutter interfering with his efforts to convince his professors that he was taking their lectures to heart. I had an urge to reach out and touch his gloved hand and reassure him that I had my stutter as well.

But I doubted that he would understand, and before I could speak he gave me a sidelong glance of nervous perplexity and said, "You used to stare like that as a child. I wager your daughter will do the same." He looked away. "Never mind. This arrangement I offer you, is it not what you came here for?"

"Of course," I said, and showed him my teeth. "What else?"

Thus, as I made my way out of the city for a destination I could not name, I found myself more and more clutched by need of the most banal sort. The roads were lonely, the tavernas and inns even more so; the world busied itself with its pleasures and pains but was utterly unaware of mine. It was bad enough to lack a back upon which to warm one's feet, but how to replace so exquisite and absorbing a preoccupation as hating one's wife because one does not love her?

Memory poured its myriad tortures into the empty hours; hallucination greeted me at every turning, causing the brass faces on a fountain to grin at me, all mothers and their children to look at me accusingly, and several voices, but one most painful and small, to call my name in the gloaming.

I whirl, but nobody is there. It can come at any moment, wistful and loving, close at my shoulder. In time I learn not to look around, but the voice keeps calling. Surely someday the tears will cease to brim each time I turn and learn that it is only myself who calls so wistfully.

In addition, the horse that I had bought was proving to be of an uneven, often melancholy disposition, and given to an eccentric gait, that is, prone to move haltingly, stopping without warning, as if holding back from some invisible threat, then lurching drunkenly ahead again, as if fleeing from some terror behind. I mean, the animal also stuttered, and Sidi Retardo is what I called him as I put the spurs to his ribs, shouting, "In God's name, the future lies wide open before us! Onward!"

So that it was in a somewhat rattled and headlong mood that I finally came to a place that promised some fun. Hornachuelas, it was called, and its inhabitants lived in the earth, like gnomes, in a beehive of chambers cut out of the earth with pickaxes. Coming closer, I saw narrow doorways and pinched windows cut out of the clay, then little chimneys sticking up from the tops of the hills. But what decided me to stay was a large placard proclaiming that there would be a fiesta the coming Monday, including the festive slaughter of some bulls.

Outside, it was ungodly hot; inside the tunnels and chambers it was close but cool, and here some three hundred troglodytes crawled about at what they called living, pale and squinting like moles against the cooking smoke that drifted everywhere. There was even what passed for an inn: the cave of an elderly widow, who rented me her very best hole; and here I settled down to await the bull-baiting.

Out through one window I could see the dark-jawed troglodyte men, propped all in a row against the clay, waiting for work that never came. For it was their trade to bake and paint tiles, and Spain was by then so thoroughly pasted with tiles that the market was in abeyance. Among them sat a womb-wrenched dimwit with a damp bib hanging from his neck and the welts of the tongs above his ears. Every few minutes, with uncanny regularity, this creature, all unbidden, raised his voice into the sun-blasted silence and offered the wasteland his imitation of a chicken, first giving himself over to a paroxysm of clucking, then thrusting a finger into his cheek and popping it out again, the which manipulation produced a sound meant to indicate the laying of an egg. After which the idiot would indulge in a good deal of cackling and self-applause, while the whole row of glowering rustics sat unmoved and unmoving, waiting patiently for the upcoming fiesta, the wine bath and the bloodletting.

There was another window that looked inward and downward upon a tiny courtyard which was really the bottom of a large chimney cut straight up through the hill. Here, various of the women could be seen, scuttling across from one tunnel to another, one in particular being not unpleasant to look at. She was young and very pale, but pretty, no doubt the daughter of some poor relation, and bound over for hard service in exchange for bed and board. She most often hauled firewood and water, shuffling on scarred and dusty feet; or went down on her knees and scrubbed the broken flagstones, a pewter cross swinging at her shallow breast.

The first time that I saw her thus, I stared, and she must have felt it; she gave a frightened look upward, her cheeks flushed, and her hand went to: the cross? her heart? her breasts? All four.

Life underground is not so soothing as one might think, for the earth is never entirely silent; there are small insects at work above and below and all around. At times the sense of restriction causes the lungs to labor and one suffers a sudden impulse to run up a chimney.

The first night that I was there, and the second, I several times awoke to the chilling conviction that I was entombed. I heard the million pincered nits of retribution crawling in the clay, and the inching roots coming to strangle me. I dreamed that a tiny hand patted my back, and I awoke in tearful sweat quickly turned aghast by the realization that the hand was my own. I coughed, sometimes until I retched. Several times I thought I saw a familiar ghost just outside my door. More than once I longed to fall to my knees and pray. And yet, even here in this tomb of clay, I could no longer do it.

Perhaps it is no mistake that the lionpard and other fanged predators are solitary. The deeper the forlorn yearning grew in me, the more I went about bunched and nervous, like a drawn bow restless for a target; and the more I inclined toward that impulse which had prompted me as a child to ride my rocking horse downstairs, as a boy to climb to the top of the swaying aspen, and as a young husband to leave my wife's bed and walk the rim of the city wall, drinking wine and leaning.

Finally the Monday of the fiesta arrived. They had made themselves an arena in a little plaza on the far side of the hill. Oddly enough, there were gentry amongst the terrecoles as everywhere else. No doubt they kept their best houses upriver where there was greenery, but here they had earthen townhouses, complete with tiny balconies cut out of the clay so as to appropriately elevate them above the common throng. These they had hung with a pretty assortment of velvets and damasks and sat upon them with all the prim arrogance of the lords and ladies of Madrid, while the rowt crowded arse by elbow on the wooden scaffoldings below.

The entire population of town and countryside seemed to be there, and the restive buzz of their excitement distilled mine all into the one agitation. I clambered up the rough fence, wrestled myself a place on its topmost rail, and folded my cape at the ready in my lap.

In the center of the circle stood the town well, but the scuffed earth was otherwise vacant, save for an abandoned wooden clog and several dark stains in the sand; the first bull had been killed, and they awaited their second.

The hot sun beat down, and there was the sickly-sweet pungency of the abattoir: blood, dung, and bull sweat. Suddenly there was a shout from behind and the crash of horns against wood; a splintered gate came open just below my dangling feet, and the bull burst in head up and snorting, tail arched in rage, haunches smeared with terror.

As the beast circled the plaza, the crowd's welcome faded to an attentive murmur. Hooking a horn at the well, the bull abandoned its dignity to a bronco hop of surprise, and they laughed.

Now the peones got behind barrels and shook out their patched capes. They were mostly local rustics or servants to the performing nobles, with one professional as their leader. This individual seemed oddly overstuffed in his embroidered vest and tight breeches, resembling more a pastry cook than a hired matador. There was something vaguely familiar about his gait, but I could not see his face through the dust as he stepped out with his cape and clumsily drew the bull off to the side so that the business might begin.

Now one of the local knights rode to the foot of the highest balcony, doffed his hat, and begged leave to perform. The duke, or whatever he was, waved a languid kerchief, a trumpet strained, and suddenly the arena was filled with plumed and beribboned bravos, riding this way and that and reaching down to prick the bull with their barbed rejones, but mostly posturing in the saddle for the amusement of their ladies, who fluttered their fans, made pretty circles with their lips, and threw down flowers. Finally, when the bull was too weary to run at horses, the gentlemen toreadors made their mounts bow daintily, and then retired to much cheering, leaving the less noble task of finishing off the animal to the peones and their hired chief.

Oddly shaped and heavy, the matador was nimble enough to stay out of the way, but he appeared to have little taste for close work, and seemed bent upon squaring up his target too soon. "Not so quickly!"

howled the rowt, for this man represented their more inflated ideas of themselves, otherwise to suffer their resentment and insults. "More capework, show us your buttocks!"

He ignored them, clearing his sword and taking aim. But this was a nervous goat of a bull with a cataract on its left eye, and as the man was pressing in, the beast gave an eccentric toss of its head, hooking at the fat belly, and lo: the man staggered back, and it was not bravery's gray bowel that spilled from his paunch, but long wads of cotton padding.

"Fraud!" screamed the public, jumping up and down. He glowered, retiring behind a barrel to stuff himself back together. My moment had come.

There is no describing the thrill of riding a rocking horse downstairs, swaying upon a high wall, or leaping into a bullring. Past and future are pressed away by the snorting present, all moments become the one, and there is no time for worry; the black simulacrum of death passes in a fetid rush!

With the other boys of Barrio San Marco, I had put my cape to dogs and goats and wheelbarrows; I knew the proper motions. Which is not to say that I was expert. But it felt good.

The horned pig hurtled past, rattling with barbs and snorting, then wheeled and came again to my nervous veronica. Whoof! How it stank, how it grunted, flinging spittle and blood, twirling its great ballsack as it turned, lowered its head, and came again.

Rattle, thunder, and rush; got you, toro, nose glued to my red wing. Whoof!

"Olé!"

Their cheers were only extra gravy; I was alone with myself. Whoof! again.

Again, "Olé!"

The beast slid to its knees, and I peddled back to give it room. Now it was up, but it could not come again. It swayed in place, foaming pink at the mouth and looking to be solid bone. I got my sword out, but truly, this was work for the expert.

And here he came, his face vivid with rage, his sword extended, and even as I saw the starting yellow eyes and knew that he was none other than the director of the Theater of the Jittering Chicken, Ripio de Rebombar, I saw that his blade was aimed, not at the bull, but at me.

249

"Villain, arsonist!" he thundered. "You burned my theater! You ruined my living once, now you seek to do it again! Pyromaniac, upstart! Have at you!"

Hence the fiesta brava was treated to a novel variation not usually included in the price of admission: two men hacking at one another, while the bull looked on.

"Fraud, mockery!" screamed the rowt, always traditionalist. They threw clods. A man jumped into the arena, then a dozen, and in a moment the entire male population of Hornachuelas was pouring over the fence.

Fortunately, Ripio's knowledge of swordplay was mainly of a theatrical sort and designed more for display than drawing blood, so that while he looked good, he did no harm, and I was able to fend him off until the crowd swept between us and swarmed upon the bull.

I saw the director draw away down a tide of tossing heads, his mouth making indignant obscenities, while I backed to the fence and slumped there, still swollen with hot blood and thwarted supersaliency. A row of rustics was scythed down by a last rush of the bull, and one tumbled into the well. But a hundred more swarmed up from behind, flailing with knives and cudgels, and finally the beast went down.

And then, as I swept my heated gaze over the crowd and through the rails of the fence, and the black tail went pinwheeling into the air, flinging blood, I discovered the bound girl alone at the back, and saw that she was watching me. Her eyes widened as I clambered through the fence and pushed toward her. I saw her throat flush and her hand go to her breast as she whirled and ducked into the tunnel, and I dove after her.

We were alone in the honeycomb, so it was not hard to follow the delicate echo of her running feet. Finally I found her, cornered and crouched at the end of a narrow chamber, beside a shallow ditch supplied by some underground spring, pretending to wash her hair.

Her slender white neck gleamed in the light of her candle, and her hinderlings fattened beneath their rags as she bent above the ditch. I let her hear my footstep, saw her eyes spy sideways at me through the hang of her hair and her hand clutch at the tin cross.

I did not rush, but went to her like the fox to the chicken run, with a deliberate semblance of charmed unhurry, laying on my warmest smile and confiding my astonishment at finding such a bright sun as herself in such a forsaken place, locked away from her appointed heaven, as it were.

"But I have no choice, sir," she said, plucking at her cross. "My mother is ill and my father dead, the one of the king's evil, the other of his capital statute condemning smugglers."

"All the more reason to look for some other benefactor who might free you from this gnomish existence." I stepped closer. How pretty she was beneath the smut: drawn and blue, delicate as china. "Have you seen Madrid?"

"Oh, no. But I hope to someday." Her eye showed a flicker of hope no fainter than its complimentary suspicion. "But please, sir, you stand too close."

"Not nearly so close as I would like to, were it not that your ladylike demeanor demands such respect." I sighed and touched her hair. "How the great ladies of the capital would envy you this honeyed wonder. Is it this magic spring here which gives it its glorious sheen?"

She laughed and shied away, her cheeks gone full of color. "I must go now."

"Back to breaking your knees on the flagstones?"

She frowned and made as if to step around, but I blocked her way. Faintly, from the far reaches of the maze, there came the shouts of the crowd and the clucking of the dimwit. I lunged, locking her in my arms.

"Oh, no," she said.

Now the parted lips and the wide, bright stare of the quarry. And I wait, savoring the moment before the pounce, watching it thrill in her eyes.

"Beast!"

"Beauty." And I bore her down into the mud.

She whimpered and cried out, but faintly. She banged her head and thrashed as I struggled to arrange our limbs. "In the name of God, don't be cruel!"

I hesitated and might well have come unbunched, had she not lost heart herself, falling back so precipitously that her head bounced, then

251

was still. Encouraged, I reached down to find a way around her undergunnies, and discovered with a passing chill that I was not much more ready than she.

It is no small matter to put an oyster into a dry purse, but I managed, and once I was past the first portals, there was a certain stiffening, and I was able to draw back a little and push in again with something like purpose. And then a faint, bubbling sound reached my ears, and at first I thought it might be the running spring, then I knew it was not.

At the second sob, I felt myself fatten, and, horror of horrors, at the next, I was huge.

"Don't cry," I said against her streaming cheek. "I can't stand to see a girl cry," and my hips gave another tremendous twitch.

Soon, I became aware of a change in the fleshly terrain beneath me and went up on stiffened arms to look. Name of God, she was suddenly a dusty Dorita, bucking and squirming, moaning and banging her head.

"Hello!" I shouted. "Señorita!" But she gave no sign that she knew who I was or that I was there: only the moans and the head cranking right, left; one could have cracked almonds with it.

"Hola!" Still no response. There was no capturing the mouth; I gave up on the small breasts as well. "Hey there!" I lurched again. Hey! (*pound*). Hola! (*whack*). Sweat scattered from my hair, and juices shot from between our bellies.

Hello! Her eyes suddenly opened wide and fixed upon me with intensity, growing wider, wider.

Flinging out a hand, I struck the candle from its rock and dropped darkness over that awful stare, then proceeded to my jolting finish.

After a long moment, I bestirred myself. With trembling hands I fumbled with my flint-match and lit the candle.

She stood with one leg on the ditch, splashing water on her parts and fixing me with the tearful gaze of an unfairly punished child. "You hate me. You don't even know me, and you hate me."

Hate? Long after she had got her clothes straight and left me, I sat in that empty chamber and struggled to arrange my plea.

How could I hate a woman I scarcely knew? Was it all women that I hated? There were signs of it, I had to admit. There was no denying the furia which swept over me each time that I was confronted by my lady's moonfit: the pounding of my blood, the swelling of my braincase, the punishing thud of my hips against hers. But what of the abject fascination with which I studied every passing doxy and veiled stranger? What of this eternal ache and yearning which caused me to dream all night of ideal beauty, of her wondrous roundness and sweet smile, of the touch of her forgiving lips to my cheek?

Did the iron hate the magnet? Did Perceval hate the Grail?

And if I hated women, then who was it that I loved?

The question conjured another childhood nightmare, subtle complement to the dream of the nursery: a ball of string as big as a cathedral, black as God's rock, towering like a thundercloud. It moves, slowly at first, then faster and faster, careening and tumbling, inexorably unrolling, any moment to peel the last concealing layers away and reveal the unknown terror at its core.

21

ENOUGH of priapic paradox. What I
wanted from a woman was simple enough. Not to hate, but merely to
meet and mutually admire, agree to love in the moment, and do so.
Surely the world could not be designed to prevent so frank and
equitable a conjunction. All that was needed was to discover the right
partner.

Finding myself in Almeria by the Sea, I was strolling down their
Strand one afternoon, when I happened to notice a pretty young thing
seated on a bench between two men. I had once again reached that
state where proximity to a wench eased certain aches, and so I strolled
over.

But it seemed that the only space on the bench was occupied by a
leather purse. I was turning away again, when one of the young men
said, "It is not ours, brother. It was there when we sat down."

My heart jumped; could he mean the girl? "I beg your pardon?"

"The purse," he said. "Being honest folk, we have left it untouched,
but have speculated that it was probably tossed there after being
emptied by some ruffianly pickpocket."

"I congratulate you on your virtue," I said, again turning away, for I
did not like the look of the men, and one of them was better looking
than I, in an oily way.

"But is it perchance yours?" this one hurriedly inquired, his bright
glance giving an effect of open clarity, yet with a certain filmy quality.

But, oh, what a sweet picture was the girl, round and ripe, and greeting my glance with a welcoming smile.

"No, it is not mine," I said.

"Well then, why not move it, and you may rest your bones." The speaker made as if to move the bag but fumbled the job, knocking it to the ground, where it landed with a clink.

They glanced at one another in surprise, but none moved. Clearly I was meant to pick it up, so I did, bending with a flourish and a wink at the girl. The thing had weight and substance, and when I spread its mouth and looked in, I saw a dull glint of gold.

I sat down on the bench. "Well, well."

"What is it, brother?" the nearest stranger took the bag and looked in. "Caramba! Pieces of eight. Some raw bullion as well!"

"Let me see," said the other, snatching the bag, pulling out a rough bit and biting into it. "By God, you are right, it is pure Indies cob. Try it, brother."

It was gold all right. "Sure enough," I said, handing it back.

The two now launched into a sprightly dialogue. "It must have been dropped by some rich man, doubtless one of the nabobs of the town."

"A member of the Council, perhaps the comendador, who knows."

"If so, the aguaciles will be along shortly, and if they find us with it, it will be the pulley and stocks or worse."

"On the other hand, if it was forgotten by someone without influence, some smuggler or other variety of criminal, then we are in no danger and the gold is ours by right."

"Yes, yes, ours! Come, let us divide it at once!"

"Wait, you are hasty. First we must go to the town hall and discover whether or not the money is being searched for. If nothing else, there may be a reward. I suggest that I hold the purse here, while you go to the ayuntamiento and find out what you can."

"No you don't. I will hold the purse, while you go."

"I beg your pardon, but I detect in myself an inability to trust you with such a task."

"Your inability is nothing to mine. Give me the purse!"

A brief struggle followed, with the two wrestling the purse between them to the accompaniment of much cursing. Finally the first turned to me. "As an interested third party, brother, would you be willing to watch over this purse while we discover if it is ours to divide?"

"Him?" his companion objected. "But we saw it first!"

"Ah, but he had the courage to examine it," said the one with a sweet smile at me. "And besides, the mere fact that he knows about it now makes him our partner."

"I suppose so," grumbled the other. "But who will watch him while we are gone?"

The young man indicated the girl. "Why, Paprika, of course." He again appealed to me. "What about it, brother? Will you hold the treasure while we are gone?"

In the corner of my eye, the girl was all dark abundance and rosy flush. "Very well," I said. "But do not be too long."

"Only so long as it takes us to win the confidence of the appropriate official." Grasping the elbow of his companion, he prepared to leave, then turned back with a worried frown. "It has just occurred to me that it will undoubtedly cost us a modest bribe to find out what we want to know."

"Hellfire, I hadn't thought of that," said the other. Then his face brightened. "But we have plenty of money." He pulled the purse out of my hands. "In here!"

"Fool," said the other, snatching it back. "Can you guess the reaction of a policeman if offered raw gold by the likes of us? Why, he would have us in the stocks in a trice. And what if the purse has been stolen and its owner finds his gold short? No, we dare not. It must be copper." He appealed to me. "You wouldn't happen to have a few coins, would you, brother?"

"Of course," I said, pulling my own purse from my waist and smiling at the girl. "I am sure there are some strangers one can trust in this cruel world."

"I am sure there are, brother," he said, accepting my coins with one hand and handing me the bag with the other.

"Somewhere," he added, as he turned away with his companion. And in a moment they were gone around the corner.

I turned to the girl. There was much of the unformed child about her face: large eyes, pert chip of a nose, moist and heavy underlip, the other puckered upward into a suckling button. But her bosom was deep enough, gold bangles swung from her ears, and her head was wrapped in a cloth of exotic design. "Paprika," I said, "is not a usual name."

A rosy flush seeped up through the dark patina of her cheeks. "Only he calls me that. I am known to others as La Chispa."

"And to the king's census officer?"

"I have never met him," she said, "and I do not want to." She craned toward the place where the other two had disappeared.

"I shouldn't expect them back very soon," I observed. "By now, they are only just reaching the town hall. If, indeed, that is where they are headed." I indulged in a luxuriating yawn. "No, I think we two shall be here for some time."

She glared, I grinned, she looked away. I hefted the leather bag. "Of course, we could pass the time counting our gold."

"No!" She turned so sharply that a wealth of oiled curls tumbled from her burnoose. "That is, ought we to meddle? What if the real owner should happen by and discover us with our fists in his—"

"Pebbles?" I said. "Or is it grapeshot?" I tipped the purse. A shower of lead pellets spilled out.

I grinned, and she mustered an indignant glare. "What is this nonsense?"

"What, indeed. Hokkano baro, isn't that what you people call it? The Great Trick?" I smiled. "That was a badly gnawed old cob in the other bag. How many fools have bit into it before me?"

She stared a moment more, then the veil fell away from her gaze. "Many." She tossed her head and showed her teeth. "And none more of a fool than you, for you gave your coppers, and plenty of them."

"Indeed, I did," I allowed. "But only so that I might be alone with you." I leaned confidingly, attempting to insinuate the bag into her sumptuous lap. "Come, take your silly purse, and let us refresh ourselves in the bodega at yonder inn."

"Gajo, alien!" She struck my hand away, wriggled off the far end of the bench and crouched, teeth grinding. "Touch me, and your member will wither and evil glanders grow in your nose!" She pulled a villainous-looking knife from her waist and made savage gestures with it. "It is prohibited for the Gajo to touch the chabi of the Rom without permission. It is marhime!"

"I can see that," I said admiringly. "But tell me, where can I get this permission?"

"I put you in ndui!" she replied, biting her thumbnail and flinging spittle at me. "I put you in seven nduis!" And with that, she turned in a whirl of vivid petticoats and fled away down the Strand.

"Should the impulse come over you to put me in eight nduis," I shouted after her, "I will be at the inn!"

There is a childish dream which I had long cherished in wistful resistance to its opposite, the nightmare of the nursery. I am deep asleep, when I feel a gentle touch of lips to mine. I awaken to find perfect prettiness bent above my bed and smiling, and I reach up to clutch her dark hair and draw her down beside me.

I did not expect to see the gitana girl again. It is a lucky man who sits next to a gypsy and comes away with his fingernails, as they say in Badajoz. But it was not easy to forget her fresh beauty and suckling lip, and that night I had the dream. Deep asleep, I felt the touch of soft lips to mine, then looked up to find her bent above and smiling.

"By whose permission am I allowed to defy taboo?" I wondered in my sleep.

"By the only proper authority," she whispered. "Mine."

She puckered her marvelous lip and I grasped her oily ringlets and drew her down.

In our most menacing nightmares we awaken just before the worst occurs. In this, my sweetest fancy, I was accustomed to awaken just before the best. But this time there was no interruption. Strange language garbled the air, all the abundant marvel of her squirmed beneath me, and she laughed to see my wondering unbelief. Immediately as I sensed the impossible was in progress, I was overcome by worry about its continuance. And so I went up on stiffened arms, whence to proceed in my usual fashion, until such time as my whipping spine might crack all doubt loose from my brain. I collapsed, clamping one hand to a breast and burrowing back into protective dreamsleep, desperate to preserve the miracle against morning's cruel light.

But lo, the dream had life beyond the night. I awoke to find her curled at my side and chuckling over my yard, the which she had sheathed in a length of gut of gypsy make, very fine and transparent; and afterward she always had one handy when we needed it.

"I cannot believe you are really here," I said. "How did it happen?"

She sighed. "Yojo and Pulinka did not meet me as they had promised. I went to the camp of the kumpania, but neither were they there. In fact, they have run off to spend your money. Canail!" How fierce she could be, baring her teeth and grinding them.

"Rascals, indeed. One of them was your man?"

"Pulinka is my brother," she said. "Yojo, the prettier one, was my chabo." She frowned. "But not my husband." Abruptly she brightened; emotions came and went with her as the weather sweeps the middle latitudes, sunshine close on the heels of tempest. "So when I found them gone, I remembered your clear and innocent Gajo eye and the hunger in it, and I came to prove that it was never my wish to gull you."

She leaped up and whirled twice in the light from the shutter, her breasts standing admirably out. Then, suddenly and as unabashedly as a little girl crouching to pick a flower, she let herself down on the cuckstool and proceeded to pizzle.

"I was right, was I not?" she inquired, smiling brightly up as she bore down at her business. "You did love me at first sight, did you not?"

I was enraptured. Such blithe unembarrassment, such a display of flesh unashamed. But I held back the words, not wanting the guilt of hasty fabrication.

Her glance darkened and her plump lip pouted. "Or is it the opposite?" She glowered. "You hate me, don't you? Because I am a gypsy?"

"O my God, no!" I said, and the knife which the bound girl had planted gave an extra twist in my gizzard. "Not for that reason or any other!"

"Then?" she prompted, brightening again.

I took a deep breath. "Of course," I said, and once started, finished headlong. "Yes, love of the first quality. Why, I knew it even before I looked at you. I felt it in the air, your aura drawing to mine."

She beamed, triumphant upon her pot.

"Chispa, wild flower of my dreams!" I cried. "Wipe yourself and come to bed!"

For a fortnight she came and went like a spring breeze, warm and quick and fickle. She might appear at any time of the day or night, to stay with me one night or two, then away again to visit the gypsy horde, only to reappear without warning a day or two later, chuckling out of the darkness and into my bed, or waiting outside my door in the morning with her hands on her hips and wild violets tangled in her hair.

To be with her was to be sent back to the breathless wonder and giddy expectancies of childhood. She reveled in all odors, pungent or spicy, in tastes both sweet and tart, in all touch that was warm or titillating. She refused shoes and bade me shed mine when we ran hand in hand down the beach. She went like a puppy, turned aside by every novelty. Plucking up the shell of a sea snail, she would dart out a pointed tongue to get its taste. With the same tongue she tasted me, plucked up my yard and peered at it, burrowed her nose along the nap of my chest.

Never had I been so thoroughly caressed and explored, nor had I ever come so clear-eyed to another's body. Her flesh was firm and of a dusky hue, both breasts roundly formed and large. But one was twice the size of the other. What a rare delight, to decide between large and larger: to have a choice!

Her coony, she called it her yoni, was an elaborate Gothic portal, with a small pink wart at its apex, the which she called her *hundunare lala vurdon*—the little soldier in the boat.

Like many another boy of fixed station and protected upbringing, I had long envied the people who called themselves Zincali, Errate, children of Romany. They gave no thought to yesterday or tomorrow, it was said, but lived only for today. Their larder was the fields and the chicken yards of tamer folk, their houses went on wheels, and the starry heaven was their blanket.

"To the children of Egypt, time is only now," La Chispa assured me. "To the Rom, a candle is not made of wax, but is all flame."

The ideal way to live, it seemed to me. I would learn this blithe uncare and share in these reckless liberties, and that without any effort beyond natural ardor, any cost beyond the spending of the moment. For she said that she wanted nothing but my love. And was it not common knowledge that no gitana ever took an outsider for a permanent husband?

It was also part of common lore that the gypsies knew more about venery than others. Certainly La Chispa seemed neither mad nor desperate nor cold nor angry at the business, but only took delight in it, as she relished all sensual endeavor. She offered herself to me from all angles and cleaved to me with tender unrestraint. Hour upon hour we wrestled and rolled on the bed, and all was open and unlimbered and hearty. For the first time, I knew play and jokes at what had always been a tense and deadly business.

And then one afternoon, she arrived in a muted mood, made unhappy by an argument with her father, she said. And when I drew her to the bed, she gave a shake of her head and pushed free. Casting her eyes down, she inquired if her mouth would do.

My flesh had gone ahead of me, and so I lay back against the pillows and tried to let her. I was not unflattered, and it felt good as well, but there was a reversal in it that made me uneasy. Even assuming that such service gave her pleasure, why did she prefer this to the other except because she found our usual tumble to be not wholly satisfying?

Suddenly the present procedure was an offense to my sense of self and various of its cherished proprieties. I lifted her up and asked, in as dignified a tone as I could muster, "When we make love, do you, have you, did you . . . have a spasm?"

She regarded me solemnly. I had not seen her so serious. There was even a certain slackness; for the first time her prettiness did not seem entire. Finally, she took her eyes from mine, and then her face began to soften and glow, somewhat as it did at those moments when we gazed at one another, given over to a mutual dream. "We call it *patshiva baribu*, the miraculous conjunction, the plenty of double love."

"That's it!" I said. "The diazinsiper. The Golden Moment. But do you? I mean, have we?"

"Sometimes I do, but it is a delicate thing. We call one who cannot, *trushalo odji*, a thirsty soul. I have been thirsty." She lifted her eyes, and they were oh so dark and solemn. "And I have drunk deep."

"But can we, you and I? I want to make you as happy as myself."

"You can try," she murmured, and now she eyed me sidelong. "If you are willing to travel."

261

Her kumpania was in readiness to set out on their annual summer wanderings, she explained. Her former lover and her brother had not yet returned, while her father demanded that she follow the horde, of which he was chief; not to do so would be to lose his approval and her wagon.

"Come with me, my Gajo," she said. "I will teach you to be the best lover of all, and we will follow the evening star to the home of perfect love."

"Chispa!" I cried, drunk with new ambition. "Child of Egypt, lead on!"

22

A̲ₕ, ᴛʜᴇ storied freedoms of the footloose life. I was loved, but safe from capture, free but not alone. Or so I was pleased to believe.

Chispa's father was a square-built man with drooping black mustaches and a heavy blue jaw, and it is descriptive of his nature that when he had first suffered from the toothache in his youth, a surgeon had examined him and announced that he was that rare thing, a dentolith; that is, his teeth were not fitted into sockets, but were part and parcel of the jaw and could not be removed without breaking bone. Whereupon Butsulo, for that was his Romany name, had taken to his diseased tusk with a hammer, breaking off a piece of his jaw in the process and afterward hanging the relic about his neck on a thread and boasting that he was in possession of the world's most effective charm against toothache; and indeed, he was never heard to complain of the malady again, despite the fact that when he smiled, which was rarely, his mouth gave the appearance of a rotten hay rake.

He was a man of deep waters and many secret sorrows, La Chispa assured me. Her mother had put an early crack in his heart by running away with a soldier from Galicia. Refusing to remarry, he had devoted himself to raising his daughter and becoming a cacique of the horde. He treated me politely, but kept a glowering distance, making it clear that he did not relish the thought of his daughter either marrying or running off with a Gajo. This I found regrettable, I assured La Chispa.

But in truth, I was not all that disappointed that he denied me the parental embrace.

Of her former lover, my gypsy sweetheart said only that he had not been adequate to her purpose. "We were betrothed and the dowry had been argued and paid, and with it my father right away bought two new wheels for his wagon. But Yojo failed to fulfill me, and he knew it, and that is why he went away."

Now her face was all gloom. "And now no gitano dares ask for me, lest Yojo come back and claim me, or demand return of the dowry in my stead. Thus I must seek my companionship outside the kumpania."

Now her expression brightened, and she pressed her suckling lip to mine and reached down to test my gristle. "But you are my chabo now. And see how bright our candle burns!"

And so we wandered all in a tattered gather; a dozen wagons, twenty gitanos and as many children and dogs. When we found a clear stream near a likely village, we stopped beside its banks and stayed that night and perhaps the next, but seldom more than three, for if the king's cuadrillos did not discover us, the local señorio was sure to send his churls to harass us and make us move on.

During the days, the men and older boys went off to trade in faulty horses, to confiscate whatever small article or edible might be left unattended, and otherwise to work Hokkano baro upon the Gajo world. In the evenings, there was often music and dancing around the fires and always storytelling, and La Chispa was very good at the first, and always delighted in the last.

And later, while the fires dwindled and most of the kumpania snored, we lay closed up in our wagon or on the ground beside it, covered by her goosefeather quilt and hunting down the patshiva baribu.

She spoke of the prize wistfully, feverishly, as Teresa might speak of her Angel, Anthony of his Devils, the pope of the Trinity, Lerma of a Balanced Economy. And yet it seemed simple enough in its practical essence: that she should enjoy a spasm more or less equal to mine, and beyond that, that we should thus shudder simultaneously and be wrenched out of reason's reach both at once and altogether.

"Not merely your pleasure, and not merely mine," she explained. "But both of us together in the same joy, each not only receiving pleasure, but giving it as well. And that is why it is called the plenty of double love, for it promises twice the delight that any two can enjoy apart from one another."

Here, it seemed to me, was a way to get and still give, to swive and not be guilty, to be at once both loving and manly, both good and great.

Clearly the first objective was to catch her spasm. Beneath a thin moon outside Almanzora, I sought to rout it into the open by application of pure vigor, pounding and waiting for word. But none came, and I finally collapsed in a lonely foam of sweat and spunk, then to hear her winsome voice inform me, "You cannot force love, you must coax it into being. Be more gentle at the start, and do not neglect the little soldier in the boat."

For three nights on the banks of the Secaseca near Lorca, I lay grinding my teeth and commanding my flesh to patience, while I twiddled her little soldier, rowed her boat, and otherwise adjusted my gestures to unaccustomed delicacy, with the result that my head became so stuffed with thunder that all restraint left me in a rush rather than by stages, and before I knew it I was into her and already gouting, then crashing again into the goosefeathers, this time to hear her sigh, "Better, my sweet Gajo, but why so far away at the end? You must come closer to me, for the secret is in the snugness. Do not despair, you will be good at loving yet."

Snug it was two nights later, on the Segura outside Calasperra, but as I lay imponed upon her, allowing only the least separation necessary to movement and otherwise striving to glue us flesh to flesh, my usual frame of mind suddenly fomented rebellion in the form of a terror that my yard might have gone soft, and, as I drew back for a reassuring glance, the sudden friction conspired with the pressures of previous restraint to undo me yet again. Bad enough it had always been to be a retardo, but I had never dreamed what a shame and torment it could be to be a rapido.

"O God, O diamerdes!" I said.

"Never mind," she soothed me. "Next time."

And so it went from Hellin to Chinchilla, then on to Albacete:

"Is that good?"

"Yes, but slower."

"Like that?"

265

"Closer."
"All right?"
"Faster."
"Fast enough?"
"Harder."
"Now?"
"Nearly."
"Nearly?"
"Almost."
"Faster?"
"Slower."
"Closer?"
"Harder."
"Now?"
"No."
"No?"
"Yes."
"Yes?"
"No!"

———

———

"O God, O diamerdes."
"Never mind, my darling Gajo, next time."

Curiously enough, even when I had thus missed the mark, she still urged me to remain in place a while, explaining that a man's love could be measured by how long he left it in afterward. For my part, I found that such dalliance could be excruciating, and surely there was a lesson in that.

On occasion I became so impatient with the campaign that I allowed myself to be overcome with angry furia and proceeded to pummel her. And, strangely, although this sort of violence never elicited the prize, she didn't accuse me of hating her. And on several such occasions she seemed to take some pleasure in it, as though even this kind of attention was better than none at all.

Quite another lesson came on that occasion when, having labored like a galley slave for nearly an hour, and suffering from the vapors as well, I collapsed upon her without having spent. She was curiously disturbed, and this time she did inquire if I hated her. And when she begged me to resume and at least come to my own conclusion, I decided that there is something in a woman which, once started, wants to see a man finish, patshiva baribu or no patshiva baribu.

I was also learning some lessons about myself. Where my yard had so long been hard only by virtue of cold terror and its complementary rage, I was now becoming aware of a distant tingling, as with a frostbit limb just beginning to thaw. Where I had known only furia's frenzy, I was now learning to sort out its various incitements and was beginning to get a dim idea of its more profitable usage.

I also learned to put my fancy to use, as I had long done so whilst brandling. To invoke the specter of apandry was to surge desperately ahead. The dread memory of retardismo could chill and slow me, while still keeping me ready. Reaching into the darker reservoirs of my mind, I found vile hatred with which to give my efforts a knifing thrust. Remembering the long-lost dream of the bath, I could soften my insistence and arrest urgency, so as to wait. Sometimes, in order to encourage delay, I would divert my thoughts to some idea or object suitable to my purpose. Holding her close, I would dream of porcupines; pushing in and out, I would imagine myself in ice; about to spend too soon, I would visualize my funeral; once capitulated, I was Vesuvius and let go my lava with a roar.

However, such feverish mindplay was not without its subtle dangers. As I lurched at my labors night after night, anxiously studying her face for signs of success, I found myself striving to be herself as well as myself, to feel me inside her as I thought she might or should or wanted to feel me. In short, in my desire to swive her well, I was also, in a certain sense, swiving myself.

Not that I saw it that way at the time. I was only taking La Chispa's word for it that the proper study of man is woman.

When we reached Alicante, I slipped away to see my uncle, the count, who was still in hiding from the king's ire, and to whom Don Diego had sent my next stipend.

I found him in a comfortable villa overlooking the palm trees of the beach, himself as suavelegant as ever and dressed to the hilt of fashion, which that season leaned away from lace and more to velvets, replacing the starched ruff with the flat golilla; nor was there any sign of gray in his hair.

"Well, well, nephew, I understand that matrimony weighed too heavily upon you and you have fled the ties that bind." His appraisal was, as always, sharp and amused. "I must say, it looks to be working hard on you. You are haggard."

I shrugged, longing to consult his worldliness, but afraid of his cynicism. "I have been with the gypsies, and they are on the road much of the time."

He grinned. "And on their backs the rest of the time, eh? Especially the wenches."

"That is jealous rumor," I said.

His eye glinted. "And is it also rumor that they work magical charms? I mean, you look to be enchanted, nephew. Are you?"

I declined to answer, but he could read me.

"Your rapturous melancholy only deepens," he observed. "Were the answer no, you would have cheered up." He gave a wistful sigh, getting my money from his table. "In a way, I envy you. I had a gypsy girl once." He indulged a nostalgic smile. "She chewed snuff and used to spit over my shoulder as we did it. Here is your money. Diego writes that your family is as well as can be expected, and your mother diverted from her plumbing by the antics of her grandchild."

He gave me the coins, and I thanked him and turned to go. "One thing more, nephew. When love begins to wane, as, like the moon, it must—"

I glared, and he raised a hand. "Sorry. You want to say that you love but are not in love. Very well, have it your way, and in the end you will be right enough. The trouble with running from marriage is that your conscience demands that you keep on running. I know, for my wife and children are still in Madrid. I know you as I remember myself, you see. And it is my guess that when it comes time to leave, your conscience will demand an excuse."

He wrote something on a piece of paper and gave it to me. "This is the address of an amusing place of retreat outside Barcelona. I'll also put the name and address of someone who stopped by asking for you, and who is now in Barcelona. This place, where I have spent a few weeks myself, is a kind of monastery. But more fun, and should speed up your education, which looks to need it. When the time comes, tell your gypsy that you are overcome by contrition and have it in mind to renounce the world. I daresay such will be more or less the case at the time, and this will give your argument the grace of conviction."

He leaned back to give me a farewell grin, twirling his dyed mustachios. "And try not to take it all too seriously, nephew."

The second address was that of Felicio Mariposa-Cid, my erstwhile house poof and salad-day nemesis.

It was the first time I had been so long away from her, and she greeted me watchfully, while I did my best to hide my bemusement and the addresses in my pocket. But by now she knew me, and she looked worried.

And yet that night, under a full moon outside Torrellana, she suddenly began to thrash and moan most heartily. At first I scarcely noticed, for we had come thus far before.

"Closer?"

——

"Harder?"

——

"I mean, do you want it slower but harder, or would you prefer it faster but—"

"Aiee! Slower, harder, closer, faster! Just don't stop . . . ohhhhh!"

The silence that followed was drawn and dense. I could not quite believe it. But she was shuddering and sinking slowly back into the quilting, a most sweet and peaceful look upon her face. And yet, beneath the first rush of pride, I suffered a certain hollow bewilderment. "Was it because it was closer?" I inquired.

"Was it closer?" she murmured. Her eyelids drooped, her head sank deeper into the pillow.

"I mean, before it was faster."

"Faster? Closer? I disremember."

"But why, then? Chispa, can you hear me? Why!"

"Oh . . ." She lifted a shoulder and let it fall; her eyes closed, her voice dwindled. "I suppose it was just time for it, that's all." And then she was asleep.

Sure enough, although to my mind nothing was different, on the following night, it failed to happen. I began a secret campaign to chart her menses. With one eye on the moon and the other on her undergunnies, I spent endless hours in mathematical calculation, cut notches on our wagon shaft, and strove to adjust my efforts to the heat of her cheeks, the pace of the calendar, the wheeling rhythms of the heavens.

But it was not so easy. The moon was thin over Jijuna, she had been only a week from the rag, and her cheeks were cool, yet it happened. On the other hand, the moon was very nearly full above Callosa de Ensarria, there were fourteen notches past the first on the wagon shaft, and her body was a furnace against mine, yet I made no catch.

I began to be restive under a new annoyance. It came to me that she had been gradually but steadily reducing the frequency of our attempts. Now she often had a headache or protested that the campground was too rocky. I traced the process back and decided that it had begun more or less after I had agreed to travel with her. From that time on, the closer and more accustomed we got, the more she seemed inclined to ration her compliance. A most awful and unwanted possibility began to haunt me: could it be that women were not inclined to swive as frequently or regularly as men would wish?

In the week that it took us to traverse the narrow mountain road between Alcoy and Onteniente, I became convinced that it was a matter of size and spent much of my time aboard her staring anxiously down at my yard to make sure it was at its most tumescent. But when I warily inquired about the matter, she only chuckled, crooked a forefinger to make a cross below her thumb's first knuckle, and assured me that she had enjoyed much satisfaction with a man "no bigger than that."

I was astonished and demanded to know who the prodigy had been. She hesitated, but I badgered her, and she finally told me: "Yojo."

Now a new and most deathly chill: "But you said he had been inadequate to your purpose."

She looked away. "Not that purpose." Then she hastened to turn back and soothe me. "If you are worried about size, do not. Yours is the biggest I have ever seen." My heart soared, only to sink again promptly as she added thoughtfully, "When soft, anyway."

As we neared Valencia, I noticed an increasing irritability in myself and a resultant compulsion to find fault with her. In the beginning I had been only charmed by her infatuation with the idea of love, but gradually I began to see that it was less a pretty absolute than a treacherous cipher. "Sometimes I think you don't love me at all" became too clearly a protest of neglect in some matter, large or small. "Sometimes I wonder if you have ever really loved" was an even crueler cut, employed when the first had lost its power. And finally, "Sometimes I think you are incapable of love" several times crushed me, until I realized that it was not incapability that I was really being accused of, but only unwillingness to make that crucial commitment which was never mentioned, yet was more and more on both our minds.

At the same time, the thought of relinquishing her company brought a terrible pain. As the now-familiar signs of the idyl's dissolution began to show themselves, panic began to turn me in a corner; I could not bear the thought of suffering another such drawn-out agony of withdrawal as I had with Dorita.

Now when I put my face close to hers and gazed, the sweet flush of enchantment was not always there, and at such moments I felt my own face stiffen in return; and from such experience I came to understand that the magical look I had seen before, I had seen as in a mirror. That gaze of absolute trust and adoration had been only the reflection of my own.

It began to annoy me beyond reason that one of her breasts was so much larger than the other. And then one night at dinner, I suddenly became aware, to my most heartsick horror, that I was cringing from the moist diligence of her mastication.

She said that her gypsy lover had caught her fish regularly and easily. If so, how so? Had his small tool been otherwise rare, perhaps forked or warted? Had he known arcane and exotic tricks not available to me? Was she holding back from me while awaiting his return? If I were to reduce all exercise, even to lying prone through the day, would I be better able to succeed at night?

But even if I were to succeed before we reached Barcelona, there would remain the better half and greater challenge of double love's ideal, and that was that we should spend together, at the very same moment, in exactly the same intensity, so that neither was more nor less satisfied or selfish than the other. But how? Only a few days remained to me; I must swallow my pride and ask advice.

The matriarch of the kumpania was Butsulo's mother, and it was said that despite the fact that she was a hundred years old and without speech, she could read the future, cause trees to wither, and otherwise achieve unnatural effects by esoteric means.

Butsulo lay wrapped in a quilt and snoring beneath his wagon. I crept up the stairs, listened at the door, then pushed in. It was as they said: the old witch never slept. She sat hunched at her wheel in the light of a single candle, spinning, spinning. Closing the door behind me, I crouched down before her, and only then did she cast a filmy white eye at me, never pausing at her work. I had no knowledge of their sign language, but I knew she had at least one good ear. "I am here, mother, for your wisdom."

She took one claw from her wheel and held it out, and I put the silver into her palm. "I seek the patshiva baribu, but do not find it. Perhaps you have noticed."

She nodded once, and her head came loose from its kerchief and was nearly bald and covered with liver spots; the wheel softly whirred.

"Can you tell me how I might achieve my goal?"

She shook her head, feeding the spindle.

"Is it because it is your granddaughter I court?"

She nodded.

"But why can't I catch her spasm? What does she want?"

She turned with a dry rustling, her foot still busy at the trundle, and reached out and grasped my hand and held it near the spindle, and as she pumped the trundle and gripped the distaff under her arm, the clinging threads went round and round my hand, then my wrist, fragile as gossamer, yet steadily binding me. And her small eyes snapped and her toothless mouth opened and her white tongue curled with her silent cackling, as she took my free hand and placed it on my cod and moved it up and down: spinning, stroking, laughing noiselessly.

272

I fled into the night to wander the dead campfires and dodge the snarling dogs. Dawn found me leaning upon the poles of the corral. Soon enough the gypsy cacique came, cast a dark glance at me, then took a bridle and went close to a horse and began to whisper into its ear.

"Butsulo, I would have a word with you."

He glowered and passed a remark to the horse.

I went closer. "You know my trouble, what can you tell me?"

"My mother told you enough," he muttered, working the bridle into place. "But if you must have more, consider this: to the Rom, there is no marriage until there is a child. That is why Yojo went away. He was unable to give her one."

I felt the blood grow heavy in my fingertips, and my knees gone feeble. "But I never talked of marriage. Nor of children."

The gray stone of his face broke open and he showed his rotten hay rake. "The Great Trick only works with one who thinks he is getting something for nothing."

A furnace of mortification stoked up behind my brow. "You are wrong," I cried indignantly. "We are in love with each other."

He cocked his heavy head. "Pretty words, but tell me, have you ever heard of the tournament of genders?"

I frowned. "Of course I have."

"And what do you think it is?"

"Why, knights vying for the favor of their ladies. Men fighting over women."

He grunted, chuckling to himself. "I was afraid of that. Que Gajismo!"

"Never mind," I said. "Whatever happens between Chispa and me, I still want to know it all."

His eye brightened. "You are leaving, then?"

"It could be that I should and must."

"Very well. I was married once, but that poor creature over there can tell you better, for he still is." He gave an unpleasant chuckle and pointed to a stooped figure cutting wood at the far side of the camp.

The young gypsy was close to my own age, but what a gaunt and

273

wasted figure he was. As I approached, and he looked up from his work, I saw the twitching cheek and rolling eye of a man nearly consumed by some monstrous frustration.

Yes indeed, he knew of the patshiva baribu; his sweetheart had told him about it some years before, when they had been only lovers. He too had quickly become addicted to its pursuit. The harder he tried and the more often he failed, the more fierce became his ardor. The more stubbornly elusive the goal, the more profound became his conviction that once he had made the catch, life would not be the same again.

"We are men, are we not, and born fools," he sighed. "She told me that she could not fully give herself to me until she knew I loved her, and that would be when she got with child. And so I got her with child, and sure enough, I won the patshiva. But now the struggle was to catch the baribu, and for this she said she needed further proof of my love. And so we got married, and sure enough: the plenty of double love. But a month later, not so good, and I was soon given to understand that she had her eye on a new cooking pot. And then a child, and then a new wagon, and then a corner for her mother's chair, and then another child, and so on. You see before you a mere trace of the man I once was. Ah, but we are men, are we not, and born for the chase?"

He grasped my shirt and pressed his twitching face closer. "In fact, I have solved it at last, after these many years of struggle, and I will tell you my secret. If she does not want to spend, well then, refuse to do so yourself! You are startled. Never mind, try it. Sooner or later, she will come around." His expression faltered, one eye rolled outward, and he gave an anguished shudder. "Of course, it requires patience, it often takes a bit of time." He cast a fuddled gaze about, then shook his head to clear the cobwebs. "Let me see, yes, six weeks so far this time. I do not feel so well and have a nervous bowel and hives, but I will triumph in the end. We are men, are we not, brother?" He staggered back, fighting for balance. "Made for the hunt and determined to win, or bound to die in the trying!"

To look into that wild eye and tortured face was to know overweening ambition in new guise; and to glimpse its awful comeuppance. I murmured my thanks, turned, and left, my mind made up. To be sure, I would always want to be a good lover. But not that good.

274

That night, as we huddled in her quilt beneath a clear and starry sky, I told her that I was already married.

For a long time she stared, while liquid moonlight brimmed from the corners of her eyes and ran slowly down her cheeks.

"Are you surprised?"

"No. My grandmother guessed it long ago. It is that you have decided to say it." Suddenly she clutched at me. "But we can go away! Or you can marry me in the Romany manner and we will stay with the horde. Here, no census taker can count us, nor any bishop come to arrest you for bigamy!"

"But I have a child as well."

How haggard that little-girl face could look, and so deathly pale in surrender. "So you must leave," she whispered.

"Only because I have already done them harm and would betray them further this way. Only because I am not meant for domestic permanence and am cursed to wander—"

"Gajo nonsense!" she suddenly shouted.

"But it is true!" I protested. "There is a monastery in Barcelona, and I am going there. I cannot stand the world, I tell you, the way it gives and takes away, never letting us rest. There has to be something more!"

As quickly as it had come, her storm passed and her expression softened, and to my great surprise, she nodded thoughtfully. "Oh, I believe you mean the various things you say. There is something of the religious maniac in every coony fiend." She sighed and looked away. "But you can keep your games to yourself now, and I will do the same with mine. It is done. The tournament is over, and there is no longer any point in trying to work Hokkano boro upon one another."

Now she turned back to face me, and her smile was sunshine through an afternoon rain. "No longer in love, we are now free to love. So come to me, my dear, desperate Gajo. Hurry and go slow, madden me and give me peace, take me apart and make me whole!"

And I did, and she did, and we did. And this time when I hurtled headlong into the sweet abyss, she was there to meet me. O patshiva! she cried, O baribu!

And that was the rarest news, and most bittersweet lesson of all.

275

23

O MNE ANIMALE POST COITU TRISTE,
goes the proverb. Sad after swive is every beast. How absurd I had
always thought these words. Ever since my failure on the hill with
Carolina, and no matter how short of perfect the event had proved to
be, if I had managed to spend, I had been relieved at worst, and at best
had experienced a joy akin to that which must have warmed Lazarus.
But now I was beginning to perceive the long view of the saying.

Not that I was not glad to have escaped; it took only a day's ride to
let the giddy expectancies of freedom back in. But with the coming of
night I discovered that my sweats and hallucinations were also back,
with a new sense of loss added to the old. I could not forget her oily
ringlets and suckling lip. Now a new voice called my name, and when I
turned, nobody was there.

I tried to reassure myself that I had learned much and was now
better armored. But it seemed that as I became colder outside I only
grew the hotter within; and in my worst moments I caught myself
railing at her memory, "How could you have let me leave you!"

My mistake, I decided, had been in taking too deep a liking to her.
Next time, I would choose a creature I could not possibly care for.

I found Felicio in a tidy posada in Barcelona's Barrio Arrabal. He
had grown a beard to hide his scar, but otherwise seemed the same, only
the more permanently perpotated.

"Juan, my darling, you have come to carry me away!"

"Not at all, I only want to ask you how it is with my wife and children."

He pretended to pout. "Nevertheless, I am coming with you to this so-called monastery. You can't stop me."

"God's nose," I groaned.

"As always, you have it backward," he said. "You are the nose, I am the daisy, and God regards us with equal indifference."

As we rode out of the city, he told me that he had left Dorita after an argument with Cristobal, from whom he had recently had a letter telling him that Dorita was well provided for by Don Diego, in exchange for which she let my mother spoil our daughter.

"Such a serious little girl," he said. "More than once I came into her room at night to find her wide awake and staring solemnly at the ceiling. But I am sorry, Juan."

"Never mind." I said. "And the Marquis Mendo? Or did you know that blustering pornocrat?"

"I knew him." His snigger lacked pleasure. "Better than you can imagine."

"Don't tell me about it." I made a face.

"Very well. But I last saw him at the mentidero on Lion Street, drunk as I am now and declaring that he had it in mind to become a saint in advance of his death and sell a certain part of himself as the relic of relics."

I chuckled. "He has not changed."

"Oh yes, he grows older. Soon his peppery caudle will no longer fire him up, and he will have to resort to the Chinese Symphony and put a plumball and violin string up his arse and hire a boy to play upon it with a bow." His face tightened along the scar, and his voice trembled with some abiding hurt. "The which turnabout I would not mind seeing, after what he did to me."

"What did he do?"

His glance was weary and pained. "You asked me not to tell you. But the heart of it is this: to be queer is still to be only half queer. When two men go to bed together, they are still men."

The place called itself the Hospice of San Placido Pordetras and stood atop a large rock some ten leagues north of the Catalan capital. It

277

seemed large and impressive enough from the high road, but as we rode closer, I noted that one of the towers lacked a bell, and there were bricks gone from the walls.

"As though somebody has been selling the place piecemeal," said Felicio. "And look."

Heaped about the base of the rock was trash of a sort not usually associated with renunciation, such as bent playing cards, ruptured wine barrels, and even a torn petticoat hanging from a fig tree. Leaving our horses under a thatched shelter, we started up the winding path and were scarcely halfway when ribald laughter sounded above, and an empty bottle came flying and shattered on the rocks below.

"Oh, I am going to like this place," said my companion.

When we had found the entrance, I put my uncle's note on the locutory and pushed it inward, to be immediately rewarded by a spate of girlish laughter from the other side, whereupon the turntable swung back to present us with two dented chalices, each filled with what proved to be a fairly good Jerez, and a floating camilla.

"Some monastery."

Once inside, we were separated, and I found myself alone in a small entrada. Suddenly a monk was shambling forward to greet me, drawing back his hood and causing me to swear softly at the sight of those bulging eyes, that turnip nose, that pugnacious grin.

"Brother Gabriel Tellez!"

"More or less." He had a paunch now, and considerable of his hair had disappeared.

"But the last I saw you was at Osuna. Did the rector finally turn around on you, if you will excuse the reference?"

He looked sour. "In a sense. It got around that one of my plays was on the boards of the local corrale, and the giddy fool took the bishop to see it. It was my *La Venganza de Tamar*, a thoroughly religious piece, but unfortunately dealing with incest. The bishop denounced me to the Board of Censors, and Gaspar could not stand the gaff. The Brotherhood has even suspended me, and so I have had to move to Cataluña."

"I suppose I am sorry to hear it," I said.

"I suppose you are not. But never mind, they will relent, and in the meantime I am doing well enough." He rubbed his hands and bulged his eyes at me. "But what can we do for you?" He gave a nasty chuckle. "That has not already been done."

His grin recalled my own dismissal from the university, and I entertained an impulse to get out my sword. But I remembered what my uncle had said of this place.

"Why, I am here to take retreat," I said to him with a wink. "It looks to be a lively place for it. Those were nuns who let me in here?"

"They weren't choir boys, although we have them, too." Then he decided to be solemn. "But please be assured that we are a serious community, in our way. Many who come here suffer from acute inward trials and difficulties, and we attempt to help them through the practice of certain novel exercises of my invention."

"Novel enough, as I hear it, to attract the more eccentric from amongst the Catalan gentry."

He gave what passed for a modest bow. "We have been privileged to help various titled or influential persons to find spiritual consolation."

"I'll wager. And what does Barcelona's bishop say about all this?"

He smirked. " 'Not bad' were his words as he left us last month after a fortnight under our care." Then he went solemn again. "Nonetheless, we are all Christians here—"

"Christians!"

He fixed me with a morose stare. "Your odium theologicum, Lucero. Are you sure it is not really odium veneris?"

"Perhaps," I said. "But at least I know which one I hate the most."

"But must you hate at all?" he grumbled. "It is possible, you know, to be a Christian without being also a frigid ass."

It truly was a novel establishment from which he now made his living. A colorful assortment of inmates populated the cells, argued in the halls, and strolled in the colonnaded cloisters. Some seemed to have brought their wives or husbands, flocks of children shrieked; there were monks, nuns, elegant lords and ladies, and not a few of what looked to be plain maniacs: a man in full armor, another wearing nothing but codpiece and cape, a nun with a pillowcase over her head.

During the day, there were prayer meetings and debates in various halls, and certain inmates were got together to practice Fray Gabriel's plays. Meals were plain but not bad. At night, some went straightaway to bed, while others devoted themselves to drinking, mutual prayer, and other, more private play. Twice a week, one or another of the monk's comedies was put on the boards out in the cloisters. Once a week, I was told, there would be a fete known as *La Fiesta de la Potencia Libre,* which was to say, a Celebration of Free Will.

But my first introduction to my fellow eccentrics came during one of those afternoon discussions which Fray Gabriel called *Duelos de Alma,* or Soul Battles. His claim for this invention was that argument clarified the earnest person's view of himself.

But join us for the second, or perhaps it was the third gathering of that small group with which he proposed to introduce me to his method. Felicio was still elsewhere. Otherwise, there were several dour monks, an extremely fat merchant who mostly slept, the nun with the sack over her head, the bearded and mournful Duke of Montril, and his duchess, a blond-haired woman in her middle years, yet with such overwhelming pornocrastic power over the arcane habits of my mind that immediately upon meeting her I had felt my yard rise, and it was still stiff.

"True peace," the duke was informing us, "true equanimity, I say, lies in an understanding of the infinite totality."

"The infinite what?" I inquired.

He loved to talk as much as he hated being interrupted, and so ignored me. "There is no pure chance, you see, but only meaningful coincidence. If we can but comprehend the pattern, we can experience the All and thereby be relieved of earthly pain and confusion."

"That will be the day!" scoffed Gabriel, shifting his bulk and casting an ogling eye at the duchess.

"It is done by direct study and contemplation," the doleful illuminist continued. "Perhaps by looking at the stars or gazing upon a sacred symbol. One need only know the way and be patient, and suddenly one is seized by the Universal Spirit and raised above all mundane consideration in one blinding, Transcendental Moment."

"Would that by chance be related to the so-called Golden Moment?" I inquired, sliding a suggestive eye at the duchess. But she seemed more interested in penetrating the nun's pillowcase.

Fray Gabriel let loose a shattering roar. "You poor misguided aristocrat, you cannot deny chance, no matter how desperately you itch to fix God in place."

The duke looked hurt and fell silent, whereupon the monster monk proceeded noisily to eulogize that famous miscreant whom he claimed to have been the inspiration for the founding of his new order. "There is no equanimity, only God's marvelous contrariness. Give me a man who can both pray and fornicate with the same hearty will. Such as the noble Fray Zapata, who made it a habit to say, 'Up little Peter, and let the people look at you,' whilst elevating the host and simultaneously exposing his privy part before the altar."

He laughed, flinging his crassitude this way and that, and let go a mighty fart for emphasis.

"Some monk," I said. "And did he then pee in the chalice?"

Gabriel glared. "You are an odd one, Lucero. One minute it is rut, the next minute righteousness. Can't you accept that all men seek union with a pleasing woman?"

"I did not say there was anything wrong with lust," I grumbled. "I only want to call it by its real name."

This time my glance did get an appreciate return from the duchess, causing Gabriel to scowl enviously. "With that I agree," she said to me.

Her voice was vibrant and deep. Esclavo twitched in his hammock.

But she turned back to the nun. "I see you are a Carmelite, my dear. A nurse?"

"I have been," came from the pillowcase. "But no more. All those wounded soldiers groaning for their bedpans. I had a husband once, and that was not much different. No more, thank you."

"The same for me," said the duchess. "And I will tell you why. In my younger days, I sought to dedicate myself to this absolute love they are so fond of separating from plain rut. While the other girls went about in society, I assisted the Sisters of Charity at the hospital. My task was to sit up at night with an ancient and decayed general who was dying. But he was so long at it, and smelled so bad, that I took to slipping out of his room while he slept, in order to visit a most handsome and dextrous surgeon on the first floor. But it seems that one night whilst the doctor was operating on me downstairs, the old fool was gasping his last just above. For I was gone some hours, and when I returned to the bedside, I found him cold as a mackerel. Why, it took two dozen hot water bottles to warm up that corpse enough so that I could tell the mother superior that the old fellow had just died, with me in charitable attendance. And even then, he had wet the bed."

"Disgusting," said the nun, doubling over with laughter.

"Wasn't it?" replied the duchess with equal hilarity, pressing one hand to her own ribs and with the nthdr, rtroking the nun's plump knee.

With what depth of loathing and hatred I glared at her. And decided she was just the girl for me.

It so happened that the next night I attended my first Fiesta of Free Will. Musicians played languid, tinkling tunes from dark corners, the food was overrich and taken by candlelight and accubation, which is to say, lying prone in the Roman manner.

Felicio was happily whooping about with what looked to be a pampered stable boy. Fray Gabriel was everywhere, shouting, ogling the girls, and eating. He ate for three, and once started, seemed prone to make his gullet God. And yet he stirred his gaspacho with gingersticks and thickened his wine with pepper sauce, as though he trusted no food to be good unless it also hurt him.

Sometimes there came trailing along behind him one whom I thought must be the mother superior of the place; and, sure enough, I was told that she was the mother of the monk's fourteen children. She had a most astonishing head of red hair, but I paid little heed to her beyond that, for my eye was peeled for the duchess.

Fat gleamed on chins and ran down billowing breasts, dissolute chatter ebbed and flowed, somebody was leading Vespers in the chapel, and the slatternly evening evolved toward that moment when the guests wandered one by one into the shadows, there to blend and drift by twos and threes, and sometimes more, down the long arcades. Sandals scraped on distant tiles, light laughter echoed in the tower, Gabriel roared like a lion, then was silent. I think he must have lost the scent.

But I found her alone at the end of the hallway, glancing sharply about, no doubt for the nun with the pillowcase. "You," she said in mild surprise.

"Do I frighten you?" I inquired pleasantly, stepping closer.

"Not at all," she said. "It is just that I had figured you for a poof."

I clung to my pleasant expression, but it was not easy. "Quickly, into this closet!" I lunged at her, desperate to get it done before revulsion intervened.

"My, you are in a hurry." She leaned back against my arm to fire a laugh into my face, but I closed my teeth on my smile and kept at it, and in the end she let me haul her in and lay her on a bed. It took only a moment to disrobe her, then myself.

"My, my, look at the poor lost little thing," she mocked, and it really was unfair, for Esclavo had never looked less lost or little. I ground my teeth and prepared to get between her legs.

She was as expected: sumptuous and firm in all her parts, the ideal cuerpo. And yet my heart could not seem to find purpose equal to the enthusiasm of the flesh. To my unsettled fancy I probed a windy cave rather than a welcoming furnace. I turned her face down so as to shut out sight of that narrow eye and mean lip. Again I turned her and tried her and turned her again, for all the world like a befuddled baker looking for virtue in a bad loaf.

Soon enough she noticed. Raising herself on her elbow, she fixed me with a glare that was briefly rueful, then irate. "What have we here, a crossbreed of venereal lion and moral mouse?" With a snort, she pushed me onto my back, her voice going deeper by an octave. "Never mind, there is a way to beard the lion in his den and make the mouse roar."

Grinning hideously, she grasped my yard around its middle, poised her slavoring mouth, and engulfed it.

While she went at it, I told myself that she did me obeisance by thus applying herself to my ripe region, and at first I tried to let go, if only to have it over with. But this time I could not avoid understanding. Just as on that occasion when Dorita had got suddenly astride me, I knew that regardless of the fact that my flesh was extended, it was receiving. I lay pinned to the mattress, while her blond head went up and down above my belly like a piston, devouring me. The difference was in the initiate source and direction of energy: she demanded to set the terms by which satisfaction would be had.

A fat vein throbbed at her neck as she labored; sweat ran down her temple. Finally she let out a croaking curse and rolled away. "It is as I thought," she muttered. "You are not a real man."

"I beg your pardon," I said. "It seems to me that the person deciding who is and who is not a man should at the very least be a member of that sex."

She turned up a shrewd glance and said with maternal authority, "But you cannot let go of your precious pudding, poor thing. My, but you certainly must hate women."

"Not particularly," I said, getting her over on her back with her legs in the air. "But I will tell you this, I certainly don't much care for you." And with that, I gave a few brisk strokes and spent.

I did not see her again until the next gathering of our clapperclaw tertulia, and then she would not look at me, nor did I much care.

"I am a dedicated aspheterist and disbelieve in private property," Fray Gabriel was declaring. "I am a doctrinaire communista, and believe in the Platonic sharing of property and responsibility. As Rojas says in *Celestina*, 'Goods which are not shared are not goods.' Or, to put it more plainly, from Plautus, 'What is yours is mine, and all mine is yours.' The model society—"

"Is the spintria!" cried Felicio, in his cups and eager to play at giganticide. "Surely you have heard of it, Gabriel. Invented by Tiberius and since employed to their pleasure by innumerable Capuchins and other devoted communistas, consisting of thirteen citizens fitted dagger to bum in a closed circle. What a delightfully democratic minimization of advantage and equitable sharing of profit and labor. Could there be a better solution to the problem of human relations?"

"Yes!" roared the monk, and the stools rattled on their legs. "I know a better solution: my dagger at the rear and the whole world ahead of me!"

With that, the company dispersed, except for the monk, who called me back from the door and bade me sit beside him.

"Do I sometimes seem to you to be inconsistent?" he inquired, fabricating green innocence.

"Not sometimes."

He bulged his eyes. "That, damn you, is because I am human!" With great effort he swallowed his ire, leaned his bulk closer and gave me a nudging leer. "But tell me, how did it go with the duchess the other night?"

I shrugged. "She is not my cut of cheese."

He shook his head incredulously. "Personally, I like it sharp." Now he spoke confidingly. "At any rate, your giddy friend Felicio may be on the right track about sharing the fun. About us all being in this together, I mean. In fact, I have evolved a theory. It seems to me that there are three kinds of love that men and women may discover, just as there are three main categories of potation: fiery, mild, and mixed. The first is the aguardiente of love: hot, sharp, crystal clear, going at once to the head, the heart, and the loins. This is first rut and first infatuation, that marvelous sense of utter abandon which seizes a man and woman when they first meet, and keeps them in its grip for weeks or months, but seldom beyond the first year.

"For few of us can stand the heat at the heart of the furnace for too long; the smoke clears and the cipher breaks, and blisters are noticed. What seemed a tight and perfect fit goes loose again, the heat has gone out of the liquor and the blood out of the yard, and there is grave danger of hangover. And so we have recourse to a blander brew, the good mild wine of accustomed love. It must be nurtured from the vine and expertly cared for. The feet learn just how to trample the particular grape. Patience and a proper climate must be maintained while the fermentation takes its time. Nourishing, steady, somewhat short of stunning, but better than nothing at all: practiced and knowing conjugation is the table wine of love.

"Yet who does not suffer a certain slackness of desire upon facing the same board each night, filling the same glass, drinking the same liquor. We itch back to the fire of the aguardiente, the fine madness of drunken abandon. At the same time, we know the dangers of seeking another table, another tavern; we are likely to ruin our welcome at home and waste all that time and effort spent upon the careful making of daily wine. Here is where adroit and canny lovers have recourse to the other diversion, and that is the tasting and mixing of assorted liquors: what I call experimental love.

"A little of this, a little of that one night, then the reverse the next. And for fresh spice to replace the spontaneous fire of first love, one might bring in a third brewer from outside, a neighbor, a good friend, one who can be trusted to bring his own bottle and perhaps some new ideas. In short, to help make one of those private fiestas of dalliance which divert one from the essential dilemma."

The silence was long, and if I may say it, pregnant. Finally he was obliged to prompt me. "Well, what do you say?"

"Mixed liquors do not agree with me."

He glowered from his mask of flaming lumps. "You are afraid of something, Lucero."

I showed him my teeth. "Aren't we all, Brother Gabriel?"

"We shall see about that," he muttered as he shambled from the room.

It was that evening that I happened to pass the duke's chamber when the door was open, and discovered him rapt before a small painting affixed to the wall. Stepping closer, I made out what looked to be a strangely decorated biscuit, the which was, he explained, a kind of mystic cipher and map by which he was guided to an understanding of the Infinite Totality.

"But I am no longer in need of such artificial incitements to Transcendence," he assured me. "Nor do I any longer believe that it can be achieved with my wife's help. True understanding of the Oneness cannot be achieved through the flesh. For there is a venality in the body which will not admit of peace. But the Transcendental Moment lifts the soul to a totally spiritual plane where not just two but all souls may come together in rarefied embrace, and every single grain of the universe is seen to be in absolute harmony with all the rest. And this is not comprehended through direct effort, but through passive unresistance and acceptance."

"All very fine," I said. "But I find anything so unsubstantial hard to believe in."

He grasped my sleeve, his lip damp and trembling. "I tell you, it has happened to me! I have experienced the Transcendental Moment, and it lifted me out of this clay shell and raised me above this carnivorous world. I saw the eternal nimbus, I tell you. Just there, above my wife's empty pillow!"

"What night was that?" I asked him.

Sure enough, it was the night I had banged his wife.

24

F<small>RAY</small> G<small>ABRIEL</small>'s mother superior had very much the boneless and rubescent look of one of those German housewives one sometimes sees in Barcelona. Her face was round as a plate, her nose scarcely there, her eyes green as new grass, her complexion pudding-pale. But it was her hair that made a wonder of an otherwise bland design. Becomingly crinkled and deep red as nothing else on earth, unless it be fresh blood, it fell about her shoulders in solid abundance, yet was so delicate that it stirred in the lightest breeze. And when the sun got behind it, one saw subtleties of light beyond reason.

It was her habit not to attend the daily tertulias, but to stay in their apartments at the back of the monastery, drinking barley beer and sorting her fourteen children and as many cats and dogs. Seated at her table, she said her progeny like beads. Reassured by the multitudinous twigs of her tree, she looked with bland green eyes out upon the disordered world and judged it according to her own fevered and feckless lights, deciding who was good and who was bad, who was saintly and who a minion of the Devil.

My spontaneous inner calculator had been at work since my bout with the duchess, and it informed me that there might be safety but there was short pleasure in coupling with a creature one detested. Better would be a woman one didn't mind, but who did not want to get married. But what woman not dead or deranged did not want to get married? One already married, of course.

And this prodigious Twigger did come out at night. It was as though she felt that the dusk, like her dingy rags, provided the forbidding obscurity by which she might test the world's intentions. At any rate, she would suffer Fray Gabriel to enjoy his freedom only during the day, and whenever he went for the door after dark, she went with him. On those nights when there was no fete, we gathered in the wine cellar, and here I soon found myself regularly attending, while she gave him vinegar and blisters and saved her sweetest sauce for me.

"Here, sit beside me, Juan, not by that big slab of suet. Give him some of your wine, Gabriel."

The monk obeyed, smirking. "By all means, share and share alike, Lucero."

"No, thank you."

"What, are you soaked already?"

"No, but I am thinking of leaving in the morning."

"All the more reason to get drunk so as to forget your cowardice." The Twigger pegged him with her scornful laugh. "This from you, who fear your own bed?"

He went red but would not look at her. "You are such a Catharist at heart," he said to me. "So full of the need for renunciations and other wasteful worry. My God, if I had your looks, your family name, your money—"

"You don't, so leave him alone," she said. "Juan is not just another pretty aristocrat, he is a sensitive person. What does it matter if he is drunk or sober?"

"That is my point. It does not matter, except as it matters to him." He leaned his long nose and bulging eyes at me. "You are not running to, Lucero, you are running away."

"All right, then." I let him fill my cup and drank it down.

But he only pressed the harder. "See our bold adventurer! Witness all ye of knightly persuasion, who sallies forth from the ruined castle of unkind matrimony, mounted upon his faithful nightmare of diminution, girt in armor of sweat and tears, brain a-whirl with dreams of maidens yet to rescue from the ennui of his absence." He put his awful mask closer, spewing fumes of garlic. "Oh yes, I know you better than you think. But be assured, you will never be a real licentiate. You have no talent for moral freedom. In fact, you will end up a monk, no matter how much you drink, I am sure of it."

"You tell me that?" I said. "You, who dress in monkscloth so as to give your thin rebellion false glamour? You, who have twigged yourself eternal sackcloth of paternity and drink your gullet full of ashes nightly?"

"I do tell it to you!" he roared. "You, who have tonsured your soul by separating yourself from your child, as you told me yourself. And who are scourging yourself even now with some fond and furtively hidden whip."

Wincing, I drew myself up, risking my most delicate treasure. "Wrong! I have a vision, a goal. I suffer pain to a purpose!"

"There, you see," triumphantly said the Twigger. "This man is very nearly a saint."

Thus we ranted and toyed nightly, and a very tight knot we made. For in his scathing way, the monk also encouraged me, and the two of them were acting in curious concert. Three is not merely a crowd, but is the protoplast of the tentigo. All we needed now was a catalyst, some unaligned fourth to untie the triad and set us to doing what we were by now bound to do.

Soon enough our fatal fourth revealed herself; the Carmelite took off her pillowcase. I will not bother to describe her face, except to say that she had once been married but had been widowed by the sleeping sickness. It seems that her husband, a professor of dialectics and a chronic narcolept, had been falling asleep during his own lectures for several years and had finally been advised by the doctors to take henbane and nightshade, the which had kept him wide awake day and night for six months, until he had suddenly gone to sleep in bed with, and I rather think, astride, his wife, and had not waked up since.

At any rate, Fandanga was the name she preferred, and she was not pretty, but had a hungry heart, a tart nature, and capacious hips. She joined our nightly tertulia, and to my puzzlement, the Twigger took to her at once, while Fray Gabriel studied her guardedly and without any excess of enthusiasm. Nonetheless, on the third or fourth night, the pot suddenly boiled over.

Fray Gabriel and the Twigger had come out after a day of hot dispute, and the monk was in his most rabiating mood and looking for a way to cause discomfort equal to his own.

"Lucero, you are holding back again," he accused me, leaning close to pop his eyes. "What is it, my dandyish friend, do you fear the evil you might do, should you unleash?"

"I have no more fear than you do," I told him. "And I have the advantage that should I let go and explode, I am not likely to spread so much bile and suet abroad."

He glared. "You are sharp. Take care that you do not do yourself an injury."

"I am not dull. Take care that you do not get cut."

"My God!" He burlesqued shock. "Harken, the scaldobanco speaks! He preaches moderation one day and threatens us with murder the next, and all because he feels himself swept up in currents he does not understand and cannot control." He swayed closer. "There is only one thing worse than a man who is afraid of others, and that is one who is afraid of himself."

"I am no more afraid than you, and I think less so," I told him. "I have heard that the walrus, when terrified, is prone to bite his parts off."

"That is the castor, you fool, the beaver!" he roared, pointing a finger at my nose. "This dreary winter worker and busy builder of tidy dams against the spring flood!" He was in a barking frenzy now. "I will show you who is the moral slave here, and who is free!" Grasping the hand of the simpering Fandanga, he pushed her before him and out the door, and his farewell howl drifted back, bearing Puncinello's curtain line: "Hurrah! The Devil is dead, now we can all do as we like!"

Urgent and intimate silence pressed in upon the wake of his going. At the corner of my eye, the Twigger smoldered in her dingy rags like some red-hot coal enticing the tongs.

"Now what in the world is wrong with him," I said, maintaining a comradely tone.

"Aaaaaaa," she shrugged, turning the florid dumpling of her face and bending a heated green gaze upon me. "He envies you, for he is the illegitimate son of the Duke of Osuna, poor and not pretty to boot. Also, his left huevo never descended or something. I keep telling him that Aristotle had the first two disabilities and Alexander the last, but he will no longer listen to me."

290

We made our way, softly stumbling and bumping, to their apartments, and she seemed unsurprised to find the monk not at home. We groped through a restive stirring of children and livestock, so that it was as much a journey for the nose as for any other part. In the small back room, my knees bumped the edge of a bed. She let herself down into the humid sheeting and was silent, drawing me to her as the placid lake draws the shout. She was all puddled pudding and heat rash in the shuttered starlight, her knees crooked over my shoulders, her expression dimly passive and blandly fevered, the lips slackening to let pass an occasional ruminating moan.

While I labored to make the moment memorable, she seemed to have already forgotten it. Feverishly I kneaded the compliant tits, arranged the unresistant limbs, and dredged the bottomless swamp. And yet for all this dim distance and vague dispersal, we were both excited, for that other promise thrummed our fibers: the possibility of a third party looming in the darkness.

As I finished my fit and fell against the wall, she squirmed free, and I watched her go barefoot to a bassinet and bend above two pudgy legs kicking from the wicker. Murmuring motherly nonsense, she lifted up a laden diaper. While a large black poodle watched from the corner, its bright eyes glinting from beneath its woolly brow.

Thus we got started, and thus we carried on. Coming together in the wine cellar each evening like witches at a common brew, we swilled and nudged, and otherwise attenuated the tentigo to that point where the first two clutched together and fled, leaving the other two to do the same. Sometimes it was Fray Gabriel and Fandanga who rushed out first, sometimes the Twigger and me.

Several times I tried to coax her into the fields and once tried to make stairwork of her on the way to their apartments, but she would have it nowhere else but at home. Always there was the squirm and mutter of other life and its pungent effluvium; once I tripped over a crawling child, another time I skidded on dog dirt whilst fumbling my way toward ecstasy. It was almost as though the act had no meaning for her away from her domestic zoo.

Still, it seemed that I had solved my dilemma. Was this not true moral freedom? We came together only because we wanted to, only when we wanted to, with no promises made, and therefore none broken. Gabriel neither denounced nor threatened me beyond his habitual browbeating, and why should he, since he was enjoying equal license. Freedom could be earned only by giving it in return, as he was fond of iterating. It seemed that at last I had found the formula for guiltless love.

And yet on the odd night that I spent in my own bed, I had nightmares. Split yellow eyes looked in the window. A black creature ran on all fours, barking inanely up and down the halls, past my door, then away to the cloisters, then at my door again! I sat bolt upright, running with sweat, and strained to hear the insistent yap-yap-yap receding back down the stairs toward the cellar.

The truth was that I was ashamed, but beyond that, I was suffering an increasingly pressing sense of being outnumbered and a mere cipher in somebody else's game. I decided to break the formula.

"Well, well, here we are all together again," said the monk. "The loose and easy lovers of freedom. And what about you tonight, Lucero, weren't you planning to leave this place and go back to painting? Or are you still not finished grinding your pigments in another man's mortar?"

"I grind my pigments where I find them," I said. "As do you. But you complain. Could it be that moral freedom is too much for you? Are you perhaps thinking of revising your communista theories out of worry for your property? I mean that mortar you mention."

"Hah!" He reared back. "Do not confuse the interests of others with your own, Lucero, that is a bad habit you have. I advise you to simply face the fact that you will never make a libertine of yourself, and let it go at that. As for my aspheterism, I do and always shall advocate the sharing of property. Not out of morality, mind you, but because it is the only practical way for mankind."

"You mean the women too, I presume," I said, waving a hand to indicate those two present.

He glared watchfully. "I mean humankind."

"And what is mine is yours, what is yours mine?" I looked in the Twigger's direction.

He beamed at his wife. "Precisely. After all, the only true freedom is the freedom to choose. . . ."

"Very well," I said, reaching for Fandanga's hand. She resisted for only an instant. "As Plautus has said it, so it shall be," I said, towing her to the door.

And as I glanced back, I saw the remaining two standing rigid, looking for all the world like a stone priest and his nunmutton suddenly without encouragement to their odium veneris. But I underestimated the monk's gluttony. And the depth of her passion.

Having fandangoed Fandanga, I went to my cell, for I hoped that the evening's turnabout might earn me a peaceful sleep. However, no sooner had I laid my head on my pillow and slipped myself into sleep's stunning envelope, when the same black nightmare began to gallop to and fro upon my brain, up and down the hallways, suddenly outside my door! Again I awoke to find it real, but this time leaped from my bed, snatched up my sword, and went out in my nightshirt.

The night was clear, the moon full above the cloisters, and I was crazed yet scarcely knew it, for the yapping was real enough. Now it seemed to come from the great hall. Barefoot, I winced my way hence, but now it sounded elsewhere. The creature was circling me. Turning, I saw a black form pass the far door, running soundlessly. I crouched in a shadowed niche, waiting to kill it.

Then I glimpsed a new silhouette out through the window, in the cloisters, against the lowering moon: two figures strolling arm in arm, the one big-headed and shambling, the other slight, with long hair. And while I knew at once that the taller one was Fray Gabriel, I could not be sure about the other, except that her hair was not brown, nor was it red.

Next morning, I dallied in my cell for some time before admitting that I could not stay away. That day's play rehearsal had been called off, I was told, and I could find evidence of Fray Gabriel in neither chapel nor wine cellar. Nor was there any sign of him in his apartments, where the Twigger shuffled about amongst her squawling troops with her hem down and her hair in her face.

My greeting being received with a russet glower and some mumbled obscenities, I trailed her into the kitchen, followed in turn by the black poodle. While the sun streamed in through the window, she glumly stirred a vast stew, now and then ferociously adding more hot sauce.

"I hope," I said, "that you were happily reunited with your husband last night, and that your domestic tranquillity has been restored."

"In a pig's arse," was her reply, and next she flung her spoon into the stew and the sauce jug after it, and turned on me in a flaming rage. "He went to her last night, thanks to you!"

"Fandanga? Well, he must have had a swampy time of it—"

"Not her, *her!*" she shouted. "That prissy duchess, that simpering shortheel. Oh, it's not the first time. I can hear her now, 'Oooo, Gabriel, what a Caesar to the world, what a Lope with the pen, what a bull in bed.'"

She was in a real fit, mincing and rolling her eyes in inspired mimicry, then gnashing her teeth and strangling the air with her fists. "He is still there!" she boiled. "They are probably at it at this very moment!"

Never once in all the times that she had kissed and clutched and lain beneath me had she showed the tenth part of such a fine passion. I could no longer avoid the fact that I had grown fond of her. My furia gathered itself.

"Oh that bitch, that whore," she gasped, slumping against the table and clutching at the air. "I hate her as I hate him! I hate them, I hate them! There is a stick in my throat, a knife in my heart . . ."

Compared to all that, of what possible help could be a mere yard in her coony? Nevertheless, I was bound to try. Kicking the door shut, I went at her right there on the tiles, while her zoo bawled and scratched in the next room; and this time I put her face down, spread her rump with my thumbs and proceeded to give her what for on the kitchen floor through the back door.

"We could go away," she gasped against the tiles. "I could take the children. It would break the bastard's heart."

At this further sign of her deepest allegiance, I gave it to her all the harder, my sockets aching, the sweat whipping from my hair.

And then I became aware of close pursuit, that is, that the kitchen door had swung open behind us. At first I thought it must be the poodle, and then I turned my head and saw the third party looming in person and lifting high his robe; and whatever the disposition of his left bollock, Brother Gabriel was not without a ready yard.

His eyes burst from the enflamed patchwork of his face, his cheeks ballooned, and he let loose his mad and exultant roar. "Got you at last, you cuckolding coxcomb, got you!"

But I was just that little bit quicker. Dodging to the side, I let him have my target, and with a grunt of unbelieving horror, he went up to the nuts in his domestic dilemma.

I would very much like to have stayed a moment longer to savor their expressions, but it seemed to me a most propitious moment to retire from the contemplative life.

Felicio watched from a bench while I got on my horse. Claiming to have found a home in that place, he had decided to stay awhile.

"Watch out," I said. "They will use you as they were using me."

He laughed, pointing a flower. "I beg your pardon, who using whom?"

I had to grin, but it also was painful; I remembered the feather-soft touch of the Twigger's hair. "Shut up."

He turned his head as I went past. "My dear Juan, the only way you will ever get me to shut up is to let me savor your yard."

Heading south, I stopped at my uncle's villa in Valencia, and who should I find on his doorstoop but a battered scarecrow which, when it croaked a solicitous greeting, proved to be old Catalinon. And old he was, too, white-haired and sunken-eyed and scarcely able to leer. With much tugging of the forelock, he let me know that he had long ago drunk up his inheritance, and had come here looking for service, but the count wouldn't have him.

"But surely, young master, you wouldn't turn out an old family retainer, and crippled at that," he said, sidling closer to show some new scars, then cocking up a wily eye. "I recall one time when me and the upstairs scullery was bundling, and you come down the hall all saucer-eyed from something you'd heard—"

"Never mind about that," I said, considering his proposition. After all, a squire would be a cheap enough hedge against bare loneliness, and for well-executed seductions one often needed an extra hand. "I might take you on," I told him. "If I get my money."

My uncle had word from Don Diego that I might now return to Sevilla, provided I avoid scandal. But I must stay away from Madrid.

"But my child is there. I want to see her."

He shook his head. "I am sorry, nephew, but my brother is the one with the money and influence these days. I have written to the king offering my services to help liberate the heathen somewhere. Anywhere. But until then, I need Diego's help." He held up a small bag of coins. "And so I must have your promise before I give you this."

It was gall, but I gave my word to stay away from Madrid.

"Did you have a good time at the monastery?" he wanted to know.

I told him what had happened, down to the touching reunion of husband and wife.

He allowed himself amusement. "Marvelous! Your friend Fray Gabriel sounds quite an attractive fellow."

"Friend!" I made a face.

He came closer to give me my money together with a knowing smile. "Is soulmate a better term? Don't you know yet that contention is a kind of flirtation? Ah, Juanito, you are no less a self-deceiving rascal than ever, but still pretty. And look how you jitter and caracole to hear it. How spoiled you always were, and still are. Perhaps it is because you had no father. Tell me, while you claim women to be the only goad and goal of your hunger, how is it that you also flirt with men?"

"Flirt?" I strangled. "What do you mean?"

He leaned so close I could smell his perfume and see the vein jumping in his caressing eye. "My dear nephew, I have watched you for a long time now, and I think it is time you knew that what you need is nothing more or less than a good stiff yard up your—"

"Damn you, uncle!"

But my furia forgot that this was the hero of Antwerp and Zante. How quick he was, taking my lunge along his blade and very nearly sending my sword from my hand.

"I could stick you, you know," he hissed through his very white teeth.

But as quickly as it had appeared, the icy ardor drained from his eye, and he put his point to the floor and turned half away. "You see how we spoil you, Juanito? Now go. You may yet find a way."

25

NEVER MIND, it seemed to me that there was nothing new to be learned, nor any illusions left to modify. Love was the function of some insatiable need, like the leech which the quack phlebotomist wears beneath his shirt, feeding his pet until he finds his next patient. The sighs and wistful fixations of that need were like sticking plaster and could be stuck anywhere; when love went rancid on one beloved, we were always ready to transfer it to another.

Woman was not the custodian of man's virtue, as was often claimed; she was too much troubled with getting a good price for her own. As for the Golden Moment, its carnal equivalent was not exclusive to any particular woman, but could be enjoyed by a skillful fornicator with any one or all of them. As for a more deep and lasting surcease of need, I began to wonder if there was any such at the top of Climax's ladder. It seemed we must be content with that one moment of meaningless release which came at the end of any good swive.

But at least the winning of that moment now held less terror for me; I knew how to get it and still get away. Or so I told myself, and I determined to test the new temper of my heart and the sharpness of my skill at the very next opportunity.

With Catalinon a respectful pace behind, I went aboard a coastal barque at Valencia, and five days later was put down with my horse and squire in sunny Málaga. We were making our way along the shore, looking for a hay bargain, when we rounded a sandy hillock and glimpsed a young girl perched on a rock and dangling a fishing line into the water. She was a typical country maiden, which is to say that she wore an exceedingly smug look on her prettiness, and a pink ribbon on her pigtail as a sign that she still had her maidenhead.

"Hold and hush," I said to Catalinon, making him duck down with me below the rock. She had not yet seen us, and we could hear her musing aloud, as only a pampered virgin can:

"Foolish little fish that lashes the sea, just like a foolish man. Like Anfriso, who haunts my door and decks the roof with evergreen, and still means nothing to me. Immune to love, that's me. Play with the men as I play with the fish. Better cast my bait windward. Oh, how I would like to catch some new and pretty plaything today. Tum-dee-dum-dum-dum."

"You shall, my little darling," I muttered, taking off my cloak and hat. How scrubbed and chaste she was, fairly crying out to be soiled. "You shall have yourself a shark of many hues."

"Rather full of herself, isn't she?" Catalinon was saying, watching the girl preen. "Rump-proud, but unpoxed, I daresay." Then he saw me testing the water with my toe. "Going wading at a time like this?"

"Going fishing," I said, letting myself down into the water. "Do not show yourself until she has pulled in this drowning nobleman. And play the game well, rascal, or you'll lose your living."

I swam underwater to her bait, put the hook into my shirt, and surfaced, gurgling. With a cry of excitement, she proceeded to pull me in; that is, I let her. Crawling like a crab onto the sand, I rolled over, and disembogued a quantity of sea water. Through my salty squint I could see her hilarious unbelief as she bent above me, but she hadn't the sharpest wit in the world, and when Catalinon came running to enrich the event, she began eagerly to believe.

"Is he all right? Thank God you have found him!" cried Catalinon. "We have both just now fallen from a ship, and I thought he must have drowned, robbing a most noble and well-fixed house of its only son. And I would be blamed, being his handservant. Quick, let's pump the water out of him."

"Poor thing," she murmured, kneeling to help push at my ribs. "But he does look healthy enough, and not bad-looking. Noble house, did you say? And is he married?"

"No, poor man, he is only rich."

I groaned becomingly, and she lifted my head into her lap and began to pick seaweed from my hair. "Gallant man of noble brow, return, I pray, to life." She must have got her language from reading romances.

I opened my eyes. Over her shoulder I could see Catalinon, blown up like a toad with stifled laughter. "Where am I?"

"Safe from all perils, in a woman's arms," she said. "My name is Thisbe. Which noble house did you say?"

"I am a Lucero," I said. "Call me Diego. My God, what an experience. I perished in the sea, but you are life. Just a moment ago I was in the hellish depths, and now I soar skyward and find myself in radiant heaven, and you my angel . . ."

Oh yes, I laid it on from the start, and why not; no doubt her loutish country swains were close-mouthed, for all their fawning love. And it worked. Her problem was boredom, her dilemma that her humble station and rustic suitors were no match for her inflated idea of her worth. Vain little fool, I told her outright that (1) I was in love with her on sight; (2) I would make her a rich lady; (3) I needed care and shelter. The three infallible keys to a woman's gate.

With Catalinon helping and me pretending vertigo, we got into her little fisher hut by the shore, and I lay wincing down upon her narrow cot, while she lit a candle.

"How sad to see so fine a gentleman thus fallen and helpless," she sighed, not sad at all, but fairly quivering over her catch; and she ran out for some water and fresh flowers for her hair.

"Get my horse ready and bring it to the back of this hovel," I whispered to my lackey. "This promises to be a quick one."

"What if her swain comes, or her father?" he said. "You are asking for trouble."

"Why not? Damn you, get going, here she comes."

He went out as she came running in. "Ah, you are here, thank God," she said, pink-cheeked and breathless. "I had the most awful feeling as I was picking violets that it had not happened, that you were not really here, and I was once again a neglected bloom amongst the thistles."

"I am here, pretty blossom," I said, reaching for her hand. "Feel how my heart beats."

She let me hold her hand, then drew it quickly back. "I feel so strange today," she confessed. "For the first time since my First Communion, I feel lost."

I could see it, the pitiable mingling of ambition and fear in her pretty little face. I could feel it, the tug of sympathy under my ribs. I knew her giddy confusions as I knew myself, and worse: the pain of loss and waste she was soon to suffer. But in her eye I also saw calculation and greed equal to her innocence. The question was, was it equal to my own?

"You are not lost, you are found," I assured her, then pretended to pout. "But your words do not convince me of your feelings."

"Why is that?"

"If you loved me as your eyes say you do, you would lessen my pain."

"Your hand is warm and gentle," she murmured. "Surely you are a good and honest man. But you go too fast! I have suitors in the village and a good name to guard."

"They do not know I am here," I reminded her.

"Oh, I don't know," she said in some consternation. "I fear that love has found me out at last, and you are my punishment for being so cruel to Anfriso. Are you really a Lucero?"

I showed her my signet ring, with Don Diego's coat of arms and his motto: BY VIRTUE, NOT BY CLEVERNESS.

"How sweet," she said. "And is it real gold?"

"The purest," I assured her. "And this as well." Around my neck hung the small crucifix that was also the key to my grandmama's escape hatch, and I lifted it up so that she might see that I was a good Christian. "As for your fears, they are nonsense. I know lasting love when I feel it, if you do not. I want more than mere dalliance, if you know what I mean."

Now she really was excited, twisting violets in her lap. "But my birth is not the same as yours."

"Love is like a king who levels all who come beneath his rule," I assured her, getting a grip on both her wrists. "And often it's his way to match sackcloth with silk to the benefit of both."

As always, it was all gabble on top, all dicker at bottom; I swore by my life and soul that I longed to marry, then proceeded to the rest: be like a peacock; the key is deceit; treat her like a person until she decides she wants to be treated like a woman; when in doubt, out! Her country swains had been too worshipful of her; all it took was a few lies, patience, and then a sudden push.

"Oh, please don't do that!"

Virgin, virgin, my first! I was trembling myself as I pegged her down on her back and wedged a hip between her legs, knocking over our candle in the process.

"Oh, oh!" she wailed, but the only answer was the pounding sea.

I forgot the candle while I insinuated my tongue into her shouting mouth to give her a preview and teach her some basics. Oh, oh! again, but she loved it. And now, to quell all doubt, out! I unlimbered with my free hand and put hers on my gristle.

"Oh, oh, *OH!*" Mustering all that was left of her small strength, she arched back and fixed me with pleading eyes. "But why? Why have you chosen me? Why do you want me?"

Did I now pause to consider? Did I rein in the loin for sententious cogitation in the name of truth? No. But I gave her an honest answer. I stuck it in her.

"Yeow! Fire, O fire! I am burning!"

Delicious to hear her gratifying cries as I went at it. Delightful to hear her final small shriek as Esclavo bludgeoned his way through the spongy veil. Tight too, as she thrashed, and I stirred that hot little stew of blood, piss, and tears, teaching her to feel beyond first shock, to know that there was a squeeze and clutch in her the likes of which she had never dreamed; making sure she would never forget, nor ever be young again.

"O God! Forgive and pity me!"

For pity, I gave her seven more strokes and spent; and simultaneously as it happened, the whole little hut went up in flames, and as I pushed her out ahead of me, then went staggering past her through the smoke, I was laughing as hard and heartily as ever I had since boyhood.

"Run, you idiot," I said to Catalinon, flinging myself onto my horse. "She'll have the bumpkins after us once she finds a pair of dry drawers and knows the full extent of her lesson."

"So you did it."

"Yes, and a thorough job of it, I must say."

302

"And now you are ending it."

"My dear fellow, I have just begun."

How straightforward and satisfying to write one's own license, to consider no other needs but one's own. It was, I speculated, like being a bull in his finest rage or a bullet from the harquebus, propelled by overwhelming force from behind, all committed to one purpose ahead.

A ride of ten not notable days brought us home to Sevilla, and it was all joy to stroll down the Arenal amongst the sailors and their trulls, to watch the merchants squabble on the steps of the Orangery, and once again to be a part of that circus of prayer and corruption which is our greatest city. I went straight to the bodegas of the Calle Sierpes, and in no time found Esteban Guzman.

But the former venereal prodigy of Snake Street had changed. His shoulders were stooped, the top of his nose had grown uncommonly thick and red, and there was a new quaver in his voice. "Juanito, you look well. There is even racy rumor of you from Barcelona." He managed a faint smile and twiddled his long fingers at his chin. "So you have left the amateur ranks at last."

"I hope so," I said, unable to take my eyes from his nose. "What's wrong with your nozzle?"

The little rabbit of fear ran past his eyeholes, and he lowered his voice. "Well, frankly, the bleeders tell me I have the Gallic pox. Two years ago I was clapt, you see, and, as you know, the best cure for that is a virgin." He wet his lips and gave a feeble smile. "Unfortunately, I got hold of some bad medicine. I mean, she was no virgin, and within the month I was sitting on a pot of fuming sulphur. And lately I have this infernal knot on my nose."

"A virgin, you say?" I put a nervous hand to my cod. "Well, what about other women? What of Carolina?"

"Ah," he sighed. "A piteous sight. She is going bald and shedding eyelashes."

"A shame, I had some unfinished business with her. But she's no good to me in such a condition."

He widened an eye. "You have changed."

"So have you."

He let go another sigh. "For the worst, I am afraid. I have even been losing at cards. And I have a woman in my house. . . ." He stopped himself, and the faintest touch of the old wile stirred in his glance. "Listen, she is young and not bad looking. There is even a rumor that she is the only daughter of some rich and powerful man and in hiding from her father, although she denies it. Would you like to meet her?"

"And get the pox?"

"Not likely," he said, gloomily fingering his nose. "The doctors say my troubles are all mine now and can't be given away."

"Well then, what's wrong with her?"

He attempted a shrug of innocence, but to look into his fugitive eye was to glimpse the bitter leavings of some unspeakable ecstasy. "Nothing at all, only that she has certain . . . habits."

"No thanks," I said. "I recall a widow you recommended."

He had even learned to blush. "Yes, I'm sorry about that. Well then, at least you can come to dine at my house."

"Oh, very well," I said, giving way to curiosity, for, of course, I knew she would be there. He fairly shivered with relief, and his lips seemed to mutter a soundless prayer. How, I wondered, could such a man, once so well armored, have gone so very transparent?

It was no common attraction that pinned me like a fly the moment I was close to her. At a distance she might have seemed only another pinched and spindly young girl. But some secret and furious fever burned in her and emanated with such force that I could actually feel its powerful mischief.

She wore a flowing forest-green gown of some clinging stuff, from which her thin arms thrust out at sharp angles, touched at elbows and wrists with a faint flush of rose. Her neck was long and thin and her head narrow, with tilted blue eyes, rather close together and tightly crossed, accounting for the peculiar intensity of her gaze. Her nose was thin-bladed but strong, and beneath it she had a small mouth, meager of lip, almost mean, yet curled in a smile which seemed passionately to declare, "I am wonderful."

"Peregrina, allow me to present Don Juan Lucero," said Estaban in the uncomfortable tone of a man opening his most secret and awful closet. "Juan, meet Peregrina Lagarta-Martin. Or at least she says that is her name." He attempted a playful smile, but she ignored him. "She also claims to have been at court as companion to the Marquesa of Castellon."

She smiled. Where had I seen that pinched face before, that baiting smile? She reminded me of somebody. "The Marquesa of Castellon," I said. "Isn't that lady noted for her loose tongue and tight purse?"

"Nowadays for her uncertain bowel," she said ever so sweetly. "You see, the day before she dismissed me, I put a powerful purge into her morning chocolate, causing her an acute embarrassment that noon at court. The king afterward remarked that he had never seen the marquesa run so fast."

Her narrow breast shook with girlish laughter; it was quite incredible to see such a measure of wicked glee in one face.

"Audacious," I said. "But why?"

Her face wizened with sudden ferocity. "She had found certain garments of mine in the marqués's possession the day before and had flown into a rage and thrown my darling Sheba into the fish pond, nearly drowning him." At that moment, a lean but powerful black cat appeared, seemingly from beneath her skirts, leaped to her shoulder, and crouched there.

"Dear Sheba, she tried to do away with you, didn't she?" she murmured in a purring voice, caressing the cat and eying me. "There, there, sweet thing, do not be afraid, Peregrina will see to it that you get what you deserve."

But the evening took its most arresting turn following dinner. The serving girls removed the dishes, and Peregrina turned a smile to our host. "I believe it is time for my medicine."

Esteban looked sickly. "If you insist."

I was amused as she produced a lady's small wicker sewing basket, but my chitterlings went tight as she opened it and proceeded to lay certain paraphernalia upon the table, beginning with a glass jug full of clear liquid and with dark leeches clinging to its inside surface.

"Are you," I asked with uncertain humor, "planning to bleed yourself?"

"Oh, quite the contrary." She shot me a small smile, and the cat watched me, its tail lashing her shoulder. Now she took out what looked to be a brass sacking needle, then a short stub of candle, a pewter spoon, and a fold of pale blue silk with a lump of something wrapped in it. "My precious diapapaver," she said, unrolling the silk and holding up a lump of some dark and tarry substance about the size of the end of her forefinger. "Happy dust from the blossoms of the East, most genial dreamstuff and noble enemy of pain," she murmured, handling it with quite the same reverence and fondness with which she had petted her cat. "Would Don Juan care to quaff the breath of heaven?"

With a challenging glance, she thrust the lump under my nose.

I sniffed. It had a peculiar odor, something like pitch but sweeter; I was put in mind of tar taken from between the toes of an ebony idol; it suggested removal, trance.

"Opium?" Ah, how calmly I said it, how level my gaze, even as my fibers jittered.

"A guess?" she murmured sweetly, and set about cooking her second dinner. In fact, she had eaten little before and seemed quite indifferent to food. But now, with what a fond absorption she proceeded, nor were the two of us any less attentive as she lit the candle, then poured aqua regia into the spoon and spit the lump on the end of the needle. Holding the spoon above the flame, she waited for the liquid to bubble, then took the needle with her other hand and lowered the lump into the liquid. It sizzled and swiftly melted into a thin dark syrup. "Laudanum," she murmured, and this she delicately stirred for a moment, then lay the spoon aside and reached for the jar of leeches.

I felt my stomach turn, and Esteban went a shade paler as she lowered a pair of pewter pincers into the jar and drew out a worm. The leech wriggled and changed form, fattening first to one side of the pincers, then the other; but for all its protean gymnastics, it could not escape. It was a big one, nearly six inches when extended, but flaccid and loose: empty.

"Ah, he is hungry," she murmured. "It is best when they are fairly snapping with famine."

What delight she took in nausea, her own and that of others. What a childish pride in her knowledge of obscure and grisly dicta.

"They can vary in size from a few fingers up to three palms long, and it is said that they can appropriate three times their weight in liquid." Putting the beast on the table beside the spoon, she laid the pincers aside and glanced at each of us in turn. The air was tense with choice considered, and Esteban's stony stare said no. She returned him a disdainful glance, as if to deny the offer, and turned to me. "Might I borrow your belt, Don Juan?"

Flattered and flustered, I pulled my waist cord free and handed it to her.

"Now comes the problematical part," she murmured. She looped the cord around her arm just below the elbow, held one end tightly in her fist, and took the other between her teeth, then laid her forearm upon the table, tender side up, and began to rub the skin briskly, bending to peer at its surface.

"I have such thin and fugitive veins, you see," she murmured as she rubbed and peered, peered and rubbed. "They are far below the surface as it is, and they only retreat the deeper when I most want them up and ready to drink." She spied an eye up at me. "I often have conversations with them. Up, little vein, don't hide, come on, you know you cannot escape, we are in this together, and you know you always like it once the painful part is over. . . ."

She went on like that for some moments, while I struggled to deny the excitement that fattened my own veins to bursting; and Esteban gawked, his shoulder blades grinding the back of his chair.

"Diamerdes!" She spit out the cord and turned to me, readjusting the knot and holding out the two ends.

Even as instinct signals the crucial moments, delusion obscures their meaning. I preferred to see it as a challenge to my courage, and took hold of the cords as the dog takes the other end of its leash in its teeth, out of the desire to play his own master.

And she smiled coyly, exultantly, then bent again to her search: rubbing, peering. "There, I see one! Be ready to let go when I say the word. Tighter, one is coming up, tighter!"

I tightened, the cord turned the flesh red where it bit, Esteban leaned away, and slowly, as she rubbed and we both bent to look, and I bore down on her bonds, a faint green vein appeared deep in the flesh.

"There it is," she muttered, poising a thumb and forefinger above the leech. "Remember to let go when I say so. A little tighter, now hold . . ."

She snatched up the leech and squeezed it. There was a moist whistle of air, and thin liquid sprayed from the worm's front end. She plunged it head first into the dark soup and loosened her grip on its middle, causing the beast to inhale, much as a wineskin does, sucking up nearly the entire contents of the spoon and becoming instantly fat as a sausage. The which gorged creature she swiftly clapped to her arm, positioning the head just over the vein, then flicked its nether end with her forefinger, once, twice, the third time causing the beast to open its fangs and sink them into the vein.

"Now!"

I flung the cords from me, blood spurted from the wound, and with a cry of triumph, she gave the worm a mighty squeeze, shooting the soup into her.

"Ah!" she said, writhing on her seat. "Ohhh," she groaned, trying to give it an extra pinch. "Oh, that was good, good." Her arm stretched out on the table, the depleted creature dangling from a rosette of blood. And even as I saw the leech detach itself and slowly curl up and die, I raised my glance to her face, and it seemed to my incredulous study that she was becoming another creature, no longer so sharp with challenge, but soft and pliant. In fact, her eyes slowly came uncrossed, and to my astonished gaze, she became the picture of perfect peace and beauty.

Soon after, I found myself on my feet and started for the door, with Esteban in mute attendance, looking as stunned as I, yet with a certain furtive expectancy in his eye.

"I can't bear to be involved myself," he muttered. "But once it is done . . ." He gave a sheepish shrug.

I would have continued out without a farewell, had she not stirred in her chair and called out in a voice gone languid, yet still mischievous: "Thank you for your help, Don Juan. You must try it yourself sometime, I do believe you might be one of us. I can most often be found at the Court of Elms."

And then I remembered who it was she reminded me of: Felicio.

26

I HAD thought there was nothing more I wanted from women, and therefore nothing more they could do to me. But venereal adventure had again become an arena of doors. Once I had thought there was only one, but going through it, found that there were others. And now I trembled and turned at the crimson locus, confronted by a strangely marked portal, the most beguiling of all. I could not forget the heat of her mischief, the bite of the cord, the mystery of the leech. To choose right might be to find surcease. But to choose wrong could be to confront the Minotaur.

And so I determined to make no choice, but to eschew the enchantments of women, indeed, of the whole world, until my nerves were better. I decided once again to marry the muse, and took a house on the opposite side of town from Snake Street, entirely surrounded by a thicket of thorny woodbine, and with a shed out back for Catalinon.

But I found that I could not put my mind to it. My determination wavered and my brush fell idly on the canvas. At night I dreamed that a tiny hand tried to comfort me, while a great ball of string tumbled, unwinding. I awoke to find my pillow wet and my teeth rattling. Each morning I drove myself into my studio, only to see a dim figure out of the corner of my eye: a man all the dull gray of ashes, seated in a chair beside the door, reaching out a hand, inviting me to come closer. When I turned, the ghost was gone. But the next time I passed through the doorway, he was there again, imploring. I was suddenly overcome with raging furia at the sight. All my life it seemed he had been dogging me, again and again sending me fleeing from his unsubstantial presence toward flesh that could be touched, from the grave to the coony, from the paella pan into the fire. "Monster!" I howled, and went for him with my sword. Only to come up against the blank wall, plaster showering down upon my bruised knuckles, my blade once again badly bent.

We love solitude only when the world crowds us. Apanthropy is not a natural passion, but only another ruse by which we struggle against our master, desire. I had been in seclusion scarcely a week when I instructed Catalinon to follow at a discreet distance and headed for the Court of Elms.

Located beside the cathedral and well within the chains that marked ecclesiastical jurisdiction, the Corral de Los Olmos was sanctuary to all manner of picaros: ring-piggers, pickpockets, unemployed soldiers, false monks, and murderers. And here also gathered the women of the streets to keep the rogues company. She was just turning from one of the stalls that sold colored ices, and we saw one another at the same instant.

"That one?" muttered Catalinon behind me. "Master, I do not know the creature, but these old bones tell me bad weather is coming."

My bones agreed, and yet I stood rooted to the flagstones as she came toward me. How pinched her face, how slovenly her ambling movements. Her smile curled, and she darted the point of her tongue at the confection in her fist. "You are early. I thought you might resist at least for a fortnight."

I glowered. The sun beat down and neither of us moved, and yet the mania came from her like a furnace glow. Or was it coming from me? Which burns brightest at the moment of conflagration, the flame or the moth?

She showed her small, pointed dog teeth. "Would you like to come with me and have a lick of my ice?"

"No," I said.

"Good," she said. "My apartments are just down the street."

She had the third floor of a broken-down house just behind the prison at the end of Sierpes Street. Halting on the doorstep, she turned a sharp glance upon Catalinon. "Get us some pastries and candles, and find some musicians to play for us. Go!"

He looked to me. "And a dollop of rum for yourself," I added, giving him some money.

"Who commands the servant owns the master," he muttered, going away.

Once inside her high and heavy door, the noise of the street was silenced, and those few rooms became all the world. She led me past a small kitchen to her large bedroom at the back.

Clearly this was where she lived, for all the furniture was there, and a heap of her dresses in a corner. Night and day were all the same, for the windows had heavy curtains, and there were only candles all around the walls, making a circle of light that scarcely encompassed the bed, for it took up most of the room and was the largest I had ever seen.

"Is your house nice?" she asked.

"Larger than this," I heard myself say, and I tried a grin. "But the bed is a bench compared to yours."

"And are you happy there all alone?"

"At times yes, at times no," I said, and the wariness clutched for purchase again, and again lost its grip to the trembling tide.

"And just now?"

I stepped closer. "Quite a bit of both."

"Poor thing." She laughed, but turned restlessly away, as though she had used up her last energy in getting me there, and now was gone irritable with some unknown emptiness.

Her ankles were thick, I told myself, her knees were knobby and her breasts too small. She was a flamingo, a pink stork. And I stepped helplessly closer.

"One moment," she whispered, her hands to my chest. What a wealth of perversity she could put into the politest plea. "Why don't you make some cocoa, while I prepare my medicine."

I put the chocolate on the coals and returned to find her opening her sewing basket and laying out her paraphernalia. I went cold in the bowel and suffered renewed compulsion to flee.

She must have sensed it, for she glanced up, and from her tensioned face came sly, serpentine challenge. "Shall I cook some for you?"

My head gave a desperate shake.

She smiled, but her fingers shook as she lit a candle. "All the more for me, then."

And now the lump, the spoon, the jug of worms. Again the sizzling of the syrup, the knotting of the cord, then the muttering search for a vein. I made an attempt to give my fascination a mask of disdain. But I also had that other drama in mind, and so I waited in a growing fever of impatience, the ghastly tension of the one ritual stoking me toward the other.

Suddenly she snatched up the leech, filled it at the spoon, and clapped it to her arm. "Now!" she cried, and I let go the cord, and she gave the worm a mighty squeeze, splattering blood and syrup, squirting it home. "Oh!" she whispered, pinching the creature again. "Ohhhhh," she murmured, sinking back and closing her eyes. "That was good. So terrible and so sweet, like a blinding flash of light, a golden flame. And now, only sweetness and ease."

And as the leech detached itself and slowly curled and died, the crisscross tension unloosed its grip on her eyes, the rosette flush spread delicately upon her cheeks, the small lines left her brow and the contours softly assembled toward harmony. And she was once again beautiful.

I watched this miracle, aghast and stunned, and more: vaguely estranged. Did she sense envy's furtive misery? She lay herself on the bed and looked up, her eyes all the blue of some pale lake, the tiny centers chips of flotsam. "At least join me by smoking a little ganga. A gift from Uncle Hashish, in my basket there, the pipe and the little brick."

I brought it, and she got upon one elbow and showed me how to crumble the stuff into the bowl of the pipe, how to light and draw in the grassy smoke. All pinch had gone from her face now, and the lips were a delicate peach color, molded and seashell smooth. She smiled, and the wickedness was no longer so hard in her eyes but only playful, nor did the dog teeth any longer seem sharp.

"A basin," she murmured. "I may retch, but pay no heed, it does not hurt. Nothing hurts now."

My eyes burned in the dark of the kitchen, and my mouth seemed unaccountably dry. I became fretful at my work, whatever it was, for it seemed I had been in the kitchen for three days, and still had accomplished nothing. Suddenly I became alarmed; by now she had surely escaped. Reminded of the need for the basin in my hand, I paused for a moment, or was it a week, beguiled by the idea of Time. That is, that it was not what it seemed to be, but something else, likely immeasurable, but very probably marvelous. It was difficult to comprehend it exactly, due to the passage of it.

The latter thought, while quite fatuous to me now, spurred me to a seizure of hilarity so delightful and violent that I found myself on my back on the tiles, holding the basin to my stomach and choking with laughter.

Eventually, during which time it seemed that the kingdom must have changed hands several times, I found myself back beside the bed, eager to tell her about my hilarious insight, the which I could not seem to remember, but was obliged instead to stand in dim attendance whilst she disembogued into the basin, and I amused myself with meandering a millennium of thought. Unable immediately to come upon any conception sufficiently humorous to explain my good feelings, I proceeded to giggle as briskly as before, but this time at absolutely nothing.

It did not occur to me that the behavior of my mind and body might be related to the stuff I had smoked in the little pipe. And besides, all that was only prelude to an equally delirious but more strenuous business.

Soon I had her clothes off and mine as well, and then was gliding into an eternity of engrossment. Every moment and fraction thereof became a granule of delight in an endless succession of sensual joys, one slide of membrane upon membrane taking me from the beginning of time to the end, then back again in the long glide from then to now, every tingle one amongst a mosaic of sweet millions.

It was a delirium of absolute uncare, with no names, no faces, no doubts; I could have swived a goat as joyously, had there been a way not to know that my beloved had cloven feet and a beard. But it came to me, at first distantly, that there were sounds which sought to reach me. I looked, to see her making wincing faces and turning her head this way and that and calling out invitingly, "Oh, it hurts, you are so big, didn't you know that I have a malady and have been swollen shut for a week!"

"Well, you are open now," I muttered from my trance, and sank back into sensual uncare.

But she was insistent, all moaning theatrics beneath me. "You invade me, you assault me, you lacerate me, you defile me!"

"In the name of God," I cried indignantly, "I am only swiving you!"

But she chose not to hear. "Oh, oh, it hurts, murderer, rapist, beast!" Beating at me with her fists, yet clinging all the tighter, she reached up her head and sank her teeth into my shoulder. I mean through to the gristle; the spasm went all the way to my huevos.

"Bitch!" I slapped her and found myself to be so unraveled that I promptly whacked her again.

And she beamed. She positively glowed with triumph, while down below, her flesh made a hotter fist.

The precise allure was new, but I knew the invitation, and instinct whispered of a trap. But at the same time, her blandishments had their effect on my vanity, and besides, I was too far into it to stop. Going up on stiffened arms, I proceeded to twist the opposite thongs of retardismo and perfuncturation into the one aching knot of cunctation, pummeling until the two cysts, one at the base of my root, the other at the back of my neck, swelled and finally popped.

But it was not to be so easy. Her voice was a dog tooth at my ear, nibbling.

"Well, my ten-minute wonder, did you have a good time?"

"Not bad." I looked away from her smile.

"I really was swollen, you know," she murmured coyly.

I shrugged. "But not so closed up that you did not open."

Her reply was suddenly stern. "Nor am I now so open that I am ready to close up."

I winced. Her voice flowed like honey, yet was the subtlest of commands. "I think you would like to smoke some more ganga. And then, what if you were to tie me to the bed?"

What can one tell of such a long groan of night? How did she get me to do it? For one thing, I had become addicted, to thunder in my blood.

314

I had come to believe that whatever mal event occurred, a good swive would cure it. In another sense, I had learned to do it, as I had often brandled, in the desperate hope that if I went at it hard and furiously enough, I might somehow get it over with once and for all. And in this new instance, there was, of course, the more shameful incitement; it was so good to be the opposite of afraid.

In fact, not all moments were to be remembered this first time, for I was new to the region, and although I had long been headed this way, arrival was too boggling for detail. Enough to remember how my hands trembled as I tied first one wrist to the bedpost, then the other, then one ankle, then the other. Spread like the captured Hottentot upon the ant heap, she squirmed and babbled ingenious incitement, and oh, the exultation and delight that choked me as I gazed upon her. Submission, utter and absolute. At last, a woman for my slave, an exclavo apart from my own easy flesh.

Gone were the treacherous slope, the shame of my prick in the rubble. Gone the shuttered windows, the foiling mockery of the veil, the running sands of retardismo, the punishing tears of the conspurcated, the fickle demands of the distaff spasm. She was mine by her own request, to use as I wished, for so long as I should desire. She said so. She was bound, and I was free. I could do anything to her I wished, anything!

And what did I do? I swived her for six hours, by her calculation and subsequent gleeful announcement. Spending a second time and going at it again, until I glanced back to see the morning light gleaming upon my knotted buttocks.

Aghast and unbelieving, I paused. But she let go a most woeful and thrilling plea: "Oh, please do not do that, do not put it in my other place! Oh, please, do not! Oh, please!"

By now I knew the invitation from the rhetoric; her objection was my command. I untied her and rolled her onto her belly. Did I now gaze out the window and pass an idle comment upon the weather? Did I chuckle, applying grease to the nozzle?

No, I was without humor, a tranced familiar, gazing into the crusty eye of the puckered posticum. For the anus was the Devil's place, and the fundament the seat of death. Dirty, dirty, cursed from birth to disintegrate in the running black bowel of the earth. I was bad, very bad. But also big, very big. Balked, I butted; groan became squeal, thrash became scuffle, then I was past the collar and into the soup, then off at a neck-cracking gallop, fishing the fundament for my dishonored infancy.

Bad enough her final strangled cry and sacrificial quiverings. Bad enough the painful withdrawal, the squishing farewell of her closure. But worst of all, her gloating chuckle, coming muffled from the pillow: "You enjoyed every filthy minute of it. And you want more, more!"

No, I would not believe it, I was not that rabiating satyr. And yet when I woke some hours later, there she was asleep beside me, the fetters still on the bedpost, and to stir my cocoa was only to make it bitter, for the spoon had been used to cook her tacky potion. Getting into my clothes, I made for the door, only to step on a sated worm and nearly crash to the tiles.

She heard me and sat up, wizened and sharp-eyed. "Fleeing the scene of your crimes?"

How quickly she had learned my strings. "Not at all!" I protested. "That is, I mean, I thought I might get some sunshine."

"There is likely to be a shortage. It is the middle of the night."

I went to the door and came back. "You are right."

She smiled, holding her spoon over the candle. "Never mind, my darling, from now on, we shall be our own night and day. Scratch when you itch, eat when you are hungry, drink when you are dry."

She held up a swollen worm, and the creature wriggled and squirmed but could not get away. "When I have taken my medicine, you shall have a little ganga. And then we shall do exactly as we please." Her cold lips brushed my cheek and she gave a little laugh. "Be assured of that, you are doing what you want to. Otherwise, you wouldn't be here, would you?"

And now for the long saturnalia of dreams and dread. I have mentioned how ganga brought new proportions to time, denegating past and future and letting now, that is, each successive moment, take the stronger hand. As it seemed to uncumber the mind and give every thought the giddy lift of discovery, so it did the same for the body, leaving the flesh free to feel in the moment and thrill to all experience that was pleasant.

Drifting and dulled in the weedy swaddling of Uncle Hashish, I discovered the hedonist in me, and was amazed. Naked in our nest, we played and chattered, utterly without regard for time or consequence. Sometimes the bed was a boat, and we sailed the great sea of uncharted time; sometimes it was a flying carpet, often it was the catasta. Somewhere the sun crawled the heavens and after it the moon, but we knew nothing of that. When the musicians played outside the door, we sometimes listened, sometimes slept, sometimes asked for a more insistent rhythm, and then made long and melodious love to the beat.

I seem to remember Catalinon leaving food and drink in the doorway once or twice, his rum-raddled eyes gone saucers. Otherwise, we were alone and sufficient unto ourselves. The circle of candles was our eternal penumbra and the bed our home, and the only other party to our fevers was her cat.

She showed me how she kept him happy, manipulating his small yard until it emerged, cone-shaped and covered with little white knobs, and shot out its mighty droplet. We stroked the creature and it purred; we blew ganga into its face, and it lay back as we did, indolent and delirious; and when she lifted up its tail, that appendage held erect a moment, then fell sinuously, languidly down, exactly expressing our voluptuous mood.

As she made her cat beholden by spoiling him, she cannily did the same with me. "How beautiful you are," she would murmur, petting me. "And what a nice big yard. If it were any larger, I would have to leave you."

And I was appalled to know I had such vanity, yet was helplessly warmed by her blandishments. As for what we did in bed, she soothed my unease by reminding me of that tenet from the Koran which holds that each man may till his field as he wishes. And when I said that I thought I sometimes hated women, she said, "Of course you do, every man does. Just as every woman harbors some dislike for men."

How she loved to talk, and considered all the pharmacopeia to be her province and all exotic and potent powers to be her study. She never tired of discussing various herbs, perpotations, and charms, exploring and debating their powers, their histories, their usage. Where another might take pious comfort in reciting the names of God, she reverently named the narcotics: ganga, hashish, cantharides, wolfbane, nightshade, hellebore, wormwort, theageline, and all the progeny of the poppy: candoo, madak, laudanum, and the bitter dross. Where another might find solace in dipping into the font, kissing the cross, and nibbling the host, she was soothed by fondling the stylet and pipe, handling the spoon, squeezing the worm, nibbling the diapapaver. Where another might be prone to extol the virtues of the saints, she was likely to hail the deeds of the pimps, the poisoners, the mind-wrenchers and anarchists.

But it was the poppy that she loved most. She confided that she had been introduced to the stuff two years before by a soldier of the Ifni legion, who had reduced her resistance with several pipes full of ganga and then, while she slept, had put the leech to her. He had subsequently kept her for several months, infusing her alternately with the poppy's juice and his own, then one day had disappeared, leaving her alone and deep in the thrall of her new devotion.

To my surprise, she bore him no ill will. "We knew we would not stay together. As for the leech, the truth is that I wanted to try, and he knew it. Just as most rapes are not rape at all, so few come to the embrace of Morpheus against their whole will."

When she was honest, she was utterly so. And yet she also loved to shock and insinuate, to prod and rouse me with hair-raising suggestion. Did I know, she inquired, that in Constantinople there was a bordello where one could purchase living creatures, to be availed of exactly as the purchaser wished? Here were kept young boys and old men, maidens and grown women, dwarfs, hunchbacks, elephants, and peacocks, all for sale to the highest bidder. Customers came from all over the world, either to violate their purchases on the premises, or to have them wrapped in chains and delivered. Terrible things, incredible in their variety and all unspeakable, were done in that place, she told me. Pretty young boys and pregnant women were at a premium, but the most expensive item on the menu was a double-bodied wonder, a girl with four legs, reportedly still a double virgin at forty-seven years, since no customer had yet been able to pay her tremendous price.

Such tales she had learned from an acquaintance named Pedro

Urdemalas, an old and dear friend, she assured me, and I soon learned to hate him, whoever he was.

Sometimes she giggled and wriggled like a young girl daring to pronounce naughty words, and sometimes she spoke in solemn tones, rebuffing any attempt to make light of her fantastic speculations. So that I scarcely knew when she was serious and when she was not, when she was telling the truth and when inventing.

"Feel," she said, lifting away the pale hair and proffering her left ear; and I reached gingerly out and found the fingerling of flesh just behind the lobe. "It is called the witch's tit," she said, relishing my shudder. "It is where she gives the Devil suck. I have had it since I was a child. And here." She guided my hand down to her right heel, and I felt the horny patch there, about the size of a gold doubloon. "At birth I was covered all over thus, but my father had in a necromancer, and the wizard took me by the heel and lowered me into a vat of cold rose tea, and it made me as you see me now, although the spot where he grasped me remains."

"Nonsense," I said, but not steadily. "If you are a witch, I am—"

"Bewitched?"

"I was going to say Perceval del Santo Grial," I muttered.

She smiled. "I don't deny your claim. As for mine, if you do not believe me, then watch. This is how I used to get to stay in bed when I did not want to go to the nuns." She lay back, closing her eyes, and it was uncanny, she became a wheedling child. "Oh, mama, I cannot go to school, see how feverish I am, and all over in a rash." And even as I stared, faint splotches began to appear upon the flesh of her upper arms, seeping up through the pale flesh, slowly turning it a mottled red. She gestured toward her thighs, and they began to go piebald as well.

"My God!"

She opened her eyes, and the patches quickly seeped away. She drank in my horror and turned to jounce and snigger gleefully, scribbling obscure hieroglyphics on the air and waggling taloned fingers at my face. "Beware, I will diabolify you and sell your soul as my own. I will put a curse upon your parts and cause them to wither. Akan gatha orim zalee gum agathar . . ."

"Stop!"

Just as sure as it began in fascination and proceeded through disgust

319

to anger, so it invariably ended in a rageful desire to be free of all thought, to be shed of cruel contradiction, if I had to crack my brain to do it. My fingers sank into the pale flesh of her arms and the red spots that flared there spread to crimson in my brain. But now, my furia was only another's triumph.

She laughed. "You are hurting me." She whimpered, glee glistening in her eyes. "Oh, you are so cruel, you do whatever you wish to me, no matter how I protest! You are torturing me, you are corrupting me! Oh, don't, please don't!"

Thus she taught me, and thus I learned, all in a dull hemp sopor. I believe there were eight such days of swive and swoon, for one morning she said it was Saturday and that her rent was due. She even told me how much, smiling and watching me squirm.

"Very well," I said after a moment. "I will pay it." And then, with faint conviction. "But tomorrow I must be on my way."

"Which way is that?" she inquired with gloating glee. "I mean, which way around the circle?"

I glowered. "If you are that sure I will be back, why do you ask for money?"

She widened her eyes in astonishment. "Why, because I need it to pay the rent." And now she put the tip of one nail between her teeth and pretended to meditate, then rolled up a playful eye. "Of course, it would save money if I were to move in with you at once."

Sometime later, as I pounded to her chorus of incitement, I found myself locking my hands about her slender neck and closing my thumbs on her gullet, exactly as the tongs of my two disparate wills were pinching my tender soul.

To kill or not to kill; it made for a consummate swelling of the tentigo. Not the words, but the deathlock of angel and fiend in my bunched shoulders. Then, at the very last instant, I fled from the meeting of the two propensities, and instead, let my brain crack open and all sensibility be swept away on the howling winds of release.

Afterward was the slow ache of awakening, the quake of nerves and heart, and I stared down at my own and that other emptied worm, then took up her mirror and saw that the explosion yet lived in my right eyeball; the veins had burst and all the white had turned to crimson.

Beside me, she slept on in sweet contentment. But come by at such a cost, for she has told me that each time the leech bit into her, she felt a bit of her brain crumble like cake. A little death, she called it, suffered for the bliss that waited on the other side. How terrible to see her killing herself again and again like this. Surely patience and love might drive the worm from the rose and make it bloom into innocence once more.

In the meantime, I told the red-eyed face in the mirror, I would have what it now seemed I had been looking for all along: my way with a woman's body.

27

THE MORNING sun slides its blade beneath my eyelids and prizes them open, telling me that it is close to midday. I crawl from the bed, am staggered by a multitude of aches, and go groaning to the kitchen for my cocoa. She has been with me for two months now, or is it three? And this is what our days have come to.

While I dab at my canvas, she lies wrapped in bed like the chrysalis of some night-blooming moth. Perhaps cords still hang from the bedposts. My pipe lies on its side in a bowl of ganga ashes beside two or three defunct worms, and there are deplorable stains on the bedsheets.

This part of my day has become increasingly precious to me. She is mute as a felled tree, and I am free to dwell wistfully upon our better moments, to gaze with painful fondness upon her, and to puzzle over how such a woman could come to be.

Her mother had died of plague when she was four, and henceforth she had spent much of her childhood with an "aunt," who was really one of her father's mistresses. She still refused to give his name, admitting only that he was a powerful man, and she hated him. This mistress had an illegitimate son by him, and whenever the woman decided that Peregrina had been naughty, she would instruct her boy to flail the little girl with a wooden spoon, whilst chanting, "I am a bastard, but you are a little bitch."

Or so she has told me, giving me a new fragment of her tale each night, feeding my fascination and making me care.

No matter how sharp the blows, she would refuse to cry. But when it was done, she would bury her head in a pillow, sometimes for hours, and when the mistress finally gave way to contrition and begged to see her smile, she would show the woman ferociously crisscrossed eyes. "Someday you will do that for too long," the woman promised, "and they will get stuck that way."

Growing long in the leg, she had climbed trees with the boys, but in her thirteenth year had suffered from hot cheeks and nervousness, and suddenly found that the boys had become stronger than she. Exiled from their games of champery, she had darted out one afternoon and stolen their Grail, a broken piece of jug, and fled with it into the distaff privy at the corner of the nunnery. But they had invaded the sanctum and dragged her out into the dust of the field, and there she had fiercely curled herself about the trophy. While her muscles were no good for lifting and striking, they could enclose mightily, and for four hours she clamped herself about the prize, until finally they went away, leaving her stiff but triumphant, having once again prevailed against superior force by virtue of her fierce and bitter will.

But one small hair appeared below her belly, then a second, then more; and her breasts began to swell and her hips to flesh. She learned about dresses and ribbons; that the most indifferent boy could be turned with a show of ankle, the most disdainful silenced by the lift of a breast. Once in church she sucked a priest's knuckle as he gave her the host, so distressing him that he spilled the wine.

A young officer home from Flanders invited her to go walking alone with him, and she went, vain of her wit and proud of the enfeebling powers of her flesh, taunting him just to see him twitch. Whereupon he threw her down at the edge of the catchspell court and raped her. And when they were done, she found that she could not forget the event, for there was a sign to remind her forever: her eyes had crossed and stuck.

Midday, and she stirs from her winding sheets and calls for cocoa. I carry it in to her, and she gets herself upright, all the rose of her cheeks gone to ashes, her voice like a whip left out to freeze. "Too hot."

"Let it cool."

"And how do I cool these?" She glares, rubbing bracelets of chafed skin. "You tied it too tight, you churl. And I burn elsewhere too."

The downside, she calls it, when the drug has worn off. In these hours she is like a vixen that has whelped stillborn and burns with treble afterpang. All raw womb, desolation, and loss, she snaps at anything that moves, herself included. "Swine, you had your way with me last night. A pig has been rooting in me."

"There is no swine without swill." But immediately I am sorry. The more lurid the memories of the night before, the more I feel obliged to play handmaiden to her the morning after. There is so little time between her awakening and the first leech, and I must exorcise all guilt so as to be free to proceed to the crimes of the night ahead. So I add with a certain furtive pride, "Sometimes I fear that I am insatiable."

Her smile is pinched, and there are beads of sweat on her upper lip. Some mornings she shakes with chill; once she broke out in welts. "On the contrary, it seemed to me that you became satiated quite early last night. I lay awake for hours after you deserted me for snoring sleep." She lifts her lip to show the dog teeth. "Have you forgotten what I told you, that in any given period, a woman can manage ten times as much swiving as any man."

I hide my wince and match her grin with one of my own. "We shall see about that tonight."

Then back to my easel. For without the illusion of nobility now, how can I justify the ignobility to come?

But as her body comes to faint revival, her craving grows stronger also. She grumbles, restive in the sheets, biting her fingernails. "Did you know that most men wear their huevos on the right side of the cod, but some poofs wear them on the left so as to recognize one another more readily. I notice you have yours on the left this morning."

Through clenched teeth: "A coincidence. Let me work."

But even the silence is apprehension; I can almost hear her butter teeth nipping at her fingernails, the frenzied spinning of her brain cogs. Now she will indulge in calumny, feverishly mining the misfortunes of others for recompense.

"Poor Esteban, to think that he has squandered his inheritance on women, drink, and playing cards. His father was once with Mendoza in New Castile and owned one million red Indians, while Esteban hopes for his huevos to appear on the dice. Do you look for the same on your canvas?"

"I do not look to own slaves."

"Perhaps you should, then you could mistreat them instead of me."

"I do no more than you invite. Read a book. Go for a walk, leave me alone!"

More nipping of the claws, fits of sneezing. She might begin to toy nervously with what she calls her twiddly, twisting and weaving the hair of her coony into a little penis, giving little thrusts of her hips and sniggering. Or she might get up and pace about in her nightdress, or make a bad meal, afterward gleefully informing me that she has laced it with hashish. Or she might suddenly screech that there is a moth in the room and I must kill it. It is the only insect she dislikes; the only thing, in fact, that she seems to fear. Then back to bed, perhaps to nap fitfully, soon enough to awaken and nag again.

"The chills have started. I am patient, but my illness is not. And besides, why should I deny myself pleasure, when God commands us to seek it."

For this she has a philosophy, recommended to her by the mysterious Pedro Urdemalas, and confirmed by Epicurus: "Morality is only the rationalization of past events by those who survive them and the restriction of the future by those who fear it. Pleasure is the first and kindred good."

Further, she is wont to claim invalidism, solemnly explaining that she has in common with all opium fiends that she was born with an infested soul, and that it is only by virtue of the poppy that she can quiet her duende, and therefore, her use of the drug is her beneficent gift to the world.

God knows, she is sharp when she is without it.

"Try exercising your famous will," I suggest.

"That from you," she sneers, "who have let yourself be led through life by your unruly member?"

She gets out her sewing basket and goes to sorting her paraphernalia. "Let me see, I have five leeches left. If I use one now, that leaves one for tonight, but only three for the four days before I see Pedro again. . . ."

"You could cut one in half with a scissor."

"How cruel you are. To make the one half suffer until it follows its other half to the final delight."

Her little joke. Yet she claims strong sympathy for insects, leeches in

325

particular, but also that tall locust, the female of which is said to offer her mate a fly, then invites him to eat the tidbit and swive her at the same time. And while he humps, she reaches back with her fangs and slowly consumes her lover right down to the part that does the poking, the which goes on twitching to the very end, whereupon she has it for dessert.

"We have agreed that I must work until the sun touches the rooftops," I remind her.

"I have agreed not to take my medicine until then. But that does not mean we cannot have a pull on the pipe. It might inspire you."

"To put down my brush." It is true; ganga mollified my muse; all idea of a loftier reality dissolved away before the palpability of the present.

"Oh, but please!" She makes the abject face of a pleading child, while all the time her eye gleams to see the effect on me. "Please let me take my medicine now, please!" she croons, wriggling on her bed and turning her considerable backside toward me. "If you do, I will be oh so nice to you."

"No." But faintly.

She sticks out her lower lip and turns her hinderlings away. "Very well then, there will be no swiving tonight."

So there it is: the fulcrum of our love: my old dilemma brought to new extremity. I would play her savior, and yet if I am to deprive her, I must also deprive myself. If I am to save her from the monster Morpheus, I must separate myself from my own master, Venery.

In fact, we have tried several times to eschew our respective anodynes, herself the poppy, myself the spasm. With the result that after three days she stayed all the time in bed, snarling and gnawing her nails, and I did the same in my corner, cursing and fondling Esclavo.

And so I sigh. "Just let me clean my brushes." And do so, meticulously, as the thief says his beads before prying open the alms box, as the drunkard shaves before going to the tavern.

Then once again the cord and the swollen insect, the muttering search for a vein, the splashing rosette of blood, her ecstatic croak, and she falls back, poleaxed and happy.

Silence. Peace. Her lids flutter, she presses a bit of cloth to the lesion, turning dreamily to invite me to my milder anodyne. "Smoke a pipe and lie down beside me."

I do so, and in due time I lift the hem of her gown.

But she shakes her head and claims nausea, for this is her favorite time, when I must wait, and she is free of pain. "I wish it was a little beast," she murmurs. "And when you called, it would come forth all hairy and gnashing its teeth."

These times of feverish thralldom often last for an hour, two, even three, and yet they are not all unpleasant to me, for the ganga brings patience, and her ramblings now delight, now chill me with fantastic news.

"How did you ever come to be such a devil?"

"Indeed," she murmurs, "how did you?"

"Our sufferings were similar," I observe, conjuring a picture of each as a martyr to his childhood. "Our parents were cruel to us."

She gives a pretty snort. "Ah, but I haven't yet told you that I was born one of twins, but my sister died at the age of thirteen under mysterious circumstances."

As the ganga can encourage bliss, it can also conjure ghastly apprehensions. Can it be true, and is her fear of moths a fear of retribution? "My God, are you telling me that you murdered her?"

She smiles. "That we were alone together when it happened."

I am thrilled, incredulous. Is she mocking me again? Increasingly it is thus: I can never be sure if she tells the truth, but she is always assured of my fascination. "But you were also thirteen when that officer conspurcated you."

"So I was." A private irony curls her lip. "Well then, I suppose you could say that he and I both killed her. And good riddance, she was such an innocent fool." Her eye narrows. "Afterwards I gathered a dozen street rascals and paid them to wreck his apartments."

She gives a fierce little chortle, then gives her nails a nip. "But it was small satisfaction and not nearly enough. Because there was no way to make these feeble fists of mine do what I wanted them to do."

She shakes them before her, the knuckles gone white. Then she rolls

327

close to me, showing her fangs. "And that was to beat the diamerdes out of him. You have no idea how humiliating it is to be helpless as a woman is helpless. There is a strength and fury in a man that every woman hates and covets."

"Yes, and would take away if she could," I mutter.

"Sometimes when I go to the well," she whispers, "I whisper down into it, 'Juan is a beast, Juan is a beast!' "

"No more than most." But even as I say the words, their contradiction fattens my veins, almost as though the struggle against the demon is the fuel that feeds it.

"Oh yes, more than most," she corrects me. "And do you know why? Because you are a venereal fiend with a conscience. Wouldn't you love to tie me to the bed right now and do what you wished with me? And wouldn't you feel terrible afterward? Exactly as you felt good before? Wouldn't it be delicious to just roll me over like a sack of barley and—"

"No!"

"—and spread my hinderlings like a peach, and—"

"Damn you!"

The mark of my slap is white on her cheek, already turning scarlet, and she smiles her triumph. "You see, you are the worst beast of all, the one that thinks. If Torquemada could have had a wife to beat, there would be a million heretics alive today." Reaching out her frail arms, she croons and shows her dog teeth, drawing me in like a fish. "But, don't worry, it is all in the fancy anyway. So come, my cruel and necessary beast, do not be afraid."

"But I am," I mutter, crushing my cheek to her breast. "I am afraid."

"Not of women," she murmurs. "But of something in yourself. Of the strings they can pull to make you twitch and dance like a puppet, helpless for all your superior sinews. Strings that your mother put there for my use, and which you simply cannot resist."

"It is true," I groaned. "I love the doxies, every one!"

"If you must call it that," she murmurs. "Now get us a swatch of willow. And tonight I will teach you how to flail me with this love of yours."

Thus the lessons came, crowding closer and closer, one upon the heels of the other.

Prodding me awake on a succession of nights, she proved to me that I slept with my hand on Esclavo, clutching like a child to his stuffed rabbit. "Oh, how you love that thing."

Musing in bed beside me, she tallied the men she had lain with, and the summation filled me with an awful mingle of admiration and envy. "Fifty-four," she gloated. "I'll wager you can't match that, my jealous darling."

Returning from an afternoon of marketing, she was likely to mention, not the cloth goods or vegetables, but the men she had seen, commending a well-turned calf here, a bulging cod there. "You didn't know a woman could think that way, did you? If you knew it all, I daresay you would jump right out the window."

Groaning beneath me, she somehow taught me what I must do, even as it was being done to her. Retardismo was no longer an affliction; it allowed time to make her feel the final moment readying itself in my flesh and hers, to sense the coming explosion in every fiber, and desperately to crave it, no matter if it took three hours. She must be beguiled to do so, commanded to do so, by contained furia, by wile, by subtle or sudden changes of pace. She must be made to bow stark naked and needy before her beloved nightmare, and beg for it to fill her to bursting.

For this the old games of my mind had to be played again. I would imagine I was her original rapist, watching the young virgin go agog as I cornered her at the edge of the catchspell court and pushed her down on the grass, and oh, what a delight of injured cries and whimpering protests she offered up as spice to our mutual illusion.

At other times, I would let myself be also herself, the raped, and there were moments, in the roiling distractions of the ganga dream, when I was not sure whether my yard was me, or I was the hot fist that served it.

One morning, after a night of this, during which I had flailed her with reeds as well, she glowered and burned in the beginnings of the downside and inquired if I would like her to beat me. And when I declined with a threat from the back of my hand, she only sniggered.

329

"Never mind, perhaps later. Today's fustigator is tomorrow's victim."

But the hardest lesson of all was the one I could not accept: that life was a cockpit, and men and women, in their essentials, were natural cannibals.

For some time now she had gone alone to Pedro Urdemalas to get her diapapaver and my ganga, but one day she demanded that I go with her. He frequently changed his place of residence, she said, and so we must go first to the Court of Elms. Once there, we found a certain beggar, whose face was covered with the most vividly colored sores I had ever seen. "Kiss my dish," said this grotesque, thrusting up a wooden bowl.

And when he had my copper coin, he lifted a black patch to spy up an unclouded eye. "Urdemalas, the artful dodger. I use his scars and sores, the best in the city." Peeling a most spectacular chancre from his cheek, he showed it to be paper, then replaced it. "Next to the Abattoir Trampista, second floor." And with that, he strode briskly away, to become suddenly crippled as he slid around the corner.

The house was a crumbling wreck. To all sides were the boneyards and huts of sausage makers and scavengers, and from the abattoir came the screams of pigs and the angry shouts of the b·· ¬hers.

"Must he live here?"

She shook her head, giving the door an elaborate knock. "He is rich from parental leavings as well as on his own account. But he is much in the arms of Morpheus and inclined to be indifferent to the look of his surroundings." She smiled to see my distaste. "Besides, he enjoys the disreputable associations to be had in the neighborhood and claims that the noise is music to his ears."

A great number of bolts and chains shot and rattled, and the door swung slowly open.

He was a Portugee, I decided at once, not a pretty man, but neither was he hideous. He wore a Morisco caftan, embroidered but recklessly stained, open at the front to reveal a cotton breechcloth and nothing else. He was neither short nor tall, square-built and with enough flesh on him so that there was no telling if he had muscle or was only jelly. His face might have been handsome with its black curls and forked beard, were it not for the sickly gray of the skin and the eyes which seemed ghastly pale, for the irises were shrunken to pinpoints. They gazed, bland and unblinking, while the voice drawled the same. "My dear Peregrina, how good to see you."

He bent to kiss her hand, then turned his fish-eye to me. "So this is the fine fellow you have told me about." His hand was cool, his grasp loose and careless.

"And she has told me about you," I said.

"Has she?" He looked at her, smiling, and their glances locked in conspiratorial struggle, somewhat fond, mostly wary. "Well, I suppose she knows me as well as anyone does," he murmured, turning and leading us into a large sala. "We have done one another harm in the past, but we have helped one another as well. And now we have a kind of truce."

It was he who had taken her in after the soldier had abandoned her, and she had returned the favor since. Like cripples, they knew each other's pain, but also that the other was capable of kicking a crutch. He had once asked her to marry him, but she dared not cohabit with a fellow Morphean, she said, lest they drag one another into ruin all the faster.

"Let's say we understand one another," she said, sitting down and showing him her most taunting smile. My God, how she could glow when she wanted to be looked at. "But I hope you haven't forgotten that you are in debt one strong favor to me."

"Ah," he said, letting himself into a chair opposite. "I see. And if I am unable to return that favor just now?"

She smiled. "But you are. You forget that I know you. However low your stock, you will always keep at least one portion for yourself."

"Won't we all," he murmured, and made a languid gesture toward a nearby table. Upon its elegant surface stubs of candles sprouted like mushrooms; in a barber's basin, the curled cadavers of a hundred leeches stuck in dried blood. "However, I have not been able to find it in myself to go down to the port for several weeks now. And, as you can see, I have been something of a glutton." His voice faded, his eyes closed, and he seemed suddenly to doze, his lips twitching a satisfied smile.

I looked about at the slovenly disorder of the room, the fine divans littered with trash, the ripped brocades, a spider drawn in soap upon a

331

gold-framed mirror. In a far corner, several baskets were heaped high with eye patches, painted sores, and false bandages.

My mistress pressed him angrily. "You are lying, Pedro. You have more than one leech left. We agree on the first rule, but only when it applies. Look me in the eye!"

From what seemed a coma, he came forth as sudden as a miracle, but with his pasty gaze fixed on me. "You look sick, Lucero. You resist your lessons. Or has our darling failed to tell you all she knows? Are you familiar with the first rule?"

"Perhaps not," I muttered.

He smiled. "But you have your suspicions. Well then, let us complete your education here and now."

"Leave him alone and remember your debt to me," she said. "As you once said in a weak moment, your respect for me is all the love you have left for justice."

But Urdemalas only continued to smile at me. "To love both women and justice, that is not easy, eh Lucero?" And he arose and brought forth a small tin box and took it to the table.

Her glare faltered, and she set to gnawing her finger ends, her crossed eyes tracing his every move. He cooked the stuff and filled the worm, then held it up between his fingers. "Time for school."

"But such a waste!" she cried.

"First the lesson, then I pay my debt." With a sardonic bow to me, he led the way to the large doors at the back of the chamber and threw them open.

There was a small courtyard, enclosed on all sides, open to the sky. At opposite ends there were wooden doors, and in the center, a small table, variously stained but otherwise bare. Holding the worm above the center of the table, he called out, "Pico! Paco!"

Almost at once, the doors banged open and two scrawny creatures scuttled in a flurry of rags to the table, crouching opposite each other, their sunken eyes fixed upon the worm, their mouths gaping open and running with slavor.

"Who would believe that they were once scholars of the church," said Urdemalas over his shoulder. "Note that they are evenly matched, both in bodily strength and the depth of their addiction, for I introduced them to Morpheus on the same day two years ago. More: they were born natural brothers. Let me repeat that: they are blood brothers."

So saying, he lowered his hand, placed the gorged leech in the center of the table, and stepped swiftly back.

Two clutching hands reached out at once, caught upon one another and tangled above the prize, and in an instant they were locked in a death struggle, falling to the flagstones, kicking and howling.

"Observe and learn," murmured my host close beside me. "Surely no pair of hogs quibbling over a melon rind ever went at it with such fury. For these are not common animals, but men, graced with awareness, intelligence, language."

"Let go of my leech, you chince-faced, gundy guts, pedantical, plow-jobbing, nose-picking, bum-kissing crack-halter cornuto!" howled the one.

"May God conspute your mother's milk," the other replied. "And the hangman excarnificate your father, and the boghouse of heaven befoul you with ordure, you rumbling, grumbling, ill-begotten, runagate whaw-drover!"

"Bravo!" called Urdemalas, patting his hands together like a courtier at a game of shuttlecock. "Quite inventive that last, don't you think? A credit to language and delightfully human, wouldn't you say so?"

"Heathen!" screeched the one, biting off the other's ear and spitting it into his face.

"Heretic, degenerate, thief!" shrieked the other, getting a thumb into his antagonist's eye and gouging it out. And while the exoculated one writhed on the tiles, the other careened to his feet, snatched up the insect and slapped it to a bulging vein on his lower arm. "Ah!" he cried, as the bug bit in. "Oh, good! Oh, what bliss!" he gasped, slumping to a chair and rolling his eyes heavenward. "Thank God, from whom all blessings flow. I feel nothing! I think nothing! I am so happy!"

"And there you have it," Urdemalas murmured with the pious satisfaction of a priest who has just witnessed the Passion. Backing into the salon, he pulled the door shut upon the scene. "Human relations in a nutshell, and the first and last lesson of the poppy. What do you say to that, Lucero?"

"I am disgusted."

"I can see that. But do you understand what you have seen?"

"I understand that the lure of the poppy makes beasts of men."

333

"Ah, but is it so simple?" he murmured, moving again to his tin box, while Peregrina watched. "Be reminded, please, that the poppy knows nothing of right and wrong, whereas men claim to. Many would pretend to be something other than beasts, and are willing to suffer all manner of torture in order to go on deceiving themselves."

His nod indicated my mistress, his glance dripped mock pity upon me. "Even to the Cross."

"Enough!" she put in. "Pay your debt."

"I will, but you will pay the usual price, of course." Without taking his glance from mine, he held out a lump of the tar, and she snatched it away. Now he held up a little bag of weed, smiling. "And some ganga, I suppose?"

I cleared my throat. "Perhaps Peregrina mentioned it to you, I am out of money just now—"

He waved a hand. "Don't worry about it. . . ."

She was beaming above her frittering spoon, busy as a little girl with a mud cake. "Today is our anniversary, darling Juan, and you have bought me such a nice gift. . . ."

But it was his flat and passionless eye that chilled me, and his words that stuck: ". . . something can be arranged."

One night some weeks later, while I was pummeling away at her prodigious podex, she suddenly cast a speculative smile back over her shoulder and inquired, "What would you do if you came in and found some other man doing that to me?"

"I would throw him out, beat you, and leave for good."

"Are you sure?"

"I am."

"I am not," she said, looking thoughtful whilst I proceeded.

And, in truth, neither any longer was I. Her audacious wit, her ready rump, the reeds, the ropes, the ganga: all were knots of a net that cinched me tighter daily, breeding a species of fear which I had heretofore been pleased to think was suffered only by others. I even said it aloud one night, bringing a catch to my heart that astounded me: "When the time comes that I can no longer leave you, then you will leave me."

And her nodding smile was sad and pleased, both.

334

"Bad seed, bad seed," Catalinon had many times muttered as he broomed out my studio or watched from his shed behind the house. "Get free of her, get free."

And now he said it again, creeping mournfully up behind me where I sat in a hempweed stupor. "Young master, I cannot keep silent. If you do not value your soul, then think of your huevos. She will see them poached, then swallow them whole. She is too much for you."

"Too much for me?" I glared.

"Get the Devil's daughter out of your house," he pleaded.

"But she needs me," I said. "Who will keep her from destroying herself?"

"Forgive me, but she is better able to look after herself than you are. Look at you, you are already half a corpse. Do you want to be buried before you are dead?"

That night in the midst of our wrestle, I found courage in a vengeful impulse, and pulled out and rolled away.

But she only smiled and quoted the verse about the broad-tailed beaver, whose codlings are much sought after by hunters.

> "That wise castor who,
> Pursued by foes,
> Biteth off his stones,
> And among them throws."

"Nevertheless, I am leaving," I said, getting out of bed and looking for my saddlebags.

"And where will you find one to abuse as you abuse me?" she mocked. "How will you get your ganga? Where will you ever find another who gives you what I do?"

"What I do not earn," I muttered, stuffing my bags, "I will have to do without."

"But what about me!" she wailed, suddenly beginning to thrash and weep. "I will be alone, I will die of a poppy seizure, you will have my death on your conscience!"

I looked away to hide my wince. "The rent is paid to the end of the month. Go to Urdemalas after that. You were meant for one another."

"But we owe him money. You owe him! And besides, we would tear one another to pieces. Don't go! I will kill myself, I swear it!"

"Nonsense," I said, strapping my bag shut.

She crouched, her face pinched and glaring. "You don't believe me. I'll show you that I mean it. Look!" She held aloft a lump of black tar. "It is enough to fell a horse. I told you that when I went it would be this way. I will die of bliss, but you will be to blame. Look!"

I tried to look away; I could not; I saw her push the lump at her face, saw her throat convulse as she swallowed, saw her waver a moment, then collapse slowly to the bed, pale and smiling, triumphant.

How long did I stand, gawking and chilled to my soul? Almost at once, her eyes came unstuck, her cheeks filled and softened, and she smiled wearily, lifting an arm. "Come, it is all over but the weeping now, and there need be none of that. It is done and there is no undoing it. Smoke a pipe and talk to me, it won't take long, perhaps half an hour. Come and kiss me good-by, Juan. Soon you will be free."

Holding back the tears, I took up the pipe and lay down. What a torment of confusions whirled in me; time crawled to the leaden beat of my heart, and even as the ganga gave the drama a nightmare's reality, my blood began to thicken in its tubes. How beautiful she suddenly was again. How I admired her courage to choose ecstasy with its terrible price, rather than hang on and die so slowly, year after year, as most did. She had never seemed so much a marvel, nor so delectably lovely as she slipped toward the final peace.

"I can feel it now," she whispered. "The first distant chill. No, no, don't cry, Juan, it is all right. Only hold me, let me know that you loved me until the end. Kiss me, my darling."

I did so. Momentary alarm chilled me. The police! Should I force some vinegar down her, a spoonful of sulphur?

But all worry melted away before her tender touch, the wrenching emotions of the moment. I could feel the unrecalcitrant worm growing thick between our bellies. For shame, and yet, why not? Was that not the only life-affirming act, after all? She stirred against me and let loose her appealing little moans, and I began to tremble and lurch. "Yes, yes," she whispered.

Was it so horrible, really? Was it not, instead, the final kindness? Surely I could do at least that much for her before she left. And besides,

336

what a rare event; surely it was given to few men; surely it would be a crime to waste it. Yet I must hurry, for by the look of her, she wouldn't long be warm.

She moaned; I was between her legs. She thrashed; was it the final throes? I fitted myself in and lifted up on my arms so as to observe the tragedy better. She was going, going. It was clear from the frenzied convulsions of her body, the rolling of her eyes, her gaping mouth, her sawing moans, the spittle on her swollen lips. At any moment she would cry out and grip me with that last powerful dying spasm. I must not be too late! Good-by, I cried out in my heart, pumping toward cataclysm. Good-by, my darling, oh that's good, farewell, that's delicious, good-by, ahhhhh!

I had suspected a ruse all along, of course, but in a region of my mind carefully apart from that which was having the fun. At any rate, there eventually came to me through the fading roar of my brain, a faint and mocking, "Hello again."

Reluctantly I opened an eye and saw the sharp teeth, the gleeful eyes.

"I said, hello there, grave-robber. Corpse-swiver."

What could I do but groan and laugh, then groan again? Fleeing headlong, I had only come home. Flinging myself from her creel, I had only landed in her frying pan.

She pressed close her succubine grin and held up the chunk of opium. "Do you think I would waste it like that? Never. I only wanted to prove to you your utter bestiality. That, once started, you would swive a dead woman if you hadn't yet had your spasm."

28

WHAT Urdemalas wanted was that I should paint false bandages for him, and also ryparography, that is, lewd and sordid pictures. The bogus wounds were sold to skelders and beggars, the paintings to certain sybarites in the city and at court in Madrid. "Turning out sores is simply a matter of keeping your nose to the ulcer," he told me with his bland and nasty smile. "I suggest you pay a visit to the hospital to get the feel of it. As for the pictures, like all art, they are best when they come from the artista's own most powerful and secret dedications. I understand from our mutual friend that you are capable of the required reversals. Do I make myself clear?"

"Too much so."

"Don't complain, you will be paid in the best-quality ganga and poppy tar."

Now he fiddled with a piece of paper. "To begin with, however, I would like you to illustrate this private item. It's nothing, really, just something I've worked up in my spare time."

He made a face, displaying that spiteful uncertainty which the novice calls his modesty. "I don't think it's entirely bad, rather poetical in fact, and besides . . ." Here he recovered himself with a snide smile. ". . . I know what I like."

It was his version of the Beatitudes, and was titled *The Bestiatudes:*

Blessed are the rich, for theirs is the kingdom of the earth.

Blessed are the bold, for they shall possess the earth.

Blessed are they who mourn not, for they do not wish to be mourned.

Blessed are they who neither thirst nor hunger for justice, for they shall not be disappointed.

Blessed are the unmerciful, for they shall have no need of mercy.

Blessed are the hard of heart, who see God only too clearly.

Blessed are the makers of war, for they shall be called victors.

Blessed are they who suffer no persecution for justice's sake, for theirs is the kingdom of now.

There was a wealth of revulsion in the work, but also a kind of awful fascination, and at least it took me out of my right mind for a space. I worked day and night for an entire week, for the first time making no attempt to reconcile my work to any rarefied ambition.

"Delightful," said my employer, reviving from his sopor long enough to study my lurid ochtich. "Revolting, heretical. You are a natural, Lucero. Here is your ganga and here your sweetheart's candy."

"I've always said you had talent," said my mistress, tearing into the package. "Why don't you do a little work while I prepare my medicine? For heaven's sake, don't let me keep you from your easel."

So it went for a month or so. I went to the hospital, and there amongst the sweating consumptives and groaning amputees, I made sketches, then went home and painted sores. At my easel, I mined the fetid tunnels of my imagination for pornerastic rubies, and when I was finished, took my payment in grassy anodyne with which to shut out memory of what I had done. And then my mistress and I dallied away an equal time, reenacting the very sordid rituals I had pictured.

Soon enough, however, there came that morning when I awoke dry as a husk from the acrobatics of the night before, unable to take up my brush and make the picture needed toward the next orgy. It was all I could do to stagger to Urdemalas's den and beg for credit.

"But you already owe me," he mentioned. "Instead of burdening yourself with further obligation, I suggest that you try this. Take it, and your brush will fairly fly to its work."

It was an agrypnotic, a powder designed to keep one awake. I washed it down, and in less than an hour I began to feel a rush of energy the likes of which I had never dreamed could be. Where the ganga dulled all ambition, this concoction brought all sense of time into one great and overwhelming urgency. All the memories and apprehensions were there, yet I knew no fear of consequence or failure. All in a sweating frenzy, I worked two days and two nights without stopping, producing no less than fifteen pictures, as vivid and consummately lascivious as any I had done.

The which did not mean, however, that I was ahead of the game. When the effect of the medicine wore off, the collapse was swift and devastating. My brain quaked in its casing, my fingernails ached, and it was very much as though my soul were slipping down my spine like soggy trousers.

Now I had a downside of my own, and I and my mistress could exchange symptoms and proceed all the more quickly to alter our senses and retire to bed, there to indulge in that wild removal for which we would soon have to pay the price again.

And the price always doubled in proportion as we took our pleasure. If I took my manic medicine and worked through one day and night, I was sick for two days following, and that much more inclined to extend the escape into the ganga dream to three, even four days hence. Which meant that subsequently I would be obliged to take a stronger dose of agrypnotic in order to paint the more and pay the higher price of the next escape.

She was still the other girl in her poppy stupor: beautiful and playful, and at such times she told me she loved me and forgave my assaults. Step by step she had made herself my touchstone and sibyl, the mother of my will and my authority on matters venereal and moral. There was one secret which she had not yet told me, she said: a key to both our fevers, but she would save it for a special time; and I suspected that she meant when and if I married her; and so I did not press to hear it.

In the meantime, the downside came more and more to outweigh the upside. And when I sought to take her to bed then, she became resistant and bitter, and if she did acquiesce, it was often only to practice some bizarre imposition, as on that occasion when she held her hand mirror up before my face whilst I was in my fit, and I saw for the first time the anguished strain, the lunatic twist and snarl of my ecstasy.

On yet another night, she took one of my huevos in her mouth, and while I was observing this with a certain astonishment, she suddenly rolled up an eye and indistinctly said, "I cannot get it out! Oh, what will we do?"

340

A chill made my backbone itch. "Spit it out."

"But I cannot," she insisted. "I fear we will have to remain this way forever." Somehow she managed a coy expression. "Unless, of course, you prefer that I bite it off."

I ground my teeth, but stopped myself, fearful it might be catching. "You got it in there, now you get it out."

"But I cannot!" she wailed out of the side of her mouth. "It has swelled up from your tremendous passion."

For what seemed half an eternity, I could only glare, frozen by gory possibility. All along she had been suggesting that there was something a woman wanted from a man, and once she had it, she no longer wanted him. Was this that moment of truth I had been dreading?

Mustering all the sense of self that remained to me, I drew back my hand and brought it smartly alongside her ear. With an appreciative gasp, she let go my codling and rolled back, whimpering and inviting more.

Nonetheless, and such moving displays notwithstanding, I was more and more afraid that I could no longer swive without ganga, paint without the agrypnotic, live without my terrible love.

"Get rid of her," Catalinon continued to mutter as he pushed his broom past my easel. "You haven't got long, master. Get free!"

"But how, you rascal, how?"

He gave me a pitying glance as he swept away. "How do you think? Decline to swive her."

So deep had my nervousness reached that I had returned to furtive consultations with Esclavo.

MYSELF: Wake up.

ITSELF: Go away, I need all the rest I can get.

MYSELF: But I need your help. If we could just resist her for a week, a few days. She cannot stand to be that long without venereal attention, I know that much. Perhaps she will find some other unfortunate, if we give her the chance. And after that, I promise you a lifetime of rest.

ITSELF: We don't have a lifetime left.

341

MYSELF: At any rate, it is you who have got us into this.

ITSELF: On the contrary, it is you who put me head first into the shit and now cannot get us unstuck. The feeling you have for her is incomprehensible to me, so you alone can cure it. Now let me rest, unless you want to burst a blood vessel tonight. My God, I tell you, I am aging fast.

"I cannot go on like this," I told her some days later. "I have not done a real painting in months, and I come closer to madness with each picture I make for Urdemalas. But most of all, the agrypnotic has exhausted me and I can no longer work. I will have to go back to my family and beg subsistence." And I added a hangdog sigh and one or two more or less heartfelt tears. "We must part, my darling. It is over."

But she was ready for me. "Never mind," she said, and could it be eagerly? "Pedro has offered to introduce me to certain well-fixed merchants of the Casa de Contración. I shall go back to work as a courtesan, and that will bring in great bags of money. Why, you can even think of yourself as a suave pander and powerful coony farmer. I'll wager that tickles your fancy."

It has been well said that a whore rests from man to man, but the poor pimp never can. She put on her most gaudy rags and went straightway to Urdemalas, and soon he had her entertaining gentlemen merchants at night and harassing me during the day.

At first I was much puffed by the delusion that she suffered such usage for me, and she in her turn was able to take some triumph in exercising the tricks of the trade, and glee from the antics of her clients. But soon enough the fun paled on her, while I began to suspect that I was not her reason at all, nor was I getting more profit than trouble.

Urdemalas did not run a trigging house, but only arranged discreet appointments for her, and hence she considered herself six cuts above the common street trull. But in fact, although she never chilled her buttocks upon bare steps, she suffered all the qualms and sought the same recompense as any whore; which is to say that each morning when she was done, she hurried home to make her lover suffer those retaliations which her customers had escaped by paying well and getting away in a hurry.

342

The main objective of the true professional, she informed me, was to induce the customer to spend as swiftly and with as little effort from herself as possible. Urdemalas had once before helped her find her living on her back, and she had long ago learned to tell the leapers from the snivelers, by biting.

"If he winces when my teeth sink into his shoulder," she told me, "he is most likely of the median cut. If he squeals with delight, he is a prick-me-daintie. If he strikes back, he is a potential fustigator."

And again I had to wince, remembering our first night. And worse: I could not help wondering what happened when she came upon such as the last, although she steadfastly assured me that she saved her truly loving responses for me.

She and her fellow courtesans referred to their clients as "Juans," the which quite scalded and enfuriated me. And how she delighted in their foibles, in mocking their manly pretensions and disdaining them for the very hunger that brought them to her. Half of them never got between her legs, she boasted, and of those that did, few could resist for more than a few minutes those techniques by which she tripped capitulation: a whimpering wince at entry and the winsome complaint, "Oh, too big!" a series of ecstatic moans and theatrical thrashings, a sudden wring of her muscular coony, even a bite on the neck, if that was the key.

Again I suffered sickly recognition, wondering. While she more and more revealed her huge contempt for malekind, at the same time embellishing her own lurid version of how she would behave, were she a man:

"I would never pay a woman, but would take what I wished by guile or by force, nor would I ever linger with one creature for a moment after I had grown weary of her, but would go straightaway to another. But only for my immediate pleasure, for I do not much like the company of most women, as I have mentioned. In short, I would make of myself a most charming but merciless rogue and certainly no Juan, if you know what I mean."

Here was a whole new complexity of torments, including a sharp reduction in our fun. Some mornings she arrived so stunned and weary that she would not suffer me to touch her. Often she complained that her breasts ached from mishandling, and on one occasion she an-

343

nounced that her underside had broken out in a rash. In fact, she was raw; but then, there was her childhood talent for inflaming her skin when she wished. Again, I did not know what to believe.

No woman wanted a man night after night, she now assured me. I must study her feelings and the phases of the moon, and adjust myself to the idea of less now so as to have better later. By now I knew that one of the contentions that heated up the tournament of genders was the struggle over who should set the terms by which satisfaction was to be had.

But she also told me that many a solicitrix of her acquaintance turned trig full willingly, not for money at bottom, but because she loved to do it. She told of the client who had unlimbered a yard like a truncheon, and she had declined, or so she claimed. But the other bawd had eagerly taken the allcock between her legs, "For with her, it is the bigger the better."

Behind my vanity I knew that the average woman could accommodate a quart-sized cucumber, should she put her mind to it. Was this second creature she described actually herself?

In short, and encouraged by the twisted apprehensions of the ganga, I began to suspect that my pleasures were being curtailed so that others might better enjoy themselves, that there was a secret campaign to cheat me. I even began to shudder at a horrendous possibility: that her true aim was and always had been gradually to reduce my swiving to the true goal of her womanly vengeance: none at all!

And yet, sometimes, with neither warning nor explanation, she would arrive home on fire, put the leech to herself, and invite me to do everything vile to her, only requiring that I do it for a long time and to the point of mutual exhaustion.

And once again I would do as she bade me, and now there was no avoiding the fact: there was a beast inside me. I could feel it in the heat of my head, drawing back my lip from my teeth, pinching my nostrils and raising pockets of dry, hot air to my head cavities. The more I knew of her and myself, the more I loved to pin her down, to rend and stab, and even to drink blood. But always I pulled back at the last moment, held by her command, controlling the beast for her usage, giving her just as much as she needed, for as long as she demanded.

344

"Oh, you are punishing me for being a whore," she would moan, pressing her face into the pillow and putting her backside into the air. "You are doing exactly as you wish with me. You are taking it out of there and putting it into the other, then out of the other and into the one. How humiliating, how cruel!"

And I pummeled and cunctated, toying with speculative visions of her night's work: and more and more in my ganga fever, the one vision mixed with the other, and sometimes I was the client exacting his due, sometimes the jilt giving a dollar's worth, and sometimes both at once. With the result that, just as I was no longer sure when I was in the drugged dream and when out of it, I was not sure whether I was myself or some other Juan, even a Juanita.

Less and less did we chat happily in bed before the fray, more and more our confidences were only bitter. "What do you want?" I demanded. "In God's name, you have everything from me!"

"Do I?" She glared.

The itch to bring the blister to a head inspired a desperate challenge; if only she would agree, I might find the strength to leap out the window. "Is it marriage, then? That's what you want, isn't it? Isn't it!"

Oh yes, I saw the small, dim flicker of hope deep in her eye, and got ready to seize upon it. But she only muttered, "Don't flatter yourself. Just tell me what it is you want. If you can tell me, I can tell you."

"Freedom!" I shouted. "It is all I have ever wanted."

The worm curled on her lip. "But I have told you: I want the same." That much was true; she talked incessantly of traveling the world, seeing and knowing all of life that she could. Indeed, she had already sacrificed much so that she could taste and know more than most ever did. During all those long nights following her rape, she had made a life plan, she said. To simply get as much pleasure as possible before she died.

"Then there is no problem," I said.

But she was too smart for me. "Really? Then how do you account for the fact that neither one of us is free?"

One afternoon on our way to Urdemalas, we took a different route,

345

and she suddenly halted the sedan chair opposite a large building which I knew to be one of the retreats of the order of MonteSeca. "Thinking of becoming a monk?" I inquired in scathing tones.

"My father is sometimes there with his latest mistress," she muttered, and added scornfully: "She is a creole."

"They are often beautiful," I said.

Her eyes narrowed and her lips went white. "He wanted a son, did I tell you? That's why he put me out with my auntie. I wasn't good enough for him. That thick brute! I will never go back to him, never!"

I had not seen her in quite such a hissing fury, and was reminded of the Twigger's passion. "Are you sure this man is only a father to you?"

Her slap did not hurt, but it seems the mark of her fingers was still there when Urdemalas let us in, for he cast a fishy eye at me and smiled. "Been beating yourself again, Lucero?"

I shrugged, no longer fencing with him, having decided that it would be murder or nothing at all.

The furniture was filthy, the brocades worse, and there were new basins of dried blood on the table. He prepared a worm and held it up, looking steadily at her, as he said to me, "Perhaps you would rather put the bite to your beloved, Lucero?"

He knew better. She had lately found it increasingly difficult to find a vein not toughened by worm bites, and had been begging me to put it to her, pointing out that Urdemalas was expert at it. But it was the one thing she had invited me to which I could not do. The refusal was my last claim to self-esteem; if I still pretended to save her from Morpheus, how could I serve as his agent?

She freed her gaze from his and turned imploring eyes to me. But I could only shake my head and turn away.

"I thought not," he said, crooking a finger at her. "Come then, my darling. It looks as though you must depend on your old friend Pedro. Jesus is sweet, you say, but hardly sufficient to all of a lady's needs. Now isn't that the truth."

Thus envy's stepchild, jealousy, turned me daily a more putrid green. Sometimes now she did not come home in the morning, but remained away until noon and into the evening. Always in the grip of either ganga or the agrypnotic, I more and more lived in my nightmares, and

346

so did she. Every other day our separate moods reached such divergence that we could neither talk nor disperse our rage in bed, but could only rail, one at the other; and once she tried to claw my eyes out, and I struck out with something very near to murderous intent.

"No, not in the face, do not mark me!" she cried, and I found myself trembling and alone in the room, staring at the bruised knuckles of my fist.

The next evening, she did not come home at all, and I woke up the following morning to find her deep asleep beside me and pale as death. She had promised to couple only with paying customers, to do her best to unenjoy it, and never to give them the special things she gave me. But I no longer believed it.

Furtively I examined her body for the telltale marks and found them: red welts across the backs of her legs, rosy bracelets around her wrists and ankles. Urdemalas? Some other? Did it matter? What an odd mingling of pain and exultation jealousy can be, once you give it the reins. I was almost glad. Thrilled and burning, I held in my fury until she had gone off on quick service at some nearby mansion. She would be back in an hour, she told me.

I gulped down four doses of agrypnotic, and immediately my heart began to speed, the blood rushed to my brain, and I was infused with a conviction of undoubted purpose and power.

Putting on my best hose, doublet, and cape, I sallied into the street. It was a balmy and beguiling day and many people were out. Disdaining to seek my quarry in a more populous district, I leaned against a hitch post on the corner and there preened and waited. Sure enough, soon enough, here she came: a street urchin, to all outward appearance a young slattern, but a prize beneath the rags and smut; a pretty child on the verge of sooty womanhood.

"Pardon me, my dear, your age?" I inquired, doffing my plumes and giving her a display the likes of which she had only dreamed of.

She gawked out from under her tangled hair; did I smell strong aguardiente wafting from those sweet lips? She glanced behind her, then incredulously at me again. She saw me not, but only a gentleman, privilege, a dream of change.

"Thirteen," she whispered in a frightened voice. "Am I to be arrested?"

347

Thirteen! I was inspired. "Quite the contrary, my child, you are to be immortalized."

Her small hand went to her mouth. "Oh my God, what is that!"

"Painted upon canvas and left to be adored beyond your natural death by generations of admiring gentlemen like myself. I am Don Francisco Zurbaran, painter to the court, and I have been watching you upon this street for several days now and have decided that you are the perfect model for the Virgin in my next masterpiece. . . ."

In short, I gave her ten times her praise in hogwash, and she was a penny muffin, sweet as any other, but cut-rate by social measure, and I had little trouble in coaxing her into my studio, there to offer her a smoke of hempweed, finally cinching my suit by confiding to her that her rare perfection had only one serious flaw, her breath, and that as an artist and expert on beauty, as well as 'a doctor and learned pharmacologist, I knew the best cure for halitosis.

"And what is that?" she asked, her eyes red-shot with ganga, her mouth all moist and trembly.

"The exercise may be familiar to you," I murmured, putting the latch on the door, then coming closer. "At least its gentle beginning," I added, bending to put my lips to hers. "But be assured that the way I do it, you will come out at the end with the breath of a peony and the comportment of a queen," and I bore her firmly down onto the bed.

Delicious. She was truly a little gem, and most compliant, once started. It seemed that the cure was not, after all, unfamiliar to her. But when it was done, she made a rueful face, all the time watching me knowingly, and said, "Well, I hope you enjoyed yourself."

"I did," I assured her, and added the question she fished for: "And what about you?"

She heaved a regretful sigh. "Sometimes I do and sometimes I do not." She twined her fingers and fixed me with a sly and appealing eye. "It all depends on whether I am truly loved, you see."

"Well now, I can understand that," I said. "In fact, I am not yet sure myself if I truly love you." And with that I put her onto her back again and proceeded to have at her a second time.

It was while we were in the midst of this that I was given precisely the thrill I hoped for: a hand rattled the latch, knuckles rapped the door, and my mistress's voice called out my name.

My partner's eyes widened and she made as if to sit up. "Who can that be!"

"The wind, a spirit," I said, pushing her back.

"Oh, I am afraid!"

"Hold tight to me and you will be safe."

"Juan, let me in there!"

The door heaved, but the bolt held firm.

"But the spirit sounds like a wife!"

"Her shade, I am a widower."

"Oh, you poor thing, what can I do?"

"Just hold still, please."

"Juan, are you there?"

"Nearly, my dear, nearly." Spread, my little treasure, how invigorating to plow a fresh field, how swollen with double delight the heady sword of vengeance . . ."

"Juan, I hear you through the door. The servants saw you with a girl. I know what you are doing, and I command you to bring this nonsense to a stop at once!"

Whatever you say, dearest. "Ah, ah, AHH!"

I had not felt so much myself in a year. The event recalled sweet memories of my grovel with Pandema Meraviglia-Gros, minus the clap, I hoped. God's nose, what a joy simply to swive. And to defy her hold on me: what a triumph!

Even if it was, and somehow I knew it: my last.

Once I had given the girl some coins and put her out the window, there was nothing for it but to let my punishment in through the door. With deadly calm she stalked in, sniffing at the telltale effluvium, fixing her squinting eye on me. If I had hoped she would go away in a jealous rage, I had underestimated her, she informed me. And when I burst out with my charges against her, she simply shook her head. No, I was mistaken, apparently off my noodle; she was innocent. Nor did it do any good to quote her own advice to adulterers: "Never admit, always deny, even to the scaffold, deny." No, it was I who had broken the rules, and therefore I who must pay in kind. It was to be a tooth for a tooth, a cuckle for a cuckle.

Urdemalas had recently introduced her to a new client, she wanted me to know. A young gentleman, well-built and good-looking, scarcely twenty, a champion swordsman and a Greek. Very much a Greek, she added.

I winced. She smiled. And the next morning she spent several hours preparing herself, kissed me good-by at the door, and went to him in her sedan chair.

I might have followed, but found myself delaying for some reason. Finally I choked down my agrypnotic, then hurried to Urdemalas to demand my rival's name and residence.

There were new rips in the draperies, more dead worms on the table, and he looked gray as ashes. "I know only that his name is Octavio," he said. "And that he is not a Greek but a Neapolitan, and said to be scion to the third richest dukedom in Cantabria. Unfortunately, I do not know where he lives. But be assured that I will find out. She told you that she will not take his money?"

I gave a miserable nod.

With him, rage seemed only to flatten his moribund gaze. "That I cannot tolerate. It is an offense to my professional pride. A man has to draw the line somewhere, eh, Lucero?" A loathsome chuckle flapped his lip, then his eyelids drooped, then suddenly he was wide awake again, staring at the spider on the mirror. "Our sweetheart's father is Don Garganto de Utero, comendador of MonteSeca. Do you know him?"

"I know of him," I said. "Defender of Chastity and Enemy of License."

He nodded. "That's what he calls himself, and is pleased to convert the rich to charity, the poor to indifference, and the bold to the galleys." His pale eyes plucked the legs from the spider, and a bubble formed at the corner of his mouth. "The mailed fist of righteousness. And yet he hankers for his daughter since she fled his jurisdiction. By God, I'll wager he would pay a fortune to know where she is. A fortune . . ."

But I scarcely heard the last, for I was letting myself out the door, anxious to be clear of the stench of his dissolution, and preoccupied by a thought which brought me up short on the porch; the fact was that I was relieved not to interfere and had delayed my pursuit out of a furtive hope that she might fall in love with this Octavio. For that matter, any Octavio.

29

A<small>ND YET</small> I still could not seem to come unstuck. My mind gave me warning and urged me to flee, yet my heart trembled with fear and bade me cling. To lose this one, it seemed to my worst apprehension, would not be merely to lose again, but to lose forever.

More and more she was out the whole night and the next day, sometimes two days. Once I happened to be at the end of Snake Street and saw her pass in her chair with another courtesan, and were the two comely heads bent together in tender intimacy?

By now, I could not paint for more than an hour or two every other day; the equilibrious intervals between manic agrypnia and ganga sopor had narrowed to nearly nothing. My mind would speed ahead of my hand for an hour, then would come the downside pain, and I would quickly retreat into a ganga stupor and go to my bed, as often as not without her. Soon, I was convinced, I would either lose my brain through an ear like a rocket, or would take root in my winding sheets and become, myself, a weed.

Finally, one night when she had incited me with her feverish nagging, I drew back my hand to strike her a practiced and harmless blow, but found that I could not.

Suddenly I knew it: to strike her was only to strike myself the harder. Her pain was not my pleasure after all, nor even was my own pain any longer mine. That too was hers.

All at once, everything was hers.

351

Now the agonizing slide of the final downside. "What a woman needs in a man and wants from him, she will take away if she can," she had told me. And my own words: "When I can no longer leave you, that is when you will leave me."

I even threw her naked into the courtyard one night, then went into my studio and again forced myself to pack my bags, only to collapse upon them, inciting myself, "Go, it is now or never. Go, it is now or never. . . ."

But never was now. Her claws scrambled at the door and she crooned my name, and in another moment she was back inside, and in another, in the bed, mocking me, even as I tied her hands. "Oh, it hurts, oh, it humiliates, oh, I am your slave." But it was I who winced at each and every whisk of the reeds.

In her way, she tried to stop me. Many a time I discovered her gazing at me in dim sorrow and perplexity. Once she said accusingly, "You are disappearing from me, you are melting away before my eyes."

And I had neither strength nor reason to say my answering thought aloud: that of course I was disappearing, for I was that green insect she had mentioned, and between us we had eaten me down to the torso, and even that tidbit twitched but feebly now, dying between her thighs.

She was gone almost every night now, but one evening she came home early and looking girlish again, rousing me from my ganga fog and dropping a ribboned package into my lap. "Happy saint's day."

"Oh is it? I had forgotten." In fact, I had not, but had passed the entire day staring at the backs of my hands, which had seemed to my melancholy gaze to be those of a man twice my age.

"Open it."

It was heavy. The paper came free from what looked to be a brass idol, a pagan priest in long robes and puffed cowl. But when she reached out and turned it so that it thrust out from my fist, it was a stiff and turose yard.

"Yours." Her smile was gleeful. "I made an impression of Esclavo in plaster while you were deep in the arms of Uncle Hashish. Then had a founder cast it in bronze, and a gilder give it a skin of soft gold. Isn't it beautiful?"

Was it? I was no longer sure. She put no less than three leeches to herself that night, and when the nausea had passed, she wooed my furia with quite a vivid display. Ah, but how mortifying it can be to have a woman prostrate herself like some naked heathen before the craven semblance of your flesh. How sour to know the turnabout at the heart of this fantastical worship. How hurtful to the emperor to know that he is praised to a purpose not his own, that his scepter is hollow, and he does not love his fate.

Sure enough, wherever I put it that night, my yard would not respond, and in the end I was obliged to employ its metal simulacrum, to which substitute she objected at first, "Too inflexible, too cold!" but in the end gave over to the usage as better than nothing at all. "Oh, it is so big and getting bigger, so hot and mighty and maddening!"

What mockery such flattery, come by through her frenzy and someone else's metallurgy. How cruel not to be loved for oneself, not even for one's yard, but only for the part one played in someone else's dream.

She had said it more than once: "It is all fancy, at bottom; men and women make love, not to one another, but to their own wishes and fears."

I even agreed. But I could not bear it.

Now she was away more than she was with me, and when we were together, she often talked of Octavio. Not as a lover, of course, but as a friend she had met on the steps of the Orangery.

"He is so young," she would muse condescendingly. "Quite a coxcomb and not sure what he wants."

And I knew she was teaching him what he wanted.

"He knows Italy well," she would mention, "and has been to Constantinople."

And I knew she was preparing him for travel.

"He is from quite a good family," she would say, "and has never married, although his mother wants him to."

And I knew she was closing the pincers on him.

"But what do you think of him, Juan?" she finally inquired, as she might have of a father. "From what I have told you, I mean."

"Why?" I said in as neutered a tone as I could muster, "he seems not a bad fellow at all."

God's nose, what that cost me in bile! For even as I encouraged her in her campaign, my heart was grinding with assorted hurts. Once I even followed as she went to meet him, and stood unseen in a doorway while he helped her into his carriage. How dashing he was in his black-and-white checkered cape, with a fine rapier at his side and his hand never far from its jeweled hilt. How bold and large his mustaches, how warm his eye as he bent to kiss her hand. How hot the bile in my belly as I saw his one hand come to rest, quite at home, on her hinderlings.

And yet I also nursed a furtive and hopeful gratitude, as well as a fondness, almost an amused pity for this eager and arrogant young hotspur. He reminded me of myself not twenty months before.

And then, one afternoon, after I had been away for a day and a night, I returned to find a checkered black-and-white cape in our closet. And when I decided to leave it where it was and not mention the matter, I knew that it was nearly over.

Soon she was not home at all, but only came occasionally, like a visiting nurse maid, most often to find me nodding with ganga before some unfinished canvas. I made no complaints, but only waited for it to be done, clinging to custom simply because I had no other handhold. I was the man who covers the cage each night long after the bird has flown, and sits with puckered lips in the dark, forgetting even to whistle.

It was while in such a stupor that I one night had the most vivid and horrible nightmare of all. I dreamed that I had escaped from her, but only to find myself suddenly before the mouth of a gigantic cave from which there came forth a fetid, hot, and insistent wind. And as I staggered and fumbled at my cod and brought forth my piteously inadequate tool, it came to me that the massive mouth before me was not a mere cave after all, but the great, indestructible, and insatiable maw of the world: a bottomless coony.

Finally, she came home with a mushroom she had got from Urdemalas, which had come from the Indies, she claimed, was similar to theagaline, and was a means by which the red wizards conjured images unknown to sober men. It was sometimes given as a cure to those possessed by demons, but did not drive the sprites out of the mind so much as it revealed their meaning, and had brought peace to many a tortured mind. Or so she insisted.

"Perhaps it will help you." There was a flicker of yearning in her agitated gaze. "Perhaps it will even help us." She reached out a hand, and there was no telling which was colder, her fingertips or my trembling shoulder. "Please, Juan, it may be our last chance."

I agreed to try the thing, not out of anticipation of where it might take me, but out of the weary speculation that it might not bring me back. A bad enough beginning, but worse to come: she discovered that her last two leeches had died. Even as I was swallowing the bitter fungus, she was beginning to gnaw her fingernails, her face clenching against the downside pain.

But I soon forgot her in the diversion of a powerful nausea. Vomiting twice, I then watched the world around me take on a new and vibrant insistence. I could not believe my eyes at first, and yet my soul seemed strangely unsurprised, and soon enough there was no question at all; everything had life, the chairs, the walls, the very air itself.

I gasped, longing to know more, but of a sudden she was there, her face twisted with the downside pain. "What do you see?"

"I am not sure," I murmured. It was so unexpected; there had been no straining, no sweat running down my spine, no cathedral to lift. "I think I see it all, the whole reason for it, the secret—"

"You see nothing of the kind!" Suddenly she was crouched on my chest, her eyes crossed in a fierce and jealous stare. Plucking up a mirror, she thrust it before my face. "This is what you see!"

I looked, and for a moment I did not know who it was. How terrible, I thought, poor man, what could have brought him to this. And then I did know, and not for a moment afterward did I doubt that what I saw was true. What a phiz! Time had gnawed it with his iron tooth. I was so much older than wily vanity had let me know, and clearly it was almost too late.

Envy, avarice, ambition, cowardice, hatred, superstition, blackmail, rape, and pimpery: all my scars and all my crimes were there. The arrow in Paco's shoulder, the forlorn droop of Pechita's breasts, Maxima's hungry bulk, the accusing gaze of the baby wrencher, the nameless orphan, the stone tears running down Dorita's cheeks, all the dead infants in the nun's deep-blue eyes, the tiny hand patting my back, the bound girl weeping into the mud, La Chispa's frail song of the

355

perfection of double love, Peregrina with Morpheus grinning at her shoulder.

All there in the gray and rotting flesh, the cynical twist of the mouth, the red-rimmed, suspicious eyes. I don't know how long I stared, but surely hours passed as I struggled to find some sign of hope on that desolate landscape. The left side of the face seemed the worst; that eye gazed back at me with incredible malevolence, red-shot and split up the middle, twitching left, then right, then fixed on me.

Satan, of course. Not Urdemalas after all, but resident within me. I stared back. I had no choice. Hours passed. Gradually, oh, so reluctantly, the baleful gaze seemed to dull, then to waver, as the beast behind the mask backed off to wait for another time.

Now I turned my attention to the other side of my face. It was not young, but neither was it so terribly old. There was a modicum of decency, a touch of gentleness, a hint of humor, a suggestion of acceptance. The faint outlines of the original angel still showed through, the flame of hope was not yet snuffed.

Now I could put away her mirror and renew my dazzled study of the life of color and the colors of life. The whole room, the whole world, seethed with that vitality one senses in the lambent swarming of dust motes in a shaft of sunlight. Substance held to ordained shape, yet churned and flowed with countless granules, aglow with the colors particular to it, but brighter and more vivid than before, as though the spectrum only filtered the vital energy into its tones, while it all remained the same music. The candle flame was a protean vial of honey, the brass door knob was a swarm of golden bees, my wine a living ruby; all matter was composed of infinite particles, all life was disparate and in motion, yet all fragments of the same deathless and swarming fire.

Now I saw all this ethereal light begin to gather and shimmer like the duke's transcendental biscuit, like the glow at the top of Climax's ladder. All became one, and the great light leaned, calling to me, and I was climbing, while the green cacodemons sniggered and clutched below; I was climbing, climbing. . . .

But I never got there. I heard laughter, low and savoring in her throat, and came back to my senses in a wrench of most worldly recollection. Turning onto my side, I saw her looming in the door,

356

outlined against the light through folds of Flemish chiffon, gliding closer, leaning over my bed. And what was this which hung on straps from her waist and thrust out from her thighs, heavily bobbing, big-headed, and glossy gold, aimed straight for my naked hinderlings?

I knocked her all the way across the room, and these were my hands strangling the air, and that was my voice shrieking, "If I were going to let anybody do it, it would not be the likes of you! By God, I would get somebody with a real yard!"

She crouched against the wall, pulling the phallus from her waist, clutching her cat to her breast and edging toward the door; and suddenly her eyes came uncrossed. "I am in love!" she cried. "I love the Duke Octavio!"

All the storms were of a sudden one, and my howl was the fading thunder of a gratefully dying day:

"THEN GO TO HIM!"

It might have ended there. It should have. But I took a dose of agrypnotic to revive my spirits. For an hour after she fled, I tried to tell myself it was for the best. Then I remembered my astonishing declaration regarding yards, and to turn my mind from that, I smoked some ganga. Presently my thoughts began to seesaw from bland to violent intention. Now in my mind I begged her to return, now I beat her black and blue, now I asked only to touch the hem of her gown, now I opened a second grin in her gullet.

And still it might not have happened, had I not decided to try to walk off my nervousness, and gone to the closet and seen Octavio's black-and-white checkered cape hanging there.

Urdemalas lay sunk deep into his chair, half-eaten pastries scattered around him, a dead worm hanging forgotten from his arm. "First she defied me for that coxcomb, and now she has left you," he murmured. "And does it hurt, Lucero?"

"I can stand it," I said without conviction.

"You mean you have to stand it." He enjoyed saying that. "Men are better at many things, my friend, but there is one thing at which women remain supreme." A smile tugged at his gray lips. "Survival."

"Be that as it may, I have got to see her just one more time."

A speculative gleam stirred his dead eye. "Are you the outraged cuckold then?"

"I only want to say a more dignified good-by," I muttered. "But I confess, I wouldn't mind running somebody through."

"I can see that." He smiled and seemed to doze, a lizard dreaming of flies. "Three birds with one stone," he mused, "and profit in it as well."

I scarcely heard him; the ganga deadened alarm, the agrypnotic made me all racing heart. Just as I was deciding that he had gone finally moribund, he bestirred himself and said, "All right, I will give you Octavio's address, and you can give him an extra cut for me. He has ruined one of my best girls."

If some part of my fevered brain suspected what he had in mind, it reassured itself that he was stuck to his chair, while I was already on my way out the door.

It did not occur to me that he could hire a messenger.

It was a large house, sitting alone at the end of Calle de La Faena. I had enough sense to study the balconies and scout an escape route, then I wrapped myself in the cape and went boldly in through the front entrance. "Tend to your duty, there are suspicious strangers in the street," I declared as I strode past, and with only a glance at my cape, the doorkeeper scuttled to do my bidding.

In fact, the black-and-white checks were my passport all the way, past liveried lackeys and dozing butlers to that corner of the house where handmaidens gossiped before a gilded door and politely parted to let me through.

I closed the doors behind me. There was a heap of embroidery on a chair in the sala, but her dueña was elsewhere, nor was there any sign of another checkered cape. Unlimbering my sword, I stepped to the bedroom doors and pushed them open.

The bed was rumpled, but there was nobody in it. A dead leech lay curled on the table, and a pewter spoon held the telltale stain of the poppy. I was about to step closer, when I heard her slovenly footfall in the sala. There was a tapestry beside the bed, and no sooner was I behind it and peering through a worn spot, when she came in, wearing her green gown and with her cat on her shoulder, then let herself with care down upon the bed. From the heaviness of her lids and the nod of her head, I could see that she was in the toils of Morpheus. Such a mingling of yearning and rage clutched me at the sight of the familiar pale angles and the rose-flushed flesh that I had to turn my gaze away.

Shortly I heard the rustle of bedclothes, then her labored breathing, and the first faint moans. Fearing the worst, I steeled myself and peeked again, only to find her still alone in the bed, her head bent back against the pillow, her hands between her upraised thighs. And then, to my astonishment, she began to speak in two voices, one her own, the other a strange and dwarfish piping, apparently meant to be the voice of that little fleshly nubbin she called her Twiddly. I was not the only one to have an intimate relationship with myself; she too had her esclavo.

HERSELF: There, my little darling, now you are coming awake.

ITSELF: Yes, all right, but go gently, for I am raw from Octavio's pummeling last night. And more to come, I'll wager.

HERSELF: Every variety of fun has its aftereffects, my darling. But until he gets here, we can have some fun for ourselves. Shall I play the bow to your fiddle, or do you want to play baton to my orchestra?

ITSELF: Fiddle me, twiddle me, oh yes, only make it delicate before the clumsy poking begins.

HERSELF: Fie: We must not think thus, lest our rebellion show.

ITSELF: I don't care, only do it! You do it so much better than anyone, man or woman, ever has or ever will.

HERSELF: Nonetheless, Octavio is a prize catch, and we must humor him.

ITSELF: You said the same of that sodomist, Don Juan, and look what a sour rag he turned out to be.

HERSELF: Come now, you're just jealous and feeling neglected. He had his moments. . . .

She suddenly stopped, for an involuntary twitch had caused my sword to press against the tapestry and make a telltale bulge.

"Who is there?" She stared, but her alarm quickly gave way before a chuckle. "Octavio, you are toying with me, naughty boy." She stretched out her arms toward my hiding place. "My darling, you were gone so long. Did you find us some ropes and reeds?"

I stepped out and showed her my sword. "Will the flat of this blade do?"

Her eyes flew wide and she sat bolt upright. But if I had expected to see fear, I was cheated. There was only mild alarm, then a chortling whoop of mischievous delight. "Juan! My, but you really do love me, don't you? He will be back any moment."

"Let him come."

She squirmed, a rosy lantern of glee; how she loved to be looked at and wanted. "He is young and quick; he will cut you to ribbons."

There was a commotion below, and a booming voice called out.

"Not if I cut him first," I said. Doors banged and servants shouted; running feet came closer. I wanted to skewer her; I wanted to bury my face in her lap and whimper.

"You once told me that when we were married you would tell me a secret," I said. "Well, you have someone else in mind now, so you have nothing to lose."

She looked blank, then incredulous, then amused again. "But don't you know by now, my darling, that the secret is this: that there is no secret?"

"Nothing?" I said. "It was all nothing?"

She shrugged. "Something, nothing, what's the difference? We try and cry and fornicate—"

More shouts cut her off, another door banged open, there was a heavy tread upon the sala tiles, then a bullish voice just outside the door. "I know she is in there! God knows, I paid the pimp enough to know it. Open up, I am the comendador!"

Her eyes fixed on the door, two stiletto points of hatred. "Him!" she hissed.

"Open up, I have come for my daughter!" boomed the voice. "Damn you, stand aside!"

The doors burst open, and there he was: large and square and red as a lobster: Don Garganto de Utero, her father.

Her blazing stare swung to me, and green spittle came flying. "Traitor!" she cried. "Betrayer! You have ruined my life and wrecked my future!"

Now her father's small and swinish eyes fastened on me as well. "So you are the one who has ruined my little girl!" His beard stood up, his jowls flopped, he grew redder and groped for his sword.

"Yes!" she screeched, pointing a trembling finger at me. "He is the one, he is the one!"

"Oh, yes, to be sure, I am the one," I said, throwing my cape over his head as he came at me, "and the Segovia aqueduct has just sprouted oranges."

And after that, I am told, I laughed very loudly and then killed him.

INTERLUDE

For almost two days the king had been reading the memoir, skipping pages, stopping here and there. "Well, well," he now said, letting the book fall shut. " 'Awakening,' indeed."

He put his gloved hand to his fat red lips and began to chew upon a swanskin thumb. And while the blue eyes rolled and roamed, the courtier, the monk, and the little nun waited to see which way the royal wind would blow.

They sat amongst the king's retinue on his balcony, whence they had removed so that Philip might continue his reading while also attending to the play. Below on the boards, the actor who impersonated Don Juan Tenorio was again executing his final and most complicated seduction. It was the sixth evening that the king had enjoyed the comedy, but all of a sudden the relish seemed to have gone out of him, and there was a brittle glint in his eye.

"Have you read this part of the memoir, Marco?"

The courtier nodded. "Why, yes, Your Majesty, I did glance through it last night while you were sorting your collection of mandrake roots."

"And did you find it interesting?"

"Well, yes, I suppose so," said the courtier, making a gesture of dismissal. "As a bit of light fancy, an amusing fiction . . ."

But the king had already turned an enigmatic smile upon the monk. "Tell me, Fray Gabriel, how did you come by this confession?"

"Your Majesty, as I recall it," said the monk, "I was strolling along the Arenal one afternoon, saying my prayers, when a masked stranger importuned me, offering a plain-wrapped package—"

"Never mind." The king waved a fretful hand. "No need to perjure yourself. I think the count has told you, sir, that there has been much speculation at court and amongst the public as to who might have been the model for your hero. Some have suggested it might be Lerma, but the only affairs he was ever interested in were affairs of state, and he lately finds himself retired even from that."

From the royal retinue came a tootle of light laughter at this reference to Lerma's recent fall from favor. The king enjoyed himself, but waxed serious again. "Others have suggested that you might have had Cervantes in mind, but that is unlikely, since the old boy is just now on his deathbed and never got much excited about women anyway."

Below on the stage, a lovely lady was protesting, "False friend, you hide behind the marqués's cloak. You have deceived me!" The king paused to watch while the hero silenced the lady's protest with a steaming kiss.

"Many say that it is the great Lope," he then continued. "But Lope has denied it to me personally, and everybody knows that he is a hopeless romantic and very religious man like myself. Perhaps he has raped, but never without feeling sorry about it afterward. Unlike that heartless devil down there."

Below, Don Juan was just bearing the lady down upon the bed, when a door burst open and another appeared, sword in hand.

With one eye on the play and the other on the monk, the king wet his lips, preparing one of the royal cruelties. "By the way, Lope called your play, as I recall, a venal piece of dander on the pate of the muse."

The monk half rose in his chair, but the courtier grasped his belt rope and held him down.

While on the stage, the hero of the play pulled out his sword and skewered the intruder. As he fell, the victim cried out, "Alas, you have slain me. But my furia will track you down!"

The king made a wan and sour smile. "A noble hope, but did it happen?" His blue eyes wandered. He tapped a finger on the book in his lap. "At any rate, I think we need look no farther than these pages for your inspiration, playwright. The only question remaining, I suppose, is whether the person in question wrote the confession, or you wrote it yourself."

"It was the last, I admit," the monk hastened to say. "I had it in mind to try my hand at a novel—"

"Never mind, never mind." The king looked weary and opened his fan. "It does not matter now. What does matter is that the Crown's integrity should remain intact, and that the Holy Office shall discover no excuse to reopen this matter." He turned to the courtier, and his glance was at once aggrieved and malevolent. "I only want to be sure that the rascal is truly dead, do you understand that, Marco?"

"I do, Your Majesty," said the courtier. "I will begin reading the third and last part immediately—"

"And I," said the king, his blue eyes roaming again, "will take my own measures." His eye lit upon the little nun's bosom and fixed there.

The courtier arose with elaborate unhaste. "Your pleasure is mine, Your Majesty."

"Not always," murmured the king, removing his spectacles so as to study the nun better. And when she arose to leave with the other two, the king put his fan on her shoulder. "I would beg you to stay, my dear. Baffled by worldly confusion, we find it soothing to have innocence near by."

"Baffled he is not," muttered the courtier when he and the monk were once again behind the stage. "He suspects, and he is planning something."

"He is not the sort to know what he does not want to know," said the monk. "Let him take his measures, he cannot raise the dead."

A grisly smile formed itself beneath his long nose, and he pushed the third volume at the other. "Read on ànd see what I mean."

The courtier opened the book and did so.

DEATH

30

Excuse my scrawl, but I am in haste. You will recall that I am to be hanged for murder at New Year. The fatal hour awaits me only a few days hence, and they have finished building my gibbet. Out through my grating I can see the scaffold, and today they are testing the trap. It works too noisily for my taste; the hinges need oil.

"My God," said Catalinon, eying the blood on my doublet and glove. "Did you go too far?"

"Up to the knuckles," I told him. "I have killed a powerful man and friend of the king. I dare not show myself on a horse. Bring the caravan, and hurry!"

The painted wagon was all he had left of my grandmama's bequest, and he had kept it well. When we had the horses hitched, I put my bags in, and my parcel of ganga, some agrypnotic, and the leech and bit of poppy tar Peregrina had left behind.

"You do not look well, master."

"The hardest-fought love of my life has just come to a sorry end."

"Never mind, it was a bad graft. Where to?"

"To hell, if we can find it."

He gave a wry and rummy grin. "We are just leaving it."

"Then beyond." I climbed into the back. "South to Barbary, and don't bother to stop at any shrines."

My father's portrait still swung from its nail at the back of the caravan, but after a day with that smug smile, I turned him to the wall and lay down on my hip and smoked ganga.

Had I been asked to describe my feelings, I would only have snarled. My sword still quaked from its deed, and the death of the comendador had started a new gnawing in me. But it was my other shock that brought the more intimate and pressing hurt. It has been said that madness arises from the inability to decide whether to laugh or cry. It was as though a gangrenous limb had been torn from me. On the one hand I was giddy with elation at its going, but on the other, my God, how the socket ached. She had been my touchstone and sibyl, keeper of my most cherished illusions and darkest secrets. What was more, for the first time it was I who had been abandoned and was the castaway.

Try as I would, I could not keep my mind from my memories. I missed her goatish will and merciless intelligence. Even as I thanked God I was free of that brambled thicket, I felt only half alive without its thorns tugging at me. In my worst moments, I recalled her wistful invocations of death as the final peace, and for the first time in my life, I began to wonder if it was true.

On the other hand, in my best moments I could see it all clearly for the comedy it was. I imagined Octavio doing the jig of rut to her winsome and wily piping. I saw him puffed by her flattery, fascinated by her novelties, panting and waiting, while she babbled endlessly. Then laboring over her like a gravedigger, while all the time the suspicion grew that it was his own grave he was digging. Now it was his face that twisted with passion's ludicrous apoplexy, and his body which twitched and thrashed like a dying frog between her insatiable thighs.

At this picture, I was struck with such a burst of ganga hilarity that I fell to the floor in a kind of shrieking cramp and made such a rumpus that Catalinon stopped the wagon and came around to peer in at me.

"Drive on," I gasped, laughing and wincing and laughing again. "I am undergoing a cure."

"The cure that kills," he muttered, but did as he was bidden.

We finally came to Algeciras Bay. "Yonder lies Africa, out of sight in this bad weather," said Catalinon. "And just there at the end of the bay is Jebel Tarik, the northern Pillar of Hercules. My cousin knows of a cave up there."

We went first to the port, but sure enough, a squad of the king's cuadrillos had joined the usual customs officers at the quayside and patroled the beaches. They had got ahead of us on their faster mounts.

"We could try to bribe them," said Catalinon. "But perhaps we should change direction and try for Portugal."

"Take me to this cave atop Gibraltar rock."

"But won't it be dangerous to linger?"

"Everything is dangerous now. Get your cousin and hurry."

There was a garrison which the king, in concert with the Duke of Medina Sidonia, kept against incursions from the Barbary shore. But Catalinon's cousin knew a back path which took us safely to the cave at the top. Once we had placed my stores inside, I told them to go. "Come only on Saturdays, unless you have special news. I want to think."

Catalinon grinned. "Like San Antonio. Or that other, Francisco, eh, master?" He gestured toward the rocks above my door. "Except that instead of the Devil or the birds, you shall have those fellows."

And when I turned to look, one of the several hairy apes on the rocks above solemnly turned about and pointed its vivid red bottom at me.

I lay on my hip in the mouth of the cave and smoked ganga and let the days run one into the other, waiting for that morning when I might look down the mountain and see the soldiers climbing up with the sun behind them. Just below, there was a shelf of rocks and dirt where the Barbary apes gathered: their town placita, so to speak.

With faint hope and gingerly, I proceeded to review my life and add up my account. All the lessons, so hard won, now seemed so obvious. How surely each bright illusion had been discredited and made dull and redundant. Within every dream of surcease, it seemed there lurked infinite cruelties of contradiction.

How sweet had been my childhood vision of that wedding in the cathedral, the bride soft and joyous, the groom heroic and proud, the bishop bestowing God's blessing upon the union. How sudden and arbitrary that septic lobster and mysterious will which had felled the groom and ended the dream before it was scarce begun.

371

As I had learned that the bishop's blessing did not banish sudden death, so I had come step by step to understand the rest: that to create a turd was not to own it, to win a mother's attention was not to enjoy the clyster, to snatch bloomers was not to escape scorn, to pray was not to spend, to spend was not to be relieved, to find one's way between legs was not to find oneself, to be great-souled was not to be greatly satisfied, to unveil perfect beauty was not to encompass it, to be famous was not to be flattered, to swive regularly was not to swive well, to pledge troth was not to fix time, to lust carelessly was not to dodge the clap, to confess betrayal was not to defray revenge, to embrace art was not to find a living, to make a baby was not to be reborn, to find a sister was not to be less starved, to go with a gypsy was not to be fancy-free, to flee the poof was not to escape the propensity, to cause pain was not to own power, to detect eternity was not to transcend the downside, to be in love was to be no less alone, to kill was not to be more alive.

Bringing all the small voices of experience together, I let them say it aloud: perhaps there was no Grail at all, nor Golden Moment, nor solution, nor cipher, nor surcease. The saying of it brought a numbing, as of amputation, and a fleeting disdain for those poor souls who still dreamed of happiness. But the missing limb continued to itch and the smugness soon left me. Perhaps, I told myself, if I wrote it down, I might make some sense of it and recover some fragment of faith.

I had some paper and a quill and began to write this confession. But I was only made the more mortified to see myself painted in words. Such childish illusions, such confusions of intent, such pitiable desperation and need. Was this a hero worthy of admiration, this moral pincushion, this emotional squid, this venereal jumping jack?

God's nose, if only I had known what I knew now. If only I could begin again. If only I were another man . . .

Remembering old Ripio de Rebombar and the Theater of the Jittering Chicken, I decided to write a play instead. I felt a deep need to leave behind some kind of testament, and besides, it might make money with which to bring a little ease to my daughter's life, if not to mine. With that in mind, I this time bent true events to a purpose, condensing here, embellishing there, hiding uncertainty, concealing contradiction. My hero suffered no youthful qualms or confusions, he came full-blown upon the stage, wild in the eye and ever ready between the legs. His

Peregrina was an easy dupe to his merciless seductions, and he had her all his way. His forlorn Pechita inspired not an iota of uneasiness in him; he plugged her and went blithely on to his next. And his next, and his next.

For a time, I enjoyed myself. All indomitable cucumber and fanciful furia, I scribbled with a freedom I had not been able to manage in life, and created a most charming monster who was every man's wistful dream of license and conquest, every woman's dearest dread. I called him Juan, since that name comes easily to me, and added my father's surname, Tenorio, out of an old and wishful suspicion that the portrait might be a true one.

And then I came to the murder of the comendador, and once I had put that down, suddenly I could write no more.

That was when I noticed Monita, by far the most comely and attractive of the apes living in that neighborhood.

It had come to me slowly as I watched the hairy tribe cavort about their placita that I could see all of life's span in that bunch of monkeys: birth and infancy, courting and marriage, politics and religion, old age and death.

There sat their king, perched on the highest rock, gazing imperiously about him whilst toying absently with the royal genitalia. Large and aloof and always alert, he was spoiled by the ladies of his harem, who picked the nits from his pelt all day and solicitously combed his long cape of hair with their fingers. The largest of them was only half his size, and when they approached him, they came backward, dipping their bright red hinderlings in inviting curtsy. When one of them was ripe, he went after her, but she most often coyly ran away and thrashed and shrieked when he caught her, offering all the coquettish resistance she could, before he finally got aboard and gave her the royal what for.

Sometimes male courtiers also approached, offering their bums in salute, and occasionally he would mount one of these and give the minion a cursory poke: there, now we know who is king here. But most often he need only yawn and display the royal armory: yellowed eyeteeth as long as those of a full-grown panther.

But he paid the price of privilege and must be always on the alert, his limbs twitching, his head forever swiveling to watch his subjects. When there was a threat to all, he must lead the charge alone, unlike our modern kings. Once, I approached their placita to test them, and he was the first to let out a thundering bark and come running at me with the hair of his back all on end. Nor could he trust his ministers, who were ever ready to turn upon him and bring him down, or to run off with a choice doxy from his harem. If he was not baring his tusks at some marauding bachelor, he was punishing some straying concubine with a nip at the back of her neck.

And, be assured, they strayed, for he had more than he needed. There was one in particular, the sprightly little darling whom I came to call Monita. On one occasion, when the king had run around one side of his throne to punish one of his other ladies, she promptly scurried to the other side and lifted her backside under the nose of one of the young bachelors. From my comfortable distance, I could admire her independent spirit, and I think she detected my interest, for several times I caught her glancing my way and fluttering her white eyelids.

I came to think of her young suitor as Juanito, and I could read his life from the antics of those younger and older than he. Born to a mother and spoiled, he had then been suddenly weaned. Coming into maturity with his female peers, he had found them to be more interested in the king and his ministers than in his own callow invitations. Exiled to the edge of the placita with the other bachelors, he was obliged to wait and yearn. How tortured he looked, twitching and grimacing each time one of the king's doxies went by. How shamefaced, as he crouched behind a bush to brandle furtively.

He was secretive about this private solution with good reason. While the females seemed to be receptive to their swains only in their time, which was to say, probably one week out of four, when they were ready, they were utterly and jealously so. Here was one of Juanito's older brothers approaching a swollen lady some years his senior. How inviting her glances, how bright her hinderlings. But in this case, the young bachelor had but little experience at the business. In fact, so excited was he made by the sight of that vivid bottom that he suddenly interrupted his courting and began to brandle. Whereupon the female turned in outrage and savagely attacked him, imposing bloody punishment for his nervous defection.

Clearly it was here, as I had found it to be elsewhere, that in the last analysis and despite her protests, it was the lady who decided when. Also, that she would brook no neglect or hesitancy in the matter, and that at the heart of the tournament of genders there was that immensely complex and insoluble argument over who should enjoy the most satisfaction.

Poor Juanito, my heart went out to him. If he did not lose his life to a leopard whilst defending the tribe, or to some rival in a duel over Monita, he might finally win her. But by then he would be already into his prime. By the time he became a minister and owned a harem, his strength would already be fading from him. And yet, even when he was old, he would be like that white-pelted elder who most often crouched alone at the fringe of the company, palsied and feeble, yet still haplessly rolling a rheumy eye whenever a ripe lady passed by.

As for Monita, my study of her older sisters made it clear that this was the best year of her life. Now she was indulged by the other ladies and eagerly attended by all the machos. But soon enough she would need protection of a single lord, for she would be with child. And from then on, virtually every day of her life until death, she would be either nursing an infant, swollen at the rear, or paggled in front.

Perhaps that is why, each and every morning, she was among those who solemnly sat with hands on knees, facing east, and greeted the rising sun with a delirious crescendo of barking. And why, when the white-haired patriarch finally breathed his last, the whole tribe gathered with their backs to the body and, for the first time to my knowledge, crooned a woeful and yearning farewell to the setting sun.

And so it seemed to me as I watched them, day after day, that at last I was beginning to see the whole pattern and reason for it. The entire objective of life was its continuance through procreation, and such purpose could not allow for individual peace. The fate of the smaller and weaker female was unremitting humiliation and labor. The fate of the male was less diverse but as sharp. He was simply doomed to be in a state of continuous and unsatisfied rut, forever bunched toward supersaliency. When he could not fornicate, he had to fight. Nature desired that he should be drawn to the female in such a state of agitation and compulsion, forced to beat through resistance at every turn, hers as well as that of his rivals, that when he finally arrived, his mind and body would be clenched by such a fury of lustfit that the spunk would be fired as from an exploding cannon, so as to be all that much more effectively sent to her egg.

To God, the woman was a vessel, a pot to be used until it finally dried out and was cast aside. The man was a piston, a harquebus, an instrument of insertion and assault, to be pumped full, then blown out, then loaded again, eventually to burst or collapse, and be also cast away.

It was as I had been told years before at the Marquis Mendo's mentidero. Beyond the securing of food and shelter, the woman's first concern was to find protection for herself and her child, and the man's overwhelming urge and function was to spend. But not necessarily for his pleasure or that of his partner, but only to God's implacable ends.

As the monkeys keened and the sun sank, I cooked up the dark soup, trembling only a little, and filled the leech, rubbed up a vein, and clamped the insect to it. There was a faint nip of hurt, then a rush of sweet, loose ecstasy that seemed to tear me all at once from every origin, melting the soul's desperate noise into a kind of pissy silver music.

I retched painlessly into the clay, then went on into a longer peace that lasted hours and was devoid of pain.

I mean its absolute absence. I took up my dagger and thrust its point into the tip of my forefinger, and I bled but felt nothing. But it was not mere physical pain that was banished. I was also relieved of those pangs of the heart and mind which can be the worst of all. I knew my troubles, and I knew they would be back with me soon enough, but I did not care. Nor was it only pain's modification or reduction, as by infatuation, euphoria, torpor, hilarity, daydream, ejaculation. The absence was complete: it was bliss.

However, as dawn crept across the sky, Morpheus began to abandon me, and in that gray penumbra between cool-blue bliss and crimson rage, all the pangs began to niggle, then to burn like the coals of hell. My God, the downside of the agrypnotic was nothing to this. Every fiber in my body ached, even the root of each fingernail. Sweat streamed down my ribs, and my skin began to prickle and itch. Black clouds crawled my mind, bearing all the hurtful memories, the mistakes, the guilts, the lies, the fractured dreams.

As I had felt no pain when drugged, so I had felt not the slightest

376

twinge, in mind or flesh, of lustful desire. But now, as I clutched at my knees and cursed and mewed, my mind began desperately to conjure lascivious images, while my blood began to pound fiercely.

If I had not been sure before, I now knew what it was that Peregrina had wanted: not to want. We had been brother and sister in that. But there was something else that returned with the downside: a certain reversal of faith which I could not quite put my finger on.

For the furia was again burning red within me. Where before I had lacked for nothing and wanted nothing, now all of a sudden I wanted it all. Every sight and sound, every offering of reality, seemed designed to thwart and deny me and filled me with a raging fury.

I heard sounds below my cave: some fading moans of mourning, then a restless chattering. Turning on my hip, I looked down to the ape's placita, and there in the dim morning light I saw them gathering in a loose circle about the body of the dead elder, muttering and scuttling closer, then shrinking back. Suddenly the king rushed forward and the others converged with him, and with a communal shriek of fear and revulsion, they pitched the corpse down the mountain.

Then, as I came naked from my cave, I saw Monita. She sat gazing reflectively down the hill and picking at her posteriors. When she saw me looking at her, she blinked her white eyelids, looked away, then coyly at me again.

All around amongst the rocks, the apes were chattering and shrieking, half the population either fornicating or getting ready to. Monita rolled an eye, and the hair stood up on the back of my neck. How glossy her coat, how exquisite her little pink ears, how moist and blindingly rubescent her swollen hinderlings. Did I detect some exotic pungency in the air? I stepped closer. She shivered and made as if to flee, yet did not. She glanced at me from under fluttering lids, and turned ever so slightly, tilting her scarlet bustle. I could feel it, the itching anguish in the quick, the command to pounce.

But at that moment I heard a yakking roar and turned to find the monarch of monkeys bearing down upon me, his huge mouth yawning, his tusks agleam with spittle. Naked, I had to flee, with him close behind and barking. At the entrance to the cave, I snatched up my sword and turned just as the enraged cuckold hurled himself upon me.

There was no time to parry or wound. I took him recibiendo, letting

377

the weight of his body carry the point past the breastbone, into and through him. His eyes popped and a gaseous croak came from deep in his bowel and out his mouth, and a tremendous shudder passed from the ruptured heart along the bloody blade to mine. And as the weight pulled the quivering body down and off my sword, it seemed to me that it tried to draw me with it.

For some time I could not take my eyes from the body. Long after the last quiver, I watched it. Then, suddenly wrenched by nausea, I turned against a rock and closed my eyes. Ah, how I wanted another leech and dose of the poppy now. But there had been only the one.

I was thus for some time, then I heard a soft chittering and opened my eyes to discover Monita peering out from a nearby rock, hair on end and tiny eyes fixed on her fallen lord. She came closer to sniff at the body, but what my eyes had seen, her nose told her. She looked at me. Fluttering her pretty eyelids, she turned slowly, delicately, put her head on the ground and lifted her backside, presenting the flaming prize to me. The king is dead, long live the king.

The furia rose again to choke my spout and send me raving. "No!" I howled. "No, I will not accept it!"

The monkey cringed back, looking startled, then uncertain. She touched a finger gingerly to the corpse, looked at me again, then turned and slipped into the rocks, her last disgusted glance making it clear that she considered me to have gone quite off my noggin.

31

DESPITE what old soldiers and writers of romantic adventure might like to think, it is not good fun to kill. It is true that there is a purgative effect, as with other cathartic evacuations. But this release soon becomes a firmer capture, for a heavy apprehension follows on the deed. To skewer is only to know how easily one might, oneself, be punctured. To kill, even in self-defense, is not to escape death, but only to become that much more intimate with its awful wonder. And thereby to deepen the dread.

My crime had left something dull and deadly working in me, and I was seized by a skittish hurry, as though I must hasten to learn my lessons before retribution caught up.

"What now?" asked Catalinon as I came down from the mountain and strode up to his cousin's house. "You are posted as a murderer in every cathedral in Spain. Let us make for Portugal at once."

"No," I said. "I have debts to pay and scores to settle."

"O my God," he groaned, "can't you do it by mail?"

"Get the wagon, we are going home."

"Home to death," he grumbled.

"You dramatize," I told him. "Now do as you are told."

But in truth, his instincts were good. Feverish and heady impulses were growing in me. I continued fascinated by the deaths of the comendador and then the monkey. One moment the life had been in the flesh, the next moment it had gone. Where to?

A conversation with an unemployed actor in Estepona directed us to

379

the little village of Pierdapan del Rio, north of Arcos de la Frontera, and there we came upon the director, Ripio de Rebombar, standing upon the edge of a show wagon and pitching mightily into a whirl of chaff. For it was the season for beating the hearts out of the wheat in that region, and they had built the village downwind from the threshing circles in hopes of blocking all loss with their hovels. Yellow chaff drifted up against the walls and filled the air, and the women went about winnowing the leavings and putting what they could into their aprons, hoping to keep this small bonus from the landlord's knowledge and make secret bread against the winter. They stooped here and there around the little plaza, dim and shifting figures in the golden haze, ignoring the stout showman who stood on the wagon, holding up his bottle of ground hyssop and colored spirits, and bellowing.

"Housewives of Wasted Bread Upon the Waters, do not despair before the cruel vicissitudes of life and the sad susceptibilities of the body, for I hold here in my hand, I say, here in my hand, Professor Ripio de Rebombar's Miracle Preservative and Universal Balm, otherwise known as Solomon's Panpharmicon or Fantastico!"

He gestured at the great lump of gray suet on the wagon behind him. "Do you fear the ruinous rub of the weather, the erosions of old age? Then behold the great fish, Leviathan, preserved from decay by this very liquor I hold in my hand. Indeed, like certain persons I could mention, this whale is not sorry to be pickled, for in life he was not without dire difficulty. Ergo: the female of the species is often plagued with encrustations of sharp barnacles upon her private underparts. And yet the oceans abound in baby whales. Which only goes to show, my friends, that on the sea as on the land, love knows no bounds, ho ho ho."

I stepped closer and said my name. He looked older than when I had last seen him swept away in the crowd at the bullfight; his yellow eye had a dull and weary roll, even as he saw me and began to rave.

"You! Arsonist, false matador, traitor!" There was some kind of harpoon there, and he snatched it up and aimed it.

"Wait!" I showed him my manuscript. "I have a play here, and if I am not mistaken, it is the very thing you need to restore your reputation."

He glared. "You burned down my theater and my reputation, then trod the ashes into the dust at that bull-baiting."

"I am sorry," I said. "But are you too proud to accept payment of my debts now?" I thrust the folio into his hands. "Here, I call it *The Rake of Sevilla.* I promise it will make you some money."

"Money." He savored it like a forgotten wine. Abruptly he sat down on the edge of the wagon to read, while Catalinon and I squinted against the blowing chaff and put kerchiefs to our noses, for his whale had a powerful presence.

"It is good," he finally announced, and the curds of his face seemed already to be gathering shape, and his saffron-ringed eyes to be bright again. "It lacks professional polish and a strong form, but the meat and fire are here. By God, yes, the makings of a character sure to warm the hearts of the public: gay, charming, a murderer." He struck his fist into his palm. "By God, I can raise money with this! The Teatro del Pollo Punzando will live again!"

"I am glad," I said.

"I suppose you want to play the lead yourself," he grumbled. "Well, you might be able to handle a character of this sort, with shrewd make-up and my coaching—"

"No, no," I said, putting a hand to his shoulder. "Only a modest share of the royalties, should you get a success."

His eyes narrowed. "I don't believe such generosity. Why?"

It popped from me unbidden: "I am not an ape, sir."

His damper fell open and he gawked. Pressing a finger to his temple, he turned an inquiring glance to Catalinon.

"I fear it might be so, yes I do," whispered my lackey.

But I was already on my way to the wagon.

"Wait!" cried the director, waving the folio. "It lacks an ending!"

"If I discover one, I will send it," I called back.

"But where will you be?"

Again I took pause, again the reply came as from some other apprehension: "If not in hell, then in the garden."

As we drove away, I looked out from the back of the caravan and saw the director in brisk conversation with the local lord, no doubt arranging to sell his whale toward the enrichment of next year's wheat crop. As the sorry cluster of huts disappeared into the blowing haze, I could still hear his stentorian holler.

"You are not serious!" Catalinon protested. "Sevilla? Of all places, you are the best known there, and sure to be recognized!"

"It is Corpus Cristi, is it not?" I said. "We will go through at night. And in this hood and chains, they will not know me from the other penitents." I made a face. "I may not even know myself."

"Nonetheless," he grumbled, "it seems to me you are asking for trouble."

It was true that I had another goal in mind, and we had to go through the city to get there. Soon enough we were caught in the crowds. All the dark enchantments of Semana Santa had Sevilla in its annual thrall. The church bells rang all day and all night, and endless streams of painted tarasques and hooded penitentes toiled the streets, holy figures gleamed with lacquer in the light of the torches, and from the balconies mighty-lunged widows sang the saeta above their favorite images.

"So alone in birth
So alone in love
So alone in life
So alone in death."

By chance we found ourselves in procession with the Confraternity of Bankers and Moneylenders, myself toiling along in purple cloak and high conical hat and mask, and festooned in light chains; while Catalinon flailed me from behind, except that, unlike the other lackeys, his whip had leathers of felt, and the bladder of blood with which he sprinkled me had been come by at the butcher's the day before.

As we staggered along, chanting prayers and moaning counterpoint to the whistle and crack of the whips, many a good-looking wench watched from her balcony, all in black and weeping with mingled sorrow and joy to see her husband, her lover, her suitor prove his love for Christ and her by having himself beat bloody in her sight.

I certainly had no plan to join in this stupid business beyond getting to the other side of the city, but the agrypnotic was working in me, and it happened that just ahead of us was the richest banker in town. I found myself falling into competition with this famous money-breeder.

So enormously rich was he that it was all his four muscular servants could do to administer him penance equal to his just deserts. How they did lay on, and yet as we approached the front of the little chapel of the Carmelites on Assencion Street, he cried out for more. Following his gaze, I saw his target, a tiny nun, radiant in her red-crossed gown amongst the monks on the church steps, and I swear it: with a visible aura of light glowing behind her small and pretty head, although it might have been a torch.

"Lay on," I muttered over my shoulder to Catalinon, and he rolled his eye in alarm, but increased his efforts with our harmless whip.

Just ahead of me, the banker bent double in agony, shot me a jealous look, and shouted to his lackeys to equal my servant's efforts and more. Grunting, they laid into him, and the back of his cloak began to take on the look of bloody lace.

"More blood," I muttered to Catalinon, and he squirted me from the bag hidden in his sleeve, then went at it with the whip some more.

Step by step we came closer to the chapel, its ranks of praying monks, and the famous Carmelite, said to be more than the common run of nuns. Just ahead, the banker glared and began to belabor himself with a hand flail, all the time casting a mooning eye toward her.

"More whip, more blood," I muttered, and Catalinon hurled himself into a last spectacular exhibition of pretended fustigation, while the banker's whippers rose furiously to the occasion, and the whole procession halted, frozen before the chapel while this grisly duel reached its final frenzy. With a shriek of agony and a gurgling invocation of the Virgin, the banker staggered forward and fell to his knees at the little nun's feet. But I did him one better, falling flat out and stiff, managing to position my bag of blood beneath me, so that as I struck the cobbles, a gigantic splash of lurid crimson squirted out from beneath my body.

"Such faith!" cried Teresa in a booming voice, pointing a finger at me. "Surely this one is the more exalted. I will salve his wounds and pray for his soul. Bring him to our hospital."

"I knew it," whispered Catalinon, as they prepared to lift me up. "Your crime has affected your reason!"

"Never mind," I muttered. "I am into it now. Meet me behind the hospital in a few minutes."

The clinic was a single room with a narrow bed and little else. Once they had laid me out, the monks went away, and she bent to loosen my clothing, praying all the while in her thick and hiccuping voice. "Sweet Son of God, pity this poor penitent and give him absolution, as you have done the same for me. Although some say that I should be burned, I ask only this humble work, to salve the wounds of deserving souls. . . ."

Studying her through my eyeholes, I now saw that she had a little girl's face, yet was as finely lined as old leather, as though some part of her had remained a child, even as three score years and more had passed through her. But the halo was still there behind her head, although it might have been the candle.

"May our Holy Mother forgive you for such an abundance of sin that has brought you to this," she said in that odd and girlish groan. "How thrilling to see you suffer so for the love of Our Savior. And yet we are none of us that much above the flesh and that far removed from the Devil that we can look down upon such devotion. I myself have been tormented by demons since my twelfth year, and have many times struggled with Satan himself, and once he threw me downstairs and broke my arm. . . ."

Her smug bemusement made my eyes burn from behind. Now she laid my hood back, and now she put a finger to the false blood on my chest, but found no wound. Disappointment pinched the glow from her face. She looked at me, and her eyes grew wider, wider. . . .

"Yes my little saint," a grunting voice said from my gullet. "My wounds have healed, the stone has rolled aside, and I am risen. But it is not your arm that we will break this time. . . ."

As a purge it was cold comfort, the passing pop of a winter blister. What once had been at least relief and sometimes triumph was now only gall and ennui. Rapine had lost its charm.

Palsied and sickened to my toes, I got off her when I was finished and climbed to the window ledge, then turned for one last look. She was on her knees on the stones and wringing her hands. Tears streamed down her cheeks and her face was bright and blank with stubborn chastity. "I was alone, Holy Mother," she declared to a plaster Virgin on a shelf. "I was praying, and then I saw a beautiful angel beside me, and I saw in his hands a long dart of gold, and this he thrust through my heart several times so that it reached my very entrails, and as he withdrew it, I thought that he brought them out with it, and left me all burning with a great love of God. And so great was the pain that it made me give those moans, and so utter the sweetness that there was no wanting to stop, nor was there any contenting of the soul with less. . . ."

Pious lunatic! I wanted to spew obscenities and puke with loathing. God, how I envied her!

"Welcome to the House of the Crazy Dead," I said as we rode in under the gargoyles of the Camposanto de Los Illustrios & Etc.

"Amen," muttered Catalinon. "Now I know you have gone mad."

"And here the Shrine of Celestial Readiness, and there the Hospital of the Bleeding Heart, and up in that tower, the Chamber of Divine Intervention. . . ."

"O Jesus."

"Watch your language, San Pedro is near."

"It is the police I worry about," he grumbled, thumbing a cross on his chest. "I am beginning to think you want to be captured."

Broken seashells crunched underfoot, the cypress writhed stock-still against the quarter moon, and in the quemadero across the way, the ashes of recently burned heretics still smouldered. We came to the place, and I stood looking at the name chiseled into the tomb: TENORIO. As I stared into the black entrance, a small and clammy wind fingered the back of my neck, and I could feel my yearning coming home. Was Catalinon right? For an instant I wanted to enter.

I turned sharply away. Then I saw a new statue on that side of the path. It was cut from marble, blue-veined and pale: a square-built, bearded man with a face the best sculptor in Spain had failed to make pleasant. Still I was not sure. I stepped closer and read the words cut into the pedestal:

DON GARGANTO DE UTERO

Comendador de Calatrava

Here, trusting in the Lord for Vengeance
on a murderer, the most Noble of Knights
lies buried.

"God, but it has gone cold," muttered Catalinon, chaffing his arms and gawking at me. "Why are you laughing?"

It seems I was. Laughing and choking, as I climbed the pedestal. The hollow eyes stared, the arrogant jaw jutted. What had he croaked as he had fallen gushing at the foot of his daughter's bed? "My spirit will see you in hell!"

"Whenever you are ready, old man," I said, and grasped the stone beard and gave it a yank.

"O my God, master, no!" gasped Catalinon. "Never did any great man since the Cid allow another to yank his beard and stay alive!"

"All the more reason," I said, and tugged again.

32

"Not Madrid, master!" cried my lackey. "The king's own city!"

"I must see my daughter once before it is over."

"Over? What do you mean, over?"

"Never mind. I've still credit to spare. Drive on!"

As we lurched along northward, I smoked my pipe and washed down my giddifying medicine with wine, so that I hardly knew if I was drugged, drunk, or in an agrypnotic fit, and as often as not it was all three. Sometimes I dozed, but the moment my stupor was threatened by a dream, I awoke and clutched for my gristle. But awakedness now held as vivid and novel nightmares as did sleep. One morning, midway through my usual conversation with Esclavo, his manner suddenly underwent a change.

MYSELF: All right, out with you.

ITSELF: My God, death dogs your heels, and you hound me. Can't you leave me alone for a day?

MYSELF: Not when our days are numbered.

ITSELF: They are always numbered.

MYSELF: Our little corporal has become a philosopher. Perhaps you wish me to let some poof get at you before we die?

ITSELF: Not particularly. But then, what's the difference between that and this?

MYSELF: Surely you are joking. There is all the difference. We are rehearsing manly endeavor.

ITSELF: Oh, of course, sweetie. Goodness yes, you are the only one. Darling, do it to me.

MYSELF: What's wrong with you? Stop that!

ITSELF: I'm in ecstasy, you brute. Your fist is so horny and manly, oh I love it, do it to me, do, do, do . . .

MYSELF: Damn you, stop that lisping!

ITSELF: . . . so sweet, so terrible, and I am so helpless, harder, drive me mad, make me scream for it, harder . . .

MYSELF: O my God, there is a woman in me!

Did Catalinon hear the words or only the bellow? He stopped the wagon and came around to peer in at me, and there seemed a hot and suggestive gleam in his eye. "What is it, master? Might I be of use?"

"You may put your whip to the horses," I shouted at him. "On to the capital, damn you, or I will stick it in you too!"

I stayed inside the wagon as we rattled past the king's park, through the Puerta del Sol, to Don Diego's house on the Plaza Real. Leaving Catalinon and the wagon around the corner, I put my cloak well up before my face and made my way to the front door. There were no soldiers in sight; I swung the knocker. A servant came, and then a thick and slow-moving figure, black against the light, then closer.

"Mother?"

The haggard look of her wrenched my heart, and I reached out my arms. But she shrank back, still shying from the bath and other memories. "O my God, Juanito, you have done it again. My own son, posted in the cathedral as a reprobate! And you badly need a haircut as well."

"I must see my daughter," I told her.

"First, you must give yourself up," she said, waggling a finger before my nose. "Poor Diego has had a stroke, but he can still intercede with the king. You must go to the palace before it is too late, and throw yourself upon the royal mercy."

"Perhaps I will," I said. "But first, where is the child?"

"Perhaps? You said perhaps?" Her feverish glance turned aside, and did it also go sly? "Very well." She heaved a sigh. "Come and wait, and I will try to bring your daughter to you."

I followed her down a corridor and stepped into a small library, then turned to receive the door in my face, followed by the shooting of a bolt on the other side. "God's nose, mother!"

"You must stay there, Juanito," she called, and was that the old compulsive chuckle I heard? "I am sorry, but I will not let you out. I am going to consult with Diego on how we might put a good face on your surrender."

"But my daughter!"

"She is in the countryside with your wife."

"Where in the countryside?"

"I shall not tell you. You will see them once things are set right with the king. It is all for your own good, Juanito."

I bloodied my knuckles on the door. "My own mother!" The gas of a lifetime came all in one weeping belch. "Take my love," I bellowed, "and push it up your posticum!"

There was a long silence from the other side. But in the end it was just as I had long suspected it would be. It didn't matter what you said or where you put it, and it never would. She simply declined to acknowledge the assault. It had not happened.

"Yes, well, be that as it may, Juanito, you really must get a haircut. And now I am going to find Diego. And why don't you take a little nap, you seem to need it."

I beat my fists and swore some more. But once her shuffling footsteps had faded away and I had satisfied myself that the door would not break, I rummaged about in a large desk that was there, then saw Don Diego's favorite book, *Rewards of Honor*. As a child I had discovered that it was hollow, and now I found that there was money in it. Next, I broke a chair in two and pried at the bars until the window frame came away and let me out.

Dread and delirium, these were ganga's gifts, and the one could become the other at a twitch from fate. I was not thinking of Peregrina but of Dorita, for we had just driven past the river, only to discover that the houseboat was gone, nor was there even any sign of the swan. I had then directed Catalinon to go past the old bodega, and was peering out in hopes of spotting the Marquis Mendo, when I saw a figure moving along the street ahead and felt my heart come up to plug my throat like a potato.

There was no mistaking that mincing and slovenly amble, proclaiming to whomever cared to follow: I itch, I roil, I want! Nor was there any mistaking the rosy flush at the back of the neck, the wisps of pale hair escaping the colorful burnoose. I was out of the wagon in a trice, and yet I could not seem to hurry, and it was all the suspension of a dream, as though we were separate stars wheeling the sky, forever pursuing, forever apart. I remembered the cruelest lesson, that love was a bit of sticking plaster, and further, that I had killed her father. I had a moment of cringing good sense and nearly turned back.

But the small heels flashed white beneath the forest-green gown, calling me to the chase. Would I never be cured? My answer was to quicken my pace, drawing close enough to see the rouged cheek, then all of the face turning, the narrow eyes measuring, then opening in delight, the small lip worming, the entire presence proclaiming, Take me, I am wonderful!

"Damn you," I groaned, and leaned close and crushed the pink mouth with mine, then clamped a hand to a breast and found it curiously like an orange.

"Juan, darling! At last!"

God's nose, it was Felicio. And yet, after the first shock had staggered me back a pace, I suffered nothing like the crushing devastation and shame long anticipated. In fact, as one of his tits ran down his leg and rolled across the cobbles, a hearty hilarity doubled me over. "Quick!" I cried, pointing, "there goes your figure!"

He retrieved it, ruefully rubbing his mouth and glaring. "Diamerdes, how I hate being kissed!" Indignation faded, and he wriggled his hips and simpered. "But you must tell me, who did you think I was?"

"You don't know her," I said, still choking. "And it's just as well."

He made a petulant face and plucked at his frilled bodice. "But do I look so unappealing, I mean, so unlikely?"

"I suppose you are presentable from the rear, although a little meager. But from the front, well, you must admit—"

"I always have," he said, his eye gone nasty again. "But do you?"

It was my turn to be uncomfortable. "Right now I am concerned with a more crucial matter," I said tartly.

"I know," he said, "I saw your name in the cathedral." Plucking up his skirts, he gave a nervous glance up and down the alley. "Well, we had better not stand here, there is a bastonero roaming the neighborhood and yesterday there were some cuadrillos asking after you at the bodega. Do you need a jar of wine?"

"These days, always," I said.

"I have apartments up these stairs."

We looked at one another.

"A place to hide and rest," he softly said.

"All right," I said. "But mind you, only for the night."

He changed his clothes and we had dinner, and when his servant had gone away, and Catalinon was sent to the stable loft, we settled down upon some stuffed cusions to drink mint tea and smoke what he said was the best kifi north of Granada. His apartments were a crossbreed of seraglio and boudoir, decked out with the fussy frivolity peculiar to such playpens. And yet, as the weed took hold, I found myself sinking into the same miasmic languor I remembered from similar evenings shared with Peregrina. As the imagination has had a childhood too, so it is ever eager to turn back to those dreamier years, with a storybook divan for a crib, candlelight for swaddling, a pipe to suck in place of a thumb.

"Have you seen Dorita since your return from Barcelona?" I asked him.

"I'm afraid not," he murmured, watching me.

"My daughter, have you seen her?"

"I'm sorry, no, not since she was an infant. Do you like my flute?" He held up a little brown tube, tootled some notes, then gave a baiting smile. "The Moor who sold it to me said it is the mummified member of a young prince who died of love for the Grand Vizier."

"Dreams," I said, offering a pitying smile. "Why is it that we must feed on dreams."

"Because we have nothing else," he said. "And if that is our fate, then why not?" From behind closed lids, I heard the slither of his silks as he slipped from his cushion. "Why are you so stubborn, Juan?" His murmuring voice leaned closer. "Why do you go on denying? Why must you keep resisting?"

He stood above me. I opened an eye. "Resisting what?"

His blue eyes seemed to narrow in upon his muzzle, and the scar stood out like suet. "Life," he said. But quickly shook his head. "No, no," he groaned. "Me!" And he fell like a stone between my knees, clutched a thigh under each elbow, and lifted up a face of feverish entreaty. "Please, let me."

A humid sweat stood all of a sudden on my temples, and my clothing was gone all clammy. Taking him by his considerable shoulders, I pushed him back on his haunches. He got up, gnawing a lip and looking away.

"Dorita always said you were selfish," he muttered. "Once you knew what the other wanted, she said, you were compelled to refuse it." He kicked at a cushion and went into a corner to pout. "For all your flirting, you are closed up, unreachable, a pretty stone."

I poured a glass of wine and drank it down.

"It is not," I said, "that simple." I drank some more. Each word came away from my tongue like a corn husk. "It is only that I have never been much fond of it . . . that way."

He turned to peer at me, his eyes gone bright and his nose twitching, like a ferret on a new scent. "Juan! Do you mean . . . ?"

My chitterlings gave a squirm, but, like a boy who has thrust a pin into the skin of his forearm, I had to see it come out the other side. "I confess," I said hoarsely, "that I have always wondered if poofs have more fun."

"Oh, but they do!" he cried, going up on his toes and coming for me with outstretched arms. "They do!"

"Wait." I held up my hand.

He gave a fretful frown, but sat on a cushion.

Mortification let the words loose between frequent clearings of my throat. "I have always thought of it as death, you see. As a simulacrum for suicide—"

"Or perhaps as the naughtiest of the naughty things?" he suggested shrewdly.

"Maybe. At any rate, considering my present circumstances, and since it seems to have been boiling at the back of my mind for a long time, I can't help thinking that at this point, at rope's end so to speak, why not—"

"Indeed, why not?" he echoed, lifting his palms and beaming.

I looked away from this too-obvious relish. "Yes, well, I have given the matter much surreptitious speculation, as I imagine most men do at one time or another, ahem."

"Oh, yes," he nodded encouragingly. "All men."

"Yes, well." I drank some wine; God, it was dry stuff. "It has long seemed to me, you see, that to play the man to a man is unappealing, since one backhole is pretty much the same as another, and I have discovered such to be quite inferior to the longer grip and less gritty squeeze and quake of a good juicy coony."

He made a sniffing face. "Ugh! Must you?"

"And so I sometime ago concluded," I went on, "that the only truly novel and untested exchange that poofery has to offer me, aside from relief from the more annoying traits of womankind, is the assumption of the passive part. I mean, women have long had this excruciating power over me, and I have done much sweating labor to satisfy them, only to fail each time in the end. I cannot help wondering what it would be like to have the shoe on the other foot. Surely it is easier to be pursued than to pursue."

I looked at my hands and waited, but the silence stretched on, and I had to look up.

"My God," he said, "the way you put it. No subtleties, no romance at all." He went to a closet and threw it open. "Anything you want, except for the green silk, it's my favorite. I'll be back in a few minutes, so be ready." And without a backward glance, he strode out, growing more manly, it seemed, with every step.

The closet was crammed with feminine trumpery.

Yes, I had long suspected that she was there inside me, longing to betray me, and take vengeance for all the sordid things I had done to her sisters. As I fumbled in the closet, sweating like a hog, handling and hefting the very rigmutton, ribbons, and silks that had long been flags to my passion, I could feel her expanding to full power, struggling to take control of the mechanism and submit me to the clyster.

If she had not been there from the beginning, surely all these years of

393

cunctation and enflamed fancy had given her life. After all, I had long
revered these bits of gaudy rag as erotic in their own right; for years
they had decorated the objects of my deepest anxiety and desire. The
same was true of the flesh they packaged, the which I had studied with
such feverish concentration as almost to merge with it.

Now I was merging. As I put on the bloomers, then the shift, then the
lace hose, then the ribboned petticoats, then the light falbala, then the
long chiton, then slipped my feet into the high-heeled slippers, then put
rouge on my cheeks and kohl on my eyes, then fitted the veil over my
nose, I watched in the mirror, and after a bubble of derisive amusement
had burst from me and passed away like my last remaining remnant of
resistance, the reversal took full possession, and it seemed that even as I
was transposed in the mirror, I was changing inside. Even as I created
the creature in the glass, I lusted after her, and even as I lusted, I
quivered and felt my vanity flutter and my loins go hot in response to
such ardent attention.

The figure in the mirror wriggled and minced, all aglow with
magnetic insistence, proclaiming with every inviting quiver: I am
precious, I am wonderful, I am rare. Come to me, prove to me that I
have value beyond the common, empty your purse and break your arse
for my delight, and I am yours.

God's nose, it was disgusting. But also exciting.

Felicio appeared in the doorway, wearing the heavy boots and
leather jerkin of a foot soldier, even to thick mustaches pasted beneath
his delicate nose, and once again a bubble of irreverent laughter
threatened to burst from me, but was quickly smothered in the heat of
the illusion, and more: restrained by a deeper, cooler desire once and
for all to know.

"Aha, my sweet, you look to be a delicate confection," he began in as
deep a voice as he could manage, twirling his mustaches and flexing his
thighs.

I made a face and looked away, and he looked indignant but fell
silent. Taking up a full flagon of wine and drinking it down, I got to my
feet, hoisted my skirts, bent over and let him see his target.

"How pretty," he said, and was on me in a single bound.

There is no describing the furia that seized me at the arrogant grip of his hands on my hips, the alien, muscled, and intrusive push of his prick at my puckered grommet.

But I had to know. And so I let him do it.

And this time there were no more games, save only the one. I let it happen, and there was soon no doubt about it, she was really there. I was there as well, but between us, Felicio and I saw to it that for a brief while she came into her full presence. For all his expressed distaste for this side of the coin, he was clever at the role, holding back, drawing it out, wanting and making me want. For my part, I found it hard at first to hold myself still and move only to his bidding, but soon enough the coin was all the way turned, and as the longing built and I ached toward the final release, it came to my removed self that beyond custom and fancy, beyond pitch and catch, the agonizing attenuation was the same, only turned inside out. And when the tooth finally began to creak and the pincers to draw, we two were together and not different at all. And when the final wrench took me out of the world, and when I then came drifting back upon the tacky tide, I found the lusterless truth awaiting me.

It was the same, all and always the same: the same little death that was flight from death yet only brought us back to death. The same sailing out, the same fleeting bliss, the same regretful returning. Whatever fancy's quaint ruses, it was the same in the end for omne animale, poof or otherwise: post coitu triste.

One spasm was, after all, in essence just the same as any other. The news was that there was nothing new at all.

The revelation was at once a relief and an awful desolation. I had not guessed how precious this final illusion had been to me. There was no venereal taboo left to fascinate, only dull disappointment, the abiding dread and the bittersweet yearning.

It came to me that Felicio was busy at his closet. I turned my head and discovered him no longer in boots, but now got up as a harem girl. He struck a pose and came mincing, simpering behind his veil. "Now it's your turn to throw and mine to catch."

"Enough," I told him. "I've had enough."

"Oh have you?" he said indignantly, hands on hips. "Well, I have

395

not. Do you think I played the bull because I like it? Damnit, you are a selfish creature. . . ."

And this much was also not different: the same querulous and insoluble argument over who should get the most satisfaction.

"Oh, go swive yourself," I groaned, and, wrapping the blanket around my burning buttocks, rolled over and went to sleep.

At breakfast he was fretful, and as I arose to go, he put a hand on my leg and dropped his gaze to my cod. "Let me just once."

"There is no point in it," I said.

He moved his hand further. "You are afraid you will like it."

"On the contrary, I know I don't much."

"But why?"

"Because I know what it is."

"Then what is it?" he muttered.

"A devouring. A desire to drain me and make me impotent," I told him. "An attempt to keep me from going to a woman. It is a jealous act." I could not help smiling. "You see, despite all your insistence to the contrary, you want the women too."

He glared, and the scar went white. "How disgusting. How untrue."

"Is it?"

His lip trembled and he looked away. "God, you are a bitch." Then he turned back, hissing. "Or perhaps I should make that bastard."

I shrugged. "What's the difference?"

The two halves of his face seemed to slip along the fracture and threatened to crumble. "No difference?" he cried indignantly. "Are you mad? No difference? . . ."

"All right," I said, getting to my feet and patting his shoulder. "If you must insist, your mother is still a virgin."

He sat with bowed head as I went to the door. "Everybody needs to believe in something," I heard him murmur as I went down the stairs.

33

"Not back south to Sevilla!" cried Catalinon. "This time you are sure to be recognized!"

"Now stop quaking and drive on, damn you. I've still credit to spare."

Credit, perhaps, but small reason. And yet something still drove me; some nameless enticement still beckoned beyond the grimmest prospect. Even at the rim of the precipice, we look to the far horizon.

But, oh, how my despair was deepening, how the black choler was burning in me. Even my conversations with Esclavo came to a mortifying impasse.

MYSELF: Come on, out with you.

ITSELF: I beg you, turn westward for Portugal, and do not waste time with me.

MYSELF: There is still a place I must visit in Sevilla.

ITSELF: Give up this fruitless searching. You and me, we are our own homeland. You know no other coupling has ever equaled ours, no other method ever provided such superbly managed titillation. It is just as Peregrina's Twiddly was saying—

MYSELF: Shut up about that, I will not hear it!

ITSELF: Nonetheless, you know it. We are alone. We always have been. Come, accept it, and let us run away together.

MYSELF: I said, shut up!

ITSELF: Very well, I shall. There, I quit. You can take your fist
elsewhere now, for it'll get no response from me.

MYSELF: Damn you, up! Up, I say! You have never done this to me
before. Traitorous worm! By God, it will be a pleasure to hang, if
only to see you punished!

We stopped in Toledo to rest ourselves and the horses, taking rooms
with a poor converso family, less likely to betray us, since they had their
own secrets to guard. That night, after I had enveloped myself in a
cloud of ganga, I heard a knocking at our attic door, and it was an
awful thunder to my ear, like giant knuckles drumming on my noggin.

"Well, answer it," I said to Catalinon.

"But what, master?" He looked perplexed.

"The knocking," I said. "At the door, damnit."

"But I hear no knocking."

"Then the rum has made you deaf." I got up to put my hand to the
latch but snatched it back. Red hot! Or seemed to be. But surely it was
a deception of the ganga. At any rate, the knocking had stopped. I
turned away, only to discover a gray figure seated at our table. It was
much like the one I had seen on other occasions, except that it wore a
checkered cape over its head. I felt an odd and grisly thrill of delight.

"Welcome," I said, and sat down. "Catalinon, set another place."

"But what for?"

"For our guest there."

He gawked all around, gnawing bread. "Are you gone mad again?"

"Could be," I said, and a spurt of inane laughter escaped me. "Never
mind the dishes, it wants a song."

"O Jesus." He reached for his rum jar.

"You have the better voice," I said. "Sing."

He drank. "Oh, all right."

While he cleared his throat, the thing just sat there. I was beginning
to think it might be real.

"If you, my lady, day by day deny," my lackey sang, "Possession of
love's prize until I die, The lease on life you give me is too long—"

"Not that one!" I shouted, and discovered myself on my feet, sword
in hand. "Leave us, it wants to be alone with me."

"And welcome to you, I'm sure," he muttered, grabbing up his jug and getting away in a hurry.

I sat there for a long time, and sometimes it was there and sometimes it was not. I felt a dull and fevered sweetness, a hint of some timeless propriety soon to be satisfied. I could feel my mind balanced on a pinnacle of apprehension, aching to go spinning off toward the stars and not come back. I laughed some, spoke nonsense, and eventually took in this response from the apparition: "Next time you shall dine with me."

"I am not afraid!" I shouted.

At this, it began to drift backward, its arm beckoning like a ribbon of fire. "Then come," it intoned. "Come."

Ah, the cool promise in that fiery invitation. Flames licked about its feet as it went, drawing me toward peace, and I stumbled headlong after it, into the hallway, toward the window where it hovered, beckoning.

The next I remember, I came to myself on a wave of pain and looked toward its source and saw that one of my legs was apparently spit upon a giant spindle. "Master, you walked right out the window!" cried my lackey's voice nearby.

I looked up and saw the gaping opening above, then saw that I lay in the bed of a hay cart, and that one of its tapered poles had thrust through my hose and badly cut my leg.

"You barely missed being impaled," said Catalinon as he cut me loose and wrapped a rag around my wound. "My God, did you want to die?"

"Die? Nonsense." And yet I looked about me with a melancholy fascination. There was no sign of the specter, only the faintest tang of sulphur. Unless it was the sweet stink of hemp.

With myself hidden in the wagon, we finally came to Sevilla and found our way roundabout to Barrio San Marco. My childhood's neighborhood had fallen into double decay and disrepute. Ramshackle huts crowded up against the walls of crumbling mansions, the streets were heaped with rubbish, and ragged Morisco children quarreled over orange rinds. We came to the house and garden of my innocence, and I got myself down with the aid of a stick for a crutch.

"Unhitch the horses," I told Catalinon. "I'll keep the mare, you take the gelding. Now get going and save yourself."

"It is not too late for Portugal," he protested.

"I cannot cross Extremadura with this leg," I said, breathing through my mouth, for the wound had already gone ripe. "Besides, there will be soldiers at the frontier stations." I turned to look at the greenery that spilled above the wall, and the sight was sweet.

"Then north to your Uncle Adan's house in New Castilla . . ."

I shook my head. "It would only bring trouble for him, and I would still be captured. No, I am weary of running."

"But it is natural to run for your life."

I handed him what was left of the money I had stolen from Don Diego. "Take this, and if you can, see that my daughter gets half of it, and keep the other portion for yourself. Buy yourself a little house somewhere and take a wife."

"I would rather adjust sundials," he said, getting onto the horse.

"What you want then," I said, looking to the greenery. "Now go."

He turned his horse. "I am ashamed to desert you like this."

"Better ashamed than hanged by a rope."

He gave a regretful nod, shook the reins, then paused again. "Don Juan, do you remember one night when you was a little tyke and me and the upstairs maid was bundling in the hall, and you came to us all scared and angry?"

"Yes?"

He blinked, but decided to say it. "You still have some of that look in your face. By my soul, you have never quite lost it."

"Wretch." I brought the flat of my sword down on the horse's rump. "Farewell." And before the sound of hooves had faded away, I had hobbled through the rotting gate and was in the garden.

Nothing had changed; all of it was only more so. The old villa was in disrepair and uninhabited, the plaster crumbling and the windows and doors blocked up with masonry. The house next door seemed also to be abandoned. Many a slate tile had slipped from its roof since I had snatched away the bloomers of the narrow-headed girl, the surgeon had reminded me of the wages of venery, her mother had mocked my nakedness, and I had fled over the wall.

Above the wild hedges I could make out that same window, and for an instant I thought I saw a figure there, but surely it was only a shadow conjured by my various fevers. Besides, it was the garden I had returned to, and the garden which now took me in.

Ah, the cool green welcome of fondest memory. More than ever, it was rampant, unpeopled, and vast, seeming one world and all the world, with no beginning and no end, only moist gestation, pungent decay and the hum and chitter of ceaseless interchange. Birds and grasshoppers sang and whirred in the leaning grasses, blood poppies were sudden in the greenery. As I pushed my way through the sweet-smelling tangle, the splashing dew cooled me and the gentle branches brushed away the worst of my memories.

I came to the center where the glorieta stood, now a mountain of honeysuckle, and beside this little sunhouse I found a place and lay me down. Once again the humus seethed beneath my shoulders and life sprang green between my fingers. High above, the clouds of summer trundled the sky, and here below, I was a boy again in the grass. Surely I would stay as I was, as the garden was itself eternal.

Here I had the only things that were left to me to want. Here I could watch a bee kicking into a nodding blossom. Here I could allow myself a whimpering sigh and a grateful surrender to Adam's sleep.

I discovered myself sitting upright, yet felt no alarm. Was it singing that had awakened me? I heard no clatter of arms nor soldiers shouting, only the drowsy hum of afternoon. Then the sound again, a woman's voice from across the thicketed hedge, and my gaze needed no guide to the house next door, the familiar window and the dim form there, the starched white cap bent in shadow, the small hands busy at lace, while the voice toyed dreamily upon the air.

> "Life is a toil, and love is a trouble,
>   Beauty will fade, and riches they flee,
>   Pleasures they dwindle, and prices they double,
>   Nothing is what I could wish it to be."

401

A bitter lyric, yet sung so sweetly as to convey an opposite meaning, drawing me helplessly to my feet and through the grass to the foot of the hedge, where it abruptly came to me that I was in considerable pain, and worse; a rattling crash informed me that I had fallen face down into her shrubbery.

Now a long and stormy time on a red sea of delirium. A dark figure rode waves of fire and beckoned to me to join him, whilst small white hands held me back, pressing me to my bed and putting cool cloths upon my leg and against my brow. In the mornings, brief bursts of clarity burned away the scarlet, and I saw green lacework of light above my head and from that knew that I was in the glorieta, and saw the large, soft eyes of my nurse, and her watchful smile, and learned that she had a name: Aminta.

But for a long time it was mostly fever, storm and struggle, with the shrouded specter always there, beckoning me to the final secret, while slender tendrils stubbornly held me fast to life. Sometimes I heard myself groan, and several times I heard my hoarsened voice cry out, "Let me go, damn you! Let me go!"

And the voice which I had heard singing now deepened to a boisterous boom and firmly denied me flight. "No!"

Finally one night the apparition retired, the scarlet tide ebbed, and dawn's cool clarity this time prevailed. My senses sharp again, I still clung to my aspect of coma, watching with hooded eyes as she moved about the glorieta, directing the activities of a servant. She was a tiny creature, but dark as my mother was dark, as Carolina had been so, with glossy black hair and a hint of swarthiness in the flesh, a trace of smut beneath the scrubbed, translucent skin. Brown eyes, blood-dark lips around a rueful smile, buttocks and breasts that were never quite lost to the drapery.

Sending the servant away, she came across the chamber of leaves to my couch and bent above me with a cloth. Swiftly clamping a hand to her wrist, I opened an eye and spied up at her. "Tell me, madam," I said, "do you by any chance have a rose on your belly?"

She went a little pale, but showed no fear. "Not madam," she said, "señorita." And, looking watchful and pretty: "If you mean a birthmark, perhaps I do."

"Catch a rabbit," I recited from memory, "Catch a hare—"

A gentle mischief brightened her glance. "Catch a housemaid on the stair?"

"Bird in the bush, Bird in the hand—"

"Hide rubbed wrong, Too soon tanned!" She let out a shriek of girlish delight. "O my God, after all these years! I thought so, something told me. It's you, you nasty boy!"

"Indeed it is," I grinned. "Juanito Lucero, at your service." She made as if to free her wrist, but I tightened my grip. "And still nasty."

Annoyance plucked at her brow. "You are ungrateful."

"On the contrary, I have an old debt to settle with you, in addition to my more recent one, and I have been saving a present for you." Sweat splashed from my brow as I pulled her down to the bed. "For, as you can see, in ridding me of the one fever, you have only roused another."

She struggled, finally frightened, her eyes huge. "No, please, I know I teased you once, but that was long ago and I am someone else now. Not like this, please!" Tears scattered from her and she trembled in my grip, gone cold as ice.

"Damn." I let her go. She slumped against the wall, but made no further move to flee. Her weeping broke off, resumed, then ceased again. An odd snuffling sound came from her handkerchief, and she spied up through her misery. "Why are you clutching at your privy part?"

"I am not," I said, hastily removing my hand.

"Are you afraid it will disappear?"

"I am dangerous," I warned.

"No doubt, but there is something else in you," she murmured. "Something, well, decent, even noble—"

I knew the trap; of a sudden the hunter would be the hunted. "Enough of that." Closing a hand on her bodice, I tore it down the front.

She did not look down, but only at me, her eyes gone wide and wet again. "I will scream."

"A lot of good it will do you. I'll wager there is only that one scullery maid to hear, and if there are others, I will kill them. Gladly, do you hear me?"

I was on fire and running with sweat; my cure was not so complete as

403

I had thought. "Because I am no longer like other men. Tears and talk of goodness no longer have any power to move me. I have killed, and I am made of stone, I feel nothing. I am ready, nay, eager to die. . . ."

As this tirade progressed, all alarm went out of her gaze, leaving her once again tenderly watchful, almost smiling. "I believe you. But wait." She put a hand to my chest, and somehow it held me there. "I will let you make love to me. But you mustn't worry so about it. It is not dangerous. It will not kill you." She put her hand on my shoulder. "I promise. There will be no punishment for this."

"Don't be sure," I said, and flung myself upon her.

But as I went at it, my fever enjoyed a renewal. Darts of light shot this way and that from my brain and sweat splashed from my hair. Beneath me, I saw surprise, then disappointment, then a saddened disbelief. I closed my eyes, but all was hellish crimson again, and the ashen specter had returned and was beckoning doggedly.

I collapsed and put my face to the wall. "It is too late," I said.

But after a moment she lifted my drenched hair back and touched my brow with cool fingers. "Never mind, it is just that you do not trust me yet, and that is all to the good. For both of us."

And as I slipped back into coma, she was dabbing a cloth at my brow with quiet determination.

When I next came to my senses, I found myself in a room in the house next door, and there I continued my convalescence under the gentle scrutiny and close attendance of my protectress. Through many a long hour we talked while she sat on the edge of my bed and did her sewing, and soon we were walking together in the garden.

Day by day, bit by bit, we each told what had happened since she had showed me her bloomers, and I had fled over the wall. I had thirty-three years, she had one less. It seemed we had traveled much the same road, except that my milestones had been women, hers men.

As a little girl, she had been often moved to tears by the story of the martyr Santa Perpetua, and her vision of the Ladder of Heaven, and of how the saint had resisted the executioner's first blow then had directed the second at her heart: "Perhaps so great a woman, feared by the unclean spirit, could not have been slain unless she so willed it."

404

Oh yes, she too had dreamed of working her will upon life. During instruction for her First Communion, she had conceived a fierce affection for a young and pretty priest of the parish and had determined to make him marry her. But when she had brought him wild flowers in her apron, he had only suggested that she cover her knees.

"Why, he was your Sister Alma," I said, and had to laugh at the comparison.

And she even knew the yearning bleat of Fray Luis de Leon:

"O Sound, O Voice,
    Descend upon my senses . . ."

She recalled her first time with a boy as only a dim sense of dull disappointment and failure. Her Carlos had been the distaff antipode of my Carolina. Through all those years that I had bumped from pillar to post, so had she. As I had learned the enfeebling force of desire, she had taught the eager boys her power. As I had finally let go my furia, she had found herself flung down and used. As I had suffered the retaliation due me, she had learned to cut a man's pride from between his legs whilst he was between hers. She had even had her Peregrina, a man who had taught her the extremes of her mind's lust and her flesh's itch, then had proceeded to break her spirit upon the rack of her body.

We had known the same blissful dreams and wrenchful awakenings, indulged the same sins of ambition, avarice, and envy, suffered the same disappointments of failure, treachery, and loss. And in the end, each had been obliged to recognize his essential aloneness.

She had come home again, and two years before, her father had developed an abscess on his right hinderling, had attempted to operate upon himself, and in the midst of strenuous contortions had suffered a heart seizure and died, whereupon her mother had fallen into a fit of melancholia and two weeks afterward been found at the bottom of the well. Aminta had then let go all the servants save one and had settled into a kind of vinous rapture, resigned to wine and spinsterhood.

"Until, that is, you fell into my hedge," she said with her shy, bright glance. "I wanted to turn my father's house into a hostel of mercy, and add the next-door garden to it, so that the poor of the neighborhood

405

might have a refuge when they took sick and a park to rest in. But I was resigned to lonely service." Her eyes sadly measured me. "Whereas you, it seems to me, have never resigned yourself to anything."

I gave a shrug. "I might have learned to, had I the time. But now, what can I be resigned to, except the noose?" I could not restrain a nervous glance toward the garden wall; each night I dreamed of horses and the clank of arms; each morning the light showed nothing there.

"You can get away," she murmured, looking miserable. "To France, to Portugal."

"I will get away one way or another," I said. "When I can travel." I took her in my arms. "But I do not want to leave you."

"Don't you?" Her glance showed rue and pity. "Last night you dreamed again of the ghost. You flailed your arms and said you would kill it."

"If only I could," I said. "But it is the fruit of a lifetime's fever, a delusion of the mind."

"You thought it real enough to try to strangle the bedpost." She gave a chuckle, but her glance was solemn and searching. "And yet, even as you raged, there was a kind of yearning in your tone. You seemed almost to be crying out for it to embrace you."

"Not likely," I muttered. "That figure is my enemy."

"I am not so sure," she murmured, watching me. "I fear it is your last and most foolish infatuation."

"Not so," I said with a clever smile, bearing her down into the bushes. "You are the one."

And, indeed, despite despair's warnings, she was beginning to be. Step by step and cautiously, we were fashioning a mutual trust. At no other time in either of our lives would we have been much good to one another, but now all of a sudden we were. Both of us had known some lovers and neither of us was an easy dupe, she the least of all.

"Am I the woman you love?" she asked me in the grass.

"The only one I ever have or ever will," came from me out of habit, by way of getting between her legs.

"I am not asking for that much," she said, holding me away. "Only that you love me right now."

"Isn't this love?" I reached again.

"Come now," she said with a stern little laugh. "We both know you would swive any willing woman not obviously poxed. But you have always held something back. You must first learn to love in the moment, before you can learn to make it stick."

"I have learned not to try," I said, glumly rolling away. "There is something deadly in love."

She eyed me solemnly. "What made you think it was supposed to be all fun?"

I gawked. "Why, every woman I have ever known."

Her voice stayed gentle but went a little cold. "You are bitter, Juan."

"I do not believe we live in the best of all possible worlds."

"But it is the only world we have. Do you know why you are disappointed?"

I shrugged. "Experience has taught me that all joys are fleeting, all pleasures but relief. Once I thought that if I could learn all there was to know about love, I might then improve it and make it what I dreamed it should be. But now I know all anodynes have a downside, all spasms are only little deaths followed by cruel resurrection. We must die again and again, only to come back each time to the same dismal hunger and dread."

"I am beginning to think," she said with a harsh little laugh, "that you would complain if you were hanged with a new rope. Why deny yourself what little you are given? Of course there is pain. That is what women know. Nothing can be whole without being rent. The flower was only so beautiful in life because it had to wither."

"Words," I grumbled. "Sophistry is a tidy game, but the cold facts remain. Life is not perfect, love least of all. And beyond, I see even less."

She went to get a book from her father's library. "Look what the great metaphysical quack Paracelsus says: 'He who would enter the kingdom of God must first enter his mother and die.' And beyond that, you told me yourself, you saw it when the baboon died, and the comendador. Life was there in the flesh, then it was gone. Where did it go? You know it went somewhere, you have always known that much. You know you believe!"

"No, no," I corrected gently. "I only know that I do not know. Do you know more?"

She looked at me with her great dark eyes. "Oh, Juan, I want to pray for you."

"Do so," I said, and I took the cross that was a key from around my neck and pressed it into her hands. "If there is any grace, it is in you, not me."

All of a sudden she wept. "Oh why are you so stubborn!" She beat her fists on my chest. "What is it you want, then? What!"

I closed my eyes. "For all the poor not to be poor and the rich not to be jealous, for the wolf to put away murder and the lamb to put away fear, for true charity to be born in the hearts of men, myself first of all. For the sun to warm eternity, while pain and doubt cease to be—"

"Oh, don't, no more!" she cried, flinging herself into my arms. "I, too, have wished it so," she wept, pulling my face to hers. "I, too, have asked too much of myself, of men, of life. But it cannot be, and there is so little time. I saw soldiers searching the marketplace today. Please, before it is too late, let us settle for what we are given."

And, clinging together against retribution's clammy breath, we tried and nearly did. All the hard dicker had by then been done, little of it regretful, for I had long since learned the concessions nature required: swiving only every third day or so, but not at regular intervals, with no brandling in between, caresses sufficient to coax reception, and plenty of gentle words throughout.

From such compromise we had made a kind of tacit contract, which had now only to be ratified in the flesh. I had been taught well by all my profesoras, including she whom I had discovered inside myself. But in the end, it was not merely skill, but trust and fellowship that turned the trick. Also that near collapse of the self which some say is the brink of faith.

While she moaned beneath me, Nuncacura ranted from his pulpit in the cathedral of trees, and the black specter slipped closer down the slope, reaching to close off my seed. But this time I only took him with me, given over and falling, marrying my death to hers, and together we burned and careened and were consumed, dying into one.

There is no joy like that of the fool newly loved. I was aware of a revived urge to sing and leap over divans, and I might even in time have roused all the way out of my despairful trance. But two nights later, as I cleaved to her like the grave, I dreamed of a flaming horizon and the apparition standing like a charred stump at the edge of the pit, and he made jealous gestures and chided me in a garbled tongue for betrayal and treachery, and as he began to beckon, I heard the clatter of hooves and the rattle of lances, and this time it was real.

Leaving her asleep, I crept to the window and watched over the hedge as the cuadrillos worked in the moonlight, some beating the bushes of the garden, others kicking in the bricked doorway and going into the empty house. After an hour they had found nothing and went away. But they would be back.

I said nothing to Aminta the next day, but once she was gone to the market, I took my horse around behind the garden wall and tethered it to the pig shed there, the same where the charcoal boy had given me my first lesson in brandling.

Returning to the house, I wrote a note. I left a rose in the bed. Returning to the stable, I found that I had to repair my rotten saddle. Finally I drew the nag to the base of the wall, stepped onto its back, and climbed to the top for one last look at the garden. A stentorian holler let me know that I had lingered too long, and I looked to see Aminta running toward me, leaving two figures beside the glorieta: Ripio de Rebombar, and as if that were not surprise enough, Brother Gabriel Tellez, looming in his habit and bulging his eyes and waving a familiar manuscript in his fist.

"Not bad for an amateur," he shouted, "but I have had to fix it for you."

"Lucero, come back," bellowed the director. "We have thought up an ending for your play!"

But it was the tiny figure below that drew my salty gaze. She stumbled and fell, and the brambles tore at her cheeks, but she got up and came stubbornly on. "Juan, stop, don't go!"

"I must," I told her. "The king's men were here last night."

"No!" she cried. "I have tried so hard! I will not give you up!"

"They will be back to search the neighborhood. I can't let them take me here, lest they take you too."

"Then flee to Portugal, and I will find you there!" She was scrambling at the vines below, tears and blood streaking her cheeks. "I will not let it happen this time, I will not!"

"You must!" I shouted. "Forget me, forget Portugal!"

The vines broke, she fell and crouched, all wild hair and weeping eyes. "I know where you are going, I can see it in your face. Don't, Juan! I will not let this happen! Somehow we must live again!"

"Twice?" It was a dead man's laughter that came from me. I turned my back upon the sweet creature and her garden, and let myself down onto my trusty nightmare.

But, as luck would have it, I roused some cuadrillos as I came from the barrio by a back alley, and they gave chase. I was still a good three leagues from the Camposanto de Los Illustrios & Etc., when they caught up with me: a squadron of eight. All in one rush, they killed my horse, broke my nose, and laid bare my lower left ribs with a pike; and I let them have me.

So that is how I have come to this dungeon cell, this grim haste, this waiting gibbet. This morning they hung a new rope from the tree, and just now they are testing the noose. A moment ago, I managed to step on a rat, but there is no time to eat it now. The condemned man's last meal will go instead into the bellies of its brothers. So much for charity.

I have no mirror but suspect that I am a sorry sight. Six months in this place has turned my skin to tripe, a large lump disfigures my nose, and my belly has nearly found my backbone. I only hope I will be able to stand upright. My jailers tell me that persons suffering from laggardly organs and impotence will be at the base of the scaffold with basins to catch my spunk. Clearly I am not the kingdom's only fool.

The sweet face of Aminta is already mercifully fading from my dreams; only the specter is left, and soon he will be gone. My quill is almost ruined, my last candle just about to go out. I have managed to bribe another prisoner to make a copy of this and smuggle it out, to whose hand I shall not say. Yes, it is time. I hear the rattle of chains, the footsteps approaching. I see a candle, a stout figure. I remember staring from my grandmama's skirts at the headsman as he stood on the town fountain, a ruttish smile on his face, his eyes looking right, left, then straight at me.

Very well then, damn you, welcome. . . .

34

Bᴜᴛ ɪᴛ was not the hangman. It was the soul-broker, Menosmal. Bald as a baby, he beamed and jiggled his small, loose corpulence and held out a water jar.

"You must be a man of influence," I said. "There are no bugs in this water."

"Nor quicklime," he said with his very ingratiating smile. "It is fresh and there is more where that came from. You are Don Juan Lucero, the profligate of Sevilla?"

"The captured, the condemned," I told him. "Yes, of Sevilla."

"I am Roberto Menosmal," he announced, looking clever and expectant. "And it is within my power and encompassed by my privilege to remove you from this place."

"When I was brought here," I said, "my guards assured me that no one but the Prince of Hell could save me now, or at the very least his bishop. Are you by any chance Satan's prelate?"

He threw up his chubby hands. "Beware, you blaspheme!"

"How is that?"

Now he clasped his hands before him and cast his eyes down, and a most pious picture he made. "I represent the most holy and determined Office of the Inquisition."

Even in the midst of my lassitude, the sounding of that name sent a chill through my chitterlings and pulled my huevos up tight. "Go away," I said. "I prefer the hangman."

"But I am here to save you."

"For the sanbenito and the stake?" I shook my head.

"Very well then," he said, looking petulant. "We will have to remove you against your will."

"But damnit," I shouted, "the secular arm has already claimed my life! What is it you want?"

His smile was most unctuous and tender. "Why, my dear fellow, your soul."

And that is how I came to be snatched from the gibbet at the last moment and taken to the Inquisition's tidier prison in the infamous former convent, Las Hermanas Sangrias. The cell in which they locked me was exactly four paces by four and without any window. Those thick walls which had once excluded my fevered ambitions now embraced their ruin.

"You should know," Menosmal told me on the second day, "that the Holy Office has jurisdiction in all the kingdoms of Spain over all heretics, whether clerics or laymen?"

"I couldn't care less," I told him.

But he only leaned closer and gave me a confiding grin. "It can be an arduous and time-consuming task to cleanse a soul." He showed me a sheaf of papers. They had confiscated my memoirs. "Especially such a besmirched exemplar as yours."

"I tell you, I do not care. Only get it over with, is all I ask."

"Very well," he said with a grumpy frown. "But be informed that there are a variety of ways in which it can end."

"I don't understand."

"You can be relaxed at the stake—"

"Burned, you mean."

"Alive." The glint of his eye went from bright to brighter. "Or you might be mercifully strangled before the torch is put to you."

Despite myself, I was moved. "All right, then, damn you, tell me how I might win the last-named delight."

He gave a shrug meant to indicate modesty. "I am only a familiar to the Tribunal. But I know this, that you must convince the gentlemen that they have saved your soul, and that is not so easy as you might think. However, I have had some experience, and if you will accept me as your advocate, perhaps I can help."

"Oh, all right," I said. "Be my lawyer and be damned. Only get on with it."

"Now, now," he chided, "haste makes waste. After all, the longer it goes on, the longer you live."

"And the more fees you collect."

He gave an acknowledging shrug. "Which reminds me. Perhaps you are not aware that while you were in the Alcazar, your Uncle Adan died and left you one-half of his lands. The property will, of course, be sequestered into the care of the Holy Office and sold at auction, the return to go toward payment of the cost of your prosecution—"

"I ask you to go now."

"I quite understand your disappointment; it was a large estate—"

"Get out!"

Even with the passage of the years and the coming of a little wisdom, it is hard to be honest about whom it is one weeps for. But I could not help myself, for the news that the old knight was dead bereaved me of a dream of honor and grace I had not known I still cherished, until it was gone. Nor were my grandfather's shield and girdings any longer mine to put on. I was finally without past or future, alone with my naked disgust.

Soon enough, unknown familiars came and took me before the Tribunal. There was a stiflement of sour ink and decayed foolscap in the high and windowless hall, and the six men in purple robes had in common a harried and disgruntled look as they muttered and scratched with their pens and called for more paper and sent clerks scuttling to and fro about their long table. I asked if my leg irons might be removed, and the constable, a thick and worried-looking man, said he could not, but gave me water. Whereupon someone called for silence and after a last flurry of writing, the papers settled, and I was addressed by the haggard individual in the center, apparently Ricardo Matamoros Casamolino, Inquisitor-General of Sevilla.

"The miscreant will sit down."

"I will stand, thank you."

"Until your soul be saved?"

"In that case," I said, and sat down.

Whereupon the invocation was hastily read by the chaplain, and also diverse prayers, after which I was informed of my right to counsel, and Menosmal was appointed as my defender.

"All right, let's get on with it," I said, and went down onto my knees. "Hail Mary, full of grace, forgive me, for I do not want to be roasted."

"You parody prayer," came a rasping voice, and it was the prosecutor, Maldonado Sinsangre, who had the dingled head feathers and hooked beak of a gyrfalcon, complete with the drop of blood: a dark wart on the end of his nose. "Constable, put this man back in his chair."

The Inquisitor-General studied me with paternal impatience. He had a nose like a spindle, oddly divided at its end; also heavy brows, pouched jowls, and a rueful mouth. "The candidate is assured that it is not the aim of the Tribunal to roast him, but to seek his voluntary and heartfelt reconciliation to the Faith. Reconciliation is not a matter of merely rehearsing verses. We must be assured of complete penitence and a true and honest desire for Grace." He made a regretful face. "It can be time-consuming, but the Ancient Instructions are explicit. Am I not correct in this matter?"

At his elbow, a shrunken elder waggled a liver-spotted head. "As Saint Thyroid has written, a man's last breath is sufficient to blow open the gates of Heaven, but the first requirement is sincerity. The Church recognizes three degrees of contrition: corrupt, imperfect, and perfect. The first arises from earthly punishment, the second from dread of perdition, the last from love of God." He looked absent, cleaning his ear with a toothpick.

"Your outburst just now belongs to the first and lowest category," the Inquisitor-General regretfully informed me, fussing with some papers. I could see my memoirs there. "Now let us proceed briskly but in a proper manner, onum post aliud, beginning at the beginning."

The clerk stood and read the charge with professional alacrity, fairly spitting out the words: "The candidate for reconciliation is here accused and charged by the Holy Office of the Inquisition, Sevilla Tribunal, coram nubis, procedure multa sunt specialia, of the following crimes against doctrine:

"Apostasy, innovation, sedition, Arianism, reading Erasmus, criticizing the Vulgate edition of the Scriptures, illustrating a parody of the

Beatitudes, aspheterism, absoloonism, offenses against philadelphy, ganga smoking, poppy leeching, heterodoxy, attempting to tip over a church, micturating on God's cornerstone, eating meat on Friday, changing the linen on Saturday, posing as a priest, soliciting in the confessional, self-pollution, trothbreach, desertion, bastardy, desecration, nun-ruin, nympholepsy, false penitence, rape, sodomy, bestiality, spermatorrhea, belief in fornication, Sebastianism, and skepticism."

"I object to the charge of Sebastianism!" I shouted. "I have never declared allegiance to the king of Lisbon. I may be damned, but thank God, I am not Portuguese!"

The Inquisitor-General studied me with mournful annoyance. "Is the candidate a lunatic?" he inquired of my advocate. "We do not prosecute lunatics, you know. We have enough trouble with the sane ones."

Menosmal scrubbed his hands in delight. "Not a lunatic, Your Honor, but possessed. We shall argue the charges in several ways, but in general, we plead not guilty by reason of demonic possession."

"Nonsense! This is imposture." Prosecutor Sinsangre arose and pointed a black nail at me. "That man is a common reprobate and nothing else."

"I beg to differ," said Menosmal, then, digging an elbow into my ribs: "Now!"

"I don't want to," I muttered back.

"You promised," he whispered.

"Oh, very well." I let out a yowl and threw myself over backward onto the tiles, foaming and gnashing my teeth, then tore my clothing open and proceeded to brandle ferociously, all the time reciting the Pater Noster backward in the dwarfish voice of Esclavo.

"There, you see, he is!" cried Menosmal.

"Is not!" said the prosecutor.

The Inquisitor-General turned away in some disgust. "Constable, remove the candidate until he quiets down." He bent muttering to his papers. "Forty souls to reconcile today, and here it is already lunchtime."

Thus it began, and went on for some weeks. I was clapped into a patented restraint called the Iron Cod, the which allowed me to perform the mundane bodily functions by means of a screen, but prevented me from touching Esclavo. However, we could still converse, prisoner-to-prisoner, through the grill.

MYSELF: Well, we are separated at last.

ITSELF: You like it, don't you? It is what you've always wanted.

MYSELF: I could say the same of you.

ITSELF: I confess that after years of abuse, I do not much mind a rest. But it is something else that has me frantic. You are not trying to save us.

MYSELF: I aim to save us once and for all.

ITSELF: Persiflage! I know what you are up to. You've always yearned to end it this way, like some kind of reverse martyr. Well, I do not want to die!

MYSELF: Death must come to us all someday.

ITSELF: Then let it come in its time.

MYSELF: I have had enough of this uncertainty, I tell you. I will not be dictated to by fate any more.

ITSELF: I knew it, I knew it! You will do anything to prove you are in control. My God, have you no heart?

MYSELF: Have you?

ITSELF: What does it matter? We are doomed. Oh, I wish I had been born a cucumber. At least salads don't think.

Meanwhile, Menosmal and Sinsangre argued their way step by step through my life history, using my written confession as their text. Did my expostulation, "God's nose!" make me suspect of the Badian heresy, which claims that God is corporal and has human members, or was it only an expression come by in childhood and therefore innocent by reason of culpa levissima? How could I be charged with sodomy, when I had backholed Peregrina in Andalusia and had bent over for Felicio in New Castile, whereas the Holy Office was authorized to punish buggery only in Aragon? How could I be charged with being an immoral cleric, when I was also being charged with posing as a priest? And so on, ad infinitum, crambe repetita, sic semper diamerdes.

And sooner or later, it always came back to the same contention: was I possessed, or was I not?

"You have read the memoirs," Menosmal reminded the Tribunal.

"Written in the Alcazar, at the very doors of death. From the beginning, the diarist speaks of this furia which drives him, this duende which infests him."

"This compulsive chasmophile is not possessed," protested the prosecutor, "he is spoiled, an incorrigible brat!"

"Gentlemen!" the Inquisitor-General finally put in. "Let us bring this matter to crux."

"I have a suggestion," said the prosecutor, bowing all in a malevolent rustle of silks. "Mind you, I do not admit of the possibility of a cure other than the stake. But we could put the candidate on the pony and see how he rides. If there is a demon, surely a few hours on the pulley will shake it loose. If not, we might at least get a proper recant and reconciliation and then we can turn him back to the civil authorities and let them hang the rogue."

"A good idea," said the Inquisitor-General, consulting his papers. "Now if we can just find a place on the schedule."

I find it painful to describe my encounters with the pulley, the water hose, and the wooden horse. Enough to say that while the constable poured the water, cranked the wheel, and otherwise did the honors, Menosmal stood to one side of the rack and Sinsangre to the other, and while I got bloated or taller, they continued in furious contention, each bidding for my attention, when, in truth, it was the constable who had it.

"You pissed on the church at Osuna," accuses the prosecutor. "Admit it."

"Do you have a family, constable?" I inquire.

"Constable, tighten the screws!"

"I pissed," I gasp.

"It was his demon did it," objects Menosmal at my other ear. "Tell them, you are possessed!"

"I am possessed," I groan.

"Nonsense, you are yourself and a heretic."

"I am a heretic."

"It is his demon that speaks!"

"He has confessed! Loosen the screws."

"He has not. Tighten!"

"Loosen!"

"Tighten!"

As they carried me from the basement, I revived enough to notice them dragging another prisoner in, and asked the constable if it was over for me, whereupon that gentleman replied regretfully that, no, it was not over, nor would be for some days, since the Ancient Instructions were quite explicit in cautioning that the accused must be tortured only once, and therefore the torture could be over only once.

All my requests for a visit from Aminta were refused, but I was allowed visits from closer kin. I was put in an iron chair, with a guard to help hold me up, for my left leg would no longer bend, and vertigo was my new companion. Five paces in front of me was an iron grille, and through its bars I saw my mother, five paces beyond, and with her a tottering creature with snow-white hair: Don Diego.

He had suffered a second stroke, she called out across the distance between us. Never had her eyes seemed so large and sorrowing, never her face so weary.

"Shit, I don't know," said the trembling skeleton earnestly. "Shit, I don't know, shit, I don't know."

"They are the only words he speaks," she explained in a straining voice, her voice beginning to jitter. "The surgeons say that the seizures have wrenched his brain. He is really trying to say other things, but his tongue has got stuck."

"Shit, I don't know," said the skeleton, nodding its head, now reflectively, now emphatically, now with the faintest of smiles, reaching out a hand toward me. "Shit, I don't know, shit, I don't know. . . ."

An awful thing began to happen. I saw my mother's face twitch and her shoulders begin to shake and heave. I sensed it coming, then I heard it, starting deep in her throat as a low and guttural choking, then bubbling forth from her lips; and at once the blade of horror sank into my heart, and the old rage prepared itself; then, while she choked and shuddered with the terrible laughter, and the tears coursed down her cheeks, all of a sudden I understood. The nightmare, the nursery, the clyster, the awful chuckle, and the mourning gaze: it was very simple after all. Just as simple as what Don Diego was struggling to say, even out of the dim ruin and impending end of his life:

"Shit, I don't know, shit, I don't know," he said, reaching out a tremulous hand, showing me a frightened, frail, and beatific smile. "Shit, I don't know, shit, I don't know."

Then Dorita, with a small and gold-haired person holding to her hand. "Papa?" inquired the child, pointing a chubby hand at me. "Papa?"

"Yes!" shrieked my wife, her hair suddenly all on end. "He's the one, he's the one!"

And she was still shouting when they led her out, while the child trailed along behind, scowling back over her shoulder at me.

I had begun to lose track of time and even to forget the specter, when I was taken one afternoon to the Tribunal Hall, chained to a chair, and left alone. Presently the Inquisitor-General came in and sat behind his heap of papers, but despite his manner, the pouches were darker and heavier beneath his gimlet eyes, and his jowls sagged wearily.

"My God," he said, wiping his brow with a purple cloth. "What a day. We do our best, but the more we clarify doctrine, the more heresies they invent." He tugged some papers from the heap and studied them, then looked up. "The lawyers don't seem to be getting anywhere with your case."

It even hurt to shrug. "They are keeping busy."

"To their mutual profit, of course," he grumbled, hunting down another paper. "Well, the matter must be speeded up. I have a most important auto coming up in less than a week. The king and queen will be in attendance, of course, but also the vicar of Naples, as well as several papal emissaries, any number of nobles, grandees, and illustrious persons, and even, I am told, a German Lutheran interested in seeing how we do it. As for candidates for reconciliation, we have an assortment of petty reprobates, as well as a sufficiency of Moriscos and relapsed New Christians. But the public wearies of muslims and judaizers and clamors to see a genuine native heretic. You know how fiercely patriotic the rowt can be."

"Arriba España," I said sourly.

His smile was appreciative, but harried. "I can understand your bitterness, but it is too late for that now. As you may be aware, you have won some notoriety amongst the rabble. The comendador was not a popular man. And so the king has informed me through his bishop that he would very much like to see you reconciled to the faith as an example, and for once I agree. After all, we must have the cooperation of the Crown if we are to continue God's work. . . ."

At last he found the paper he was looking for. "I am obliged to ask you these questions for the record. Are you now or have you ever been in league with the Devil?"

"Not that I know of," I said.

"Are you possessed?"

"I don't know."

"Do you disbelieve in the Trinity?"

"I do not understand it."

"Do you deny Purgatory?"

An odd confusion held me silent.

"You do not answer."

"I thought—I mean, I expected another question."

"What question is that?"

"Did I believe in Heaven."

"Do you?"

"I cannot. It seems that I am without faith."

"But in your memoirs, you speak of seeing the life essence seep out of the body of your victim and go elsewhere. What could that be but the soul? And what could its transmigration imply, but an afterlife? And you claim to have several times seen a spirit."

"It was an illusion, a passing figment of madness."

"Then why do you still dream of it and cry out in your cell, now telling it to go away, now bidding it come closer?"

"Because it is also true," I said unhappily, "that I cannot not believe."

"Well, then," he said, lifting up his hands and managing a bright and haggard smile. "You are human. Nothing to be ashamed of. We are all of us born into mortal confusion and sore in need of the guidance of the Church."

"You go too far for me," I said. "The Church is an institution and by its nature refuses to acknowledge my right to make my own choices in these matters."

"You are not only misinformed about the Church, but also about the opportunities for choice." He put the paper impatiently away from him and leaned forward on his elbows. "But there is no time to instruct you in doctrine. Let us simplify. You do believe in God."

"I said that I don't know."

His smirk attempted to indicate sympathy, but his eyes had gone cold with final impatience. "I am sorry, but you are required to know. My dear fellow, we all believe in something. I have read your confession, and despite what you might like to think, you are not an exception. Think of the unlikely illusions to which you have so desperately attached your yearning. No, it is not lack of faith that the world suffers from, but only from ignorance, inefficiency, and confusion."

He made a gesture of disgust to indicate the heaped schedules, torts, and dispositions. "Nor can faith do much toward clearing up the matter. It is not lack of faith that has brought you to your present sorry estate, but the imponderable machinations of that implacable abstract: Fate. Or, to give it is proper name: God. The trouble with you, Don Juan, is that you have always had too much faith and not enough good sense. Well, God has put you on the spot, and you must soon make the final choice. There are certain Jews and Lutherans who say that if Christ came again, the Holy Office would persecute Him. More likely, we would not notice Him amongst the mass of innovators. We are too busy. More to the point, we have no desire to torture or to burn. Our aim is merely to encourage the confused and the relapsed to see the truth."

He sat back and plucked up yet another paper and read rapidly from it. "I must inform you that the Tribunal has found you guilty of heresy and other crimes, as charged. You will be placed on view at an auto-da-fé in the city of Sevilla, January 12, 1620, where you will be afforded the opportunity to recant your sins, abjure your errors, and return to the Faith, in which case you will be strangled, or you may persist in your refusal to acknowledge the One God and Jesus Christ his Son, in which case you will be burned alive."

He put the paper down and looked at me. He suddenly smiled, as if at an infinitely sad and satisfying joke. "And do you know, I think you might well make the right choice in the end. It is quite satisfying to one in my line of work to see how quickly religious excess goes out of a man when the torch of reality is passed before his face."

421

35

ACT OF Faith was the occasion's name, and fate and the Inquisitor-General had decreed that it should be held on my own saint's day.

The night before the auto-da-fé, hooded familiars came to my cell and took away my sandals and made me wear the sanbenito, an open tunic decorated with a yellow Saint Andrew's cross and various symbols and writing meant to depict my crimes and punishment. From its hem, painted flames licked upward, tended by scarlet devils with pitchforks, reminding me of the same that had menaced San Juan Climax as he had climbed his ladder in that unforgettable painting of my childhood.

Two Dominicans each took an ear, and all night they muttered prayers and nagged me to repent, while out in the streets, other friars chanted psalms and the church bells announced special Masses. Through all this steady din, I now and then heard a faint whimpering sound and guessed that it came from my own lips, but felt little pity for its owner, for I was no longer entirely present, but was dulled by a sense of time crowding close to its appropriate end. Whatever happened, it would be final, and a kind of relief was promised in that.

Morning, and after bread and milk, a rope was hung about my neck and its ends used to tie my wrists in front of me, and an unlit green candle stuck upright in my fist. Then we went into the street, where I was put at the head of some fifty other prisoners, and we began to wend our way in procession toward the cathedral square. Drums rolled and trumpets sounded; priests chanted and incense burned. All along the

422

way stood hooded familiars with torches and soldiers with pikes, and the population watched with a lively interest, but none displaying sympathy, lest they be invited to join the doomed.

Suddenly we had entered the square and were slowly going round it, and I could not help but thrill with awe to see such a spectacle. Directly across from the front of the cathedral, the king's balcony was marked by various tapestries and the royal standard draped in black crepe. Opposite this, in front of the cathedral, two great scaffolds had been erected, the larger one rising several stories to a covered rostrum lavishly draped in greens and purples. To the side of this was another, lower platform, fixed with plain benches, tier on tier, and decorated only in the most somber black. All about the periphery crowded the rabble, looking sober, but in a festive mood for all that.

We came to the cathedral, and the greenwood cross was carried in to the altar and some prayers said, then it was carried out and raised upon the larger scaffold. Now the Inquisitor-General, in his best purple satins, climbed to the highest rostrum with the rest of the Tribunal in solemn attendance, as well as the bishop and his retainers. Below them, various other clerics and notables and illustrious visitors took their seats, whiie all about the base of the platform stood the Company of Coal Merchants who had provided the fuel for the fires; and to guard it all: a multitude of soldiers.

Now the Dominicans, in white surplices and flowing black hoods, each took a prisoner by the elbow and led him up onto the plainer platform, and here we were obliged to straddle wooden ponies, myself being positioned at the forefront. To the sides were placed coffins containing the remains of persons who had been proved heretics after their deaths, and behind stood large and grotesque straw effigies meant to represent those who had failed to survive the torture or had managed to escape.

Finally the king appeared with his queen and retainers on the far balcony, his delay no doubt meant to assert the Crown's independence. And yet when the Grand Inquisitor arose and stretched out his arms and declaimed the oath of allegiance to the Holy Office, Philip was among the first to go down on his knees with the multitude.

Now they said a Mass, followed by a long sermon by the bishop concerning the advantages of repentance. All the while, attendant familiars and monks muttered and groaned into our ears, exhorting us to recant and reconcile. It was warm, and while the larger platform was drenched in burning incense, we had none, and the cadavers of the guilty dead began to stink. There was a brief scuffle and protest behind me as someone set fire to the beard of a converso, but otherwise the droning boredom was unrelieved, and several of the more lunatic amongst us began to fret and rave, one even calling out for the burning to begin; but these were quickly silenced with gags and prayed at all the more vigorously.

Midday had come and gone, and finally they began to bring the prisoners forward one by one, beginning with those accused of lesser crimes. The accusations of each were read out loudly and in great detail, and each was again exhorted to repent, and at this point many did, going down on their knees and confessing and declaring their great desire to enter the kingdom of Heaven via strangulation. Only a few responded with defiance, one wild-eyed Morisco calling upon Allah to prevent the pope from having any more children, whereupon the public was encouraged to throw refuse at him, even as the Dominicans prayed on.

The sun had gone behind the cathedral tower when my turn finally came. There was a certain not unflattering murmur of interest from the crowd, and the prosecutor read out my crimes with particular relish and vigor, although he was quite hoarse by then. Then the Inquisitor-General himself arose to offer me my chance to recant and return to the fold.

In fact, though his voice was strong with paternal authority and boomed in the hushed square, I was unable to make out the words, but it mattered little to me, for I could see the jaded eyes burning from deep in his pouched face, and the expectant, mocking smile.

He finished and waited, motionless and encastled, a figure of purple metal. The silence was long. I searched my mind for childish rebellion and found none left, only the dull and persistent desire, the last passion. I looked down and slowly shook my head. A groaning sigh went furtively round the plaza, while I somehow heard, clear as a bell, his sardonic comment to the prosecutor as he sat down again: "Retar-dismo. He knows full well that one final chance remains to him."

Now the condemned were commended to God by the bishop, then the prosecutor bade us farewell: "The Holy Office can help you no more. You are abandoned to the secular arm. This we do beseeching them to deal moderately with you and shed no blood, for our own soul's sake."

The Recording Angel, it seemed, disliked the sight of blood, but did not mind the smell of burning flesh.

And we could already smell it as we were put upon donkeys and led from the plaza in solemn procession. The cadavers had been sent on ahead and were already burning, and the straw effigies as well. Above the rooftops, the night sky was red with flame, and eager citizens scuttled past us, heading for the place. The drummers beat out a slow tattoo, and many of the prisoners were moaning and praying now, while the friars exhorted them to prepare for death.

Finally we came to a field at the river's edge: the *quemadero* or burning place. Here, stakes had been placed upright in the ground, some already engulfed in flames. Beyond the edge of the field was the open side of the Camposanto de Los Illustrios & Etc., with its black cypress trees and pale mausoleums. Only a loose line of soldiers marked the separation between consecrated ground and this. In the center of the field, rubble and bones had been heaped up to make a mound, atop which stood three bare posts thrusting up, each from its heap of dry brush and faggots. I was taken to the foot of this small hill, removed from my donkey, and led up to the center stake. Two others were brought and tied to either side of me.

From below and all around there came a great and grisly furor of violence and prayer. Hooded familiars bustled amongst the fires, thrashing figures were strapped to stakes, monks kneeled and prayed. The constable moved from group to group with a knotted cord in his hands, familiars bent with torches, the crackling flames leaped into the night, and a stifling pall drifted toward the cemetery and hung heavily amongst the monuments. To my right, the defiant blackamoor suddenly began to babble half in Spanish and half in the Muhammedan tongue, and a Dominican leaned eagerly to hear the words, making a cross upon the dusky forehead, while the constable slipped up behind with his cord.

My second companion upon the hill had stolen a wafer for use in the ritual murder of a choir boy, the constable confided to me, sweating profusely, for he had just strangled the wretch.

"Which makes you the last one unrepentant," said a voice, and I turned my head to find Inquisitor-General Casamolino standing by me, his satins covered by rough monkscloth, a breviary in his hands, an expectant sneer upon his exhausted features. "Are you ready to face the true and real?"

Below us, the screams had ceased and the praying become a murmur, and even the roar of the flames seemed to soften, as if the fires also paused to listen. "Don Juan Lucero," said the Inquisitor-General in a powerful voice, "do you believe in the One God and His Church, and in His Son, Jesus Christ, who died that you might be saved from your sins and have Everlasting Life, and Himself rose from the dead and sitteth on the right hand of God the Father, world without end, Amen?"

"I cannot," I said.

The lumps of his face multiplied and darkened, and his mad eyes bored at me. Taking the torch from the constable's hand, he passed it before my face, once, then again, crying hoarsely, "Do you believe? Do you!"

I smelled burning hair and had to turn my head away, and yet in the fierce heat there was a promise that had been too long at the center of me. I could feel neither doubt nor terror, only a giddy uncare and the longing. Now, I thought, let it be done. I shook my head. "No."

"Fanatic!" he hissed, and bent to put the torch to the tinder.

That is when a huge and sudden light of unnatural brightness lit up the monuments of the Camposanto de Los Illustrios & Etc., outshining even the bloody flames of the quemadero, and a powerful and unearthly roaring arose and seemed to shake the very trees. All eyes turned thence to see the light hover, then lower slowly sputtering and trembling above a marble statue on a pedestal. The statue shuddered, the stone head turned, and as I saw who it was, I suffered a wrench of ecstatic anguish of a sort which must have thrilled Teresa when she had seen her angel.

"It comes!" I heard a shrill voice cry, and it was my own. A part of me stood aside, even as the other part gave over to hysteria. "It has come for me!"

The crowd swayed and turned in confusion. "A ghost, a demon!" While others covered their eyes or turned their faces away.

"Nonsense," muttered the Inquisitor-General at my shoulder, but there was already a quaver in his voice.

"Don Juan's victim." The constable took a lumbering step backward. "By God, it is. That statue is alive. It is the ghost of the comendador. . . ."

"An illusion!" But the torch slipped unnoticed from the Inquisitor-General's hand. "An effect of the light, a ghost made of smoke!"

But his voice was drowned out by the shouts of the crowd. All around amongst the burning heretics, Dominicans were thudding to their knees, and a great chorus of Latin arose. Already some soldiers had thrown down their pikes and turned to flee. Now the statue was climbing down from the pedestal, all ghastly blue-white and pointing a hand toward our hill. Somehow its awful command rang out above the din: "Untie him, he is mine!"

"Do as it says," shrieked a voice. "Or it will destroy us!"

Now even the part of me that stood aside was seized by feverish belief. Doubt was no longer adequate defense, the heat and flame and grisly welcome had convinced me. I not only saw the horror and felt it, I wanted it.

The constable was fumbling at my ropes. Lightning crackled and spirits danced and spun in the trees above the monuments. Another sudden light revealed a table all glimmer and glint, as if made of glass, with napkins of crepe, plates of red-hot brass, platters of glowing coals, bowls of bubbling fire. A banquet for the damned.

"Gloria in excelsis Deo," intoned the bishop from somewhere nearby. "In te, Domini, speravi . . ."

The statue beckoned from the head of the hideous table. My hands were free. The very stake between my shoulders seemed to push me toward my fate. I started down from my hummock. Somehow I was walking, through the gawking familiars, past one flaming heretic, then another.

"Stop him, he is ours!" cried the Inquisitor-General, stumbling after me. But the line of soldiers parted as I reached them, and behind me, the Inquisitor-General shook with rage, clutched at his heart, and toppled, thrashing and cursing, into the last of the fires.

427

Some soldiers fell to their knees, others bolted. The statue nodded its glowing head, scattering ashes. Beyond its shoulder, I could see the mouth of my father's tomb and the name: TENORIO.

"I have brought you to the foods of death, the feast of Hell. Will you eat?"

Behind me I heard moans and prayer, more knees striking the earth. "What are your dishes?" I said.

The apparition seemed to float, coming closer. "Scorpions and vipers," it intoned in its stentorian voice. "Such is our diet. Will you eat?"

"I would eat," I shouted, "if it were all the asps in hell!"

Thunder rolled and strange lights swung and spun in the trees. It leaned closer, and I could feel its heat and smell its awful breath. I looked down at the hem of my sanbenito, and the painted flames came alive, licking upward at my loins, while the little devils danced and gibbered, aiming their forks at my privy region. I was fainting, careening into grateful heat. There was no mistaking the grinding ache in my head, this burning fever. Now at last all wrongs would be righted, all debts paid, and propriety and peace restored.

"Father, forgive me!" I shouted.

"He begs forgiveness of God," cried a voice from the crowd. "Don Juan's soul is saved!" shouted another. All was utter chaos now. Figures were fleeing in all directions; soldiers stumbled and fell, got up, and ran again; monks retreated on their knees, praying all the way; two priests clung together, desperately kissing one another on the mouth. If ever there was a living picture of Armageddon, this was it. The world had come apart and it was every man for himself.

"Papa, forgive me," I heard myself whimper as I reeled and sweated. "I bathed with your wife, I tried to give her my turd. . . ."

The apparition was very close now. It nodded, eyes burning, and reached out and took my hand and turned to lead me toward the tomb.

Fire! It scorched my hand, sent shooting flames of pain up my arm and down my spine. "Hell!" cried my croaking voice. "It has found me out at last! It takes me to my flaming home! Consummatum est!"

Tugged, I teetered, vomit in my throat, and prepared to hurl myself into the dark maw of the tomb. Behind us, torches were snuffing, fires dwindling, while the mob continued to tangle in terror and flight. Now was the time, now it would be over. I leaned toward the hole.

But the apparition held back, annoyance jittering its features. It bent its heavy head to mine. Ashes sprinkled down, and now I could separate the ingredients of its disgusting breath: bad sherry, mildewed sausage, aniseed.

"Don't come so easily," it muttered. "If you want to live, you must show some resistance. You are mistaking the play for the game again."

I gawked. I disbelieved. I knew.

And as the two of us thrashed in

EPILOGUE

THE PLUMED courtier turned the page and found the rest blank. A quizzical smile lifted his mustaches, and he turned to the tall monk. "Is that all there is?"

The monk nodded, scratching his shoulders against a post. On the boards just above, actors and stage attendants whispered and scuttled about, while out front, the hero of the play sat at dinner with the ghost of his murder victim.

"At least that is where the confession ends," the monk said. "I am told that in the considerable furor following the disappearance of ghost and diarist into the tomb, someone bricked it up."

"Was that done by masons attached to the Holy Office?"

The monk grinned. "Because of the confusion, it would be very difficult for anybody who was present to say. At any rate, it has remained sealed ever since. As I mentioned, the king cannot raise the dead, figuratively speaking or otherwise."

"He can try," said the courtier, thoughtfully tugging his gloves on. "It is unwise to underestimate our Philip. It is not that he is without a modest intelligence, but his tremendous advantage in life has given him little use for thought beyond the avoidance of discomfort."

They stood for a long moment, loath to face the final crisis.

Above them on the backstage boards, a stout individual all covered in gray shrouding and marble dust was drawing off a flagon of yellow liquid from a barrel, whilst simultaneously rumbling directions to the assistants bustling about him. "Dust me for the final scene, you scullions, but take care not to cloud my liquor. By God, at last I am rich enough to drink before the first-act curtain!"

The monk and the courtier set out, and as they made their way alongside the stage, a huge and sudden light illumined the scene and burning chemicals spilled from iron pots suspended in the scenery. An awesome rumbling arose, as assistants beat upon sheets of tin, and a low moaning roar, as others whirled devices on strings, and there followed a series of flashes and glowings, as pinwheels and roman candles went off in the canvas trees.

"An effective display," observed the courtier.

The monk's chuckle had some brag in it. "Think how much more so on a moonless night of superstition and terror."

On the stage, the stout individual who played the statue was just dragging Don Juan toward the paper tomb, while the captured rake gesticulated mightily and cried out, "I burn, I freeze, I am gone to its awful home!"

The courtier chuckled, enjoying his knowledge. Then he went pale. "My God, I have just remembered something," he whispered to the monk. "In that portion of the confession which His Majesty read two days ago, the grandmama dies, and Don Juan goes to wait outside her tomb. Outside the secret rear exit!"

The monk's good spirits left him and he gnashed his teeth. "Damn. Unless the king of Spain is an idiot, we are discovered."

"Or unless," the courtier said hopefully, "he is only a careless reader."

The play had ended as they let themselves onto the royal balcony, and they found Philip with his arm resting on the rail, his jaw upon that, and his lower lip protruding. "Must you punish your hero so mercilessly, playwright?" he inquired of the monk. "Could not his soul have been somehow saved?"

"Beware," muttered the courtier to the monk, "he is fond of sham."

The monk answered the king solemnly, "There being but little space in a drama, Your Majesty, I thought this the neatest conclusion. But I am, of course, confident that the soul can be saved if there is true contrition."

"Well, I certainly hope so," sighed the king, glancing over his

432

shoulder at his bishop. "Of course, I do not think any sinner should escape punishment, and certainly not the common dissemblers and felons abroad these days." The royal fan came up. "But I do think that if the sinner feels genuine shame and gives as much to charity as I do, he might be redeemed."

"I am sure of it," averred the monk. "In the present circumstance, I think that damnation might be considered as only a theatrical convention, just so much showmanship—" He stopped short and swallowed hard.

"Really," said the king, watching over his fluttering fan. "And what about the body, playwright."

"The body, Sire?"

"We have spoken of the lost soul of this Don Juan. What about his body?"

The monk's lips moved, but nothing came out. Beside him, the courtier had a coughing fit.

The king simpered, enjoying himself, and turned to place a hand on the little nun's knee. "I do hope all this vulgar talk of the flesh does not offend you, my dear."

She fixed him with her dark gaze. "Not at all, Your Majesty. Through my work in our Hostel of Mercy I am quite familiar with leprosy and other fleshly contagion."

"Ah!" The king hastily removed his hand and brought out a bottle of perfume with which he drenched himself, obliging all about him to move away.

Now he turned, his face gone dark, his fan rapping his knee. "Enough of games, the play is over. Let us get on to the post-mortem. Marco, what did you learn from the remainder of the confession?"

"Nothing that Your Majesty does not already know, I am sure," said the courtier. "It seems that young Lucero, who, as you know, was my nephew by my brother's marriage, suffered such guilt after killing the comendador that he became convinced that the ghost of his victim sought revenge. When the Holy Office put him to the torture, his madness apparently worsened—"

"Enough," the king put in impatiently. "I intend to leave for the capital tonight. Let us shorten the inquiry by consulting an outside witness."

He clapped his hands, and a stout-legged and serious officer of the Guard stepped out from behind the draperies, his helmet under his arm.

"Captain Baltazar Muñeco, of my own cuadrillos," said the king. "I sent him on a mission while waiting for you to finish your reading. What have you found out, captain?"

Below the balcony, the pit had emptied, the stage was also abandoned, and the soldier's voice rang in the empty alley. "As I have told you, Your Majesty, I and my men were there that San Juan's eve when the aforementioned Don Juan Lucero was taken by the familiars and officers of the Holy Office to the quemadero to be burned. I saw him strapped to the stake, saw him defy the Inquisitor-General's last appeal, and saw him break free and start for the Camposanto."

"And did you see this living statue, this rumored apparition?"

"Some said they saw it, Your Majesty, some said they did not. I was busy keeping my men in hand and am not sure myself. I did get a glimpse of the aforementioned Don Juan Lucero just as he tumbled into the mouth of the tomb. After that, there was a great confusion, what with many persons stumbling about and fleeing in fright, and the Inquisitor-General himself falling into one of the fires. It was chaos for quite a while, during which one of my men said he saw masons bricking up the tomb. Later, when the heretics had finally stopped burning, it was no better, for a great number of small crimes had been committed during the aforementioned excitement, and there was the painful task of trying to tell which set of burned remains had been the Inquisitor-General. As you know, they were never certain which—"

"Please," said the king, looking sick. "About the tomb, Captain. Who bricked it up?"

"Well, Sire, the inquiry into the scandal was conducted in some confusion, as you will recall, but I think it was commonly assumed that unnamed familiars of the Holy Office sealed it in order to be certain that the aforementioned heretic, Lucero, was definitely dead."

The king cocked an ear, watching the courtier, the monk, and the nun. "And is he, Captain?"

The captain stepped to the edge of the balcony. "We opened the tomb as you ordered, Your Majesty." He pointed downward to where two soldiers stood beside a canvas, and on the canvas, the blackened char of a man. "I would say that he is thoroughly dead."

Of all there who went pale, the king went palest of all. Clearly he had not expected so graphic an answer. He glanced downward, and from behind his fan came the choked query, "Well then, is it him?"

The courtier looked at the monk and the monk looked at the nun. "Is there a cross around its neck?" murmured the monk.

"Ah yes, the cross," said the courtier, stepping to the balcony's edge and calling down to the soldiers. "See if there is anything around the neck. A cross in the form of a key."

Below, one of the soldiers took out his dagger and bent to probe at the blackened neck. There was a dull scraping sound, and a stronger odor wafted up. The king looked away and gnawed the tip of his fan.

"Here it is," said the soldier, tossing up a chain and cross.

The courtier caught it and brushed away the ashes, and there was an odd lilt in his voice, though it affected a mourning tone. "Yes, it is my nephew, Don Juan Lucero, baptized Tenorio. God rest his soul."

He handed the object to the king. "If you look, you will see the Tenorio monogram incised on the medallion, and the family motto: 'Death is the key.' "

The king studied the key then handed it back, a tear moistening his eye. " 'Death is the key.' And thus it turned out to be, eh? Poor rascal. Well then, he is dead." He heaved a sigh and worked his fan. "So be it. I had suspected you of some kind of ruse, playwright, and you as well, Marco. I had recalled something, but cannot now remember it. Forgive me, it was no doubt my nerves."

With one last fitful glance at the corpse below, he got to his feet in a great rustling of silks, shaking perfume onto his handkerchief. "Yes, I believe I badly need a rest. A week of retreat and prayer, I think." He considered, the plump lips pursed. "Well, perhaps a bit of revelry at home." He nodded. "And then retreat." Crossing himself, he started for the stairs.

"But, Your Majesty," said the captain. "The body."

The king paused, arrested in much that same alert and tiptoe posture in which he was soon to be painted by Zuburan, except seen from behind. "The body, yes." He shuddered and pressed his handkerchief to his nose. "What shall we do with the body?"

435

There was a scrape of brocade and click of beads as the bishop leaned forward. "I have a suggestion, Your Grace. We have worried much over the dangerous appeal this play has to the common imagination. No doubt it would help to offset its corruptive influence if we were to hang the body of the real Don Juan up outside the theater as a lesson to the rowt. After all, a sanbenito with his name on it is presently hanging in the cathedral for the same purpose. Surely other prospective profligates and skirtlifters will be thus reminded of the promise of hellfire."

The king shuddered, but did not turn. Clutching at the royal cod, he gave a little snuffling whimper, then waved his handkerchief by way of assent, and was gone.

"All of Spain was in that face, that moment," the courtier said some time later, as they stood talking behind the stage.

There were the courtier, the tall monk, the little nun, the director, and a second monk, who had his hood well up over his head. "It seems I remember you saying that once before," said this friar.

The courtier chuckled. "I remember." He studied the other, but there was little to be seen in the shadow of the cowl, save only a nose that had once been pretty but now looked to be broken. He studied the silver chain and cross in his hand. "You know, I could conjure a happier ending for the play. The pretended ghost and our hero stumbling down the steps of the awful tomb, and perhaps Don Juan pauses to kiss the cheek of a reclining stone figure there, while others bring in a cadaver and others brick up the entrance. Then out through the hidden exit, then down the clammy passage, the glint of light ahead, the gate. Someone unlocks the gate, then rushes back to put this chain around the neck of the smoldering corpse. As for our hero: fresh air, freedom, the nun waiting, their hands reaching for the sweet embrace."

He handed the chain and cross to the friar. "Congratulations." Then: "But haven't you taken an unnecessary chance coming here?"

"I had to see my play at least once," the other said.

"Your play!" The taller monk's eyes bulged threateningly. "Who gave it polish and form? Who is the professional here?"

The director belched and waved his flagon. "And who read the

436

memoirs you sent to Aminta and suggested the fine stage effects which so enlivened the auto-da-fé of January twelfth last?"

The second monk said softly, "I'm sorry. I meant: my foolish life, your play. Be that as it may, I quite enjoyed it. What a hero. Oh, to be such an arrogant and faultless blade. It was the dream of my life."

The little nun stepped to his side and gave his arm a fond twist. "Never mind, you had your moments. Now you can leave that dream to the young fools; it is theirs by tradition and by nature. You are free of it."

"Believe me," said the friar, bending to kiss her cheek. "My bones thank God for that."

"Don't tell me he has become devout," said the courtier to the nun.

She smiled. "If it is devotion to tend the flowers and have faith in their blooming. You must come visit us at our Hostel of Mercy someday, and walk in our little park."

"I will." The courtier turned his amused gaze upon her companion. "And the tentigo, has he also rid himself of that?"

The little nun's smile was wry. "When the neighborhood maidens dance around the Maypole, he does show some signs of agitation."

The friar looked the courtier in the eye. "Oh, I am not cured of it, and hope I never shall be. But it is no longer the same thing. You would be surprised, Uncle. Once the true tentigo is separated from other expectations, it turns out to be not nearly so pressing."

The courtier's glance went briefly bleak. "So I have heard. Well then, you have come through. I am glad." He cleared his throat and lifted a smile. "Other good news. Your mother is better since my brother's death, and is getting quite beautiful again."

"I am glad to hear it."

"Until we meet again, then. Fare thee well, Juanito."

"Good-by, Uncle."

They embraced. The courtier bowed to the taller monk. "Fray Gabriel." And to the director. "Don Ripio."

And finally he paused before the little nun, then suddenly bent his knee and swept the ground with his white plumes. "Madam, I salute you."

As the friar and the little nun were passing out of the alley of the

Pollo Picando, they passed close by two clerics who stood with their hands clasped and their eyes turned upward to a large broadside advertising the present play, and tied beside it, a blackened and crumbling cadaver with a hand-lettered placard around its neck:

¡BEWARE THE WAGES OF VENERY!

"Impressive," murmured the cardinal, crossing himself and pressing his cap to his nose. "Effective."

"Indeed, devastating," gasped the bishop, breathing through his mouth. "A forceful warning to all fornicators. I can't help thinking how Inquisitor-General Casamolino would approve. If only he were here."

"Perhaps he is," murmured the friar, who had silently stepped closer.

The bishop started and turned. "I beg your pardon?"

"Figuratively speaking, of course," said the friar, and in the dense shadow of his cowl, one eye rolled heavenward.

"Ah, yes. Yes, of course," murmured the bishop. "Amen to that."

"Amen, indeed," said the friar, and held out his arm to the nun, and they continued on.